Praise for Joyce Gee
and The Altira Series

"A compelling, well thought out story which leaves you wanting more."
—*Early Reader Review*

"*Magic of Lies* is fast-paced, witty, and was instantly my new favorite fantasy series. Joyce Gee built a beautifully rich and diverse world. *The Altira Series* deserves a home on any fantasy lovers' bookshelf alongside George R.R. Martin, J.R.R. Tolkien, and Sarah J. Maas. With so many enchanting characters, you'll be rooting for them all. I highly recommend reading it!" —Alex Williams, editor

About the author Joyce Gee

Joyce Gee is an Australian author based in Mandurah, Western Australia. Growing up among the rainforests of Far North Queensland, she loved to vanish into the other worlds hidden within the trees. When she isn't writing, she enjoys drinking tea, pottering around the garden with husband and their two children, or escaping with her camera to capture the beautiful landscape of Western Australia.

Her latest release is *The Altira Series,* composed by *Magic of Lies, Blood of Husks, Grave of Dandelions, Shadows of Life, Game of Gods,* and *Fires of Unmaking.*

The Altira Series

When Princess Eirian returned home after decades away, she thought it would be a fresh start. Born with magic, she struggles to balance her ability to give life with the desire to kill. Raised a mage in a distant city, she struggles to adjust to life as a princess in a court where magic is undesired.

With assassination attempts and rumors of war, Eirian proves to those around her that she is not one to hide from confrontation. Even when it risks her life.

- 2023 -

JOYCE GEE

The Kingdom of Endara is at war and Eirian refuses to be the soft-hearted queen the enemy expects. Among her growing collection of secrets is one that can help turn the tide of battle, even if it means that her people might turn on her.

She knows she can buy the precious time needed for reinforcements to arrive, but she will have to break her promises to the ones closest to her.

- 2023 -

JOYCE GEE

With nightmares clawing at her fragile mind, Eirian embraces the whispers that have followed her for as long as she can remember. In the aftermath of the real enemy revealing herself, Eirian retreats from the allied armies to seek answers.

Accompanied by Aiden, Celiaen, and Galameyvin, they are determined to confront the spirit of the last mage and face the dark god seeking their destruction. The price for victory is one that Eirian is willing to pay, even if her friends are not.

The Altira Series (continued)

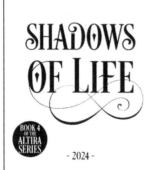

SHADOWS OF LIFE

BOOK 4 OF THE ALTIRA SERIES

- 2024 -

JOYCE GEE

Tormented by her mother's memories, Eirian fears what she will become if she accepts her duty. The gods of Death and War have waited patiently for Eirian to make her move. Willing to do whatever they must to ensure the enemy is destroyed and reborn, the gods of War and Death must risk Eirian turning Tir into dust to keep her on their path.

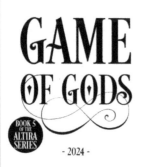

GAME OF GODS

BOOK 5 OF THE ALTIRA SERIES

- 2024 -

JOYCE GEE

There is a thin line between saving the world or destroying it, and Eirian finds staying on the right side harder with each passing day. Determined to bring down Annawyn, Eirian returns to where she grew up. No longer hiding the truth, she knows her presence will cause disruption across the land.

But with increasing attacks from the Unseelie army, Eirian cannot stand by while innocent lives are destroyed because of her mistakes.

FIRES OF UNMAKING

BOOK 6 OF THE ALTIRA SERIES

- 2024 -

JOYCE GEE

Faced with distrust, Eirian tries to protect the ones she loves with the help of War and Death. All she needs to do is find a way to force the mad god to pass over before her manipulations destroy Endara. But unraveling the darkness woven throughout the people she once ruled is not an easy task.

They know that if they do not stop the enemy's forces, countless innocent lives will be lost.

MAGIC OF LIES

BOOK 1
OF THE
ALTIRA SERIES

JOYCE GEE

MAGIC OF LIES

BOOK 1
OF THE
ALTIRA
SERIES

JOYCE GEE

5310
PUBLISHING

Published by
5310 Publishing Company
Go to 5310publishing.com for more great books!

SCAN ME

Our books may be purchased in bulk for promotional, educational, or business purposes. Please contact your local bookseller or 5310 Publishing at sales@5310publishing.com or refer to our website at 5310PUBLISHING.COM.

MAGIC OF LIES (1ˢᵗ Edition) - **ISBNs:**
Hardcover: 9781990158810
Paperback: 9781990158858
Ebook/Kindle: 9781990158865

Author: Joyce Gee
Editor: Alex Williams
Cover Design: Eric Williams
Map Illustrator: Dewi Hargreaves

MAGIC OF LIES (1ˢᵗ Edition) was released in February 2023.

ADULT FICTION (with Young Adult interest; it can be categorized as New Adult 16+)
Fantasy / Epic
Fantasy / Action & Adventure
Fantasy / General

Themes explored include: Epic fantasy; Adventure fiction; Love and relationships; Coming of age; Death, grief, loss; Interior life; Identity / belonging; Politics; Narrative theme: Social issues; Mythical creatures: elves.

In Memory of Freya Heatherbell

CAST OF CHARACTERS

Kingdom of Endara
Eirian Altira: Princess of Endara, purple mage
Nolan Altira: Eirian's father, King of Endara
Dowager Duchess Amira Altira: Nolan's sister, mother to Llewellyn
Duke Everett Altira: Eirian's cousin, next in line to the throne, Duke of Tamantal
Duke Llewellyn Altira: Eirian's cousin, third in line to the throne, Duke of Onaorbaen
Duke Marcellus: Nolan's cousin, Duke of Raellwynt
Duchess Brenna: Marcellus's wife, chief of Eirian's ladies in waiting
Countess Elena: Countess of Caerwel
Earl Alastair: Elena's husband
Countess Elyse: Countess of Periyit
Earl Craig: Elyse's husband
Earl Baeddan: Earl of Nareen
Countess Caraf: Baeddan's wife
Earl Adalardo: Earl of Gerygaen
Earl Gallagher: Earl of Jurien
Dowager Countess Kaie: Gallagher's mother
Countess Kathleen: Countess of Kaban
Earl Kendall: Kathleen's husband
Chancellor Ulric: Endaran small council
Treasure Sabine: Endaran small council
Chamberlain Wendel: Endaran small council
Justiciar Ollier: Endaran small council
General Cameron: Endaran small council, commander of the Endaran military
Lady Isabella: Eirian's lady in waiting, daughter of Countess Kathleen
Lady Romana: Eirian's lady in waiting, Elke's sister, daughter of Earl Baeddan
Lady Elke: Eirian's lady in waiting, Romana's sister, daughter of Earl Baeddan
Lady Bea: Eirian's lady in waiting, Earl Gallagher's sister
Captain Gunter: Captain of Everett's guard

Kingdom of Endara – Eirian's guards
Captain Aiden Cathasaigh: Captain of Eirian's guard
Merle: Aiden's second in command
Devin: Merle's squad
Fox: Merle's squad
John: Merle's squad
Sid: Merle's squad
Tobin: Merle's squad
Fionn: Squad leader

Kyson: Fionn's squad
Paxton: Fionn's squad
Geoff: Fionn's squad
Zack: Fionn's squad
Tyler: Fionn's squad
Fisk: Aiden's squad
Gram: Aiden's squad
Lyle: Aiden's squad
Randolph: Aiden's squad
David: Aiden's squad
Mac: Aiden's squad
Gabe: Squad leader
Jack: Gabe's squad
Layne: Gabe's squad
Kip: Gabe's squad
Wade: Gabe's squad
Andrew: Gabe's squad

Kingdom of Ensaycal

King Paienven Kaetiel: King of Ensaycal, red mage
Queen Sannaeh Zarthein: Paienven's wife, sister of Archmage Baenlin Zarthein, red mage
Princess Awena Kaetiel: Princess of Ensaycal, daughter of Paienven and Sannaeh, blue mage
Princess Nadinna Kaetiel: Princess of Ensaycal, daughter of Paienven and Sannaeh, blue mage

Kingdom of Ensaycal – Princes of Ensaycal

Prince Galameyvin Kaetiel: Prince of Ensaycal, Celiaen's cousin, blue mage
Prince Celiaen Kaetiel: Crown Prince of Ensaycal, son of Paienven and Sannaeh, red mage
Prince Yaernan: Paienven's brother, blue mage
Prince Selagan: Paienven's brother, blue mage

Kingdom of Ensaycal – Celiaen's companions

Tara: Red mage in charge
Alyse: Tara's assigned blue mage
Tynan: Blue mage assigned to Celiaen
Kenna: Red mage
Ianto: Blue mage assigned to Kenna
Lydia: Green mage
Harlow: Yellow mage

Link: Yellow mage
Tully: Red mage
Cai: Blue mage assigned to Tully
Darcie: Blue mage assigned to Imogen
Osric: Blue mage assigned to Mabel

Mages of Riane

Archmage Baenlin Zarthein: First red archmage of the high council
Archmage Azina: First green archmage of the high council
Fayleen: Yellow mage, Eirian's best friend
Soren: Blue mage assigned to Baenlin
Jaren Valkera: Red mage, friend of Eirian
Rylee: Red mage, friend of Eirian
Luke: Blue mage assigned to Rylee
Master Howell: Green mage

Kingdom of Telmia

King Neriwyn: King of Telmia
Prince Emlyn: Neriwyn's son
Lord Vartan: Neriwyn's lover and general
Lord Faolan: Telmian envoy to Eirian
Lady Saoirse: Faolan's twin sister, part of Telmian delegation
Lord Tharen: Part of Telmian delegation

Kingdom of Athnaral

King Aeyren: King of Athnaral
Ambassador Darryl: Athnaralan ambassador

Acknowledgements

I'd like to begin by acknowledging the Traditional Owners of the land on which I wrote this book, the Bindjareb of Mandjoogoordap, and pay my respects to Elders past and present. I would also like to acknowledge the Traditional Owners of the land on which I began creating this world, the Djabuguy of Ngunbay, and pay my respects to Elders past and present.

Well, this has been an adventure! First and foremost, I have to thank Anita. She has been the most amazing alpha reader. The second person I have to thank is my amazing sister from another mother, Meghan, who has propped me up for years. Without the two of them, and their enthusiasm for the world I created, I might have filed this away with all the rest.

And Callai, even though you haven't read it yet, you're an amazing bestie and I love you. You'll probably kick me for this, but it's okay, you love it really.

To my most wonderful, amazing, loving, and patient husband, Beau. Thank you for putting up with me. I know I'm a cantankerous git at times, but you love me anyway. Without you, I wouldn't be able to write as much as I do. You are a fantastic husband and father. My rock. My everything. I love you more than I can express.

To Barbara Jones and Freya Heatherbell. I hope the two of you are proud of me, wherever you are. You started the journey into this world with me way back in 2001, and neither of you stopped telling me I could do it. I grieve that you're no longer with us, but you're both always in my heart, and I'll never forget.

To everyone else who has played a part in this journey, thank you. Especially TMT! You ladies know who you are. Thank you for being such an awesome, supportive group.

—Joyce Gee, author

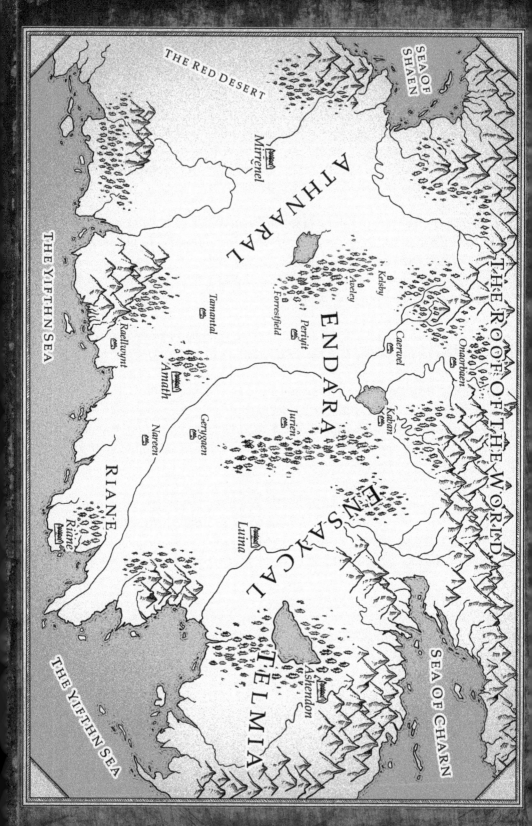

PROLOGUE

25 YEARS AGO...

L ightning lit the sky, the accompanying boom of thunder rattling the glass windowpanes. Cradling the hours-old newborn, he watched the storm unfolding in silence. His speeches had come earlier, before he forced the most powerful god in the world to pass over to her heir. The god he had loved. His balance.

Now he held a mewling baby girl that was not his, the echo of her mother's words in his mind, and an emptiness that would remain for years. He felt the loose end of a bond that would not repair until the child in his arms died. A death he would do his best to make sure was decades into the future. She would grow up before she took her place. His actions had unbalanced Tir, but it was nothing they could not manage for a few years.

With a glance at her, he said, "I'm sorry, my darling little life."

The unfocused gaze of the newborn stared back at him, and she yawned.

"You need to grow up. It won't be easy. It can't be easy. There's much you need to understand. And one day, you will." He turned back to the window. "You won't have a mother, but you'll have others who love you."

She opened her mouth again, her face screwing up.

"I know you're hungry, and I need to find someone to disguise as your mother. Better everyone believes she's dead in childbirth. Don't worry, I'll always be close, and soon enough, so will my heir."

Thumb stroking over the soft, downy hair that covered her head, he smiled.

"You'll have the other two heirs by your side in a few years. They'll love you more than anything because they won't be able to help it."

Life continued for the people outside the quiet chamber, utterly oblivious to the man watching the storm. Unaware of the destruction of their queen. Ignorant that the god of death had held a knife to the throat of their princess. Without smiling, he looked down at her.

"One day, you may remember this night. If you want to. It won't be your memory of it; it will be hers. I hope you understand why I did it and can forgive me," he said.

Turning from the window, he walked to the crib to set her down.

"We need to be reborn, darling. You're the first in a new era. Tir will be yours."

Tucking a blanket around her, he saw the signs she was preparing to cry. With a finger pressed to her cheek, he used a thread of power to calm her. He had a task to complete, and he did not need her crying to attract attention. Once it was over, he would let her cry to draw the attention she needed. All it would take was a quiet word in the ear of a guard for them to discover her and what they would see as the body of their queen. A queen dead from complications post-childbirth like so many other women. No one would know the truth, not for many years.

He kissed her forehead, saying, "You're going to think no one understands you, but that's not true. I understand you, and so will they. Everyone else, though, won't. They'll fear you, fear how powerful you are. Which you will be, and you're from my line on top of everything else, so you'll be dangerous."

She grizzled, and he smiled at her.

"Your mother did the wrong thing by taking his magic to give to you, but I can't change that now. So, you must learn to balance both sides of the coin. Life and death."

With a step back, he prepared to leave, but hesitated. Outside, the storm continued to rage, and the thunder was deafening.

"I can feel how angry she is about what happened. You'll have a few years before you notice things. Before she's free to spread her twisted ways. She'll drive them to madness and war in her desire to destroy Tir. You'll fight, and you'll die, like your mother planned, but you'll be reborn, and you'll make Tir whole."

Chuckling, he shook his head and silently scolded himself for talking to a newborn.

"Don't worry, it's nothing you won't be able to handle. Because you're Eirian Altira, and you're going to save the world."

Vanishing, he left the baby alone in the dark.

ONE

"You're never gentle with me, Eirian."

Smirking at the man beneath her, Eirian replied, "You hate it when I'm gentle with you, Jaren."

He chuckled. "True, but I thought this time might be different."

Rolling off him, Eirian lay on the sand and stared up at the tiers of stone and balconies above them. Watched the curious heads pull back to avoid her gaze, the people quickly deciding it was better to continue on their way. It was easy to gawk at Eirian when they thought she was unaware, but no one fancied drawing her attention. Beside her, Jaren used his training sword to poke Eirian's arm.

"You know, Ree, for someone who's about to leave and return to her home, you don't look very excited."

Eirian sighed. "I'm not excited. Would it excite you in my position?"

"You're the Crown Princess of Endara. Going home to Amath means you get to be a spoiled brat."

"Ass!" Eirian laughed, slapping a hand to his chest.

"Yeah, alright, I forgot, you've always been a brat. Going back to Amath won't change that," Jaren grumbled.

Feeling her magic flicker, Jaren glanced at Eirian and frowned. Her eyes were closed, cheeks flushed from their sparring match. Sand stuck to her skin, and Jaren suspected the company of mages assigned to escort Eirian to the border with Endara would have plenty to say when they found her. Sighing, Jaren pushed himself into an upright position and ran a hand through his hair.

"You don't have to go, Ree," he said.

She arched a brow, replying, "So everyone keeps telling me. The thing is, Jaren, I have to go. As you said, I'm the Crown Princess of Endara, and I have an obligation to my people."

"If you don't want to go back, you don't have to."

"I want to go back."

Looking at the entrance to the training square, Jaren spotted a familiar woman waiting for them. The yellow embroidery on her gray clothes stood out at a distance, displaying what order she belonged to. He expected her to come over and yell at them, but she remained leaning against a pillar. Sitting up, Eirian followed his gaze and smiled at their audience.

"Fay's been trying hard to convince me to stay. Everyone has. If she can't manage it, what makes you think you could?" Eirian asked.

Jaren shrugged, saying, "I don't think I could. If Fay can't manage it, the only people who could are Celiaen and Galameyvin, and they're not here."

"Then why—"

"Because you need to be reminded that it's your choice. You can say no. No one can force you to stay in Riane with your people, but no one can force you to go back to Amath."

Eirian replied, "Endarans are my people, Jaren."

Grabbing her arm, Jaren growled, "No, they're not! You're a mage, Eirian, a mage. You belong here in Riane with other mages. Not chasing some fucking crown in a distant city you haven't seen since you were five."

Her fingers curled around his wrist, and Jaren looked down at the solid purple band that adorned her left hand. It gleamed in the sunlight, brighter than the red band on his own hand. A reminder of what Eirian was, that her power was greater than his. Jaren was used to dealing with purple mages. His mother and sister belonged to the order, but neither came close to Eirian's magic.

A ward rippled around them, Eirian's brows shooting up in amusement. Her gaze shifted to Fayleen, and Jaren watched the amusement morph into sadness. Striding across the sand, Fayleen lifted her hand and closed it into a fist, magic tightening around where Eirian grasped his wrist. Jaren knew what she was trying to do, and he did not fancy facing one of her knockback wards.

"Let Jaren go, Ree," Fayleen said. "I didn't expect to find you here playing with the reds, but when I found the cliff garden empty, I figured you'd be in a square."

"I finished packing last night," Eirian muttered.

"Rylee and the others are waiting for you."

Snorting, Jaren rubbed his wrist when she let go. He scrambled to his feet and started picking up the discarded training swords. Eirian and Fayleen regarded each other silently. Neither woman wanted to make the first move, knowing what it would mean when Eirian joined Rylee. Finally sighing,

Fayleen offered a hand and braced while Eirian pulled herself up. Jaren shook his head, heading over to the weapons racks.

Clinging to Fayleen's hand, Eirian murmured, "I want you to come with me."

"I can't. The high council won't let me. You know they assigned me to Archmage Baenlin," Fayleen replied, squeezing her hand. "If I could, you know I'd follow you anywhere."

"Including Amath?"

"Anywhere means anywhere, sister."

Eirian pulled her into a hug, burying her face in Fayleen's shoulder. Watching from the side of the square, Jaren wondered how Eirian would cope without other mages around. Especially Fayleen. Hearing a sound behind him, Jaren turned to spot the short blonde woman assigned to escorting Eirian back to her homeland. Rylee stood with her arms crossed, the red of her band standing out against the silver gleam of her mail armor. Matching red bands adorned the delicately pointed tips of her ears, the piercings a result of a dare.

"Oi, Princess!" Rylee bellowed. "Move your adorable ass to the stables. We're waiting for you."

"If I called her ass adorable, she'd skewer me," Jaren joked.

Rylee rolled her eyes, replying, "Her ass is mine, Valkera, so keep your hands to yourself."

"Fuck you, Rylee."

"No thanks, Jaren, you're not my type."

Walking over to join them, Eirian shook her head at their exchange. Arm slung over her shoulders, Fayleen smirked at the two red mages and made a rude gesture that Rylee returned. Pressing her lips together to hide her laughter, Eirian tugged at her leather armor and gave Fayleen a sideways glance.

"I promise I'll finish your new armor," Fayleen said. "It will be worthy of a queen."

"I won't need new armor."

Jaren scoffed, giving her a look. "We've heard this argument before. It's why you didn't bother to keep up with training in mail."

"That's right." Rylee agreed. "I'm a princess, and I don't need mail."

Her eyes narrowed, and Eirian snapped, "I don't appreciate the two of you ganging up on me! You know the argument is valid! It's not like I'm going to be leading battles."

"No, they're going to put you in fancy dresses," Rylee mocked. "Make you whisper sweet nothings to pompous lords who wouldn't know what to do with their swords if an instruction book hit them over the head."

Snickering, Fayleen commented, "Let's not mention the dancing."

Eirian threw her hands in the air and snarled, "Fuck you!"

"I'll take you up on that offer once we stop for the night," Rylee said.

"Just rub it in, Rylee," Jaren muttered.

Her lips curled, and she gave Eirian a knowing look. "Oh, I plan to."

Eirian pulled away from Fayleen and took the few steps out of the training square to join Rylee. Following her, Jaren and Fayleen shared a look of agreement. They would make sure Eirian made it to the stables and the escort awaiting her. While Rylee and Fayleen watched on, Jaren and Eirian picked up their weapons, securing the swords to the baldrics crossing their chests. Fayleen felt a moment of pride, admiring her craftmanship adorning Eirian. The leather rippled with every movement Eirian made, and Fayleen sensed the protective wards entwined in every grain.

"She doesn't have to get on her horse," Rylee murmured. "Surely there is something you can say that will make her stay."

Fayleen answered, "I've exhausted everything. I sent letters to Celi and Gal, but I haven't heard from them. Gal could change her mind, and if Celi finally admitted the truth to Ree..."

"She belongs here."

"I know, but we can't change her mind. I've tried for years. She's determined to take her place as the future Queen of Endara."

Grunting, Rylee shot a look at where Jaren was fussing with his knives and asked, "Did you hear about his orders?"

"Yes, I did. Don't know if Ree knows."

"Think it would change her mind if she did?"

"Not in the slightest." Fayleen shrugged, adding, "Tessa being in Riane doesn't make a difference to her. It's been years since she fled, but people still make out like there is a rivalry between them."

"Wasn't there?"

"Nope, not on Ree's part. She's the most powerful bloody mage here. Do you think she's bothered by rivalries?"

"Rivalries?" Eirian asked from behind them.

Turning to her, Rylee waved over her shoulder at Jaren and said, "Did you hear?"

"No? Hear what?"

"They ordered Jaren to fetch his sister back to Riane," Fayleen answered.

Eirian looked surprised. "But the high council exiled Tessa."

"Guess with you leaving, they'd rather not have the two most powerful mages alive out of their control," Jaren said. "I'd prefer not to bring Tessa back, but orders are orders. If I don't go, they'll send someone else."

"She won't be happy."

"Which is why it's better if I go. Tessa will be less happy if the council sends hunters after her. Or worse..."

Startled, Rylee asked, "You don't think they'd put a price on her?"

"You don't think our father hasn't considered it?" Jaren replied.

Shuddering, Eirian ran a hand through her short brown hair. She sympathized with the reluctance Jaren was showing. They had witnessed the public
persecution led by her father targeting Tessa before she quietly vanished from
Riane. Eirian knew Jaren had helped Tessa escape the city. So had she. Her help
had been the distraction that kept people talking about something else for a few
days. Long enough for their disappearance to go unnoticed.

"Hugh's a fucker, that's for sure," Rylee grumbled.

"Riona is worse," Eirian commented. "I've seen the way she looks at me
like I'm dirt on her boots."

"Sorry, Jaren. They're your parents."

He shrugged. "Believe me, you'll hear no arguments. If Tessa decides she
doesn't want to come back, maybe we'll run. We could slip over the Telmian
border and vanish into the daoine lands."

Rylee nodded and said, "I'd recommend that. Screw coming back to Riane
when your fucker of a father wants Tessa dead. Do you know why they've
ordered you to bring her back?"

"No, but the order came from Azina. So, I know it's not what Hugh wants."

Eirian studied him. "Are you sure?"

"Azina and Hugh don't get on. Besides, the grand mage tried to protect
Tessa, so I don't see her husband willingly giving the orders to bring her back
to her death."

"You shouldn't be worrying about Tessa, Ree." Fayleen gave her a shove
and added, "You're supposed to be leaving Riane today. If you linger too long,
the high council might think you're hesitating."

"I'm not hesitating," she muttered.

They stared at Eirian, and she crossed her arms. Sighing, Rylee started out
of the training area, not glancing back to ensure Eirian had followed. She did
not need to look. Fayleen and Jaren would make sure Eirian came with her. The
sprawling grounds surrounding the red tower were busy, mages hurrying about
as they attended their duties. Above their heads, the shining white towers stood
out. It was mid-autumn, and the sky was an ominous gray. It hinted that rain
was on the way, but no one could ever be sure.

Looking at the main entrance to the tower, Eirian caught sight of the last
person she wanted to see before she left. He watched her hurrying across the
courtyard, a hand resting on the hilt of one of his twin blades. Following her
gaze, Fayleen groaned quietly and ducked her head, hoping he would ignore
her presence. Reaching out, Eirian threaded her fingers through Fayleen's and
gave her hand a reassuring squeeze. They had said their goodbyes that
morning, but Eirian hoped the watching archmage would not call Fayleen
away.

"Fayleen!"

"Fuck," she grumbled. "He's calling me. I should have known."

"He's doing it to make a point to me."

Chuckling, Rylee shot a glance at Jaren and commented, "Better run, Fay, before Baenlin feels a need to shout again. You might end up cleaning his office."

Snorting, Fayleen figured the task would be easier than working directly with him. Eirian looked at Baenlin and grinned, remembering the hours she had spent defiantly cleaning his office while Celiaen kept her company. Reminded of her absent friends, her smile faded, and she pulled Fayleen into a hug. Holding her tightly, Fayleen ignored the press of Baenlin's magic.

"I'm going to miss you, Ree. Don't go."

"Come to Amath as soon as they release you. I'll make a place for you in my household. If I have guards, ladies, and all that pomp, I can bloody well have a mage companion. I should have blues, but they decided it wasn't necessary." Eirian stepped back. "You could ask Celi to request you join his companions."

"They wouldn't let her. Fayleen is a human," Jaren pointed out.

"He has a point. They begrudgingly let half-elves like Kelsey serve Ensaycalan royalty, but not a human. Sorry, Jaren," Rylee apologized.

Holding Eirian's stare, Fayleen understood why she suggested it and nodded. Eirian returned the nod before giving Baenlin another look. He had left the tower, making his way towards them slowly.

"I love you, Fay, always," Eirian assured her.

Kissing Eirian's cheek, Fayleen murmured, "I'll see you when I see you."

"Find a way."

"Love you, sister."

Spinning on her heel, Fayleen rushed to intercept Baenlin before he could reach Eirian. None of them fancied the results. Grabbing Eirian's wrist, Rylee tugged her along, and Jaren gave her shoulder a shove. The faster they got away from the red tower, the less chance Baenlin would attempt to stop Eirian from leaving. He had been one of the most outspoken against Eirian returning to Endara. While Rylee agreed with him, she knew it had to be Eirian's choice.

"So, when you become queen—"

Interrupting Rylee, Eirian said, "It will be years before I become queen, so don't go making plans."

Rylee huffed. "I'm an elf. I have time to make plans."

"Point taken. What do you want?"

Jaren chuckled, unwilling to miss his chance to tease them. "Rylee doesn't have a point for you to take."

She hit him over the back of his head, and Eirian laughed. Their banter was something Eirian would miss when she went home. While she looked forward to seeing her father and cousins, Eirian knew she would be alone. The lone mage surrounded by strangers who hadn't seen her since she was a small child.

Keeping her eyes forward, Eirian did her best not to stare up at each of the towers as they followed the streets through Riane.

"That's enough," Eirian muttered. "Rylee, what do you want when I'm queen?"

"I want to attend your coronation! I mean, I bet those things are grand affairs."

"Yes, I imagine they are. Why would you want to attend?"

Holding a hand up, Rylee framed the sky with her fingers and said, "I want to laugh my ass off. Why else? Will they make you wear something fancy?"

Rolling her eyes, Eirian answered, "I'll spend the night before my coronation in the tomb of my ancestors. There's a whole formal recital of oaths before they put the crown on my head. So yes, I expect there'll be a fancy gown."

"I tell you what, I'll come to your coronation, and at the end of the day, I'll take your pretty gown off and kneel for a queen."

"Seriously, Rylee?" Jaren groaned. "Don't you ever think about anything else?"

"Nope. We're reds, Jaren. What else do we think about? We fight, drink, and then we have a bit of fun."

"A lot of fun," Eirian joked.

Waving at Eirian, Rylee laughed, "See, even the princess gets it... but I already knew that."

"A word, please, Eirian!"

They halted, turning to face the man who spoke and shared looks.

"Archmage Azina," she greeted.

Smoothing a hand over the intricate green embroidery of his coat, Azina studied the three younger mages impassively before settling his gaze on Eirian.

"I'm sure you've heard everything already, but before you left, I thought I should ask one more time."

Eirian chuckled, arching a brow as she asked, "Did the grand mage send you on her behalf?"

"Mayve understands your obligation to Endara, and so do I. However, are you sure that returning is the right thing for Endara?"

"Of course it is. I'm the rightful heir to the throne."

He crossed his arms, nodding slowly, and said, "No one is contesting that. You're the only child of King Nolan."

"Then what?"

"You're a mage. They'll never trust you, never accept you, and you'll constantly wonder if they'll turn on you. Is that how you want to live the rest of your life? Looking over your shoulder for a knife in the shadows?"

"The Endaran council has had twenty years to decide they didn't want a mage to take the throne when King Nolan dies. If they were so unhappy with it, they could have bypassed me before now. Instead, they sent tutors to instruct me in Endaran law and traditions," Eirian argued.

Azina glanced at Rylee and Jaren. "Don't go back to Endara, Eirian. Stay in Riane. You could be so much more than a princess waiting to be queen. More than a puppet on a throne, dancing to treaties with Ensaycal and the demands of lesser people."

She smiled, winking at Rylee and Jaren while they stared blankly at Azina. Their expressions did not falter, years of training as red mages keeping them in place. Azina grunted, turning back to Eirian and catching sight of her amusement.

"You could do me the decency of taking this seriously."

"I'm taking this seriously, believe me, Archmage," Eirian replied. "But when have I ever followed orders? Do you really think I'd be anyone's puppet?"

Inclining his head, Azina agreed. "Very true. You've always been obstinate. You're terrible at following orders—"

"Thank you."

"That wasn't a compliment."

"Oh, I disagree."

Rylee shifted, glancing away as she said, "Archmage, I have orders to escort Eirian to the border."

"I'm quite aware of your orders, Rylee," Azina replied. "If Eirian chose the right path, you wouldn't need to leave the city today."

Blinking, Eirian banished the shadows chasing at the edge of her mind. She knew what the right choice was, and it was not to remain in Riane. Turning to look toward the distant Yifthn sea, Eirian bowed her head.

"I'm making the right choice, Archmage. I'll do what I was born to do. I'll rule Endara when the time comes. Sitting idly by is not something I'm good at, and if I remain in Riane, that's exactly what I'll be doing."

Sighing heavily, Azina took a step back. He did not need to try anything to know he was no match for Eirian in power. Exchanging looks, Jaren and Rylee felt relieved when Eirian also took a step back. Azina held out his left hand, the green ring catching in the sunlight. Taking hold of it, Eirian bowed slightly, inclining her head in respect.

"You're a fine healer, Archmage. It's been a pleasure."

"I don't know how good a queen you'll make when the time comes, Eirian, but we will watch closely." Withdrawing his hand, Azina added, "You're still beholden to our laws."

Her lips twitched, and Eirian turned to Rylee. Bowing to Azina, Rylee ushered Eirian away while Jaren remained behind. Waiting until the two women were out of earshot, Jaren nodded to Azina.

"I'm seeing them to the stables and then leaving myself."

"Good, good. We need Tessa back in Riane, safely."

Biting the inside of his cheek, Jaren glanced after Eirian before saying, "If you tell her the grand mage is failing, she might stay."

"No. Let Eirian return to Endara. She'll change her mind when faced with their mistrust. Ride safely, Jaren, and watch your back. I don't trust your father," Azina replied and walked away.

Chasing after Eirian and Rylee, Jaren caught up with them, and they continued to the city's outskirts. Waiting for them, a company of mages stood around a loaded wagon chatting. Novices tended to horses in the complex's shade. Spotting her beloved mount, Eirian hurried over to a large brown gelding and greeted him. Joining her, Jaren patted the horse on the neck and smiled at Eirian.

"Don't give them a hard time."

She snorted. "No promises. I don't need an escort. I can ride to Amath on my own."

"They're following the expectations of your people. There will be an escort waiting for you at the border."

"I know my cousin Everett will lead it."

"You can change your mind at any point, don't forget."

Kissing his cheek, Eirian grinned and murmured, "Don't miss me too much, Jaren. Good luck finding Tessa. I'm actually sorry I won't be around to see her return."

Scratching the horse behind his ear, Jaren said, "You look after her, Halcyon. I know she's an idiot, but you're not. So, don't let her get into trouble."

"Right, you lazy fuckers!" Rylee yelled. "Let's get moving! We've got a few days of riding ahead of us to the Endaran border, and I don't want to hear any complaints."

Holding Halcyon's reins while Eirian hauled herself into the saddle, Jaren watched the others mount as well. Returning his gaze to Eirian, he wondered if he would ever see her again. A faint smile graced her lips as Eirian winked at him.

"You know where to find me, Jaren. Keep Rylee out of trouble. She has the potential to go places."

Letting go of the reins, Jaren replied, "You know I will."

Before she pressed her heels into Halcyon's side, Eirian stared at the towers and the buildings surrounding them. The city had been her home for twenty years, and she was reluctant to leave the safety of the familiar. Riane held so many memories, the good and the bad, and leaving her friends behind hurt. She had never backed down from a challenge, and Eirian knew she would adjust to life in Amath.

"You coming, Princess?" Rylee called.

Jaren muttered, "Does she ask that in bed?"

Eirian made a rude gesture in his direction and gave Halcyon a nudge to move. He was happy to follow the other horses, Rylee bringing her mount in beside Eirian. On the other side of Rylee, another elf looked bored, twirling his reins between his fingers. Glancing around, Eirian noted every person selected for her escort was an elf. It made her chuckle.

Baffled, Rylee asked, "What's funny?"

"The council really didn't want to take any chances. You're all elves."

"I asked for this task!"

"I know. They're just ensuring no one is likely to have a moment of defiance at the border. After all, I might tempt a human to come with me to Amath," Eirian explained.

"You haven't tried to tempt me."

"I don't need to. You like Riane too much, Rylee. You won't give up the chance to be a master one day to chase me. Though I wouldn't say no. You could be in charge of my protection."

"I don't want to leave Riane!"

Rylee and Eirian looked at the man and laughed. He sneered at them, rolling his eyes.

"I could ask for a new blue, Luke," Rylee said.

"You'd never! You love me too much, Rylee. I'm the one who stops you from killing people when they say you're short."

Eirian laughed, saying, "Any good blue would do that. What makes you so special?"

"Ree is right. What makes you special? Any blue would be happy to be assigned to me," Rylee said, grinning at Luke.

Watching them argue, Eirian smiled sadly. She would miss them and their banter. Looking forward, Eirian let her gaze drift over the landscape. Her magic wanted her to let go so it could turn the sparse scattering of windswept shrubs into a garden. Pushing the thought aside, Eirian indulged herself with one small thing. Something that would go unnoticed, even though it was out of place.

Behind them, a single dandelion bloomed.

TWO

"Well, there it is," Rylee said tensely.

Staring ahead at the distant gathering of people, Eirian swallowed nervously. They were waiting for her, but she did not think she was ready to face them. Banners flapped in the wind, the rearing horse crest of the royal family of Endara clear even at a distance. Eirian could pick out the flags of other families, including the house of Tamantal, the region her cousin ruled. Biting her lip, Eirian glanced at Rylee and took in the disinterested look she wore.

"There it is." Eirian agreed. "They're waiting for me."

"We're on Riane's side of the border, and you don't have to cross it. We'll back you up if you want to ride over there and tell them to fuck off."

Luke grunted in frustration. "Don't you think it's time to stop pressuring her, Rylee?"

"No, never. Until you cross that border, I have time to keep reminding you that you don't have to do this."

Eirian nodded and replied, "I know, Rylee. But no one is forcing me to do anything. I've decided to go back to my people and my family. I'm going to step up to my duty."

"Damn noble sentiment. Why do you always have to put everyone else first? Just once, Eirian. Just once, would you make a fucking choice for your own gain? Endara won't be worse off if you decide to stay in Riane!" Rylee snarled.

"No, but they'll be better off if I take my place. Think of all the good I could do!"

"You belong in Riane!"

"With a mage on the Endaran throne, think of the changes that could happen!"

Rylee snapped, "You're just one human!"

Cocking her head to the side, Eirian stared at Rylee with her eyes narrowed. Realizing what she had said, Rylee started stammering while Luke covered his face and groaned.

"Careful, Rylee, your elven superiority is showing. I'm just a human, after all."

Slipping from Halcyon's back, Eirian tossed his reins to Rylee and made her way to the wagon of goods. Her single chest of belongings was at the back, within easy reach. With it blocking the view of the distant waiting Endarans, Eirian began stripping off her weapons and armor. Balancing her twin swords on the edge of the chest, she carefully rolled her baldrics up and put them in before doing the same with her belts. Bracers followed, the jerkin resting on top. All she kept on was one belt and the two knives nestled against her back.

"What are you doing?" Rylee demanded.

"Making my introduction a little less confronting."

Holding the swords in her hands, Eirian pressed the hilts to her forehead and closed her eyes. She knew Celiaen would understand why she was doing it, but Eirian wished he was there instead of Rylee. It had been a year and a half since she last saw Celiaen and Galameyvin, the two princes who were her closest friends next to Fayleen. Eirian missed them more than she could ever miss Riane.

"Blade of my blade, song of my song," she whispered, brushing her magic against the bond she had with Celiaen.

Kissing the two hilts, Eirian put them in the chest and rummaged around to pull her clothes on top. Watching her hide the weapons and armor, Rylee muttered curses, shaking her head in disapproval.

"What would he say about this shitfuckery?"

Eirian smiled, replying, "Celi would remind me of my duty to my people. He understands because he'll be the King of Ensaycal one day."

"Princess Eirian and Prince Celiaen, the two biggest fucking idiots in the world. How Galameyvin puts up with you… well, I know how he puts up with you. The same way I do."

With a glance at her hand, Eirian slipped the purple band from her finger and let it drop into the chest. The moment it vanished into the objects, Eirian wanted to grab it back. It felt strange to remove it, to hide the symbol of her order when the people waiting for her were aware she was a mage. All she had to do was give it some time, slowly let them become accustomed to her. Bit by bit, Eirian reminded herself. Take it day by day, step by step, and they would get used to her. Shutting the lid, she turned to look at Rylee.

Rylee dismounted, and other mages held the reins to her horse and Halcyon. Joining Eirian at the back of the wagon, she slapped the chest and growled.

"Fucking fool."

Winking, Eirian replied, "Don't you know it."

Reaching up, Rylee grabbed the front of Eirian's tunic and pulled her down so they could kiss her. Eirian let her, understanding it was her way of saying goodbye. They had avoided saying it to each other on the ride to the border. This was their last chance. Cupping the back of Rylee's head, Eirian rested her forehead against hers.

"I'll miss you," she whispered.

"Don't go."

"Rylee..."

Eirian thought she saw the glimmer of tears, but Rylee blinked, and they vanished. Letting go, she stepped back and straightened her armor. Nearby, Luke sighed and shook his head at them. All the blues, not just him, felt the emotions rolling off the two women. They waited, watching as Eirian collected Halcyon and pulled herself into the saddle. Following suit, Rylee mounted her horse and returned to the front of the group, giving the wagon driver a nod. Holding back, Eirian let the group move.

"What are you doing?" Luke waited with her.

"Don't worry, I'm not bailing. Halcyon and I want a run. I don't think they'll let me have too many of those for a while."

"Alright, I'll tell Rylee. We'll hand you over and leave. Don't need to drag this out."

Watching him trot to catch up with the others, Eirian scratched Halcyon's neck under his mane. The gelding pawed at the road impatiently to express his desire to go. She chuckled, looking at the rolling green of the countryside. It was so different from the land surrounding Riane. No salt-lashed shrubs or trees bent by the harsh sea winds that frequently besieged the cliff city. Instead, it was a rich green, the white of sheep dotted about. It was a region that escaped the snows of the north and the bitter coastal storms of the south.

"Just a little longer," Eirian said.

Continuing to stare out at the land, Eirian let a small part of her power course through the earth. Not too much, just enough to make the green vibrant and a smattering of wildflowers appear. Nothing that would attract attention. None of the mages with her were aware of what she could do. Not even Rylee knew everything. Those mages who knew were far away in Ensaycal or back in Riane. Satisfied with her efforts, Eirian drew her magic back and allowed herself one last chance to consider what she was about to do.

"It's for the best."

Halcyon snorted, tossing his head.

"I know it is. Let them meet me first, without my magic in their faces. Then I'll slowly drop my shields, just enough at a time that they won't notice."

The horse did not offer her an answer, and Eirian sighed. She partially shielded her magic all the time and had done so since she was old enough to grasp how much more powerful she was than everyone around her. Having flowers blooming wherever she walked was frustrating as well. By the time Eirian finished building walls around her magic, she felt empty. The power remained, lingering in the background. She always sensed it, but it was deep, a smoldering fire that did not give any heat.

Shaking off the feeling, Eirian forced herself to smile. The escort had reached the Endarans, and she knew they were waiting on her. With a touch of her heels, Halcyon eagerly leapt into a canter, and Eirian kept enough of a grip on the reins to hold him from a gallop. She did not want the run to end too soon. Tossing her head back, Eirian laughed, enjoying the rush of air. She loved running. It felt like freedom.

Rylee shook her head, catching Luke's gaze as she watched the faces of the Endarans. They watched Eirian coming towards them, a broad smile and laughter betraying how much she enjoyed the run. Voices murmured among the crowd, shocked words expressing horror at the undignified behavior of their princess. Rylee heard a woman gasp, muttering something about trousers to the gaggle of younger ladies with her. Glancing down at her own clothes and armor, Rylee scowled, looking back at Eirian.

Walking over to join Eirian as Halcyon fought against stopping, Rylee caught the reins. Still grinning, Eirian slid from his back and glanced at the crowd, her expression never faltering. Rylee recognized it. She had seen Eirian wear that look before. A smile intended to disarm, to hide the ruthless warrior beneath jokes and wide brown eyes. Catching Eirian's wrist, Rylee realized she could not feel her magic.

"Ree?"

"I know what I'm doing, Rylee," Eirian murmured.

She protested, whispering, "It's dangerous."

"Just for a little while. Until they're used to me."

"Eirian Altira!"

Turning to the man who called her name, Eirian's smile became genuine, and she rushed over to greet him. He pulled her into a hug, lifting Eirian up to swing her around. Hearing Eirian laugh, Rylee sighed and held onto Halcyon's reins.

"Everett! I'm so glad they sent you," Eirian said.

Crinkling his nose, Everett ruffled her short hair and replied, "Who else would they send? Llewellyn?"

"Well, he is my cousin as well."

"And a proper scoundrel."

"My father could have come."

"I'm sorry, Eirian, King Nolan is busy with—"

She cut him off with a shake of her head. "I know. King Nolan has a kingdom to run. I'll see him when we get to Amath. It's not like another week will matter when I haven't seen him since I was five."

Hearing the dismissal in her voice, Everett turned to wave at a group of heavily armed men. They approached, saluting as they bowed. Eirian looked them over, meeting the gaze of the man at the front. His blue eyes studied her, and she thought they were familiar, a tug at her memories making her press her lips together. Gaze dropping to the knife hilts at her waist, his brows arched in amusement, and Eirian smiled. She had a feeling that whoever he was, he would be a fair challenge.

"Let me make some introductions," Everett said, pointing at the lead man. "This is Aiden. He's the captain of your guard and a right cantankerous bastard. I picked him for the task because he's one of the best swordsmen in Endara."

Smirking, Eirian let her gaze drift over him before saying, "I'm sure he is. A pleasure to meet you, Captain."

"It is an honor to serve you, Your Highness," Aiden replied.

Clearing her throat, Rylee muttered, "You won't be saying that once you get to know her."

"Rylee!" Eirian growled.

"Just saying, he doesn't know you like I do."

"Goodbye, Rylee."

Rylee blew a kiss to Eirian and chuckled. "You said farewell earlier. Repeatedly."

Aiden glanced at Rylee, taking in her armor and swords. She gave him a wink, and he assumed she had been the one in charge of Eirian's protection. Tossing Halcyon's reins to Eirian, Rylee turned and walked back to join the other mages watching the Endarans.

"My predecessor?"

Covering her mouth to stop herself from snorting, Eirian replied, "No, my sparring partner. I didn't need guards in Riane."

"That's right!" Everett said, looking Eirian over. "They didn't let you keep the swords and armor?"

"Something like that."

Crossing his arms, Aiden suspected she would be trouble. Sharing a look with the man next to him, he nodded at Halcyon. They took in the quivers hanging from the saddle, an unstrung bow in a comfortable position to be drawn. Catching his gaze, Eirian glanced at her horse and smiled.

"I'm a fair archer," she said.

"We'll see about that."

Glancing between them, Everett grinned. "Perhaps Aiden will let you continue to do some sparring."

"Well now." Eirian chuckled. "I'm sure the good captain wouldn't deny his princess the chance to continue learning how to use a sword."

The look on her face told Aiden that her words were a challenge. He recognized the confident gleam in her eyes. He had seen it worn by plenty of young soldiers who thought they were unbeatable. A woman spoke from behind him before he corrected Eirian's assumption, and Aiden moved out of the way to let her through.

"Your Highness! It is an absolute pleasure to meet you."

Leaning in, Everett murmured, "Brenna, Duchess of Raellwynt and wife of Marcellus. She's your mistress of the robes."

"Your Grace!" Eirian said, stepping forward.

Brenna curtsied, looking Eirian over in disapproval before watching the mages withdraw. None of them remained, and she frowned. The only thing they left was the wagon of goods from Riane that was destined for Amath. Aiden signaled for one of his men to go over and take the reins from Eirian.

"Where are your servants?" she asked with concern.

Eirian's brows rose as she replied, "I don't have any servants. No servants, no guards, and previously no need for them."

"A princess who can dress herself, how scandalous," Aiden muttered to his companion.

He chuckled. "Careful, Aiden, the Duchess will yell at you."

"Nothing new. Brenna yelled at me this morning about not being too familiar with the princess and Everett."

"Do you think she remembers you?"

Aiden watched Eirian exchanging pleasantries with Brenna. It was clear the conversation frustrated her, but she was doing her best to hide it. Catching Everett's eye, he nodded.

"I don't know, Merle, but I won't ask. There's a chance she's too polite to mention it."

Merle snorted in disbelief. "I doubt that. No offense, Captain, but I think we drew the short straw. Something tells me the princess is all sorts of trouble."

"She's one woman. How much trouble could she be?" Aiden asked.

"I can tell you don't have sisters."

"There's twenty-five of us. If we can't manage one woman, then something's not right."

They watched Everett and Brenna lead Eirian over to greet more nobles. Observing her move, Merle thought Eirian resembled a predator stalking her prey. Despite her casual comments about learning to use a sword, he had a suspicion she was better than they knew. He had watched her assess them, a cold calculation in her eyes that reminded him of seasoned officers. Merle only knew one other person who positioned their knives the way Eirian had hers nestled in the small of her back.

"Aiden, I have a feeling we shouldn't turn our backs on her," Merle said.

He agreed. "I should've brought Gabe with us."

"I'm sure she hasn't killed anyone, but she is a mage."

"Of course she hasn't. She's a princess."

Even though Eirian could not hear them, she glanced over her shoulder at her new guards and smirked. Aiden dug his nails into his palm, gazing back at her blankly. His response made her smirk widen, and Eirian winked at him. Her hand brushed against the hilt of a knife as Eirian turned back to speak to Brenna, and Aiden watched her thumb stroke the pommel.

"Oh yeah, we're in trouble." Merle chuckled, giving him a sideways look. "Or maybe just you. That look is not for my benefit."

"She's a princess."

"She's a mage."

Aiden hoped they were wrong. Everett left the nobles and approached them, grinning over his shoulder at Eirian as she dealt with bowing lords.

"What do you think?"

"Does the princess really know how to use a sword?" Aiden asked.

Everett nodded. "Yes, she does. I mean, it's been a few years since I last saw her in Riane, but Eirian can hold her own if attacked."

"I suspect the Duchess will have her hands full."

"It's Eirian. Our mothers had their hands full before she started walking. She's been a handful since she was born."

Smiling faintly at the memory, Aiden replied, "Hopefully, she doesn't still climb trees."

"I don't know, Captain. I'd like to see you climbing a tree to fetch our princess down," Merle said, grinning at the prospect.

"It wouldn't be the first time!" Everett laughed.

"Everett," Aiden grumbled.

"She didn't indicate she remembers you."

"Might be for the best."

"I feel bad. I'm delivering her to Amath and then leaving in a few weeks."

Aiden nodded and said, "You have to go home for winter. Besides, Eirian will have us, her ladies, and the court. She's got a lot to learn."

"Are you telling me what to do, Aiden?" Everett grumbled.

"I've been telling you what to do since you were born, little brother. That's never going to change. I even give Gunter tips."

"Bastard."

Hearing the affection in Everett's voice, Aiden chuckled. "Damn straight."

"I better rescue our dear princess," Everett commented. "She looks daunted by the crows."

"Merle, can you make sure they transfer her belongings off the wagon? Sid, take her horse to the rest. Make sure no one touches him. Wouldn't want our princess to take a fall."

Saluting Aiden, Sid walked off, leading Halcyon, and Merle signaled to two more guards to follow him. Going with Everett, Aiden slipped into place a step behind Eirian, smiling when she glanced over her shoulder at him. He pressed a fist to his chest, saluting her. Eirian's eyes narrowed in suspicion, but she turned back to the woman she was listening to. At her side, Everett offered his arm, cutting into the conversation.

"It's already midmorning, Your Highness. We should make our way to Amath."

Eirian glanced at the sun, frowning as she said, "Yes, we should. I'm sorry to cut this lovely chat short, Lady Beth, but His Grace is right."

She curtsied, bowing her head and replying, "Of course, Your Highness."

Letting Everett direct her to the waiting horses, Eirian took in the circle of men surrounding Halcyon. The situation did not bother the gelding. His head was high as he calmly stood, ignoring the man holding his reins.

"He's an impressive horse," Aiden commented.

"Yes, he is. Halcyon is my good boy. He's steadfast, and I can count on him to never put a hoof wrong," she said, glancing over her shoulder. "I half expected them to deny me permission to keep him, but I'm thankful they didn't."

He saw the affection in her eyes as Eirian spoke about the horse. The guards parted, letting them through, and she smiled at Sid. Watching her hands run over Halcyon, Aiden shared a look with Everett. Eirian checked the horse, fingers dancing over the tack while they observed. It was obvious she knew what she was doing. While they waited for the nobles to sort themselves out, Aiden instructed his men to prepare their horses. Taking the reins from Kip, he smiled at Eirian.

"You know your way around a horse."

Not taking her eyes off her quivers as she checked the buckles, Eirian replied, "I do. I might be a princess, Captain, but I think you'll find I'm really quite capable."

"I'll be the judge of that."

"Yes, I'm sure you will be. You strike me as the judging sort."

Aiden chuckled. "You've got snark for a princess."

Laughing, Eirian slung an arm over her saddle and leaned against Halcyon to study him. Arching a brow, Aiden noticed how similar her eyes were to Everett's. The same shade of brown, the same mischievous gleam. She drew her bottom lip between her teeth before looking him over like she was appraising him. Swallowing, Aiden decided Merle was right. She was trouble, the sort of trouble that would drive him insane.

"I've heard worse."

"Really?"

Eirian smirked. "You bet. Believe me, Captain, you can't throw anything at me I haven't heard before. I've got thicker skin than you think."

He could tell she believed it. Mulling over the options available to him, Aiden tried to unsettle Eirian. From the way she looked at him, it was clear he needed to make sure she knew who was in charge.

"Alright then, I'll give you a chance to prove it. Once we're in Amath, and you're all settled, you can join us for training."

"Excellent. I'm sure you're a talented teacher."

"I'm a hard teacher," he replied. "But I'm sure you're used to that."

Her gaze dropped briefly, a smile curling her lips. Aiden recognized the gleam in her eyes and clenched his jaw. It inspired thoughts he could not risk thinking. Watching people mount their horses, Eirian shifted her hand to grasp the back of her saddle to prepare for hauling herself up. Tossing the reins over Halcyon's neck, Aiden moved to give her a hand, but Eirian was off the ground before he could. She crinkled her nose in amusement, and he sighed.

"When they get you in dresses, you'll be begging for my help."

"I never beg." She leaned down to whisper, "I'll let you into a secret, though."

Aiden muttered, "This should be interesting."

"I don't remember the last time I wore a dress. Probably before I left for Riane."

"Never?"

"Never."

"Then you'll definitely need my help," Aiden quipped.

Eirian replied mockingly, "At least you'll have a use."

Looking around, Aiden spotted Everett leading his horse over. Most people had mounted. His men were waiting for him to take his place, Merle holding his horse's reins. Indicating she should lean down, Aiden took in the confident smile on Eirian's face as she crossed her arms on the pommel of her saddle. Moving in as close as he could, Aiden held Halcyon's reins tightly. He stared at her, wishing her smile was a little less confident. It would be easier if it was.

"Let me make one thing clear, Princess. I take my role seriously. We're going to be together for a long time, and it'll be easier for both of us if we try to get along."

"Why, Captain, you've only just met me. Don't assume we won't get along. I'm a friendly person most of the time, and I don't bite hard... unless you ask nicely."

"I mean it. Your safety is my priority, and I won't tolerate an overconfident princess putting herself in danger."

Straightening, Eirian stared down at him with a crooked smile. She considered dropping her shields and letting Aiden taste a hint of her magic. People had called her overconfident all her life, and Eirian was used to proving them wrong. Aiden would be no different. Cringing, she shook her head and stopped herself from releasing her power.

Mistaking her reaction, he nodded slowly and said, "I thought as much. If you do what you're told, Princess, we'll have no reason to argue, and you'll remain perfectly safe."

The words made Eirian bristle, and she reminded herself of the plan. She would play her abilities down, let people like Aiden think they were better than her. If allowing him to bark orders in her direction and defeat her in training was what it would take, then she would do it with a smile. They could not know what she was capable of, the lives she had taken, the blood on her hands. Returning to Amath was a fresh start. One without the preconceptions she had faced in Riane. Eirian would make it work.

Eirian replied icily, "As you wish, Captain."

Patting Halcyon's neck, Aiden let go of the reins and moved away. He paused, looking back at her, enjoying the frustrated clench of her jaw.

"Good girl."

"Captain," Eirian said, stopping him. "You don't know what I'm capable of or what I'm willing to do. Don't underestimate me. You might regret it."

Running a hand through his messy brown curls, Aiden smiled. It was a knowing smile that told Eirian he was used to boundaries being pushed by subordinates. She had seen masters in Riane direct that smile her way. Eirian had always gone out of her way to get rid of that smile. Aiden was a new challenge, and she enjoyed a good challenge. They were always the most pleasurable wins.

"Right back at you, darling."

THREE

"Welcome home, Eirian!" Everett declared.

Gazing at the city, Eirian struggled to connect it to the diagrams and drawings she had seen. It was not how she imagined. Great walls ringed the city, and the ancient keep her ancestors had built towered above everything else. Eirian had read detailed reports on the construction, the work that mages had put into every stone. She had studied it, learning everything there was to know, right down to the maps of the underground caverns that housed an ever-flowing stream of water.

It was wonderful, and Eirian rubbed her mouth while she continued to stare in awe. Every line, every stone, the smoke that rose in eddies to the wind, the tiled roofs of the mismatched buildings. All of it was magnificent to her. She imagined Celiaen making jokes about her ability to find everything beautiful. The thought made her smile, and Eirian glanced to the side, half expecting Celiaen to be there. Instead, she caught the blue eyes of Aiden, and he gave her a curious look.

"It's not quite what I expected," Eirian commented. "The maps, the drawings, the architectural reports. None of it compares to seeing Amath with my own eyes."

Snorting, Everett asked, "You've actually studied those things? Powers, Eirian, didn't you have anything better to do?"

"Of course! Mages built the castle and the reinforcing structures beneath it in the caves. I've studied the ward maps as well, but Fay helped me understand a lot of them. I'm not a yellow, and construction isn't my thing."

Brenna huffed. "I should think not! You're a princess."

"What is your thing?" Aiden asked quietly.

He had been trying for days to find out what order Eirian belonged to. No amount of hinting had convinced her to divulge the information, and asking outright had received a defiant smirk and a flippant response. Eirian's clothes were plain gray, absent of the intricate colored embroidery typically adorning mage garments. Aiden knew enough about mages to recognize that the shade of gray she wore designated her as a full mage. The slate color was darker than the silver-gray worn by novices, but not as dark as the shades worn by masters and archmages.

"I told you before, Captain, killing people is my thing."

Everett snickered. "Stop tormenting the man."

Sighing, Eirian shrugged. It was infuriating and relieving that none of them believed her when she suggested she could kill. She did not know how to explain what she could do. Her magic gave life, and it took life. There was little else. Eirian could not heal like a green, and she could not craft things like a yellow. She had some ability to manipulate emotions like a blue, but it was minor. What Eirian could do was fight like a red, her bloodlust a raging force few could resist.

"But it's so fun," she replied.

"We're on the wrong side of the city, but over that way is the large wood maintained for our use," Everett said, changing the subject.

"That's right!" Brenna confirmed.

Aiden glanced at Merle, muttering, "I'm sure the princess isn't one for hunting."

Nudging Halcyon, Eirian heard him and said cheerily, "Actually, Captain, I can drop a moving target at over two hundred yards on the run. I only need one shot. How many do you need?"

Aiden took a deep breath and watched Brenna follow Eirian, the convoy of nobles making their way towards the city. Merle and the other guards accompanied Eirian, leaving him behind with Everett.

"She's a purple."

"You're only just telling me that?" Aiden snapped.

Everett shrugged, saying, "I didn't think I'd need to. Obviously, she doesn't want it widely known."

"She doesn't wear any marks of her order."

"Like I said, she doesn't want it known. Respect her privacy, and stop trying to pry information out of your future queen. It might be better if we let the magic question fade from thought. There are enough grumbles among the nobility. Let's not give Eirian more obstacles to overcome."

"Everett." Aiden stopped him from leaving, saying, "When are you going to tell her?"

"Not yet."

"It's not fair to keep it from her. She should know what she's walking into."

Shaking his head, Everett growled, "She's my family! I'm doing what's best for her. Eirian needs time to settle in."

Aiden sighed. "I think you're underestimating her ability to adapt."

"She's been away for twenty years, Aiden. All the reading and tutors won't prepare her for life in the Endaran court."

"And how long before someone lets slip about the King's illness? What if she witnesses one of his episodes? You tasked me with protecting Eirian for the rest of our lives, but that isn't something I can protect her from. Better to tell her once she's safely in her chambers and away from gossiping nobles."

"Don't let personal grudges impede your job," he muttered.

Grinding his teeth, Aiden replied, "This has nothing to do with how I found out about our father dying! Eirian expects to get to know her father. She thinks she has years to spend with him before he dies, and she becomes queen."

"All the more reason to let Eirian think everything is fine! If she knows Nolan is unwell, that is all she'll see. It might even send her running back to Riane."

"Would that be a bad thing? Riane is what she knows, and you're what Endara knows. Your claim to the throne is as strong as hers."

Everett stared at him in silence, and Aiden crossed his arms.

"Careful, Aiden, you sound like father. Next, you'll tell me you want to be the earl."

"Don't twist my intentions, little brother. You know I was happy serving in the military, but it was your idea to make me Eirian's captain. I'm thinking about what is best for her. Maybe the best thing for her is to turn down the throne and go back to the mages."

Staring at the tail end of the people who had accompanied Eirian from the border, Everett contemplated if Aiden was right. He suspected it was the truth, but he wanted Eirian to have some untainted memories of her father. Rubbing his face, Everett slumped in the saddle and gave Aiden a frustrated look.

"I'll tell her when I return after winter."

Aiden did not look impressed with his decision, shaking his head while staring at Amath in the distance.

"If Nolan gets worse over the winter, Marcellus will tell Eirian. He'll be remaining since Brenna is in charge of Eirian's ladies."

"Have you run this past Ulric, Sabine, Wendel, and Ollier?" Aiden asked.

"No, but I will. General Cameron likely thinks the same as you, that we should get it over with and tell her."

Reminded of the general, Aiden glanced away. Cameron had been one of the first to congratulate him on his promotion to the royal guards. The suggestions Cameron made to Aiden had left him uncomfortable, and he wondered if Everett knew what some people were plotting. Especially since it involved him. It did not matter yet. The more pressing concern was the state of King Nolan's health.

"He's concerned about how Athnaral will react to Eirian's return. You know what their laws state." Aiden reminded Everett.

"That I do. I need you to support me, Aiden."

"I've always supported you, Everett, and I always will." Aiden sucked in a deep breath and continued, "But you know I take my job seriously. No matter what it is. Eirian is my priority now. She might think it's funny to have guards and for me to give her orders, but she'll learn."

Everett grinned, saying, "I'm sorry I won't be around to watch the two of you figure out who is in charge. Riane gives mages a lot of freedom, so expect her to fight you."

Shrugging, Aiden nodded at the group that had left them behind. He knew Everett wanted to be with Eirian when she entered the city.

"She's one mage. How much trouble could she give me?" he asked.

"You remember how much trouble she was when she was a child."

Laughing, Everett kicked his horse into a canter, his guards keeping him surrounded. Frowning, it left Aiden wondering what Everett knew about Eirian that he had not bothered to share. Muttering curses, he encouraged his horse to move, hurrying to catch up with everyone else. Skirting around the outside of the group of nobles, Aiden located Eirian near the front with Merle beside her. Brenna was chatting away, and Eirian was listening with a bored expression.

He caught the mention of tailors and understood why Eirian looked bored. Merle gave him an amused look, nodding at the city walls. They were close enough to see the city guards lining the parapets, watching for their arrival. Most city folk would not care about the group of nobles riding through, but the guards knew who was among them. Curiosity drove those on and off duty to watch from where they could. Glancing at Eirian, Aiden caught her staring at the guards lining the wall and took in the calculating gleam in her eyes.

"You know, they added these walls much later than the main keep and original city," Eirian commented.

"Well, yes, cities grow," Brenna replied.

"From a defensive standpoint, these walls are less resistant. This is because common laborers made them rather than master stonemasons from among the yellows."

Everett joined them and asked, "Are you expecting someone to besiege Amath?"

"Should I be?"

"No."

Brenna arched her brows at Everett, saying, "Endara is at peace. That won't change."

"Excellent. War is a messy business," Eirian said calmly. "Unfortunately, we can never be sure when Athnaral might decide to be less peaceful."

Studying her, Aiden caught the suspicious look she directed at Everett. It vanished as quickly as it appeared, but it made him wonder what Eirian knew. He doubted it was anything they did not. Eirian caught him looking at her and smiled, her short brown hair catching in the breeze. He had heard Brenna lamenting over the shortness, but Aiden thought it suited her.

"Now, once we get you to your quarters in the keep, I'll have the tailors sent for," Brenna said.

Eirian groaned. "Right away?"

"Yes. I had arranged a suitable wardrobe, but you're taller and… uh, well, the dresses are unlikely to fit."

"Taller and?"

Aiden saw the twitch of her lips. She knew precisely what Brenna was trying to avoid saying. Eirian had the figure of a soldier who trained daily. He had caught her doing stretches and exercises before breakfast each morning of the journey. Like everyone else, Brenna had expected Eirian to be a dainty woman, softly spoken and typical of the Endaran court.

"Either way, we need to sort out the right clothes for you. You can't greet the King and court in what you're wearing."

"I have formal attire," Eirian commented.

Brenna looked hopeful, asking, "You have a dress?"

"Powers no. Don't be ridiculous."

Biting back laughter, Aiden said, "While the Duchess makes those arrangements, I'll introduce you to the rest of your guards. Gabe and Fionn remained in Amath to finalize rosters and wait for the last few men to arrive."

Seeing an opportunity to irritate Aiden, Eirian asked, "Are they as pleasant as you?"

"Absolutely, Princess," Aiden replied. "We're all charming men who enjoy picnics in the woods and going for long walks in meadows."

"What a pity. I was hoping you'd say you enjoyed drinking, gambling, and wagering on brawlers. I know I do."

Clearing his throat, Everett said, "Your Highness, what do you know of brawling?"

Eirian winked at Aiden. "I've got a mean uppercut, and you wouldn't like my hook."

"Left or right?" Merle enquired.

"Both. We're taught to use our left and right hands equally in everything."

Groaning, Brenna covered her face with a hand. Fascinated by the subject, Merle ignored the look directed his way by Aiden and studied Eirian.

"Do they split you by weight in Riane?"

"Fuck no! The only hard rule in any fighting is no killing each other. Breaking a limb isn't a big deal when you've got greens to patch you up." Eirian shrugged, adding, "Besides, it's good to know hand to hand if you're disarmed in combat. Big swords aren't always best."

Aiden glanced at her knives. On the other side, Brenna looked horrified, and Everett was holding back laughter. There were murmurs from those nobles listening in as they entered the city. Around them, buildings rose almost identical in appearance and color. The dark stone was all locally quarried and commonly found in Endara. Some masons considered it the best, making Endaran stone a high commodity export. Eirian stared at everything with wide eyes, the look reminding Aiden of the child he had known.

"It's beautiful," she murmured.

"It's Amath," he replied.

There was no challenge in the smile Eirian gave him. Her eyes shone with an appreciation of what she was looking at, and Aiden wondered how she could seem so innocent.

"Captain, everything is beautiful if you know what you're looking at."

He returned the smile. "You're right."

Eirian fell silent, ignoring all attempts from Brenna and Everett to engage her in conversation. She was busy focusing on every detail of the city that she could. Aiden watched her gaze following people as they went about their lives, the gleam of appreciation never fading. He noticed the way Eirian's nose flared when the scent of fresh bread reached them. Several of his men had already commented about how much she ate. Aiden suspected Eirian would be hungry when they arrived and noted to send someone for food.

When they reached the moat surrounding the original city and castle, Eirian grinned. She dropped the reins, pushing down on the saddle with her hands to stretch up for a better look at the curtain walls that rose out of the water. They wound around the hill, inter-spaced with bastions. Only one bridge crossed the moat, a defensive chokepoint that had not lost relevance even after expanding the city. As they crossed the bridge, horns announced their arrival, giving the keep time to prepare.

Unlike the outer curtain wall, the middle curtain walls had tall towers. They carefully spaced the buildings through the outer bailey, positioning them in locations least likely to affect defensive measures. Eirian had studied all their layouts, knowing where to find the various smithies, lower stables, guard barracks, training yards, and tanneries. Passing through more gates, they entered the middle bailey, and Eirian had to crane her neck to look up at the towering keep that rose high above the inner curtain walls.

"It's huge," Eirian said.

Everett nodded, replying, "Yes, it is. I'd give you a rundown of the history, but I suspect you know more than I do."

"Most likely."

"Please, don't sound so modest."

She crinkled her nose in amusement, and Everett chuckled. When they entered the inner bailey, Eirian gasped. The large courtyard was a hive of activity, people hurrying in and out of the keep. Her gaze located the trees growing higher than the walls of the garden, and Aiden detected relief on her face. It was not the only garden on the grounds, but it was the largest. Stable staff were waiting to deal with all the horses, and people were eager to dismount. When a young man came to take Halcyon's reins from her, Eirian protested.

"I can look after him."

"Your Highness, that is not appropriate," Brenna said.

Growling, Eirian quickly unbuckled the quivers from the saddle and slung them over her shoulder. Arching a brow, Aiden shared a look with Merle while Everett walked away to greet the people waiting by the entrance. Brenna opened her mouth to argue, but the look on Eirian's face silenced her. Moving to join Everett, Eirian swept her gaze over the gathered people, taking stock of their reactions to her appearance.

"Let me introduce Her Highness Princess Eirian Altira," Everett said, waving in Eirian's direction.

"My ladies, my lords," Eirian greeted them. "It's a lovely day, wouldn't you say?"

The tallest man among them chuckled, giving Brenna a pointed look. She spread her hands, shaking her head, and Eirian assumed he was Duke Marcellus, Brenna's husband. Extending her hand to him, Eirian smiled broadly.

"Your Grace, it's good to meet you. I've heard a lot about you."

Marcellus grasped her hand, surprised by the strength of her grip. Beside her, Everett cleared his throat, and Brenna muttered something under her breath that Eirian could not quite make out. He smiled, amused by the situation.

"You're just like your father, Your Highness," Marcellus said.

"I suspect few would say that's a good thing."

Releasing her hand, he replied, "Possibly not."

Stepping out of the way, Marcellus let another man move forward. He was older, gray hair showing signs of balding, but Eirian could tell he was a shrewd man from the way he studied her.

"I'm Chancellor Ulric," he said, bowing stiffly.

Four more officials stepped forward, each bowing.

"Treasurer Sabine," a woman said.

Smiling faintly, a man introduced himself. "Chamberlain Wendel."

Beside him, the next man said, "Justiciar Ollier."

Last on the line, a heavily armed man stared at Eirian impassively with a hand on his sword. Eirian returned his stare, cocking her head to the side while she waited for his introduction. She had a good idea who he was and skipped the formalities.

"And, of course, you're General Cameron," Eirian said, extending her hand to him.

He arched a brow, eyes shifting to the bow and quivers slung over her shoulder and the glimpse of hilts he saw at her waist. Grasping Eirian's hand, Cameron held her gaze, waiting for her to look away. When she did not flinch, he chuckled and saluted.

"Your Highness. Interesting choice for a bow," he commented.

"Now, General, I'm sure I don't need to explain the reasons behind my possessing a recurve instead of a longbow."

"No swords?"

Shooting a look at Aiden, Eirian smirked and replied, "Apparently, I don't need them anymore. I've got twenty-four strapping guards and a dashing captain to wave their blades around. Are all your officers as pretty as he is?"

Cameron's booming laugh surprised everyone, and he let go of Eirian's hand. Waving at his fellow council members, he appreciated the shock on their faces.

"Your captain is one of the finest soldiers in Endara," Cameron said with a nod to Aiden.

"Yes, but unfortunately, like a lot of men, he and my other guards think that bigger is better. I look forward to teaching them otherwise."

Glancing down at her hand, Cameron noticed the lack of a band to tell him what order she belonged to. He had met many mages over the years, but sensed no magic rolling off Eirian like he expected.

"Are you a red?"

Eirian gave him a crooked smile. "Something like that. I'd pass."

"So, I don't have to translate for you?"

"Well, that depends. How many hours do you want to debate offensive moves?"

He said, "I could go all day."

"I'm one for rapid dominance, but I have an advantage as a mage. Of course, disinformation makes an ambush victory all the sweeter."

Her eyes slid in Aiden's direction, and Cameron chuckled. He did not need anyone to tell him that Eirian was dangerous, and she was doing her best to appear otherwise. From the look on Aiden's face, it was clear he was underestimating Eirian. Nodding, Cameron saluted her again and stepped back in line with the other council members. They looked at Cameron and Eirian, uncertain of what exactly they had exchanged.

"I look forward to getting to know you, Your Highness."

"And I, you, General," Eirian replied.

Cameron winked, adding, "I'll try not to underestimate you."

"Don't worry if you do. I'm used to it. Give a girl the title of princess, and people fall over their feet to underestimate you."

Clearing her throat, Brenna said, "It's been a long ride. I should get Her Highness to her chambers and settled."

Ulric agreed. "That is a fine idea. His Majesty looks forward to seeing you tomorrow, Your Highness."

Aiden saw the crack appear in her mask, disappointment flickering across her face briefly. Forcing a smile, Eirian nodded.

"Inform the King that I look forward to our reunion."

Allowing Brenna to guide Eirian up the stairs into the keep, the council members exchanged looks before turning to Everett. Glancing over his shoulder as he followed, Aiden knew they would have a conversation about how to approach informing Eirian of what was going on. Studying Eirian from the corner of his eye, Aiden did not know if her quick handling of Cameron should impress or concern him. He was the most powerful man on the small council, the general in command of the Endaran army. If Cameron did not support Eirian's right to the throne, she would have no chance.

Eirian peered at everything as they went past with the same wide-eyed fascination she had given the city. When they reached the quarters assigned to her, Aiden was pleased to see the rest of his men waiting. They opened the door, allowing Eirian to enter. Her hand shot out, catching an apple tossed in her direction without warning, and Brenna gasped in shock. Looking at the man responsible, Aiden frowned.

"Thank you," Eirian said, and took a bite. "How did you know?"

"Well, ma'am, you've been riding most of the day," he answered.

Shaking her head, Brenna huffed and went through to the next chamber. Standing in the door, she called out for two of the ladies accompanying them.

"Isabella, Romana, in here."

Introducing Eirian to the entirety of her guard, Aiden signaled for them to group up into their squads. Those who had gone to the border had been a mix from the four teams, but now they were back in Amath, they would fall into the correct rotation.

"Your Highness," Aiden said, drawing her attention.

Taking a slow bite, Eirian blinked at him without answering, and he sighed. Waving at Merle, he started with him.

"You've met Merle. He's my second-in-command. His squad is Devin, Fox, John, Sid, and Tobin."

They saluted Eirian, and she inclined her head.

"This is Fionn," Aiden said, pointing at a grinning man. "His men are Kyson, Paxton, Geoff, Zack, and Tyler."

Fionn bowed, saying, "A pleasure, fair Princess."

"Tell me again why you put Fionn in charge of a squad?" Merle muttered.

Eirian studied him and chuckled. "Are you my entertainment?"

"I could be," he answered.

"And this is Fisk, Gram, Lyle, Randolph, David, and Mac."

"Which leaves you," Eirian said, looking at the man who had given her an apple.

His face was blank, but she thought she saw the hint of a smile. There was something familiar about him that made the memories whisper at the back of her mind. He met her gaze, and Eirian recognized the coldness in his stare. She had seen it in her reflection and the eyes of countless reds.

"This is Gabe, and his men, Jack, Layne, Kip, Wade, and Andrew."

Waving the half-eaten apple at Gabe, Eirian commented, "Keep up with this. It's a sure way to earn my favor."

Gabe did not smile, asking, "Apples specifically, or any food?"

"Any food will do, but fruit is preferable. I'm particularly favorable towards berries. I'd let you get away with murder for a bowl of blackberries. Or muntries."

Several of the men choked, Aiden and Merle giving them silencing looks. Cocking his head to the side, Gabe regarded Eirian with a faint smile before looking at Aiden.

"I'll keep that in mind, ma'am."

"Good," Eirian said with a smile. "You and I might actually get along."

Clearing his throat, Fox waved at the quivers slung over her shoulder. Eirian shook her head, gripping the straps.

"I can see to those, ma'am."

"No, thank you, I'll keep them with me."

Aiden muttered, "The Duchess might not like that."

"That's her problem, not mine. I'm used to looking after my own weapons and always having them close. Just because I'm in Amath and surrounded by you lot doesn't mean that's going to change," Eirian said.

Twenty-four pairs of eyes stared at Aiden, and he sighed. The only person not looking at him was Gabe. He watched Eirian instead.

"Right, Merle, Fionn, take your men back to the barracks. Your Highness, I believe you're wanted in the next chamber."

Turning, Eirian saw Brenna glaring at her and muttered, "Yes, apparently I am."

FOUR

Sitting on the stool, Eirian wound the strips of fabric around her hands and wrists before layering leather on top. The cotton provided padding between her flesh and the leather and would take some impact out of her strikes. Wards in her leather jerkin would withstand any blows her opponent landed on her. Not that she would let anyone know. Outside the tiny room, she could hear the crowd cheering for the two men who had gone before her. It was not her first time in the dimly lit building, and so long as her guards did not find out, it would not be her last.

Several such places were in Amath, and Eirian had visited all of them in the few months since she left Riane. Thinking of her guards reminded Eirian of the travesty of a training session that morning. Another day in which she allowed Aiden to defeat her repeatedly. Every time he had her on her back, his smug smile made Eirian want to scream. Or kiss him and whisper suggestions of what he could do to her just to see his demeanor falter. She knew it would be too easy to let her control slip, to show the laughing guards what she could really do. Instead, she found her way to the brawling dens and took her frustration out on unsuspecting men who thought they could beat her for easy money.

"You ready?"

Looking up at the man in the doorway, Eirian nodded. She stood, doing some stretches as she walked over to join him. Eyeing her warily, the man took in the leather jerkin Eirian wore. It was not typical Endaran army wear, but he had heard her speak, and her accent suggested she was from the southern regions. Winking at him, Eirian slipped through the door and let him lead her to the ring in the middle of the room. People surrounded it, jeering at the man being hauled out by a couple of helpers.

"Looks like you had fun," Eirian commented.

He lifted his head, glaring at her while staggering between the other men.

"Or not so much fun."

"You got a smart mouth on you." The man leading her chuckled. "Better hope your fists are as smart."

Eirian made sure her magic was firmly behind her shields and grinned. She did not need to hope, because Eirian knew she would win against whoever they threw at her. Flexing her hands, she balled her fists and peered at the man on the other side of the ring. Snorting, Eirian arched a brow at her companion.

"They're pitting me against a mountain. I'm flattered."

He shrugged, replying, "Boss remembers what you did last time. He's got money on you, so don't disappoint."

"Win or lose?"

"What do you think?"

Laughing, Eirian rolled her shoulders and stepped into the enclosure. They set the ring below the planks of wood used as flooring for everyone else. It helped keep the sand contained and allowed the audience a better view of the fighters. Not looking at the crowd, Eirian watched her opponent move. He was heavyset, easily double her size, but only slightly taller. There was a confident swagger to his walk that told Eirian he was sure he would win. She looked forward to proving him wrong.

Crinkling her nose, Eirian waited for the caller to give the signal. Her opponent wore a sleeveless jerkin showing off the bulky muscles of his arms, hands wrapped with leather and strips of cloth. Eirian looked them over, making sure he did not have any sharp objects tucked into the strips. It was a dirty move, but when there were no strict rules to follow, those hungry for a win at any cost would do anything. Licking her lips, Eirian reminded herself that her magic was in easy reach if he proved her wrong.

"You're a big one," she said. "Are you big everywhere?"

He rumbled, "I won't go easy because you're a woman."

Those members of the crowd who heard the exchange jeered, and Eirian laughed.

"Don't worry, I never go easy."

"You got balls."

Eirian winked, saying, "I've heard that before. Has anyone told you the bigger you are, the harder you fall?"

There was laughter at her comment, and the man grunted. Whistling shrilly, the caller held up a hand, drawing the attention of the two fighters.

"Alright fuckers, you know the drill. Get the other one down for a count of three, and you win. The only rule is no help from outside the ring. You got it?"

"Got it," they replied.

The caller backed out of the ring and counted loudly before giving them the signal to begin. Eirian was quick, darting sideways out of his reach before he could take a swing. She watched her opponent, the shift of his feet, how he dropped a shoulder as he turned to locate her. It was easy to pick where his center of balance was, her years of training guiding her movements. Glancing sideways at the cheering crowd, Eirian let the man get a couple of hits in. Taking him down too fast would leave the audience unhappy.

Dropping her guard, Eirian let him land a blow to her shoulder, the wards absorbing the brunt of the impact. Winking, she pirouetted and slipped beneath his next swing, landing several jabs before switching hands to deliver a hook. Her switch came as a surprise, but she received cheers from the crowd. Keeping close, Eirian carefully blocked his attacks, letting him push her across the ring. The longer she drew it out, the better the knockout would be.

Allowing a strike past her guard, Eirian felt it catch her mouth and tasted blood. He leered at her, but Eirian moved quicker than he anticipated. She delivered a hook to his lower body and chased it with an uppercut, switching lead hands without thinking about it. Off-balance, he did not expect her to tuck a foot behind his leg, assisting his fall backward. Another uppercut had him hit the ground unconscious. Eirian peered down at him with a grin before bowing to the crowd, putting a foot on his chest while the caller counted.

They cheered, whistles of appreciation coming from throughout the crowd. Swiping the back of a hand across her mouth, Eirian saw the blood and chuckled. The caller entered the ring, grabbing her hand to hold it up. He announced her the winner before letting Eirian exit. She passed the men entering to carry the unconscious fighter out, and they gave her appreciative looks. Eirian let her gaze linger on them, considering her options. If it had been Riane, she would have hunted down Rylee or Jaren for a quick post-fight release. Unless Celiaen and Galameyvin were in the city. In which case, Celiaen would have been the one she was fighting and Galameyvin providing her with the release.

Making her way back into the room she had prepared in, it did not surprise Eirian to find the man who led her out before the fight. Another stood with him, and she did not need to look behind her to sense the two men leaning against the wall. Eirian began unwrapping the leather around her hands, taking a seat on the stool. She did not speak, keeping her focus on her task. She would let the men talk. It was safer than having to fight her way out if they did not like her attitude.

"You're a good fighter, but you're not from the army, are you?"

Glancing at the well-dressed man, Eirian shrugged, dropping the leather straps on the ground at her feet. He studied her, eyes narrowed suspiciously.

"You're not a mage. I've met mages, and there ain't no magic coming from you."

"Do you have a point?" she asked.

He chuckled, walking over to stand in front of her. Cotton strips joined the leather, Eirian flexing her fingers to make sure she had not injured herself. She felt the dull ache leftover from the hits, but she was unconcerned. By the time her ladies arrived in the morning, all signs of the bout would have healed. Eirian was terrible at healing other people, but her body recovered quickly. Even her split lip would vanish before anyone at court saw it.

"You're a switch-hitter. Noticed last time. You've been making the rounds of the fighting dens. I want that to stop."

She sighed, knowing what he was planning to say. "Thanks, but no thanks. I'm not interested."

When Eirian attempted to stand, he pushed her back onto the stool. Her nose flared, the only outward sign of her anger.

"I think you should be smart. Sit down, listen to my offer. I'd hate to call the guards to report a murder."

The threat made her freeze, but not for the reason the men thought it did. Holding his gaze, Eirian considered dropping her shields.

"You don't want to do that," Eirian said.

"I want you to fight for me. Exclusively."

"I told you, I'm not interested."

He lashed out, striking where her opponent had split her lip. Eirian's eyes narrowed, and she swiped the back of her hand over her mouth. Giving it a disdainful sneer, she lifted her gaze from the blood to the man who had caused it.

Eirian chuckled darkly. "You shouldn't have done that."

Hearing the hint of a threat in her voice, the two men leaning against the wall stepped forward, ready to defend their employer. Glancing over his shoulder at them, the man clicked his tongue and gave Eirian an amused look.

"You're good in the ring, but it's four against one."

"I've faced worse odds," she said. "Look, your offer is great, but I'm afraid I have other commitments. I hit the ring to let off frustration when I have a free night."

"I could make you wealthy. People will pay to watch you perform. You know how to make a show of it. We all saw you drag that match out to give the crowd something to cheer."

"Yes, I do enjoy putting on a show."

Picking up the straps she had used for her hands, Eirian laughed. When she moved to stand again, the man let her, taking a step back to give Eirian room. There was a row of shelves where fighters could leave belongings while they fought, and Eirian walked over to retrieve her knives and coat. She felt the tension rise when the men caught sight of the weapons before she secured them to her belt. Glancing slyly over her shoulder, Eirian smirked. If they thought she was dangerous with her fists, they did not know how much worse it was when she had a blade.

"I heard what you had to say, and I'll take it into consideration," Eirian informed him.

He crossed his arms, watching Eirian shake out her coat and pull it on before she shoved the straps for her hands into a pocket. The gray was familiar. He had seen it before during a visit to Riane, but it made little sense with the lack of magic.

"Southern accent, you grew up in the mage city. What, they kick you out because you don't have magic?"

Fed up, Eirian sighed and rolled her eyes. She wanted out of the building and away from the man pestering her. Preferably without having to kill anyone.

"I'll let you know about your offer."

When he signaled, the two men blocked the door, and Eirian crossed her arms in frustration.

"You really don't want to get in my way. It won't end well for you," she told them.

The man said, "I want your answer now."

Dropping her shields, Eirian controlled the rush of her magic. The four men felt it rolling off her, but before they could make a move, Eirian's hands shot out to grab the ones blocking her way. Gripping their shirts, she raised a brow and smirked.

"I told you, it won't end well."

Her magic demanded to kill them, but Eirian banished the whispers to the back of her mind. Feeling their heartbeats, she extended a thread of power and slowed them, letting the men drop to the ground, unconscious. Turning around, Eirian stared at the man in charge.

"They didn't kick me out because I don't have magic. I left."

Holding his hands up, his eyes darted between her and the men on the floor. Leaning against the wall, the fourth man shrugged in disinterest.

"How did you?"

"Mages can shield their magic, and you'd never know. Now, do you still have an issue with me leaving, or are we good?"

"We're good."

Eirian declared, "Excellent! You have a wonderful night."

Careful as she stepped around the sleeping men, Eirian pulled the hood of her coat over her head and used her magic to discourage anyone from looking her way. There was a back entrance used by fighters and the people who worked at the den. It meant she could avoid the crowd. Her wards were good, but Eirian did not want to use any more magic than she already had. When her hand touched the door to push it open, she paused and sighed, shoulders slumping.

"This is fucking ridiculous," she muttered. "Did someone dose the ale tonight, or have they all gone mad?"

Someone was waiting in the dark alley the door opened into. The magic warned Eirian of his presence. Warned that he had a weapon and was waiting for her to walk past. It might have annoyed Eirian to release her magic to get out of the den without a fight, but she was thankful she had done it. A hand grasped the hilt of a knife as she pushed the door open and went through into the darkness. Listening carefully, Eirian picked up the scuff of boots on the pavement and turned in the other direction.

She kept her magic close, partially shielding it to avoid letting her stalker know. Moving slowly, Eirian wanted to draw him away from the door and lessen the chance someone might become involved. It would have been easy to kill him before she walked out the door, but Eirian wanted to know why he was waiting. Her magic had picked up his intent, his desire to kill her. There was nothing else to sense about him, just a drive to destroy and a hint of darkness that felt familiar. The sort of familiar that made the forgotten memories tug at Eirian's mind, their demands for attention a distraction she could ill afford.

Pretending to trip, Eirian put a hand out to stabilize herself on the wall and waited for him to make his move. She had drawn a knife, the cold steel tucked against the inside of her wrist. Eirian enjoyed knife fighting more often than using swords. It felt more intimate, bringing her closer to her opponent, especially if she intended to kill. A hand grabbed her shoulder, the flash of a blade catching Eirian's attention before she relaxed her hold on her magic and swung. Her assailant had no chance, grunting in surprise when he felt the blade strike.

"Tell me, do you like attacking women in dark alleys?" Eirian asked.

Twisting the knife she had driven into his side, Eirian felt the blood on her hands. She had aimed carefully to ensure there was time to question him. Magic curled around them, rage urging Eirian to kill him quicker. To anyone unfamiliar with it, the bloodlust of a mage was terrifying.

He spat at her. "Endaran bitch."

"Well, hello, an Athnaralan. Now we're getting personal. It's not the first time one of you has tried to kill me, and I'm sure it won't be the last."

Lifting a hand to his face, Eirian stroked his cheek. She tasted his fear, the racing beat of his heart, and let her magic course through him. It was easy to intensify what he felt, the pain, the terror. The magic urged her to surrender, but Eirian reminded herself of where she was. Throwing up a quick ward to muffle his agonized screams, she smiled in delight.

"Did someone tell you to attack me?"

"Yes!" he whimpered.

"Who?"

"He did."

"Does he have a name?" she asked.

Nodding, he answered, "My king… Kill me before the shadows do."

Yanking her knife free, Eirian let him slump against the wall, his hands covering the wound. Studying him, she considered using her magic to end his life. Looking at the end of the alley and the quiet street beyond, Eirian decided not to risk causing an upset. It was easy to imagine the reaction when someone found a withered husk. Preparing to turn her knife on him again, Eirian paused.

"What do you mean, the shadows?"

Staring into the darkness beyond Eirian, the man did not reply straight away. She waited, the hilt of her knife gripped tightly in her hand.

"The ones in our nightmares," he whispered.

Eirian frowned. "Nightmares can't hurt anyone. They're just dreams."

"Please."

Grabbing his hair, she held his head and drove the knife into the back of his neck. Applying force, she cut through his spine and let him drop. Wiping the blade and her hands on his clothes, Eirian slipped it into the sheath and shook her head. The last thing she had expected when she snuck out of her chambers was to have to kill someone. Making sure the hood still covered her head, she turned to leave the alley and stopped short when she found a man standing there.

He stared at her, and Eirian wondered why her magic had not alerted her to his presence. There was something familiar about him, and reaching for her power, Eirian discovered it was reluctant to respond. Chuckling, he did not step towards her, keeping a short distance between them so they could talk.

"You killed him cleaner than I would have," he said.

Memories screamed in Eirian's mind, but she could not recall them. They told her she knew the man, but it was not possible. Eirian knew she had never seen him before.

She replied, "I'm not angry enough to make a mess tonight."

"You should be more careful slipping out of the keep, Eirian."

"How do you know who I am?"

Cold power oozed from him, and Eirian suspected he was no mage.

"I know a lot of things about you, darling, more than you know. You better hurry and get back. Your guards will change shifts soon."

Eirian swallowed nervously. Something soothed her magic, drawing her to him, and it was frightening. She had never felt a pull so strongly, not even to Celiaen after they found themselves bound. Chuckling again, he turned to wave at the street.

"Go on then."

"Are you going to tell anyone what you saw me do?"

He shook his head. "I'll always keep your secrets, darling. Unless they threaten Tir."

It was difficult to walk past him, but Eirian forced herself to go. She wanted to ask more questions, to find out what he meant. Halting, she glanced over her shoulder to ask him another question, only to discover he had vanished. Turning around, Eirian searched for him and found nothing. Her magic returned to normal, and glancing at her feet, she caught sight of a dandelion forcing its way through a crack in the pavement. Groaning, Eirian bowed her head and hurried off before anyone discovered the corpse in the alley.

By the time she made it back to the keep, Eirian's frustration over what happened had faded to mild irritation. None of the guards on the bridge or scattered through the baileys gave her a second glance. The wards Eirian held around herself continued to make them look in another direction. It was easy to turn their attention elsewhere to make them miss the figure in dark gray slipping through the shadows on her way back to her cage. Inside the keep, things were quiet except for the thud of boots where guards patrolled.

Eirian halted at the end of the hallway outside her quarters and studied the guards, positioned in several locations. There were four of them, and she suspected the other two would be inside the audience chamber where she left them. Recalling what the stranger had said about her guards, Eirian was thankful she had gotten back before the shift change. It meant they would be tired enough to distract easily. Extending a hand, she urged the men to turn away from the door and hurried to it.

Magic softened the sound of it opening so she could slip through. Most of the time, they never noticed, but occasionally her tricks did not work. Aiden, in particular, was adept at seeing through them. It meant Eirian had to avoid sneaking out if he would be on duty, and she was thankful he preferred to be by her side during the day. Having Aiden around at night was a far more dangerous prospect than she wanted to entertain. Using the same trick as she had outside, Eirian redirected the attention of the two guards at the table so she could enter her room.

Inside the chamber, the fire remained lit to help keep it warm. Winter had tightened its grip on the city, and with her magic shielded, Eirian had discovered she felt the cold. Pulling the coat off, she bundled it up and shoved it into the chest at the end of her bed. Her fingers loosened the cords of her jerkin, allowing Eirian to remove it. Moving closer to the fire, she looked the leather over for any signs of blood. Finding a few spots, Eirian took a damp cloth to it before chucking it in the chest and shutting the lid. Running her hands over the top, she activated the wards worked on the wood. No one would notice it sitting there.

Sitting on the side of her bed, Eirian took a deep breath and began shutting her magic behind her shields again. She hated it and hated herself for choosing to do it, but she remained confident it was the right thing to do. During what little time Eirian had spent in Amath, she had quickly picked up on the dislike for mages felt by the nobles and courtiers. People avoided mentioning her magic, very few asking questions about it or her years in Riane. They behaved as though she had always been there, expressing horror in whispers behind her back when her actions did not meet their expectations.

Hearing a knock at the door, Eirian got to her feet and wandered over to it. On the other side, Gabe waited with an apple in his hand, offering it to her when she opened the door. Smiling, Eirian accepted the fruit and took a bite, noticing when his eyes lingered curiously on her hand.

"Thought you might appreciate it," Gabe said. "Can't sleep?"

"How did you guess?"

"Well, ma'am, you often have trouble sleeping."

Eirian nodded, replying, "This is true. Sometimes I wish sleeping wasn't so necessary. I could get so much more done if I didn't need to rest."

"I just took over from Fionn. The captain will be on at dawn."

"Good to know."

His eyes dropped to her hand again, and Gabe arched a brow.

"Just in case you were thinking of doing anything about your inability to sleep," he commented. "By the way, ma'am, you missed the back of your hand and your face. You should probably clean up before anyone else notices."

She froze, muttering, "Are you going to tell on me?"

Gabe shrugged. His hand went to his chest, toying with the silver pendant Eirian had noticed a few times. It was an obscure symbol she recognized as the quaternary knot she had encountered in dusty old books. Eirian reminded herself to ask him about it like she did every time she saw it.

Instead of asking, she said, "You know Aiden would be furious with me. Again."

"Way I see it, you were here when my shift started. I know nothing about what happened on Fionn's shift except what he told me."

"All I did was go for a walk. I must have grazed the back of my hand without realizing," Eirian explained.

Turning away, Gabe said, "Just a walk and nothing more."

FIVE

C rumpling the letter, Celiaen left it on his desk and turned to the messenger who had delivered it. Her gray cloak covered most of her clothes, but Celiaen saw the red embroidery on the coat that covered her armor. It did not surprise him that Fayleen had convinced a fellow red to deliver the letter, and he extended his hand to the woman.

"Do you have any other letters?"

She nodded, replying, "I have one for Prince Galameyvin."

"Prince Galameyvin is currently on a diplomatic visit to Telmia. Unless you want to take it back to Fayleen, I suggest you give it to me," Celiaen said.

"Telmia? Lucky him."

Withdrawing the letter from a pocket in her coat, the red gave it to Celiaen without question. Smiling faintly at the familiar curl of Fayleen's writing, he shook his head in frustration at what he knew the letter would say. It would be much like the one she had sent him, and Celiaen could do nothing to change it.

"Was there anything else?"

"No, nothing else. Fayleen said everything you needed to know was in the letter. Though she mentioned something about not getting any ideas in your stupid head."

"Stupid ideas?"

"No, it was definitely stupid head," she replied.

Celiaen chuckled. "That sounds like Fay. Thank you, you can go."

Waiting until she left, Celiaen opened the letter for Galameyvin and ran a hand through his hair while he read it. His assumption was correct. It contained much the same content as the one she sent him. However, it included suggestions of what Galameyvin might do to convince Eirian to return to Riane. Taking a deep breath to control his jealousy, Celiaen took the letter to the fire in the corner of his chamber and tossed it in. The flames consumed it quickly, and he returned to his desk.

"What are you going to do?"

Glancing at the man in the doorway, Celiaen shook his head. Leaning over the table, he stared at the crumpled ball of paper.

"I don't know, Tynan."

"Want to tell me what's going on?"

"The grand mage is failing."

Tynan let out a low whistle and leaned against the doorframe to stare at the ceiling. He knew what it meant for all of them. Mayve had been the grand mage for several hundred years, and change did not come easily.

"That would explain why they sent Jaren to fetch Tessa," he remarked.

"It gets worse."

"How could it get worse, Celi?"

"Baenlin is planning to go to Amath to get Ree. They don't want Tessa. They want the most powerful mage alive, and we know who that is. She won't say yes, but I worry about what my uncle might do when she refuses him," Celiaen explained.

Turning to look into the next chamber, Tynan watched the people around the table playing cards. They knew something was troubling Celiaen, but trusted him to deal with it. He was Celiaen's assigned blue now, and it was his job.

"Soren wouldn't let Baenlin get out of hand."

Rubbing his face, Celiaen disagreed. "Soren does what Baenlin tells him. I wouldn't put it past him to try influencing Ree. He doesn't know she can't be unless she wants to be."

"Except by Gal."

"I need to go to Amath."

Clearing his throat, Tynan said, "You know you can't just go to Amath. Ree is the future Queen of Endara, and you're the future King of Ensaycal. We must follow the formalities now. We're not talking about visiting a friend in Riane."

Celiaen looked at a small box that sat on his desk. He had intended to give it to Eirian for her next birthday when he saw her in spring. A plan made before her summons to return to Endara had come. Following his gaze, Tynan sighed.

"You're planning something stupid. I can feel it."

"I need to see my father."

"That's not a good idea. You saw the King yesterday, and we know it's best if you space out your visits. Is it something your mother could help with?"

"Actually, yes," Celiaen said, glancing at him. "I'll need her help to convince Paienven to agree. Though, knowing his ambition, it shouldn't be too hard."

Tynan pinched the bridge of his nose and turned to the others. Convincing Celiaen not to follow through with whatever was on his mind would take more than him.

"Tara, Celi is planning something stupid. Can you beat some sense into him?"

She looked over from the table, the red band on her finger catching in the filtered sunlight. Next to her, another woman chuckled and laid her cards down on the surface.

"Really, you lot need to stop throwing money at me."

"Again, Alyse? Can't you give me one round?" someone else groaned.

Alyse smirked, replying, "Sorry, Osric, if you want an easy mark, ask Cai to play."

Tossing her cards on the table, Tara got up and walked over to join Tynan at the door. She studied Celiaen while he pulled on a coat, the midnight blue silk embroidered in silver. His fingers moved quickly to do up the clasps, each of them engraved with the triple sword emblem of Ensaycal. The hilts of his swords were visible through the slits on the sides as he moved. Dark eyes darted in her direction, and Tara saluted mockingly, receiving a rude gesture in return.

"What's this about stupid plans?" she asked.

"It's not a stupid plan. It's something I've wanted for years."

"You're going to quit being a prince and move to Riane to become next in line for a red archmage position?"

He snorted. "Not that plan. Though it would negate the need for formality. No, I'm talking about Ree."

Tara groaned. "No, Celi, you can't. You're the future King of Ensaycal, and she's the very human future Queen of Endara."

"Doesn't that make it more possible? Ree is likely to die long before my father fades."

"Celi."

"Tara."

"You're a fucking idiot."

He grinned, saying, "Yes, but you still put up with me. Gal is in Telmia. Without him around, Ree will finally acknowledge the truth, and she'll agree."

Frowning, Tynan worked out what they were talking about and slapped a hand to his face. His string of curses drew the attention of those at the table.

"You want to ask your father to propose marriage to Ree? Have you lost your mind completely? He'll either kill you or laugh you out of chambers. It would cause a war with Athnaral!"

Osric called out, "About fucking time you made a move, Celi!"

Meeting his gaze, Tara bit her bottom lip. She was one of the few who knew the truth of the bond between Celiaen and Eirian. All of them knew how much he loved her, despite Eirian's love for Galameyvin. Tara adored the three of them, but to her, they were the definition of complicated. If they were ordinary mages and not royalty, they might have been able to work something out between them. While it was not uncommon, it was perfectly acceptable for mages. However, it was not accepted when the future leadership of kingdoms was in question.

"Celi, you know how much I love you, don't you?" Tara said.

He answered, "I have to do this, Tara. She can't marry someone else!"

"What if Paienven agrees and gives you permission to approach the Endarans about marr—"

"He'll see the benefits!"

Tara snapped, "Don't interrupt me, Celiaen!"

Looking sheepish, Celiaen tucked his hands into the pockets of his coat. Snickering, Tynan slid off the doorframe and walked over to join the group at the table. He leaned on the back of Osric's chair, peering over his shoulder at his cards.

"So what if Paienven says yes? That doesn't mean the Endaran council will, and it certainly doesn't mean Ree will. She's not stupid, an oblivious fool but not stupid."

Watching them, Alyse put her cards down and cleared her throat. She stood, leveling a look at each of the people around the table.

"Osric, Tynan, Link, let's go for a walk."

Making vague excuses, they did not look at Tara and Celiaen as they scrambled to exit the room. Alone, Tara knew it was safe to bring up what needed to be left unsaid where others could hear. The things that could lead to their executions by the command of the high council. Celiaen stood in the middle of his chamber, avoiding her stare, mouth twisted in uncertainty.

"Celi, I don't want you to get hurt," she said.

"It's Ree, Tara. She'll agree, with our bond, she'll agree."

"I'm not Gal. I've avoided yelling at you for making the bond for the last eight years, but I think it's fair to say if the two of you were going to happen, you would've by now."

He scowled. "Gal has been in the way. Even before the bond happened, Gal has been there. Now he's not."

Crossing her arms, Tara arched a brow and stared at him.

"We didn't choose the bond, Tara. We didn't start it. Our magic decided for us. Doesn't that mean something? Doesn't it tell you that deep down, Ree loves me as much as I love her?"

"What it tells me is that you're a pair of powerful idiots."

"We're already married, Tara, but we can't tell people. I've waited patiently, and I've let Gal, and Rylee, and others have what's mine long enough."

Shaking her head, Tara threw her hands in the air and turned her back on him, walking away. Frustration stirred her magic, but not enough that the blue mages lingering outside the chambers felt the need to intervene. Celiaen wandered through to the next room, stopping at the table to study the cards scattered over it. A smattering of coins sat in the middle, unclaimed by whoever had been winning the game.

"What you did to Gal was unfair, Celi, and I won't pretend to approve. Your jealous streak will be your undoing." Tara glanced over her shoulder, asking, "What if she says yes? Then what?"

"I don't think I understand what you're asking."

"At least you can admit it."

"I mean, I don't think you mean the obvious answer. Ree and I would marry, have a family. Eventually, King Nolan would die, and they'd crown Ree as the Queen of Endara. We would rule together until she died and our eldest child took over," Celiaen said with a shrug.

"No," she replied. "That's not what I meant. I don't see Ree ever being happy if she remains in Amath. Any more than I think you'll be satisfied to continue being the Crown Prince of Ensaycal. You're both capable leaders, but you're not cut out to be rulers."

He was silent, leaning on the back of a chair. Dark hair fell over his eyes, and it reminded Tara of Celiaen's mother. He was the reflection of Queen Sannaeh, even though most called him a younger version of Baenlin. Tara had known them all her life, and she had raised Celiaen, held his hand when he learned to walk, cleaned his knees when he scraped them, picked him up when Paienven knocked him down.

"If I gave up my place."

"Awena would be the future Queen of Ensaycal, and no one wants that. Except for her, your father, and those who share their ambitions."

Celiaen sighed. "That's what you're afraid of."

"Maybe."

"You think Paienven will say yes because if Nolan agrees, it delivers Endara into his hands, and it will redeem me in his eyes."

She looked at the ground, and Celiaen waited for Tara to say something. When she finally did, he flinched at the disappointment in her voice.

"I suspect there's nothing I could say to make you change your mind. So I'll say this last thing, and then we'll find your parents, and you can get on with your insanity. Ree wouldn't marry Gal, and she won't marry you."

"Gal would never ask her. He knows we belong together!" Celiaen declared.

Tara snorted. "Yep, that's why he loves her."

"I'm going to do this, Tara."

"I know. I only hope you get something positive out of this experience."

Nodding once, Celiaen turned and made his way to the door. When it opened, he found Tynan and Alyse leaning against the wall, murmuring while they waited for him and Tara to appear. They pulled apart, and Alyse smiled at Tara, holding a hand out to her. She took it, kissing Alyse's knuckles, giving her a cheeky grin. Rolling his eyes, Tynan turned to Celiaen, cocking his head in their direction.

"Don't look at me like that." Celiaen chuckled. "Just because you don't feel attraction like the rest of us."

"I have bad news," Tynan informed him, ignoring the comment.

"Do you?"

"Her Majesty is in council with the King."

Celiaen clicked his tongue while he considered the ramifications of going to his parents with his plan. He met Tara's gaze, and she shrugged, letting him know it was his choice. Looking around, Celiaen noted that Link and Osric had vanished, which meant they were busy telling everyone else what they had overheard. If he put it off, it would allow his companions to work on changing his mind. Dismissing his concerns, Celiaen flicked a hand at the others and started walking.

"Celi, quick question," Alyse said. "What if Paienven says no?"

"Then you're all out of a job."

Tynan choked, and Tara slapped him on the back.

"That was a joke," Celiaen muttered.

"Was it, though?" Tynan asked, sharing a disbelieving look with Alyse.

Waving a hand around, Tara said, "Could you give up living here in Luina and the luxury that comes with being a prince?"

Glancing at them over his shoulder, Celiaen rolled his eyes with a faint smile. He did not need to pay attention to where he was going. He had run the marbled halls of the royal palace of Luina for most of his life. They were a cold reminder of the Kaetiel family and the empire Paienven had built. When Celiaen had been younger, his father had spoken of building a new palace. Unfortunately, years of continued instability within the united borders of Ensaycal had disrupted those ideas.

The thought made him glance at the mottled floor and wonder how Eirian was adjusting. Amath would be an unfamiliar experience for her, and a feeling frequently struck Celiaen that she was thinking about him. Missing him. It was not a new sensation. Celiaen had felt it ever since the bond had formed. Sometimes, he thought the bond felt like loneliness but dismissed it as his imagination. One day, he would ask Eirian if she ever felt anything from his end. It was one thing when they were close, but the distance between them prevented the sharing of magic, so he could not work out how they could share feelings.

"Good afternoon, Celi."

Spotting Nadinna, he smiled at her affectionately.

"Nadinna, my dear sister, what brings you to this part of the palace?" Celiaen asked.

"I heard a whisper that someone was planning to make a fool of himself in front of the King and Queen," Nadinna replied.

"Not a show to be missed?"

Kissing his cheek, she smiled at Tara, Alyse, and Tynan. Squeezing Celiaen's shoulder, Nadinna nodded at the closed doors they were preparing to go through.

"You know she's in there as well."

Celiaen sighed. "Awena is always close to the King."

Brushing a stray lock of dark hair away from his face, Nadinna studied Celiaen intently. She adored her brother. He always protected her, and given a chance, Nadinna would do anything to return the favor.

"I know how much you love Ree," she murmured. "But Awena will take this request as an opportunity to whisper vile untruths in father's ear. She'll question your loyalty to Ensaycal, claim your desire to marry a human will taint the Kaetiel legacy."

"She's an Altira."

"Ree's also the most powerful mage alive."

Frowning at Nadinna, Celiaen waited for what else she intended to say.

"Awena knows Ree. She knows how powerful she is, and she knows Ree and Gal have been something for years. If I know the real reason Gal went to Telmia, you can bet she guessed it as well."

He looked away, muttering, "Gal always wanted to visit Telmia."

Shaking her head, Nadinna tucked her loose gold curls behind her ear and met Tara's gaze. She shrugged, refusing to say a word. It was Nadinna's turn to try convincing Celiaen to change his mind.

"Oh, and I suppose his departure has nothing to do with those rings you keep on your desk?" Nadinna asked. "You've never given Ree jewelry before. I imagine they're a matching pair, like everything else you give her. One for you, one for her."

"You know, for a girl who's only forty, you're too perceptive," Celiaen snapped.

Nadinna snorted. "I'm the smartest one out of the bloody lot of us."

"Don't think Zayern would agree."

"He's a green. I don't need him to agree. I just need him to patch you up after you get your ass handed to you. Which Paienven might do, and of course, you would never stop him. Even though you're twice the mage and a far better man."

Draping an arm around her shoulders, Celiaen hugged Nadinna tightly.

"It's a pity you're not the second born. I wouldn't hesitate to give up my place if I knew you were going to be queen."

"Yes, well, can't help the accident of birth, now can we? You're still going to go in there, aren't you?"

"Yes, I am. Ree is everything to me. Is it so wrong that I want to at least put the offer on the table?" he asked.

Inhaling sharply, Nadinna replied, "I'm a blue, Celi. I know what you feel for her, what Gal feels for her, and I know what Ree feels for both of you. I've been friends with her for nearly as long, but I don't understand why the two of you love her so damn much that it turns you into idiots."

Feeling pity for Celiaen, Alyse said, "Love makes idiots of us all. I know it turns Tara into a fool."

"Hey!" Tara protested. "Don't bring me into this. I'm a respectable married woman."

"Respectable? Is that true, Alyse?" Celiaen chuckled.

She agreed. "She married me. That affords her some respectability."

"I suppose that's true," Nadinna said. "It's about the only time a red gains any respectability, to be honest."

Taking in the look that Tara and Alyse shared, Nadinna envied them. It was not an uncommon relationship. Many blue mages married their red, and they considered it an excellent match. They worked so closely together that it was natural and encouraged where appropriate. She turned away, knocking on the door to alert those inside the room of their presence. With a nod, Celiaen prepared to enter when the doors opened.

The first thing he saw was a group gathered around the central table, King Paienven standing between his brothers and his second eldest child. Awena was the first to look up at the newcomers, her blue eyes gleaming with delight at the sight of Celiaen and Nadinna. There was a sly curl to her lips that suggested she knew precisely why they were there. Opposite Paienven, Queen Sannaeh leaned on the table, her long black hair secured at the back of her head with two thin knives masquerading as pins. At her waist, the twin swords of a red mage hung.

"So, you finally graced us with your presence, Your Highness," Awena said.

Gazing at her, Celiaen observed the gold curls carefully pulled back from her face and the blue eyes that were a mirror of Paienven's. Including their cruelty. Sannaeh turned to look at Celiaen, smiling warmly and extending a hand to him in greeting. Unlike his wife, Paienven did not look at Celiaen, leaning towards Awena.

"What do you think?" Paienven waved at a document.

Awena kept her eyes on Celiaen, replying, "Show them leniency. For now. If the reports are accurate, we'll need to move legions towards Endara."

Bowing, Celiaen kissed the back of Sannaeh's hand and shared a look with his uncles. They wore carefully guarded expressions, and Celiaen inclined his head first to Yaernan and then to Selagan.

"Have there been reports out of Athnaral, sire?" Celiaen asked.

Paienven said, "Aeyren is mustering his army, and I can't have that."

Straightening, Celiaen took his place beside Sannaeh at the table, Nadinna standing on the other of him. Picking up a report, Celiaen read through the contents and frowned. He glanced at Sannaeh, and she nodded to confirm what he was reading.

"Athnaral intends to put pressure on Endara," she told him.

"We'll come to their aid, of course. We have a treaty, and we haven't neglected to uphold our side of it over the years," Awena muttered.

Celiaen smiled. "What if we renegotiated the treaty with Endara?"

Giving him a curious look, Paienven inquired, "What are you thinking?"

"I want to marry Princess Eirian."

No one spoke while Paienven regarded Celiaen in amusement. He started laughing, and the reaction surprised the others around the table, especially Awena. Sannaeh pressed her lips together, crossing her arms and looking away from Celiaen.

"Are you trying to start a war, boy?" Paienven asked mockingly.

"No, I'm not."

Sannaeh said, "You're talking about the future Queen of Endara."

"The future Queen of Endara and the purple the high council would like to see as the next grand mage. I've been cultivating her friendship for nearly twenty years. Isn't it time Ensaycal benefitted from that?" Celiaen said, holding Paienven's gaze.

"Eirian Altira is a human," he replied. "Why would you want to marry a human when you could have your pick from a nation of fine elven women? You're the future King of Ensaycal, and you can have whoever you want so long as they're an elf."

"Doesn't a king deserve a queen worthy of him?"

"You're a fool if you think Nolan would say yes. I'll make the proposal. I'll even let you deliver it to Amath yourself, so you can make your case."

Bowing, Celiaen said, "Thank you, sire."

"Are you sure, my love?" Sannaeh asked in surprise.

"I'm well aware, as is everyone in this room, that Eirian Altira has eyes for Galameyvin, not you. It's a pity he's in Telmia. I can tell you now, she won't marry you, boy. The best you could hope for is that in a few years after she has married the dutiful Endaran man her father picks for her, she might take you to bed. You'd have to wait for her to produce an heir and a spare, but if you pushed, she might have you."

Taking a deep breath to hide his anger at Paienven's words, Celiaen maintained a bored expression. Beside him, Nadinna cleared her throat, glancing away.

"A marriage between the Endaran and Ensaycalan thrones would unify our kingdoms better than any treaty could. The future heirs to Endara would be Kaetiel," Celiaen argued.

Nodding slowly, Paienven agreed. "They would. It's up to you to convince King Nolan to agree. Of course, there is the minor matter of the high council and the grand mage."

"Eirian will turn it down. She is a creature of duty and always has been. If she wasn't, she would have remained in Riane."

"Do you know who they have sent to fetch her back?" Awena asked.

Glancing at Sannaeh, Celiaen replied, "I do. Baenlin will go once the winter storms have passed. I'm told he intends to be there in time for First Planting."

Paienven scoffed. "Fucking Baenlin. If he wants the Altira princess, then I hope she turns him down. It might teach him a lesson."

"Eirian knows people seek to use her for her power. There are very few she trusts besides me, and Baenlin is not one of them. If the high council truly wants her, they should send someone else."

Agreeing with him, Awena commented, "This is true. Eirian has mentioned to me how she detests the way the archmages watch her. Particularly my uncle."

"I'm sure Baenlin was simply curious about her progress," Sannaeh murmured. "Especially since you value her friendship so highly, Celiaen."

"Or he's an ambitious fucker. Mayve rejected him in favor of Azina. Talk about an insult. Imagine rejecting a Zarthein and the Queen of Ensaycal's brother in favor of a man who used to be a woman!" Paienven laughed.

Looking at Sannaeh, Celiaen noted the frustration on her face and watched it fade when she glanced in his direction. Her dark eyes held affection for him, and he returned her faint smile. Shifting to study the others around the table, Celiaen let his gaze linger on his uncles.

Yaernan crinkled his nose, swatting a stray gold curl away from his face as he asked, "Paienven, are you sure letting Celiaen do this is a good idea?"

"What are your reasons, Yaernan?" he asked. "Besides the fact that your son has already been there? Maybe we should recall Galameyvin from Telmia and let Nolan know what his daughter has been doing. Or rather, who."

"King Aeyren won't accept an Endaran ruler with a Kaetiel consort," Yaernan replied, ignoring the comments about Galameyvin.

Selagan added, "Aeyren is unlikely to accept Eirian either way. She's a woman."

Picking up a document, Paienven flung it in his direction and laughed.

"Do you think I give a fuck what that little brat of a human will or will not accept? By the reports we've had, he wants the girl as well. I'd sooner see Eirian Altira dead than married to Athnaral."

Celiaen swallowed and glanced at Nadinna.

"I suspect Endara would prefer Celiaen over Aeyren," she said. "Ensaycal has always been there for Endara as friend and ally. If it came down to a choice between the two? Of course, they would choose us."

Turning away from the table, Paienven studied the wall behind it. It was the most extensive map Celiaen had ever seen, and it was constantly being updated. They had painted every detail of the known lands. Celiaen knew it was there to remind everyone of what Paienven had done in uniting the elven kingdoms under one king. Running his fingers over the lines that marked the border between Endara and Athnaral, Paienven nodded thoughtfully.

"Athnaral intends to strike at Endara. They'll lose, as they always do. We'll make sure of that. It'll amaze me if the Endaran council agrees to your proposal, Celiaen. So your job is to make sure they don't agree with the Athnaralan one. Either she marries you, or she marries an Endaran. Either way, get used to Amath, boy. You're going to be spending a lot of time there."

Bowing, Celiaen did not let his relief show, and he said, "Thank you, sire."

"You might prove yourself useful for a change."

Awena smirked, catching his gaze, and Celiaen knew she would use whatever happened against him.

SIX

Wildflowers broke through the carpet of green, their delicate petals varying shades of yellow and orange. Like miniature suns, they stood out as evidence that spring had arrived. Bees flitted back and forth, busy at their task of collecting nectar and spreading pollen. They disregarded Eirian, her back pressed against a tree, and they ignored Halcyon as he snatched mouthfuls of grass. Neither of them posed a risk, and the bees had a job to do.

Eirian's magic filled the air, coursing through the ground. It fueled the growth, and not for the first time. With winter over, she had shifted from sneaking out to the woods instead of the city. Rather than brawling, Eirian vented her frustrations on something that came more naturally. Putting a hand on the tree, Eirian pushed up while careful not to pull on the rein she clasped. Lifting his head, Halcyon observed as she rose. A bright yellow dandelion hung at the side of his mouth where it had caught in the bridle.

Dusting off, Eirian smiled at it. Halcyon shook his head with a snort, and the flower flapped around. His mouth twitching, Halcyon attempted to snag it, but it hung out of reach. Unable to resist, Eirian giggled and walked over, plucking the flower from his bridle. She held it out on the flat of her hand so he could finish it. Tying the end of the rein back on the bit, she ran her hand gently over his neck and rubbed him soothingly.

"Come on, Halcyon, my love, we should get back before Aiden comes for me. I'd rather he didn't march me back to the castle while yelling at me."

Halcyon snorted at her, and she grinned.

"And you know he'll give me that look. I have to be patient. It won't be much longer, and I'll stop shielding my magic around them. I'll stop pretending."

Checking the tack, Eirian tightened the girth before lifting her foot to the stirrup and swinging into the saddle. Settling into the seat, she nudged gently and guided Halcyon towards the path. He needed little encouragement, his stomach reminding him there would be a meal waiting for him. Relaxing, she reached out to touch the trunks of trees. It was a habit Eirian learned as a child before the control of her powers had developed. She felt the trees with her magic, sensing the beat of life in them while pouring a little of hers into them.

Every so often, sunlight burst through gaps in the leaves, the warmth making her skin tingle before the trees hid them away again. When she reached the edge of the woods, Eirian hovered in the shade of the trees while she unrolled her cloak. She shook it out and secured it around her shoulders, hiding her face in the hood. Continuing on her way, Eirian took the time to layer her magic beneath shields. When she slipped out, it had been needed, but for her return, it was unnecessary.

She was careful to keep her face covered as they approached the gates and hoped the fresh guards would not feel the need to check all incoming people. Now and then, the guards would get zealous. Something she suspected Aiden arranged because of her sneaking out. Watching out of the corner of her eye, Eirian noticed the guards paid her no attention. Their gaze slid over her and Halcyon like they were nothing. Her lips twitched slightly at the thought, a smirk forming.

Patting Halcyon, she chuckled. "That's right, pay us no attention. I'm no one important, just your future queen. Lucky I'm not planning to raze Amath to the ground."

Tossing his head, Halcyon seemed to agree with her. Eirian was never wholly sure how much he understood. The mage-bred horses showed more intelligence than the average horse. She supposed being around that much magic over generations had changed them. They were a breed apart, and Eirian was thankful to have kept her companion. Halcyon had been her sanctuary when the stress of her studies became too much. The taste of freedom that she envied in others.

Passing steadily through the sprawling city streets, Eirian watched the people scurrying around and going about their daily lives. Women carried baskets filled with food for their families or wares they had produced to sell at the market. Small children trooped at their feet while the older ones helped carry things and control their younger siblings. Men pulled small carts laden with goods, while others had sacks hoisted on shoulders, and many hurried on their way to their workplaces. Herders led livestock through, and horses hitched to carts took up so much room they often forced traffic to a halt.

The clang from smithies rang out over the din of shouting voices, and countless different smells lingered in the air. Cities always teemed with life. It was an all-out assault on the senses that could overwhelm the unprepared. Eirian adored it, the constant buzz of life, and when her power was free, it could become too much. While she enjoyed her solitude and being able to run free in the open air, the cities of her life held a much more significant portion of her heart. These were her people, hers to lead and protect. They expected fair leadership, as they had from generations of her family before her. The people respected her father, and Eirian hoped one day they would respect her.

She had to pause when the smell of fresh bread hit her nose. Smiling, Eirian noticed a little boy tugging at the long brown skirt of an older woman. He was watching her and her horse with the wide eyes of an awestruck child. Lifting her hand, she waved at him, careful to keep her face shrouded. His face lit up with a toothy grin, and he stopped hassling the woman long enough that she turned to look down at him to make sure he was still there. When she caught sight of the passing rider, she ruffled his hair and turned back to haggling with the shopkeeper.

When Eirian reached the castle, she pushed her hood back as Halcyon's shoes rung out on the stone bridge into the lower bailey. While hiding her identity as she passed through the city was beneficial, it was a hindrance on the castle grounds. Guards watched solemnly from the top and bottom of the gatehouses, weapons never far from reach. They knew Eirian by sight, and they did not stop her. Eirian followed the pathway upwards along the slight hill slope through the busy gate.

Guards watched from the top of the curtain walls as they patrolled. Horns sounded at intervals, used by those on duty to communicate basic instructions rather than sending runners constantly. She knew they were conveying her arrival and the path she had taken. When Eirian reached the gate to the upper bailey, a squad of royal guards waited, and she brought Halcyon to a halt. While she dismounted, Randolph took the reins, and the remaining guards saluted her, clapping fists to their chests as he led the eager horse away. Glancing them over, she nodded to Aiden. With a step forward, Eirian smiled innocently at the man who often drove her to distraction.

"Good morning, Aiden. Have they missed me?"

His eyes raked over her, lingering on her knives. They remained there for a moment before Aiden lifted his gaze to meet hers, and she saw the anger contained within.

"No, Your Highness, not yet. I thought we discussed you sneaking off?"

Falling into step with him, Eirian unclasped her cloak and draped it over her shoulder with the hood hooked on a finger. His mouth twisted, and he eyed her suspiciously.

"I wasn't expecting it, but it's always nice to know no one wants you. And yes, you have discussed my sneaking off. Repeatedly. Sometimes I even pay attention when you discuss it," Eirian said sweetly.

"Someone will always want you for something, Princess. It's the burden of leadership. Another part of the burden of leadership is not going anywhere without your guards."

Not willing to miss an opportunity to tease Aiden, Eirian cocked an eyebrow and let the hint of a smirk grace her lips. Challenging him was the highlight of her day, though she often regretted withholding her abilities. Eirian wanted his facade to become as tousled as his dark brown curls and to know she was the one responsible for it.

"And what do you want from me, Aiden?"

When one of the other guards chuckled at her question, Aiden shot him a scathing look.

Avoiding a direct answer, he replied, "Princess Eirian knows exactly what I want from her."

"Yes, I know. You'd dearly like me to behave and to stop sneaking off without you wonderful guards," she quipped.

Turning her attention to the other guards, Eirian winked.

"Besides Fisk, your captain knows my sense of humor. Don't you, Aiden?"

"Unfortunately," he answered.

Aiden directed a sideways look at her. It told Eirian he knew she was trying to lure him into an argument, and he had no intention of indulging.

Fisk commented, "If you don't mind my bluntness, ma'am, you're nothing like I expected a future queen to be. I mean, I watch you train with the boss man, and I'm amazed."

One of the other guards slapped the back of his head, and they all laughed.

"Forgive him, ma'am; he's easily impressed," Mac said.

Eirian laughed loudly, tossing her head back in delight. People turned to look at her, unsure why their princess was laughing.

"Mac, you're right. I'm not good with a sword, and I'm thankful that the boss man lets me train with him," she said, the lie slipping from her tongue.

Suspecting she was still trying to lure him into an argument, Aiden gave her another sideways look. "I wouldn't say you're not good with a sword. You're better than many I've trained with over the years. That's why I never let you win."

"Thank you, Aiden."

Giving him a faint smile, Eirian shifted her cloak from her shoulder to over her arm and let her gaze drop guiltily. Turning her eyes skyward, she took in the sight of the main keep towering above. It reminded her of the extent ambition could reach when wielded by those determined to dominate others. She constantly compared it to the mages' soaring towers, their shimmering white walls rippling with generations of magic and sea salt. Her family home was a dark relative, cold stone walls built to protect a fortress born of military function. Riane did not need walls. Some days Eirian felt it was a stone box in which they would bury her freedom beneath duty.

"Highness?" Aiden murmured. "You seem further away than normal this morning. Is something bothering you?"

Shrugging, Eirian smiled sadly and met his gaze, seeing the concern within. "I'm allowed to be pensive sometimes, Aiden. You'll get used to it."

"I hope so. Just don't let it consume you."

A cough from one of the other guards startled them, and Eirian shook herself as though she could shed her mood like a dog shaking off water. Watching her, Aiden regretted he could not offer the comfort he wished to.

"Alright, I'm going. Better clean up and at least pretend to look the part."

People moved out of the way as they approached the great doors into the keep. They were open to allow the easy flow of traffic in and out. Standing like statues on either side, guards watched constantly. Armed with pikes and bows, all of them carried swords and knives. While the kingdom was at peace with their neighbors, they never let their guard down. Endara knew from experience how quickly it could end.

Inside, tiers of balconies surrounded the greeting hall where people could observe the comings and goings. Stairways off to each side gave easy access upwards through the keep, while hallways branched off to lead them into the maze of rooms. Opposite the main entrance were the doors leading to the throne room. Tapestries depicting the noble houses hung on the walls, their bright colors a stark contrast to the stone.

Ascending flights of stairs, Eirian's barrier of guards ensured no one dared approach her. She wished she could flit through the throngs of people and chat casually, but Aiden's words were a heavy reminder. People would always want something from her. Eirian saw the disapproving looks of courtiers, who found her habit of dressing like a man disturbing, and heard them whisper loudly to each other about it.

Smiling at them, her attention let them know she was aware of their actions, and Eirian wondered how they would respond if she wore her armor and weapons. Armor and weapons that she continued to keep hidden away in her chambers and never spoke of. She found it insulting that they did not have better things to do with their time. To her, it was not dressing like a man; it was simply what she had always worn. They gave all novices the same clothing to wear, and they kept their hair cut short around their ears from the day they arrived in Riane.

They were halfway to her quarters when Randolph caught up. He offered a quick salute before delivering the news.

"Captain, I ran ahead to make sure her ladies would be prepared."

"Thank you, Randolph. That was good thinking," Aiden replied.

"A messenger was waiting from the Duke of Tamantal."

Eirian murmured, "I was wondering when Everett would return."

Determined to find out what Everett wanted, Eirian picked up the pace, and they hurried through the hallways. Guards stood outside her quarters, the same guards she slipped past on the way out earlier that morning to go for her ride. When they saw her, frustration appeared in their eyes, which faded at Aiden's glare. Inside, she saw three of her ladies chattering and a young man in messenger livery waiting. When they saw her, the messenger bowed, and the ladies gave deep curtsies, their skirts rustling against each other.

"Good morning," Eirian said. "I believe you're from the Duke of Tamantal? Has he returned to the city?"

"Yes, Your Highness, his party arrived late last night. His Grace was hoping to speak to you before the next council meeting."

"Tell him I can see him today. Ladies, shall we?"

The messenger left, and the three women ushered Eirian through to her chamber. When they entered, Brenna was with the other ladies in front of Eirian's wardrobe, discussing what gown she would wear. They had laid a clean chemise over the back of a chair, the soft white linen a stark contrast to the dark timber. Eirian doubted she would ever be completely comfortable having someone else clean and dress her.

"I'm pleased to see you're not covered in dirt again," Brenna said. "I was thinking the light blue, you only have a meeting with the chancellor later today, and I presume Everett."

"A good morning to you, Your Grace. Yes, I tried to avoid the dirt, so I'm glad you're pleased by my efforts," Eirian replied with a warm smile.

Shaking her head, Brenna drew a key from inside a pocket of her gown. "You spend more time sneaking out to get filthy than my sons do. All of your guards are going to end up quitting at this rate."

Giggling, the ladies stripping Eirian off shared an amused look as Brenna unlocked the cabinet where they kept the jewelry. Closing her eyes, Eirian took a deep breath as she waited for them to wipe her over. When satisfied, they slid the chemise over Eirian's arms and head before bringing the cornflower blue gown over.

"I look forward to your hair growing out so we can do something with it. Honestly, I don't understand why those mages insist on cutting girls' hair so short," Brenna grumbled.

Eirian replied, "Brenna, don't lie. I know you fully understand the reasons."

"But you're a princess and the future Queen of Endara!"

"Yes, and my roommate was the daughter of a shepherd."

Going silent, Brenna draped the gold chains around Eirian's neck and secured them at the back. Walking around to stand in front of her, she nodded in satisfaction.

Brenna commanded, "Elke, fetch the brushes."

There was a knock at the door, and Aiden's voice rang through the wood. "Your Highness, the duke is here."

"Thank you, Aiden. I'll join him shortly," Eirian called out.

Thrown into a flurry by the announcement, the ladies ushered Eirian to the chair so they could fuss over her hair. Trying her best not to wince as Elke dragged the brush through her barely shoulder-length hair, Eirian chewed her bottom lip. She contemplated what was so important Everett needed to see her. A swift swat to her hand startled Eirian, and she met the scowling gaze of Brenna.

"Stop chewing your lip. A princess shouldn't look like an over-enthusiastic farm boy has mauled her mouth."

Unable to help herself, Eirian joined in the chorus of giggles and shook her head in amusement. "Really, Brenna, what would you know about over-enthusiastic farm boys?"

The scowl faded into a bemused smile. "My eldest son is that age. I don't think enthusiasm differs depending on rank."

"I don't know about that. Farm boys probably get away with more than the son of a duke!" Romana replied.

They were soon wiping tears of laughter away. Stepping back, Elke cleared her throat, having finished Eirian's hair despite their laughter. Free to add to the conversation, she winked at her friends.

"What about elven men? Do you think they get away with more than the son of a duke?"

Covering their mouths, the other three women bit back howls of laughter.

Brenna shook her head and scolded, "Honestly! The Duke of Tamantal is in the next chamber."

"Yes, this is rather unbecoming for a princess and her ladies. As for elves, I can't speak for the ones I know. They never told me anything about such matters. Shoes?"

Running a hand over her skirt, Eirian avoided her companions' eyes for fear that they would see through the lie. Quickly bringing over a pair of soft leather shoes, Bea knelt and slipped them onto Eirian's feet while she held them up off the ground. Taking the hand offered by Brenna, she stood and smiled at Eirian, wiping her hands on her dress.

"I'm sorry, my lady, I had them ready for you."

"Thank you, Bea. Have you heard from your brother? How is he?"

"Oh, he's well. Mother has kept him busy, but he plans to be here by your birthday."

"No one expected your father to pass so soon. Poor Gallagher. I'm sure the Dowager is training him well."

"It has been hard," Bea murmured.

Rising, Eirian waved at the door. "I think we've kept the duke waiting long enough."

Isabella and Romana pulled back the door and allowed her to walk through. Taking in Aiden in discussion with Everett, Eirian felt an immense amount of relief. With a smile, Everett crossed the room to where she waited. Sweeping her up, he spun Eirian around as she laughed in delight before pulling her into a hug.

"I'm happy to see you!"

"And I'm overjoyed to see you, Everett. What's going on here?"

Reaching out, Eirian touched his face where Everett had grown a beard. It was the same brown as his unruly mess of wavy hair. He rubbed his chin in response and looked over at her ladies-in-waiting.

With a chuckle, he replied, "My men tell me the ladies like a nice beard."

The younger ladies giggled but were soon cowering beneath the disapproving glare of Brenna. Everett bowed and took her offered hand, placing a kiss on it. The giggling resumed, and they pretended to fan themselves when he grinned cheekily at them. Enjoying the show, Eirian glanced at the guards, who watched everything with disinterested gazes.

"Bea, please send for something to eat and drink."

Bringing the giggling to an end, Eirian walked towards the table and chairs near the window. With a curtsy, Bea left to carry out her orders. Everett joined Eirian at the table, sitting opposite and resting his elbows on the wood. They stared at each other, silently observed by the others in the room. Eirian desperately wanted to tell everyone to leave.

"How did you enjoy your first winter home?" Everett asked, leaning back in the chair and crossing his arms.

Shuddering dramatically, Eirian grimaced and replied, "Freezing! It's so much milder in Riane."

"The season certainly put on a good show for you. It was colder than the last few winters. You'll get used to it. If not, you'll endure it in silence. We don't want people thinking the queen can't handle a bit of cold."

Spotting the amusement in his expression, Eirian shrugged. Futures winters did not concern her. Eirian did not feel the cold when her magic was free, and she intended to be done with shielding by the following winter.

"It was the right decision to return before winter and spend the season learning from the council. I wish you'd been here for the company."

"You had your ladies."

"I did, but that's not the same. My ladies expect me to behave like a proper princess."

Exasperated, Brenna told him, "What Her Highness means is, we've tried to teach her how the people will expect her to appear. They don't expect to find a queen gambling and drinking in a tavern!"

Everett stared in shock and asked, "Eirian, you didn't? Aiden, where were you and your men in all this?"

The guards looked at the ground. Aiden cocked his head to the side, scratching his neck as he avoided answering immediately.

Deciding on an answer, Aiden said, "Well, we were guarding an empty room. Again."

"Honestly, Eirian!"

Slamming a hand on the table, Everett glared at her angrily, eyes filled with disappointment. Eirian did not speak, her face blank.

"I can't believe you behaved so irresponsibly! Brenna is right. People expect us to behave with a certain level of decorum. I know you were used to a lot of freedom in Riane, but you're home in Endara now and among different people."

No one said anything, and he sighed.

"You can't trust anyone! What if one of those people in the tavern had been a hired killer sent by Athnaral? Promise me, no more sneaking out."

Pursing her lips, Eirian stared at her lap. There was no way she could tell him of what had happened several months earlier. No one could know she had killed a man in an alley after Athnaral had hired him to kill her. They could not know of her nights in brawling houses fighting for money. Not for the first time, Eirian questioned her decision to keep so many things secret from them.

The doubt she felt did not stop her from replying, "I'm sorry to have disappointed you, Everett. That was never my intention. You're right. I behaved irresponsibly."

"That doesn't sound like a promise to stop sneaking out."

"I promise to stop sneaking out as much."

His expression grew darker, and he looked at the guards. "Aiden, how often does she sneak out?"

"Every few days. I mentioned we could tie her up at night and keep guards in the chamber, but Her Grace informed me that's not how you handle a princess."

Aiden shot Eirian an amused look, clearly pleased that someone was on his side over the matter who stood a chance at doing something. Embarrassed to be witnessing Everett's anger, the remaining three ladies-in-waiting excused themselves and left in search of Bea and the refreshments. Brenna stood with her hands clasped behind her, eyes never leaving Eirian. Accustomed to seeing others dressed down, the guards paid little heed to what was going on. They knew their captains would make them suffer if they made a sound.

"Does your father know?" Everett asked.

"He's said nothing," Eirian answered.

"Where do you go when you sneak out?"

"Mostly the woods. Occasionally other places."

Everett deflated and rubbed his face. "By the powers, Eirian, I can't believe how reckless you are! If Nolan doesn't know, he can't find out. It would cause him distress. Who else knows?"

"Probably half the castle. I cover my tracks, but people talk. Especially guards shown up by a princess. Fionn was careful the last time he dragged me from a tavern. He pretended I was his misbehaving wife, and the patrons found it rather amusing."

"Where were you, Aiden?"

Aiden grumbled, "Asleep. I need that sometimes. Fionn and Merle were in charge. Fionn admitted to being tempted to treat her like she was an errant child. Not that I'd have blamed him. It's not as though I haven't thought of doing it myself."

"You're bloody lucky Aunt Amira isn't here. Though I suppose Llewellyn would find it amusing and join you. I expected better from you, Eirian!"

Everett rose to his feet and walked over to the window to gaze out over the city, his mind lingering briefly on their other cousin. Resting her head on her hand, Eirian watched him, considering what she could say to reassure Everett. She could not decide and settled on apologizing.

"I'm sorry I disappointed you."

"So you say. If you're truly sorry, you'll make it up to me by going nowhere without your guards from now on. Do you have any suggestions, Brenna?"

"Perhaps we should have a lady sleep in her chambers with her."

Indignant, Eirian protested. "I may have behaved irresponsibly, but I'm not a child who needs a minder! I have guards outside my doors, and I'll stop sneaking out. I can defend myself better than you know."

"You might be a mage, but you're a woman and haven't been in real danger. It's our job to keep you alive so you can rule this kingdom. The powers know I'm not so interested in being king that I'd like to inherit the throne because you got yourself killed in a tavern brawl!"

Resting his head against the window, Everett sighed heavily. Pressing her lips together, Eirian looked away, glad none of them knew about her adventures at the fighting houses.

Brenna murmured, "Everett."

"This is not how I pictured this going. I came here to talk to you about something serious. Just promise me, Eirian, no more sneaking out. If you're so desperate for time roaming in the woods, plan it with Aiden. There is no one I trust to protect you better."

"What do you mean, Everett? Something serious?" Eirian asked.

Glancing at Brenna, he shook his head, and she nodded.

Everett told the guards, "Aiden, Gunter, you can remain. The rest of you leave."

Eirian glanced at the guards leaving the room. It stung that they would obey him so quickly. She wondered if it was because they respected Everett for being a man or because she continuously pushed the limits with them. She suspected the former. Everett would lead an army into battle, but they would not expect her to do the same. Gunter glanced at Aiden before they turned their backs on the nobles. They huddled, and Eirian heard the murmur of their voices as they found a topic to distract themselves.

"How much do you know, Brenna?" Everett asked.

Brenna stared sadly and answered, "Marcellus tells me everything. I haven't said anything to her. It's not my place."

"It's your father. Eirian, he isn't well."

"What do you mean, he isn't well? I was with him yesterday, and I saw no signs."

Confused, Eirian looked between them, hoping for an explanation. Walking over to the table, Everett knelt and gathered her hands.

"I'm sorry, Eirian, but I don't think you would see the signs. You barely know Nolan. Marcellus and I believe the King is losing his mind."

SEVEN

They could tell it surprised Eirian, and Brenna took a seat on a chair. Shaking her head in denial, she looked at them and waited for Everett to continue.

"There have been changes, and at first, only those closest to Nolan noticed. He forgets things, and his moods change suddenly. Then there is the confusion."

Brenna drummed her fingertips on the table and said, "It's getting more noticeable, but that's not a good thing. Not right now."

"You mean, not when the heir is a stranger to the nobility?" Eirian grumbled.

Yanking her hands out of Everett's grasp, Eirian closed her eyes and took a deep breath. A multitude of fears crossed her mind.

"You're correct. However, there's more to it. Athnaral is getting aggressive, and there are other rumors."

Everett said, "Oh, Brenna, surely you don't believe those blasted rumors!"

"We can't dismiss them."

"What rumors?" Eirian leaned back.

He explained, "There are rumors that the elves are looking to expand."

Amused, she laughed. "I can assure you those rumors aren't true. The elves aren't planning to invade Endara. I'd know if they were."

Silence descended on the room, and it drew the two captains to turn around to look at Eirian. Unsettled by the stares, she shrugged and uncrossed her legs, stretching them out. Exchanging confused looks, Everett and Brenna grew impatient with her lack of further explanation.

"Why would you know, Eirian?" Everett pushed.

"Because Prince Celiaen and Prince Galameyvin are two of my closest friends. If Paienven were planning such a thing, Celiaen would know, and he'd warn me."

Before they could respond, there was a knock at the door. Bea's voice came muffled through the wood to let them know they had the refreshments. Nodding to Aiden, she dismissed the suspicion in his gaze. Eirian rose to her feet and stepped around Everett to walk to the window. Rolling her head and shoulders, she stared out while she mulled over what else to tell them about her friendship with the heir to the Ensaycalan throne. She knew she could not tell them everything.

"It was maybe a year after I went to Riane that Celiaen, Galameyvin, and their companions came. You may not know, but it's normal for elves with magic to come and go. A few years here and there."

Brenna muttered, "They could have let you do that."

"A few days after they arrived, Celiaen sought me out. He reasoned that as we were the only immediate heirs to thrones with magic, we should be friends because no one else could understand our position."

"Eirian—"

Everett stopped speaking and stood, making way for the ladies, who placed trays of food and drink down on the table. When they completed their task, he continued.

"Are you saying you're courting the heir to Ensaycal?"

She scoffed. "I might be many things, but an absolute fool is not one of them. No, by a close friend, I mean exactly that. Celi is my friend and the person I trust most with my life."

"You wouldn't lie to us about this?"

"I know how serious what you are suggesting is."

Sagging in relief, Everett sat and selected a pastry from the trays. Eirian was thankful he accepted her slightly evasive answer.

"That's a relief because if you were, it would mean war with Athnaral."

The ladies hovered nearby, unsure if they should leave again, their eyes darting between their three superiors as they waited for a signal. Noticing their restlessness, Brenna nodded at the door, and they pivoted, fluttering out like a quartet of butterflies. Following Everett's lead, she selected an item to eat and resumed watching Eirian.

Eirian murmured, "I know, Everett. Celi is a good man, and I'm sure when his father arranges a match for him, she'll be a lucky woman."

"Your friendship could be extremely beneficial."

Brenna selected another item and commented, "You could use it when renegotiating the treaty."

Turning to stare at her in disbelief, Eirian noticed the food, and a pang of hunger struck. It was a reminder that she had used her powers earlier.

"I won't take advantage of our friendship."

Studying Eirian as she came towards the table, Everett considered how to phrase his next point. "You might have to."

Nibbling at the corner of a pastry, Eirian inhaled the sweet scent of the berries within. "I suppose you'd argue Paienven would tell Celiaen the same."

Sipping from a cup, Everett remained silent. Unsure what else to say, the two women followed suit and focused on eating. Satisfied with how much she had eaten, Eirian returned to her spot at the window and gazed out, watching the flurry of activity below.

"None of this is important right now. What about my father?"

Knowing it was a delicate subject, Everett was direct. "Those of us who are aware of what's going on think Nolan needs to abdicate."

Pursing her lips, Eirian said, "You're talking about asking the King to give up his throne. That would need the backing of the entire nobility."

"If it comes to it. We're hoping you might encourage Nolan to come to the idea himself. That's why I needed to see you before the next council meeting. They're going to ask you to do just that."

"You're neglecting an important factor, and I keep telling my husband this. King Nolan might not be aware of anything wrong. If Eirian goes to him with the suggestion he abdicates, Nolan could view it as treason!" Running a hand through her hair, Brenna got to her feet and paced across the room.

Everett looked away in guilt and said, "We wouldn't let that happen."

"It's asking her to put her neck on the executioner's block! We can't make any moves until we know something is wrong with him."

With a shake of her head, Eirian agreed. "Brenna is right. We can't do anything until we know he is losing his mind. I'll talk to him to find out if he has detected any changes."

Watching Brenna pace back and forth, Everett argued, "The council—"

"Can bloody well wait for me to talk to him! I'm their future queen. I'm not some commoner to be ordered around as they please!" Glancing back, Eirian caught Aiden watching her in concern.

"We're worried. A mad ruler is dangerous and a weakness to the kingdom."

"I'm meeting with the chancellor later. Ulric probably wants to discuss this matter. After that, I'll attempt to see my father. If I feel it's needed, I'll send for a green. I dare not try anything myself. Healing has never been my strong suit."

"The council may wait for a healer to assess him. I can convince Marcellus to back you on it. Though, if it is a sickness of the mind, could they do anything for him?" Pausing mid-step, Brenna glanced between them and hoped that Eirian would give a positive answer.

Shaking her head, Eirian lifted her hand to push strands of hair out of her face and said, "I'm sorry, but no. There's a reason Riane puts mages so afflicted to death. There is nothing magic can do to undo physical damage to the mind."

Getting to his feet, Everett approached and placed a hand on her arm. "I'll try to buy you time with the council."

Eirian studied him, taking in the serious look on his face. "Everett, who knows?"

"His household and the council. We can't control who talks to who, so rumors will be out there. That's why we need to start the wheels turning. If he recognizes he isn't well, Nolan can step down on his terms while he possesses himself."

"And if we do nothing?"

"One way or the other, if the King is going mad, you'll be queen soon. The nobility won't stand by while a madman is on the throne."

Gasping, Brenna shot a look at the two guards, warning them with it. "Marcellus hasn't said it out loud. You're admitting an act of treason to the heir to the throne. In front of a peer, the captain of your guard and your—"

Everett said, "Eirian knows."

She did and replied, "None of you can voice this suggestion anywhere. You don't know who might be listening. I love you, Everett, and I'd rather have you by my side. Does Llewellyn agree with you?"

"And I love you, Eirian. So does Llewellyn. There is nothing more either of us would like than to watch you grow old ruling Endara."

"But?"

"As much as I love you, I have to be loyal to the kingdom. If Nolan is going mad, trying to stop a leadership change will give the nobles cause to decide you aren't fit to be queen."

She covered his hand. "Everett, I know my duty to the land comes before familial loyalty. If he is going mad, I'll do what I must."

"Thank the powers."

Turning around, Everett looked at the captains and said, "I don't think I need to remind you of what would happen if you told anyone about what we've discussed here."

They shook their heads and saluted him. Aiden's eyes remained locked firmly on Eirian, and she gave him an annoyed look. Satisfied, Everett turned back to Eirian and leaned in, kissing her cheek lightly. She shifted her gaze to him with mild irritation, causing Everett to arch his eyebrows questioningly.

"They'll never respect me if you keep dealing out threats first. Just because I'm a woman doesn't make me less dangerous than you. Should they cross me, they'd soon discover what happens when I'm betrayed, and I doubt they'd enjoy it."

Regretting her words as they left her mouth, Eirian wondered what they thought she meant. She knew they did not understand what she was capable of.

"I'll always be the one there to do your dirty work, Eirian. It's expected of me. My father filled that role for your father, and I've been filling it since he died. It would be Marcellus or Llewellyn if it wasn't me. Don't you prefer me?"

There was concern on Everett's face, as though he feared she would tell him that yes, she would prefer someone else. Closing her eyes, Eirian took a calming breath before opening them again to stare at Everett.

"I'll keep you for now. They've already broken you in, and training replacements is such a tedious effort. Besides, I doubt Llewellyn would appreciate replacing you."

Laughing, he pulled her in for a hug, then stepped back and bowed. "Well, Your Highness, I must leave you. Are you going to proceed with your plan to meet with Ulric today?"

"Do you think I should? I suppose if I go soon, I might stand a greater chance of getting to see my father."

"Ulric would know we're meeting now. It might be his assumption that I'd discuss the matter and decide it's better to leave it to me."

"He might decide to talk to her about it, anyway. If she hears it from one of her father's most trusted men," Brenna said softly, looking between them.

Drawing her bottom lip between her teeth, Eirian bit it nervously. They looked at her, waiting to hear what she wanted to say.

"I've got a question, Everett, and I want you to answer it as my right hand. Has my father or the council made plans for me to marry?"

They stared in surprise before glancing at each other. Brenna waved her hand in the air dismissively, giving Everett a silencing look.

Brenna answered, "There have been many offers of marriage from various nobles. King Nolan has turned them all down. However, your age will shorten the grace period the council will allow you."

"So that's a no?"

"Correct, Eirian. No plans for you to marry are in the works. Not unless your father has secretly arranged something in his madness." Everett looked away, adding, "We're monitoring his correspondence. His secretary is my man, and he carefully searches everything when the King is not around."

Eirian stared at him blankly. "I presume you're telling me this because you want me to know it will be the same for me. Does Brenna already search through my letters?"

"If a time comes that we feel we need to monitor you, it would never be a peer of the realm. I'm telling you this because when everything is over, I'll have to kill a man loyal to me to protect everything he has learned."

"There's a lesson in this for me."

"Yes. You understand?"

She continued to stare at Everett, silence settling between them while Brenna shuffled nervously. The two captains observed, somewhat bemused by the exchange.

Finally, Eirian said, "I understand you better than you realize, Everett. However, I suspect you don't understand me quite so well as you think you do."

"Perhaps you're right. I hope we have many years in which we grow to understand each other better."

"I hope so, Everett. May the rest of your day be productive, but try to avoid killing anyone, and I'll do the same."

Turning, Eirian dismissed him and walked to the window once more. Shooting her a wry smile, Everett saluted Eirian, though she could not see it.

"You kill someone? That's an amusing thought. I'll see you at dinner unless you decide to dine privately."

Eirian did not turn, and her smile was unseen by the others in the room. "I assure you, Everett, I'm more than capable of killing someone."

Brenna glanced between them, watching Everett walk to where Gunter was waiting. She shook her head and joined him when he paused at the door to give Eirian one last look. Placing a hand on his arm, she leaned in, monitoring Eirian the whole time.

"I'll work on her," Brenna murmured.

His eyes searched her face. "We need her to be with us."

"I know my duty, and I won't let you down."

Giving Brenna a curt nod, he stepped back and followed Gunter out of the chamber. Taking Everett's departure as a sign, the guards filed in. They saluted Aiden and Eirian before resuming their positions. Peeking through the doorway, the ladies slipped in when Brenna nodded and began tidying things up. None of them dared to approach Eirian at the window. Quietly muttering between themselves, the ladies continued their discussion with the occasional glance at Brenna and Eirian. Leaning against a wall, Aiden watched Eirian like a hawk with a thumb hooked through his belt.

"I won't bite unless you ask me to. You don't need to be so quiet," Eirian said, turning around to frown at them. "Does anyone know when I might expect the chancellor?"

"No, Eirian, but he is a busy man." Brenna held out her hands apologetically and said, "We can send a messenger if you wish."

Contemplating it, Eirian took another glance at the position of the sun. "I'd like to get on and try to see my father. Send someone to let Ulric know. He may already be there, and I'll see him before speaking to the King. I'm sure it should work out."

"Fisk will see to it, ma'am," Aiden spoke, his tone soft.

Fisk saluted, quickly heading out the door.

"Would you also like someone sent to His Majesty's chambers to let them know you're coming?"

"No, I don't think so."

The ladies glanced at each other in surprise.

Elke asked, "My lady, do you want us to come with you?"

"Yes, that would be best. It is the proper thing, isn't it, Brenna?"

Brenna said, "Very much so."

Eirian rolled her eyes. "We should go. I imagine the later I leave it, the harder it will be to gain an audience with the King. Even for his heir."

Falling into step with her, the ladies followed the guards out the door and ignored how the heavily armed men surrounded them. Eirian's eyes constantly swept her surroundings as her long strides covered ground without hurrying. Her mind was troubled, fear of the truth behind Everett's concerns at the forefront.

The King's quarters were in a separate part of the castle. His side was a hive of activity. Courtiers lingered in hallways, hoping to advance themselves with the nobility or with others of power who had the ear of the throne. Messengers scurried back and forth, some laden with rolls of parchment and books, while others looked weary from days spent on the road. Officials of the court strode along, arrogant in their importance even when faced with Eirian's party.

Tucked away in corners and shrouded by shadows, guards observed with nonchalance and remained poised for action. They watched everything, rarely missing a trick. It was Aiden who received their respect as he passed. He acknowledged them, the action barely perceivable to those unaware of what was transpiring. When they reached the doors to the King's outer chambers, they found a crowd of people.

Many sought an audience with King Nolan, but few got past the guards. Most of those who waited were merchants trying to catch attention to gain business. When the crowd realized who had arrived, they fell back and cleared the way. Standing to attention and saluting Eirian, the guards opened the doors to allow the party through. Murmuring her thanks as she passed, Eirian did not glance at the crowd, knowing to do so would attract demands on her time.

Once inside, it was less chaotic. Officials and higher nobility filled the chamber, turning to stare at Eirian while she observed them. Her gaze swept over the clusters of people. Many gathered around tables covered in documents, while others stood in groups to talk. Large maps covered the walls, detailing parts of the kingdom and the rest of the known lands. The crowd fell into bows and curtsies, the swish of fabric filling the silence that had struck. Eirian nodded, spotting Ulric among a group as they rose.

Pushing his way to the forefront, Ulric took control of the situation and guided Eirian to the table he had been at. "Your Highness, I was preparing to come and see you, but your message just reached me."

"I'm pleased my man got here before I did, Ulric. The Duke of Tamantal has been to see me this morning," Eirian replied.

Glancing over her shoulder at Brenna, they shared a knowing look. If he understood the message in her words, his expressions did not betray him.

"They told me the duke was back. He's well, I presume?"

Leaning forward to look at the papers strewn over the table, Eirian watched him from the corner of her eye. "Of course. Everett is as hale as ever. Are these the surveys of food stores from the end of winter?"

"Yes, Your Highness, they are," Sabine said. "I believe Ulric was planning to discuss them with you once we had finished our review."

"Well, I look forward to it. I'm here to see the King and can't discuss it now, but Sabine, I'd like to hear what you have to say. You must join us when we go over it." Smiling at her briefly, Eirian enjoyed the look of surprise that struck Sabine.

Resuming her usual composure, Sabine inclined her head. "I'd be pleased to share my thoughts on the matter with you, ma'am."

"Excellent. We're going to be working together for a long time. Never feel you can't share your thoughts with me."

Reminding Eirian why she was there, Ulric said, "I haven't seen His Majesty, but several of his gentlemen are in his quarters."

"Do you expect him to appear?"

"I'm sorry, ma'am, but I can't say with any certainty if King Nolan will make an appearance. However, we have many pressing issues and need something done. May we assume you're here to help?"

Ulric met her gaze, and Eirian noted the signs of stress in his expression. "You may."

Eirian turned and walked over to the doors leading into her father's rooms. Searching for Aiden, she inclined her head slightly, signaling for him to join her. Brenna held back, remaining with Ulric as they watched the duo approach the doors. The guards standing there hesitated before knocking on the heavy timber and pushing it open. Stepping through, Eirian's gaze shifted to the handful of men sitting around a table while guards leaned against walls with their hands raised in salute.

"Thomas, where is His Majesty?" Her voice broke them out of their daze, and they jumped to their feet, sweeping into deep bows.

"He is in his chamber, Your Highness," Thomas said. "I apologize for our state, but he doesn't wish to see anyone."

Glaring at him, she refused to back down. "I'm his daughter, and he doesn't have a choice. Aiden, make sure no one disturbs us."

"Of course, Princess," Aiden replied.

His hand rested on the hilt of his sword, and he gave the occupants of the room a challenging smile. Crossing the space with quick strides, Eirian pushed the door open and slipped through. It was dark, with only a few lit candles scattered about. Searching, she found the shadowy form of her father sitting in a corner with his back to her, hunched forward and resting his head in his hands.

"I told you to get out until I called you, Thomas!" Nolan snapped.

His voice was gruffer than Eirian had heard before, and it prompted her to dawdle.

"It's not Thomas."

Jolting upright, Nolan turned and stared at her. The sight of him so disheveled distracted Eirian momentarily from the realization that he looked older than he had the day before. Unsure if it was the shadows or her mind, Eirian finished crossing the space and crouched beside his chair, taking one of his hands in her own. Silently watching each other, they waited for someone to muster the courage to speak.

She broke first, her voice cracking. "It's true then?"

Recognizing that Eirian knew something was wrong, Nolan sagged in the chair, gripping her hand tightly. "I'm so sorry, my darling girl."

"How long has this been happening?"

"I don't know when it started. I know sometimes…" Nolan sighed, shaking his head. "I'll be doing something. Then it's suddenly later, and I don't recall what happened in between. Or I forget things, names, places. I'm sure there is more."

Leaning in closer, she said, "You should've told me."

"I'm a proud man, Eirian, and I know what this means. I had days where I planned to tell you. Perhaps I forgot, I forget so much."

Resting back on her heels, Eirian rubbed her face in frustration. Anger filled her, the emotion directed at everyone who knew or suspected and had not mentioned a thing.

"It has Everett worried. He's the one who finally told me. He felt he needed to before someone else did. Father, you can't keep going like this."

Getting to his feet, Nolan stepped away from her, stumbling to the window to pull back the drape. Light flooded the room, and they both blinked uncomfortably as their eyes adjusted.

"I know what it means. They say nothing, but I've seen the fear in their eyes. You don't understand yet, but you will one day. It's hard, knowing you're growing old and your mind is escaping you."

"I hate to say this, but father, you need to abdicate while you can."

"That has crossed my mind. I don't want to give you a kingdom in chaos. Everett would've told you they'll force me from the throne if needed. He doesn't want to be king, but if you don't dance to their tune…"

Silhouetted by the light, Nolan seemed the forbidding figure of her childhood memories. Closing her eyes, Eirian reminded herself that she could not be the loving daughter. That had to wait until after following through on her promise.

"I want to send for a green to look you over."

"No, there is no need. I wasn't young when you were born, and I'm certainly not in my prime. Even though I'm not a mage, I know magic can't help this. You'll be the queen before next winter," Nolan said, returning to the chair.

"So soon?"

Standing beside her, he stroked Eirian's head gently. "I'm proud of you."

"I wish it weren't like this. I'm in no hurry to take over from you."

"I felt the same way as I watched my father grow old. Occasionally, the impertinence of youth saw me wishing he would hurry and die so I could be king. Still, I feared, loved, and respected him. He was my father. I imagine you feel the same way towards me, and one day your children will feel the same way towards you."

Gazing up at him, Eirian smiled sadly. "I do, father. A great deal. We've missed out on a lot of time together."

"We missed out on a lot of things, Eirian. I hope I can keep my mind long enough to watch you flourish as a leader." Glancing at the door, Nolan huffed. "While I'm clear-headed, I should deal with the mess out there. I imagine they're all slavering like starving hounds over a bone."

Eirian followed his glance as she rose, taking a moment to smooth the fabric of her skirt. "If someone had mentioned something to me sooner, it might not be a mess."

"Don't worry, they'll be your mess to deal with soon enough. I need to gather the full council to abdicate and tell them they can stop plotting. However, I can start the process with that lot out there."

Not sure how to respond, she did something she had not done since she was a child. Stepping up to her father, Eirian wrapped her arms around him in a hug. Nolan stiffened in her embrace before relaxing and hugging her back, resting his cheek against the top of her head. They stood there and pretended people were not outside the doors, waiting to find out what their next step would be. Sighing, Nolan kissed her forehead and pulled back, giving Eirian a sad smile.

"I wish your mother was here."

Swallowing what she had planned to say, Eirian fought harder to keep from crying.

Her voice did not break when she replied, "So do I."

"You'd best send my gentlemen in. I'll join you in the outer chamber shortly."

"Father."

Nolan walked to a table where a bowl of clean water sat. "The day is escaping us, Your Highness."

Pulling herself together, Eirian rubbed her eyes. She felt like a chastised child.

"Of course, I'll send them in and wait for you, sire."

King Nolan watched her walk towards the door and saw the similarities to his younger self. He had always been thankful to see little of his dead wife in their daughter, but at that moment, he wished she were less like him. Recalling the sweet and innocent child, Nolan struggled with the reality that her magic had destroyed that side of her. His hands tightly gripped the washcloth while the memories crossed his mind, and he hated the guilt that came with them. The knowledge that there were so many secrets he could not tell his daughter.

Letting the door fall closed behind her, Eirian faced the nervous gentlemen and impassive guards. She spotted the concern in Aiden's gaze, but focused on the gentlemen.

"His Majesty is waiting for you. Hurry, he has much to do."

Thomas bowed, a brief smile of gratefulness crossing his face, and he replied, "Of course, Your Highness. We will attend to him."

Nodding to Aiden, she kept walking, and he was not quick enough to prevent Eirian from shoving the next set of doors wide open. Cursing himself for not stopping her so he could check she was okay, Aiden followed closely. There had been changes to the people waiting, and Eirian saw Everett mingling with other council members. Breaking away from his conversation, Everett joined Eirian with a concerned look. He took her arm, meeting Aiden's gaze. Aiden gave a slight shake of his head, the action receiving a brief nod of understanding.

"Well?" Everett murmured, searching her eyes for a sign.

"His Majesty will join us soon. He's aware of what has been going on." Looking around at the people pretending they were not listening, Eirian ground her teeth. "I don't care what everyone thinks of my abilities. You should have brought this to my attention sooner."

Frowning, his grip on her arm tightened in a warning, and Everett hissed, "Eirian, this is not the time or place."

"I disagree! Everyone in this room plays a part in running the kingdom, Your Grace, and they saw what was happening."

Eirian wrenched her arm from his grip, anger filling her eyes. "Can anyone give me a reasonable excuse why you left it so long before I was told?"

Shocked faces stared at her, and Eirian met each of them with her furious gaze. Beside her, Everett froze in amazement, the look on his face making her anger fade slightly into uncertainty. Looking at Aiden, she found admiration and respect in his expression and drew strength from it. Smirking, Sabine bowed and nodded at Everett.

"Thank you for saying that, ma'am. You're right. Some of us were pushing for you to be told when you returned from Riane. Others, like Tamantal, thought it was better to wait and give you time to settle."

"What Sabine means is we didn't feel it would be useful to deliver such distressing news on your return. You had barely set foot in the kingdom after so long away," said another member of the council.

Sabine snorted, giving him a scathing look. "I'm sorry, but that's horseshit, and everyone in this room knows it."

Eirian held up her hands and snapped, "That's enough! I agree it is horseshit, Sabine, and I'm not above calling it. I accept I'm unknown to you. The heir with an unexpected gift sent away for twenty years."

Seeing Everett open his mouth to speak, she cut him off.

"But let me make this clear. I am the heir. I am the only child of King Nolan, and I will be your next ruler. You will answer to me, and you'll find I am a hard taskmaster."

"Well said, Your Highness," Ulric replied as he placed a hand on the shoulder of the noblewoman beside him. "Please understand that we need to get to know each other. We must learn about each other's strengths and weaknesses."

Eirian nodded before she said, "But that has nothing to do with what is going on here. You withheld information regarding the wellbeing of the King. Should something like that happen again, I will not be so forgiving. I'm not someone you can manipulate, and from now on, you will include me in everything."

Reaching for her arm again, Everett asked, "Does this mean?"

She cocked her head to the side, staring at him blankly, and answered, "Wait for the King to tell you about his decision."

"By the powers, Eirian, you're more like him than I realized." Everett shook his head and stepped back, looking at Brenna to say, "I don't envy you in your role, Brenna."

Grinning, Brenna shrugged and gleefully replied, "I warned you. She's her father's daughter."

"Right down to the rambunctious outbursts!" Marcellus shook his head. "Reminds me of our youth. His Majesty was always up for a bit of carousing."

Aiden gave Eirian a disgruntled look and, keeping his voice low enough that she was the only one who heard him, muttered, "Like father, like daughter with the carousing."

His words earned him a faint smirk from Eirian before the doors opened behind her. The room fell silent as they bowed. She turned, slipping into a curtsy as she came face to face with Nolan. Standing there, he regarded them with an impassive expression. Rising first, Eirian stepped to the side to allow Nolan to take command of the room.

"I see you move quickly once you set your minds to it. Well, you can be at ease now. You have your wish. Start preparing because I'm abdicating, and we will instate Princess Eirian as the queen before winter."

EIGHT

The view from the roof of the tallest tower of the inner bailey took her breath every time. Resting her arms on the stone, Eirian tilted her head back to bask in the sunlight as she gazed out over the sprawl of the city. Plumes of smoke drifted into the air and, from her position, she could barely hear the bustle of life surrounding her. A cool breeze caught strands of her growing hair, and she hooked a finger around a stray one that crossed her eyes, tucking it behind her ears without thinking.

Turning her gaze to a closer location, Eirian watched a flurry of people crossing the courtyard towards the main keep. Something about their appearance seemed familiar. Behind her, several of her guards discussed their training. Aiden had insisted on making changes, and they were still adjusting to them. Ignoring their conversation, she continued to watch the courtyard with curiosity.

"Your Highness?"

Startled out of her reverie, Eirian replied, "Yes, Merle?"

Merle stepped over to the edge of the tower and glanced down. "A messenger has come for you. It's time to head back to the keep."

Sighing, Eirian nodded and allowed herself another look over the city. "Then we'd better head back."

Leading the way, Merle signaled to his men to surround Eirian. Remaining quiet as they traipsed down the stairs, she pondered who sent the messenger. Her weeks had been busy since learning about Nolan's illness and his decision to abdicate. The council demanded her time, and the reality that she had a lot to learn had sunk in quickly. Eirian's outburst had left Everett distant towards her, and to an extent, she was thankful. It meant she could focus on learning without him interfering.

When they reached the bottom of the stairs, the remaining two guards were waiting to join them. Beside them, a young woman stood adorned in the uniform worn by castle messengers, her hair drawn back in a tight braid that swung over her shoulder as she bowed.

"You have a message for me?" Eirian said, glancing at her as they walked.

"Yes, Your Highness. Travelers from Riane have arrived. They sent me from the gate to tell you they were being taken to your receiving room."

Jolting, Eirian suddenly understood why the group had looked familiar. "Did you catch the names?"

Shaking her head, the messenger apologized. "No, ma'am, I didn't. A guard grabbed me, and I ran as fast as I could. I knew to ask at the barracks about where you might be. Guards know everything."

The men chuckled, and she blushed in response, trying her best not to look at them. Amused, Eirian thanked her and sent her back to her post. Noticing one of her guards watching the young woman stride off, Eirian cleared her throat and gave him a scathing look. His fellow guards jeered at him for being caught out. Eager to find out who had come from Riane, Eirian pushed the guards to keep up.

Ignoring everything they passed, Eirian barely blinked when several of her ladies joined her. People saw them coming and were quick to get out of the way, the path clearing without the guards needing to do anything. When they reached Eirian's quarters, they saw one of her guards in front of the door. He pushed himself off the timber when he spotted Eirian, saluting, but not moving out of the way.

"Fionn, why are you barring my door?"

He replied, "I'm not sure it's a good idea for you to go in there."

Nostrils flaring, Eirian made herself take a deep breath. "Why is that? I have visitors from Riane."

"Yes, ma'am, you have a room full of mages."

"I don't see the problem."

Fionn glanced at the guards and ladies standing behind her. "They're dangerous."

"Fionn, no one in there is more powerful than me. Am I dangerous?" Eirian stared at him, not sure she liked where this was going.

"Ma'am, I'm sure you're dangerous when you want to be, but you don't make my skin crawl like they do," Fionn said and regretted his response when her eyes gleamed.

Holding a hand up, Eirian squared her shoulders and gave him a knowing look.

Her voice dropped as she purred, "And yet here you are, standing in my way. You certainly don't seem afraid of me."

Merle made a noise, distracting the two of them as he said, "This is fine, but if the boss man were here, he'd have you at the tip of his sword, Fionn. Now apologize, get out of the way, and let Her Highness greet her visitors. Before anyone comes along to suggest we hang you."

Prepared to argue, Fionn moved when the door behind him opened. Another guard stood there with a wary look, and they knew he had been listening. Eirian looked in and saw the party dotted around the room. Stepping around Fionn, she strode inside, drawing their attention to her. No one spoke for a moment before one of the gray-clad mages leaped at Eirian with an excited squeal and pulled her into a hug, laughing.

"Sister!"

"Fay! By the powers, what are you doing here?"

Pushing Fayleen back, Eirian gaped at her. Smiling, Fayleen shook her head and pointed over her shoulder at the only person not looking at them.

"He thought it would help if I came along."

One of the other guards nudged Fionn, muttering, "Yes, so dangerous."

Letting go of Fayleen, Eirian stepped around her and towards the cloaked figure at the window. She suspected she knew exactly who it was.

Grabbing her arm, Fayleen stopped her. "Send everyone away before he tells you why we're here."

"That sounds serious."

"Ree, why can't I feel your magic? I've been trying since we reached the city, but it's like you're not here."

Frowning, Eirian gave Fayleen a guilty look and said, "I'm shielding."

The cloaked man said, "Her shields are so complete that she didn't feel us coming, either. I don't understand how you could willingly cripple yourself."

"Archmage Baenlin Zarthein. It is an honor." Eirian nervously turned to her people and said, "Everyone, please leave us."

"Your Highness, I'll remain," Merle said while signaling to the other men to go, but Eirian shook her head at him. "You can't be without a guard."

"Everyone, Merle. The archmage isn't here to do anything to me. Even if he could. You have my word."

Turning, Baenlin pushed back his charcoal gray cloak, revealing himself. Dark brown eyes took everything in, keen intelligence shimming within their depths. Eyes that reminded her of Celiaen and made her long for his company. Eirian understood why Fionn had been nervous. The power coming from Baenlin would set anyone on edge. Novices feared him, whispering horror stories of what he had done in past wars to each other in the darkest hours.

"Drop your shield, girl," he demanded, and crossed his arms.

The cloak fell away, revealing the twin swords of his order. Not willing to risk angering him, Eirian let her shields drop, and the rush of her magic was intense. Behind her, she sensed her guards freeze as they were leaving. It made her heart sink, knowing they were suddenly aware of her as a mage. Fayleen closed her eyes, head tilting back as she let Eirian's power wash over her. Glancing over her shoulder at Merle, Eirian saw fear in his eyes as he quickly saluted and hurried out of the chamber, pulling the door shut with a thud. Turning back to Baenlin, she bowed.

"I hear you're to be the Queen of Endara before winter comes," he said, continuing to stare at her.

"My father is unwell. For the sake of Endara, he is abdicating."

One of the other mages gasped, "We weren't expecting that news to be true."

Turning, she looked at the man and greeted him. "Master Howell. The reason for this visit must be serious for you to be here."

"Your father is not the only one who isn't well. The grand mage is failing."

Looking to Baenlin, Eirian hoped he would say Howell was lying. Receiving no denial, she rocked back on her heels and covered her mouth with her hand, horrified.

When she gathered her thoughts, Eirian said, "That is terrible news. However, I don't understand why it brings you here."

"We're here to bring you home to Riane," Baenlin said sharply.

"Is that a joke?" Eirian asked, her power surrounding her.

Flaring in response, Baenlin's power was a thundercloud. "I don't joke about such matters. The grand mage is failing, and you're the most powerful mage alive who can take the seat on the council."

"It's true, sister," Fayleen said, and touched her arm cautiously. "We need you."

"Has there ever been a human grand mage?" she countered.

Howell shook his head, scratching behind his ear as he muttered, "Honestly, it's hard to believe you are human. I suppose there's a first time for everything."

Walking over to the table, Eirian pulled out a chair and sat.

Looking at each of them in frustration, she said, "You're asking me to forget my duty and to return with you. I won't turn my back on my people. I made that clear when everyone was telling me not to leave Riane."

"Why not? You'll serve them far better on the high council than as a mere queen. Having a lesser mage in the highest seat is sheer folly. The council oversees everything and everyone. We are the highest power in all the lands. Why would you want to be a queen of one little kingdom when you could be the queen of them all?"

Baenlin's words reminded Eirian of how superior most mages viewed themselves.

"I barely want to be the queen of said little kingdom. Why, by the powers, would I want to be the queen of them all? I'm not driven by the desire for more power."

Catching the implication, Baenlin glared at her, and she felt suffocated by his magic. "You've always been disrespectful!"

Taking a deep breath, Eirian pushed back with her power. "Call me disrespectful, Archmage, but it won't change my mind. I have a job to do here."

"You would honestly refuse us? You would refuse the position of the grand mage?"

"Ree, please reconsider. You belong with us in Riane. We're your proper people, the ones who understand and accept you. I saw how your people reacted to us. That's why you hide from them," Fayleen said, holding her hands out.

Eirian sadly replied, "You're right, Fay. I know how much distrust there is of mages, and rightfully so. We're a terrifying force. So, I hide it and yes, doing so cripples me. But I belong here."

A shadow crossed her vision, and Baenlin crouched in front of her.

His eyes filled with concern as he said, "You can't keep shielding. Magic doesn't like it. If you were very weak, maybe it would be okay, but you're not weak, not by a long shot. Knowing you as I do, I suspect you began shielding when you crossed the border."

"I don't keep them up constantly. I release my magic daily when I'm alone."

"That will only delay the inevitable. Your power will rebel, and you'll destroy this city if you can't control it. If you're so fearful of their reactions, then don't become their queen."

Eirian did not respond. He took hold of her hands and rubbed his thumb on the middle finger of her left hand where the purple band signaling her order should have been.

Baenlin scolded, "You don't even wear your mark. We invested so much time into your potential, and you want to let it go to waste."

Swallowing, Eirian looked past him at a spot on the wall and replied, "I don't want my people to fear me."

"So, don't do it."

"Archmage, you have an ulterior motive," she said, and her lips twitched briefly.

"Yes, I do. Even if I didn't, I'd tell you the same thing. You're one of the gifted, and the power of the gods runs through you. Hiding your magic is wrong and an insult to all mages. Worse, it is dangerous for those around you."

"He speaks the truth, Eirian. If you insist on becoming queen, you need to stop shielding." Joining them at the table, Howell leaned on it and said, "I know I'm not one everyone remembers, but Baenlin hasn't seen half of what I have. You're not the first to hide their powers and believe me, the fallout is not worth it. That you're going down that path terrifies me."

"As it does me," said the previously silent woman.

Her soft voice was a caress of power, an attempt to spread calm through the room.

Glancing at her, Eirian frowned uncomfortably. "Please don't do that."

"Apologies. All this talk has made me anxious."

Pursing his lips, Baenlin threw an angry look at the woman. "They didn't pick the most disciplined of blues to accompany me this time."

She smiled at him and the expression bordered on serene. Noticing she was human, Eirian arched a brow. Reds went nowhere without a blue, their opposing natures creating a balance. Blues had to overwhelm a red on a rampage, calming the warrior with their magic. To accompany Baenlin meant she was powerful. Turning her gaze to the other silent mage, Eirian recognized him and his bored expression while he watched them.

"Are they that worried about you losing your temper with me, Archmage, that they felt the need to send a second blue? Is Soren not enough?"

Turning slightly to glance at them, Baenlin shook his head. "I'm not the only one in this room that might require their influence."

"You brought a blue for me?" She covered her mouth and laughingly said, "I'm flattered. Of course, I should have left Riane with one."

His eyes darkened as he looked at her, and Baenlin replied, "We could manipulate you into agreeing if given a chance. As you know, Soren is good at influencing."

A loud knocking at the door caused them to turn. Eirian rose to her feet, stepping away from Baenlin in one swift movement, and walked across the room. Reaching the door, she opened it and smiled calmly at Brenna standing there. Checking Eirian over, she pushed her way past and took in the five mages who dominated the room with their presence. Distrust flickered over her face before she turned back to Eirian.

"You should have sent for me."

"Don't you dare!" Eirian barked at the blue when she stepped towards Brenna.

"I could help," she murmured.

Her tone became threatening, and Eirian said, "You wouldn't enjoy what I'd do to you if you did. I'm sure you're familiar with the stories."

Taken aback, Brenna turned and stared at the stranger, asking, "Your Highness, what is happening?"

"Nothing is going on, Your Grace. Archmage, are you planning to stay for long, or will you be heading back to Riane now that you've finished what you came to do?"

Her tone carried a note of warning, and for the first time, Brenna realized the aura of power surrounding Eirian. Mouth open slightly with amazement, it was as though a shadow had lifted from her eyes as she stared at the future queen.

Brenna said, "I've never seen you like this."

Snorting, Baenlin shot up, and his movement distracted her as he declared, "This is your precious princess in almost all of her glory! She's only let you see a fraction of herself, and you don't know how magnificent she is."

"Don't do this," Fayleen muttered.

Soren agreed. "Now is not the time."

Fayleen glanced at her feet uncomfortably before she looked at Howell and said, "You're the sensible one, don't let them start a pissing match. It'll only end badly."

Howell held his hands up passively and shifted the conversation to Nolan. "You say the King is ill. I'd like to see him."

"You can't help him." Eirian shook her head and explained, "It's his mind."

"Still, I should like to see him and confirm. It may help matters."

Nodding, she looked at Brenna and asked, "Your Grace, could you take Master Howell to see the King? If anyone tries to prevent it, tell them it's on my orders."

"Do we need to arrange quarters for them?" Brenna continued looking between the two powerful mages in awe, adding, "First Planting is soon, and with the celebrations…"

"Please, yes. I may spend quite some time with him to make a diagnosis, and I'd like to rest afterward. First Planting celebrations are always a pleasure, and I should enjoy attending them. Are you fine with that, Baenlin?" Howell promoted.

There was a gleam of triumph in his dark eyes as Baenlin agreed to stay. He saw the opportunity being presented and inclined his head in agreement. Watching the flustered Brenna lead Howell out tempted him to send Fayleen with them. Left alone with the two blue mages, he could work on Eirian. More guards and the nobles they accompanied arrived, foiling his plan.

Bringing his hand to the hilt of a sword, Baenlin rubbed his fingertips against the cool metal as he studied his target. Tensions rose, the newcomers distracted by the visitors, allowing Eirian to slip behind her walls. Meeting Baenlin's disapproving stare, his hand on his sword drew her gaze. Fear the situation could spiral out of control made her swirl around and check the guards.

"Enough!" Eirian snarled in frustration.

They looked at her, quietening down while they waited for direction. Running a hand through her hair, Eirian picked one of her ladies out of the crowd. Trying her best to look demure, Isabella could not help but continue to glance warily at the mages.

"When Brenna found out you had visitors from Riane, she wanted people around. Said they were less likely to do anything if there was a crowd. Merle argued you wouldn't appreciate the interference, but she wouldn't listen."

"I see. What exactly did Brenna think they might do?"

A young nobleman Eirian did not recognize replied, "Well, they're mages. They stole you as a child, and what's stopping them from doing it again?"

Astonished, Eirian staggered at his response. Fayleen quickly darted to her side, offering her a hand. The other mages stared at him in horror.

"Stole me? Good grief, where did you come up with that rubbish?"

"That's what my parents told me." He looked less confident after seeing her reaction and the appalled faces of the mages he had insulted.

"They never stole me. The King sent me to Riane when my powers manifested. I'm a mage!"

Many faces in the crowd looked away, unhappy at being reminded. Taking stock of their expressions, Eirian wondered if Baenlin was right.

"What's going on?"

Everett arrived, his presence providing Eirian with the assurance things would not get out of hand. Seeing the thankful look appear on Eirian's face, Baenlin knew his chance to encourage the Endaran nobles to show their dislike for mages had slipped past. Exchanging a glance with Soren, he changed his direction and hoped it would not backfire.

Looking at Everett, Baenlin said, "Her Highness was about to have someone take us to our quarters for the night. We'd like to freshen up. It was a long journey."

Eyes narrowing in suspicion, Eirian nodded. "Yes, I was. Isabella, if you could please take my friends to their quarters and have refreshments delivered to them."

Curtsying, Isabella signaled for them to follow. Several nobles went along, wary of leaving any of their number alone with the mages. Sighing in relief when the room emptied, Eirian walked back over to the chair. Hearing the door shut, she glanced up and saw Everett had banished everyone. He was alone, leaning against it with one hand pressed to the timber. As he turned to face her, Eirian noticed he looked tired.

"What is going on?"

"They were traveling and thought they'd visit on their way past."

He stared at her in disappointment as he said, "That wasn't convincing. Try again."

Rubbing the back of her neck, Eirian contemplated her options and tried to think of a better story to give him. "You missed the fifth member of the party. He's one of the best healers in Riane and came to give King Nolan a diagnosis."

"I almost believe you. Yes, there is a healer, and yes, he is looking over the King, but that's not why they came. Just tell me the truth, Eirian."

"Do people believe the mages stole me?"

"I've heard that story. It's one of many floating around."

He crossed the room to the table. Taking a seat next to Eirian, he leaned in and chuckled. She bit the inside of her cheeks, avoiding his gaze.

"It's you and me, cousin. You can tell me why they are here."

"First, tell me, did you sense the power coming from them?"

"Only a dead man would have missed it. You never feel like that, which makes me assume they're more powerful than you," Everett replied with a shrug.

Chuckling softly, Eirian had to shake her head, saying, "Hardly. Even combined, they're not as powerful as me. I keep my power buried behind shields, and no one notices. It's dangerous, but I risk it."

"Why? I gather people were a bit… excited by your mage friends, but that's only because they're strangers."

"Can you look me in the eye and tell me that if I let my power be as it should, people would accept me? Because I don't think they would. They can happily pretend that Riane stole me for whatever reason they come up with so long as my power isn't in their faces."

Her words stung, and Everett pushed away.

Slamming his hand on the table, he said, "You're the heir to the throne, Eirian. Power is power! People will get used to it, but it needs to be there for them to get used to."

"You don't understand. Baenlin wasn't the most powerful person in this room. He wasn't even the most dangerous. The reason they have come is that the Endaran throne is not the only one I'm next in line to."

Holding her head high, Eirian watched him darkly. Frustration with the situation tempted her to do what he suggested and drop her shields.

"What do you mean?"

"The grand mage is dying. I'm the most powerful mage alive, which makes me the heir. They came to take me back to Riane."

Eyes widening, Everett opened and closed his mouth as he struggled to find the words to respond. Eirian watched fear and ambition flicker through his eyes before he stood and walked away.

When Everett finally spoke, he said, "You can't do that. You're the next ruler of Endara. That is your role, your duty, what you were born to be."

"That's what I said when I refused. Baenlin could try to make me go, but it would be risky. I don't want that, and I doubt they do either. If I say yes, you'll replace me, so what you want is important."

"Please, Eirian, I'm begging you to stay here and be the queen you were born to be."

Eirian dropped her shields, controlling the rush of magic. It was a slow-rolling fog as her presence grew. Feeling the magic, Everett turned to stare, watching the way she lit up. He had often thought Eirian was unimposing, but looking at her without her shields, he felt he was finally seeing her. Shivering, Everett felt a sliver of fear pierce his heart, casting doubt on his conviction that the people would grow used to her.

"Can you look me in the eye and tell me you aren't frightened of me?"

Everett stared into her eyes and marveled at the way the dark brown shimmered with flecks of gold. "I can. Besides, I visited you in Riane, and I've seen you like this before. You're still my little cousin, the girl I used to beat in a race."

She frowned and said, "You always cheated."

"Did not. Your legs were too short."

Admiring how her skin and hair had taken on a glow, Everett decided that the power made her seem earthier. They laughed at each other, the sound breaking some of the tension.

"I grew up. I could beat you now."

"How about one day we cause a scandal and race like children? Everyone will talk for days. But Eirian, you must stay here. Please, I'm begging you. I'll get down on my knees to do it. Let the high council be someone else's problem," Everett said.

"I want to stay. I know this is my duty, but I'm scared. I'm not ready to be the queen, let alone the grand mage. The way I've been shielding my powers is dangerous."

She seemed so small, and Everett approached to draw her into a hug. Tears of guilt were shimmering in Eirian's eyes, and he respected her fears.

"We all know, deep down, magic is more, and mages are special. You're not the same as the rest of us, and the ability to use magic makes you closer to the gods. Whether that is some deeply rooted instinct or conditioning from childhood when parents tell us stories that make mages the things you fear in the night."

"In Riane, Baenlin is the one we tell each other stories about in the dark."

"That's not reassuring in the slightest, Eirian. Thank you. I don't think I'll sleep tonight," Everett muttered.

Eirian giggled, wiping away her tears.

He continued, "People would fear mages less if they were around more. With you as queen, a mage who is open with her magic, Endarans will understand them better."

Intrigued by his logic, Eirian considered it and replied, "You're right. Very few human mages return to their birthplaces. Maybe they prefer the privileged life in Riane and decide it's better not to risk possible fear and distrust among the people they were born to. It could be our shorter lifespan. There is much to learn, but we don't have the time."

"The mages who are here, who are they?"

"Archmage Baenlin leads the group. Everyone knows who he is. You've met Fay previously, and you can bet they brought her along to use our friendship. I'm not sure who the other woman was. Both she and the last man are blues. He's called Soren, and I know him. He's a master, an influencer of extraordinary talent, and Baenlin's primary blue."

"I saw Fayleen. She looked at lovely as ever. It will be good to catch up."

Taking a moment to think about Nolan, Eirian said, "Then there is Master Howell, the green. He rarely leaves Riane, but they sent him to add a sense of urgency. He's a gifted healer."

Everett let go of her and sat on the edge of the table. "Who do you fear more? The archmage or the blues?"

"None of them. It would be a struggle for two blues to maintain control over me. Particularly if I wasn't cooperating."

"All they'd need was for you to refuse the throne. You wouldn't be able to take it back without revealing their actions, and doing so would put everything at risk. It would turn people against Riane, and they know you'd sooner go along with them than put lives at risk."

Shrugging, she agreed. "Baenlin missed his chance when Brenna put on her show. I'm thankful for it now. The man is a master strategist, and I don't know what he might try next. They don't like second best for the highest position in the land."

He asked, "Who is their next option?"

"Tessa Valkera. I know her, and she's brilliant, though not very popular among those in power. They see her as too different." Chuckling, Eirian recalled the last time she had seen Tessa and added, "And Mayve failing explains why they sent Jaren to fetch her."

"We can't tell anyone why they're here. Let everyone think they came because they heard about Nolan's ill health. It is a great honor for us to have such important mages here. With our reports about the King's condition, who's going to question it? No one need find out they came to steal you away for real this time."

Slinging an arm over the back of the chair, Eirian stretched out and rolled her neck, flinching when it cracked. "They can't have the position vacant. Her heir must be in place before she dies, but she's an elf. Failing can take years, and she could outlive me."

Everett silently agreed with her, looking towards the door. "I think you should talk to Aiden. Issue explicit orders that you aren't to leave the castle grounds without me agreeing. Just in case they try anything."

"Aiden will demand to know why. He gets very pushy."

"I know all too well how pushy he gets. Why do you think I chose him to be captain of your guards?" Smirking, Everett said, "He's loyal to a fault and damn near the best swordsman in the kingdom. I know I don't stand a chance. I hear you're the only one he goes the slightest bit easy on."

It was her turn to smirk, and she replied, "If I stop shielding, Aiden will find it harder to beat me. I've held back. Though for the sake of his pride and peace between us, I should probably continue to do so."

"Promise me you'll stop shielding. People will get used to it if you give them a chance. Which won't happen if you accidentally destroy us. You know what I mean?"

Chuckling to take the serious edge off his words, Everett hopped off the table and offered Eirian his hand. Placing her hand on his, Eirian let him haul her to her feet and smiled sadly.

She admitted, "I never stop shielding completely, even in Riane. I can't. I wonder what sort of joke the gods were playing when they gave me this gift."

Not answering, he swung her arm as they had as children, and Eirian gave a little twirl before stumbling.

Everett laughed. "A pity your powers couldn't help you dance. You are such a bumblefoot."

Eirian lightly stomped on his foot, scoffing. "Some people are just bad at dancing. Even Celi couldn't improve my skills, and the powers know that man is as graceful as they come."

"You're a danger to anyone who dares partner you."

"Rude."

Letting go of her hand, Everett bowed and swept his arm outwards towards the door. "Shall we get on with the day? I believe we're preparing for your birthday."

Sulking, Eirian ran her fingers through her hair, then smoothed her dress. "Do I need to freshen up before council?"

"You look better now than I've seen you look in a while. I don't think you realize the difference," Everett replied. "It's rather startling. You're more of a presence, more vibrant and alive. I feel you'll command respect this way."

Shrugging, Eirian gave him a perplexed look and started to the door. Opening it, she found the guards had cleared everyone away while they talked. Taking stock of who she had on duty, Eirian was pleased to see Fionn gone, leaving a sullen-faced Gabe in charge. Catching his gaze, she thought she saw a hint of approval as he held out an apple.

Biting it, Eirian made a noise of appreciation. "Thank you, Gabe."

"Let's get to the council chambers. They will have started without us," Everett said.

Following him, Eirian focused on ignoring anyone who crossed their path. Arriving in front of the doors, Everett nodded to the guards, and they pushed them open. People glanced their way, barely paying attention until they felt the power radiating from Eirian. She watched them freeze and stare, the startled expressions making her feel like a display. Ignoring the reactions, Everett hurried over to the table. He slipped in beside Marcellus to pick up the papers in front of him.

"Your Highness, it seems you're rather popular today!" Everett held them out, prompting Eirian to walk over to take them.

Ulric stopped her before she reached the table. "Are there mages visiting you?"

"Yes, there are. The group was passing and thought to check in on me. We're very honored to have them here. Archmage Baenlin Zarthein leads the party."

"I see. Any concerns?" Ulric asked, stepping back so Eirian could take the papers.

"Hardly!" She skimmed over the words and gasped. "When did this arrive?"

Taking the lead from Everett and Ulric, Marcellus ignored Eirian's magic and said, "Late yesterday. We've only gotten to it now. I don't know if the messenger remains."

"Send someone to find out. I don't understand why the elves are coming, but I won't deny I'll be pleased to see them." Eirian added, "We can use the opportunity to broach our treaty. With my coronation coming up, it will need to be renewed."

Giving her a calculating look, Everett wondered if she hoped Celiaen would be among the party. "Perhaps they'll be here in time for your birthday celebrations. I'm sure your good friend, Prince Celiaen, knows when your birthday is. We'd best make them something worth enjoying."

"Powers take my birthday. There are more important things to deal with. Now, where are those reports regarding the disappearing sheep in Caerwel? Who can tell me what we are doing to find out what happened?"

Eirian handed the papers back to Marcellus and relaxed slightly, finishing her apple. Several people laughed at her attitude, and Eirian felt a pang of hope that Everett was right. Letting go of her worries about her magic, she focused on the council session.

NINE

Eirian slipped through the doorway quietly with her magic held close and pulled the hood over her face. If her guards discovered her absence, she would face their anger, but she needed a break from the constantly watching eyes of her household and the court. Hardly anyone would be around to notice her witnessing the rising sun while she worked through her thoughts. Lingering in the shadows, she observed a patrol of guards pass the entrance she was aiming for.

Moving quickly, Eirian ran a hand over the door before opening it, working a ward to make it appear as if nothing had happened. The stairs were empty, flickering torches casting shadows that danced to the movement of the flames. Eirian made her way up the steps to the last door between her and the false sense of freedom she sought. Since the patrol had already passed, she did not work the same simple trick on the second door. She pushed it open and stepped through, turning her eyes skywards to take in the expanse of stars.

Letting her hood fall back, Eirian gathered her coat tightly to ward off the slight chill, and her fingers caressed the warm wool absentmindedly. The air was crisp, and she breathed deeply, relaxing the hold on her powers. Eirian was unhappy with the way people were treating her because of her magic. Most of the older council members were less bothered, providing her with some reassurance. It was the nobles outside of the council who showed an aversion. Her guards were no longer as relaxed, and Eirian felt hurt when she saw their wary looks.

Thoughts turning to Baenlin, Eirian ran a hand through her hair, tugging at it in frustration. She stared at the horizon and waited for the glow of the sun. He had barely let an hour go without reminding her of his presence. Baenlin's magic would brush against hers, his lingering rage frequently stirring her own. Her temper became harder to restrain, and several times Eirian had nearly lost control of it. The only consolation was that she got to spend time with Fayleen, and it reminded her of what she had lost by leaving Riane.

She often found Fayleen regaling her ladies and Everett with stories of their youthful adventures. Everett was enthusiastic about learning what the duo had gotten up to. Eirian was thankful that Fayleen was careful to leave out details involving Celiaen and Galameyvin. Not to mention the more dangerous incidents. Eirian did not want them to find out about what she had done, particularly with Celiaen by her side. Or the things their friends had covered up.

Feeling the approach of another mage, Eirian slumped and looked at the door. She knew it was Howell, the taste of his healing magic like a hearty soup on her tongue. The door opened, and she watched Howell dawdle. Not speaking, he crossed to Eirian and leaned against the wall, turning his face out towards the faint glow. In the flickering light, she watched a relaxed look appear as he took in the night.

"Good morning, Master Howell."

"I suppose it's a good morning," he replied tiredly. "I'm sorry for disturbing your peace."

Her hands gripping the coat tightly, she said, "I'm glad it's you."

Howell smiled faintly. "I apologize for the archmage and his behavior, but no one can stop Baenlin or make him see things differently."

"You sound like you've been up for hours. Is everything well?"

"I was with a family in the city. A child broke her leg trying to assist her father at his work, and they asked for my help. My time here has been wonderful. I've had many opportunities to use my abilities. Thank you."

Eyes wide, his revelation amazed her. "I'm not sure why you're thanking me. I'm thankful for the care you're showing my people."

Howell told her, "When I was young, I spent years traveling the lands and spending time in villages and towns. Greens have always been the most welcome. On my return to Riane, I'll push the archmages to encourage it again. It's a wonderful experience for young greens, yellows, and blues to get out there and help the people we serve."

"You disagree with Baenlin that my people will turn on me?"

"I do, but I can't say so where he can hear it. None of us can speak against him. Though I suppose none of us are brave enough to try. We're not you. Not even Archmage Calhoun defies him, and they're technically equal. Celiaen tries when he's feeling cocky, but you'd know more about that than I do." Growing serious, he shook his head and said, "I agree you belong in Riane."

Eirian looked at the horizon and at the yellows and pinks of the sky as the sun crept closer. "You can't tell anyone, but I don't entirely disagree."

"I don't know that you should be the grand mage. Mayve is dying, but she's an elf, and for all we know, she might not die before you do. We could spend years training you to take her place for it to have been a waste."

"Whereas I'll be the queen before this time next year. You're more politically minded than I gave you credit for, Master Howell."

Cocking his head to the side, he smirked. "Do I see an advantage if we leave you here as queen? A mage on the Endaran throne is an opportunity for us to assert more influence among the people. The first step to claw back a fraction of the power the high council claims to have."

"Use Endara as a steppingstone into Athnaral?"

"Yes."

"You realize I'm facing a potential war with Athnaral."

"I'm a green, not a blue. War is an opportunity for my order to come in and remind people of the positives of magic."

Rubbing her face, Eirian said, "I've never thought of greens as warmongers."

"I'm an old man, Eirian Altira. I've seen war before, and it's petty bickering. The only thing I want is for mages to be more involved."

He stopped looking at her and tilted his face into the light. Watching the sunrise, Eirian admired the way it layered the sky with color. Lingering clouds took on darker pink tones, and she was glad the dawn bode well for the day. Birds appeared, dark shapes winging their way across the line of light. Closing her eyes, Eirian imagined their song as they heralded in the new day. Faintly, she thought she heard them and, opening her eyes, looked above to see if a bird was floating in the air closer to the wall. She loved sunrises. They filled her with energy.

"Why did you come up here?" Howell asked.

Looking at him from the corner of her eye, Eirian shrugged and answered, "I couldn't sleep, but that's not unusual. Why did you?"

"I felt you up here as I was returning to the keep. I thought it might be the only opportunity I have to speak to you alone."

They fell silent again, each staring at the sky in thought.

"Your time is running out, Master Howell. I need to sneak back to my chambers before my guards know I tricked them again."

"Indeed. I'm tired. Healing broken bones takes a lot from me these days. While we grow knowledgeable with age, our bodies don't handle the outpouring of magic as they did in our youth. I fear it's a sign of my failing. I don't know what Baenlin has planned. Whatever happens, I want you to know you'll always have friends in Riane."

"I've never doubted that. Surely the city would never close to me simply because I refused the grand mage position."

Howell slumped, giving her a sad look. Eirian was confused, and he understood why.

"Don't underestimate Baenlin's vindictiveness. No one other than his sister and the grand mage has ever dared refuse him. Until you. He isn't used to being defied, and he will lash out."

"Like a child throwing a tantrum?"

"Like a princess who didn't like her teachers telling her what to do because she was more powerful," he replied.

Embarrassed by her attitude during her early years in Riane, Eirian looked away, flustered. "I see your point. Hopefully, Baenlin will accept the defeat gracefully and realize the potential good that could come of a mage ruling Endara."

"There's something else, Eirian. Something I dared not say where others could hear." Howell grabbed her shoulder, saying, "I shouldn't be telling you. My archmages have ordered us to keep it quiet. I don't know if they've shared it with the rest of the council or not, but considering your father."

"What is it, Master?" Frowning, Eirian met his fearful gaze.

"It's why I wanted to look over your father when you told us what was going on. I'll report my findings to my superiors and advise we investigate."

Feeling his grip on her shoulder tighten, Eirian did not move, her mind whirling. The words of the Athnaralan she killed came back to her, and she wondered if there was a link.

She finally asked, "You've had other reports of madness? My father isn't the only one... surely not the grand mage?"

"No, Mayve is failing, as all elves do when their time comes. We've had reports of madness in Endara and Ensaycal. Rumors of it out of Athnaral. Many of your towns ask for our help, particularly in the southern regions close to the border."

"And you're saying your order hasn't investigated? That's absurd! It's negligence!"

Her anger was apparent, and Howell felt her bloodlust stirring.

"Be calm, Eirian. I'll push for it because I want to know if they're like your father. Why so many more reported cases of madness than normal? Are they normal cases of madness or something else?"

"I can't answer your questions, Howell, though I wish I could. You need to raise this issue and find out what is going on. What if something is causing it? Perhaps something in our food supplies? Exposure to a common source, but that leaves us with who and how long before they show signs." Covering her mouth, Eirian sighed and said, "This is concerning. Are you sure I can't mention it to my council?"

He shook his head. "No, Eirian, you can't. If they find out I told you, I'd be in serious trouble. I'm defying the direct orders of my archmages. I told you because your council may receive similar reports, and if you do, I want you to request the high council investigates."

"So, I file it in the back of my mind and continue to observe. I'll send you a messenger if we receive reports, but I want you to do the same in return."

"Are you suggesting I report on the council to you?"

Howell arched a brow and let go of her to step back. Her lips curled slightly, and Eirian contemplated his assumption.

"Now you've put it in my mind, I wouldn't be averse to knowing what they were up to if it involved my kingdom. Otherwise, no, I wasn't suggesting that. My concern is purely for my people, and if the greens investigate, I want to know if we need to be worried."

"You have my word that I'll let you know. I think it's time to return to our beds."

Tilting his head, Howell listened to the horns. Flinching at the sound, Eirian nodded.

"I think you're right. The guards will change soon, so I'd best hurry."

"How do you sneak past your guards? They strike me as rather vigilant. Your captain watches you constantly." He chuckled knowingly.

Holding a hand towards the door, Howell waited for her to go past. Casting a last look at the dawn, Eirian breathed deeply.

"That's a secret."

"I sensed your ward on the door below."

Opening the door, Eirian stepped carefully onto the stairway. "Then why ask?"

"You're a purple, so I suppose it is a little trick your kind have up their sleeve."

Firmly shutting the door behind them, Howell let Eirian start down the stairs in front of him. Glancing back, Eirian did not tell him it was a trick that only she could do.

"That is a good guess. It takes a touch of power."

Hearing him chuckle, she focused on walking down the staircase.

Howell mockingly said, "Modesty from a purple, how unusual."

Eirian placed a hand on the door at the bottom of the stairs and felt her ward still there. "Thank you for the talk. It was enlightening."

"Eirian, I want you to know I'm deeply sorry about your father and the position you're in. I wish I could help him, but there is nothing I or any other green can do. Anything a blue did would be very temporary," he told her.

Turning to look at him, Eirian smiled sadly and offered Howell one of her hands.

Her voice was soft as she said, "Let me show my gratitude for what you've done."

Frowning, Howell took her hand and gasped when he felt Eirian's power flow into him. It was rejuvenating. He suddenly understood why other masters had complained that she carried Fayleen through tasks that should have been outside her abilities.

"Thank you."

"No, thank you. Thank you for healing my people. Thank you for sharing your time with my father."

"Will this tire you?"

He wanted to close his eyes and bask in the feel of her magic, but he fought to continue looking at her. Eirian winked, placing a single finger on her lips.

With a smirk, she replied, "Why ask questions you can already answer. All those stories you've heard about what purples can do? Just assume I can do them tenfold."

Feeling a loss when she let go of his hands and cut him off from her power, Howell shuddered. "I see. Now I understand why your teachers would get so frustrated with you and Fayleen."

"I look after the ones I love."

"An admirable trait, but beware those who would use it against you."

Opening the door, Eirian lifted her hood over her head and offered him a smile as she stepped out into the courtyard. Not waiting, Eirian used her magic to blend her hurrying form into the shadows as she made her way. The grounds were bustling with life. Guards preparing to change shifts were striding towards their posts, while servants rushed around getting their tasks started. Wise merchants and petitioners were entering the courtyard, knowing that the earlier they got there, the higher the chances of being seen.

She watched as eyes slid past, her magic making them look away. Inside the keep, it was less alive, but Eirian knew it was a trick of the floors and the maze of corridors surrounding her. When she arrived at her quarters, Eirian saw Aiden leaning against the door. Arms crossed, his furious expression made her want to turn around and leave again. Dropping her ward, Eirian pushed back her hood.

"You're early, Captain."

Aiden glared at her and replied, "I thought you promised to stop sneaking out."

"No, I promised to sneak out less."

Shrugging, Eirian approached the door and crossed her arms, smiling at him as they faced each other. Her rage simmered enough that she had already calculated how quickly she could disarm Aiden. All Eirian had to do was give in, and she would have him right where she wanted him. Which was pinned against the wall with her knife to his throat and his lips on hers. Aiden shifted slightly, detecting the change in her magic. The gleam in her eyes warned him not to turn his back on her.

"Don't worry, I didn't leave the keep."

"Where were you?"

"I was visiting my lover," she joked.

Batting her eyelashes, Eirian continued to smile as his eyes narrowed. Dropping his arms, Aiden took a slight step towards her, and Eirian thought she saw a flicker of jealousy cross his face. It made her smile widen.

He demanded again. "Where were you?"

Giving him a look of fake astonishment, she huffed. "You don't believe me? Do you want me to introduce you to her? Or him. I'm a mage, so I'm not fussy."

"Princess."

"Fine, I wasn't with my lover. I was on the inner ramparts watching the sunrise."

"If that was all you wanted to do, then take your guards with you."

"Or I wanted to get away from you for a little while. I haven't slipped my guard in weeks, but I needed some time to think without eyes watching me."

Eirian thought he would stop her when she pushed past him to the door, but Aiden stepped aside, letting her enter. His footsteps followed, and Eirian kept her back to him as she undid the clasps of her coat while lingering halfway to the door that opened into her chamber. Glancing over her shoulder, she shrugged the linen from her shoulders and frowned at the way he continued to glare at her.

"Look, Aiden, I'm trying. Yes, I used my powers to slip past your men. Yes, I went off alone, but do you know what it's like to have someone constantly watching? The only time I'm alone is when I go to bed, but even then, I have men watching my doors."

"We can arrange for you to be alone if you ask. That is all you must do," Aiden said, glancing at the knives on her belt. "But you never ask! You sneak out with no protection and no idea of the dangers out there. What if something happened?"

"I would've dealt with it."

"Your confidence in your abilities will get you hurt. Possibly killed."

Pursing her lips, Eirian did not turn to face him, not wanting to risk giving anything away. If Aiden knew the truth, he would lock the door and station an army outside it. He would never take his eyes off her if he knew the other thoughts she frequently entertained.

"Would you be this zealous if I was a man?"

Her question made him pause, and he frowned, answering, "Yes, I would. It's my job to be zealous. You are my life now, Princess."

"I'm not sure I believe you, Aiden. I'll go change, and we won't mention this to my ladies or anyone else. In the future, I'll try to ask you to plan for my solitude."

Closing the distance to the next door, Eirian slipped into her chamber without waiting for Aiden to respond. Shutting herself in the room, she leaned back against the door and sighed. Everything was dark, with heavy drapes covering the window. She did not need light to get around. Unbuckling her belt, Eirian placed it on the table before stripping out of her clothes and replacing them with the chemise she had slept in.

Returning the garments to their place in her wardrobe, she went to the table and picked up her belt. Tracing her fingertips over the hilts of the knives, Eirian shook her head and slipped one free. Weighing it carefully in her hand, she wrapped her fingers around the handle. Eirian squashed her memories, knowing they were dangerous territory. Glancing over her shoulder at the door, she longed to show Aiden how clueless he was.

Slipping the knife back into the sheath, she closed her eyes and sighed. Eirian reminded herself it served her better if they did not know what she was capable of. Just as it had in Riane. She knew a time might come when she would have to reveal the truth, and she dreaded the reaction. Dreaded how much they would fear her. Wrapping the belt around the knives, Eirian placed them on a shelf and closed the wardrobe. Standing with both hands on the doors, she rested her head against the timber.

Remaining there, Eirian took several deep breaths before pushing away and turning to her desk. There was a stack of reports waiting for her to review ahead of the next council meeting, and knowing sleep would remain elusive, she got on with it. Approaching the window first, she drew back the drapes. The room filled with light, and Eirian blinked while her eyes adjusted. Howell's words lingered in her mind, and she frowned. Staring at the papers as she sat, Eirian wondered how to investigate previous reports for mentions of madness.

Focused on her work, it startled Eirian when a heavy knocking came at her door, and she called, "Enter!"

Brenna slipped through the door and glanced over at Eirian, tutting. "I see you've made a start on your day."

"I couldn't sleep, and these reports were too interesting." Rubbing her eyes, Eirian looked back down at the papers strewn in front of her. "I hope they get duller because I could use something to bore myself to sleep."

"What are you reviewing?" Making her way straight to the wardrobe, Brenna opened it and pursed her lips, eyeing the selection of dresses.

"Judicial decisions made by reeves in various towns in Kaban."

Frowning, Brenna pulled out a pale-yellow dress. "Found any you disagree with yet?"

Leaning back in the chair, Eirian carefully sorted the papers into neat piles. "Not yet."

"The girls should be here shortly. I believe Bea was arranging some breakfast. A good thing she's always thinking about food because you eat a lot." Laying the dress out on the bed, Brenna shook her head at Eirian and said, "You look tired. Did you sleep at all?"

Eirian stood and stretched. "Little and restless. I'll sleep better when my friends have left Amath, and the excitement of the First Planting celebrations is over. Don't worry, I've energy enough to get me through the day, but food will assist with that."

"I'll make you a soothing tea tonight. Trust me, it will help. You need to rest properly. It won't do any good if you run yourself haggard, and we need a healthy queen taking the throne."

Chuckling, Eirian shrugged and gave Brenna a small smile. Walking to her bed, she gazed at it.

"You're right, and I'll drink your tea. I could use a decent night of sleep."

Knocks on the door announced the rest of her ladies, and Eirian glimpsed Aiden, watching the door as they trooped in. Snapping her fingers, Brenna was quick to direct the young women to where she wanted them. Eirian let them fuss, dressing her for the day while listening to their chatter. Turning her gaze to Brenna, Eirian thought about asking if she had been a giggling, gossiping young woman. She remained silent and did her best not to flinch when Elke began working on her hair, doing battle with the knots that had formed overnight.

"Right, let's get some food in you," Brenna said.

Clapping her hands, she shooed the group through to the next room and offered Eirian a warm smile. Ignoring the guards, Eirian sat at the table and selected something to eat.

She asked Brenna, "Am I supposed to be spending the morning with the council?"

"I thought you were meeting with Sabine and some merchants," she answered.

"Of course, representatives from our merchant guilds responsible for facilitating trade between Ensaycal and Athnaral. I don't envy their jobs if it comes to war."

"Neither do I."

Sighing, Eirian shook her head. "Am I meeting them here or in Sabine's offices?"

Romana smiled knowingly and said, "You're meeting at her offices. Three of them are attending, and they represent the primary resources traded between Athnaral and Ensaycal."

Surprised, Brenna looked at Romana. "Thank you, Romana."

"It's my pleasure. Unlike some here, I pay attention." She sneered at her sister.

Rolling her eyes, Elke mocked her. "You're not the only one who pays attention."

Chuckling, Eirian shared a look with Brenna. "Hush now. Romana did well to remember. Let her have her moment."

"Indeed. The rest of you should take note, you may be mistresses of a household one day, and you'll need to know such things." Giving each woman a stern look, Brenna said, "Life is not all about dresses and fancies, and you're old enough to know that."

Giving the tray of food a look, Eirian decided that she had eaten enough.

Wiping her hands off, she said, "I should like to arrive early for this meeting. If I'm in luck, Sabine can spare some time to refresh me. Romana, would you like to attend?"

Romana exclaimed, "Oh, thank you, Your Highness! Yes, please, I'd be grateful."

Rising to her feet, Eirian nodded to Brenna and asked, "Will you attend as well?"

"Yes, I think I should. The rest of you can see to your other duties." Brenna clicked her tongue, scolding, "I don't want to find out you have been neglecting anything."

Turning to walk out of the chamber, Eirian passed in front of Aiden and glanced at him briefly. "Good morning, Captain."

His eyes narrowed before shifting to Brenna, and Aiden said, "Good morning, Your Highness. I trust you slept well."

"Yes, I did. Thank you," Eirian replied, hiding how she bristled at his accusing tone.

The guards continued to give her sideways looks, frustrated by her earlier actions. Eirian hoped Brenna would not pick up on their mood. When they reached the treasurer's offices, they found a bustling area filled with people. Eirian watched officials greeting visitors and leading them off to private meeting rooms. She admired the smooth way Sabine had everything running before assistants led them to her office. Turning to Aiden, Eirian narrowed her eyes at him.

"I think it's best if you and your men remain outside the office."

"I disagree," he snapped. "I'll attend this meeting, and my men will remain outside."

Crossing his arms, Aiden's glare dared Eirian to fight with him over the matter.

Brenna scoffed. "Sabine has guards."

"She does, but they're not the guards assigned to Her Highness. Our job is to protect the princess and her ladies, which includes you, Your Grace."

Unwilling to argue with him in the middle of a corridor, Eirian huffed. "Do what you want."

Walking through into the office, Eirian glanced over her shoulder to see Aiden had followed. Her gaze crossed the large room, and she noted that Sabine only had a pair of guards lingering on either side of the doorway. It made Eirian pause and glance again at Aiden, noting the triumphant look he wore. She knew he had already assessed the two guards as she had. The men regarded him warily, as though they expected him to dress them down. Sabine was bent over a table, discussing a matter with one of her assistants.

She looked up to greet Eirian. "Good morning, Your Highness. I wasn't expecting you yet."

"I apologize if I'm imposing by arriving now." Eirian joined Sabine at the table and glanced over at the documents laid out. "I was hoping you could prepare me for what to expect from the representatives."

"Of course, ma'am, I can do that." Surprised, she signaled to an assistant and requested, "Please clear the table and bring me the documents for our meeting."

Holding up her hand, Eirian shook her head. "No, please, finish what you were doing first. I don't want to interrupt anything important. Besides, I might learn something useful."

Sabine smiled warmly and said, "You continue to surprise me. However, it won't be long before they arrive, so we best get on with it."

"If you insist. Now, tell me about who we are meeting."

"Do you recall what they are representing?" Sabine stepped over to a small desk with a jug and cups set out on it.

"I do not. Hence, why I need your help."

"I'm pleased you asked for it. As you know, Ensaycal has several resources less commonly found in both Endara and Athnaral. Gold, silk, and marble are the ones most people know of. Athnaral is rich in salt and tin. We'll discuss workable options for maintaining trade in the event of war."

Accepting a cup of water, Eirian nodded. "Because a breakdown of trade will leave entire regions suffering."

"Yes, and if the war goes on for an extended period, it could cause people to leave those areas in search of other work. People need to eat. This then has long-term consequences. It benefits all of us to maintain the trade lines for as long as possible, working ways to avoid areas of conflict." Pointing at a stack of books, Sabine smiled and said, "There is some small irony that the taxes we make from Athnaralan trade go into provisioning our army."

"You find it ironic, and I find it depressing."

Everyone looked at Eirian in surprise, and Sabine nodded slowly. "I suppose you're right about it being depressing."

"The loss of life is regrettable. Not just the lives of soldiers, but those innocent bystanders and livestock killed, and those who lose their homes and livelihoods to encroaching troops. I have to consider everything," Eirian said, and gripped the cup tightly.

"I apologize if I seem unsympathetic. It's simply my job to view all of it in terms of currency. A wealthy kingdom can help its people recover. A poor one can't."

Staring into her drink, Eirian considered the point Sabine was making. "I gather you want me to make it clear to these people that I'll do what I can to avoid a war."

"Simply, yes. Their trade doesn't need your interference. It doesn't matter to them who wears the crown. What they want are assurances the throne will protect their ability to continue doing what they do best."

Clearing her throat, Sabine crossed her arms and waited for Eirian to respond.

When Eirian did not, she said, "And that is making money, which feeds everyone."

"What if I don't feel confident making those assurances? We may not have much choice about war, and surely they know that."

Shrugging, Sabine uncrossed her arms and waved at a wall lined with books. "I don't care if you feel confident or not. I know the decision is beyond us, and yes, they know it. This is politics, ma'am, and you need to get used to telling sweet lies with a smile on your face. Reassure them, pretend you believe it, and they'll pretend they believe it as well. Those books there tell the truth because numbers rarely lie. What we want is for those numbers to keep telling a happy, bountiful truth."

"You never know when someone might believe the lies," Aiden grumbled. "You already tell them so easily. What's another one?"

Before Eirian could respond to him, one of the treasury officials knocked on the door.

They proclaimed, "They're here when you are ready for them."

Drawing herself together, Sabine ran a hand over her skirt and nodded. "Bring them in. In an hour, I'd like light refreshments served."

"Refreshments?" Romana asked.

Winking, Sabine said, "Oh yes, we'll need them. Talks like these aren't brief."

Walking around the table to face the visitors as they came in, Eirian rested her hands on the back of a chair. It was not a surprise that the representatives were men. The Athnaralans would not deal with a woman considering their views. They looked at her, and Eirian could tell they were sizing her up. Tilting her head to the side, she gave them a faint smile and let her eyes linger on each one in return, her magic curling around her like a cloak. They bowed, and their focus shifted to Sabine, who was watching in amusement.

"Gentlemen, it is my pleasure to introduce you to Her Highness Eirian Altira. You will have heard the news King Nolan is abdicating."

Their focus shifted back to Eirian, and the shortest man stepped forward.

He said, "A good morning to you, Your Highness. I see it's true you're a mage."

Her slight smile remained in place, and Eirian replied, "A good morning to you as well. Yes, it is true. I do hope that isn't an issue."

"No issue at all, in fact, quite the opposite."

TEN

Despite the sun's warmth, Eirian felt a chill. Rubbing her arms, she stared out at the lush garden. She had not been there long, but Eirian could see the difference. Her power blanketed the space, filling the plants with life. Blooms had opened, vines creeping further along the walls and arches defining the area. Birds trilled, their tiny forms darting from tree to tree, some going after insects. Others hovered over flowers, beaks seeking the nectar within.

The occasional butterfly took to the breeze, colorful wings like jewels in the light as they drifted from flower to flower. Everywhere Eirian looked, her power enhanced things. Shoots pushed through the carefully tended soil, the unfurling plants seeking the light of her magic as though she was the sun. Scattered among the shadows, her guards watched nervously. They were uncomfortable, and Eirian hated how some avoided her gaze. Aiden was the least changed, and she was thankful she could count on him to continue challenging her at every turn.

Eirian leaned back and turned her face to the sky, resting her hands on the bench behind her. She loved the energy the sun provided and how it fed her, but she was careful not to let it show. Eyes shut, Eirian listened to the sounds of the garden and allowed them to fill her mind. The noise of boots nearby and the rustle of her guard's shifting brought Eirian back into focus. She tracked the progress of Fayleen walking towards her.

Sunlight made her blonde hair shine golden, and Fayleen held a hand over her eyes as she squinted at Eirian with a broad grin. Flopping down on the seat, she groaned and rolled her shoulders, admiring the surrounding plants. She leaned back and rested her elbows on the stone bench, hanging her head back in a mirror of what Eirian had been doing when she arrived. Eirian regarded Fayleen cautiously.

"Were you sent to find me, or did you break free?"

Fayleen sighed and lifted her head to stare at Eirian. "Do you think I could sneak away from them? They know exactly where we are while they plot another way to change your mind."

"The archmage has been playing a different game."

"I know what you mean. This behavior is not what I expected from Baenlin," Fayleen said. "I mean, everyone knows he likes power. He had a thing with the grand mage a long time ago before Azina transition—"

Nostrils flaring, Eirian glanced at her guards to make sure none were too close.

She cautioned, "Hush, Fay, ears are everywhere. The archmage has been careful not to let anyone notice his attempts at persuasion."

"Are you flattered by it?"

"What do you mean?"

Waving a hand around, Fayleen said, "If it were me, I'd find it flattering."

"I don't." Eirian raised a ward, preventing her guards from hearing them.

"Few could claim that they've had Baenlin show so much interest in them. He's a stone-cold killer, and the last thing you expect to see from him is warmth and charm, let alone flirting! I didn't think he could do it, to be honest."

Pinching the bridge of her nose, Eirian closed her eyes and sighed. "He always watched me in Riane. Though who didn't? I used to think it was because of Celi, but now I think Baenlin harbored plans for me from the day they realized how powerful I am."

"That's right, you used to mutter about it." Shuffling closer, Fayleen leaned in and nudged her shoulder with a grin. "I love what you are doing to the garden. You always breathe life into your surroundings. I wish my magic grew things."

"I'd trade you in a heartbeat. Things would be easier if I had your power. I don't know if I'm making the right decision, but I know I can't afford to second guess myself. Everett is certain that people will get used to my magic."

"It's a control thing."

Eirian chuckled. "This should be good."

Turning to face Eirian, Fayleen crossed her legs on the bench, placing her hands in her lap. "Magic is common among the elves. We can skip the daoine because no one goes to Telmia. But humans? It's less common for us to be born magical."

"I suspect I know where you're going with this."

"Magic makes us more. It becomes something to control, but you can't control magic without magic. Things we can't control, we fear. What we fear, we ostracize, and we teach our children to despise. It becomes a cycle until we have an ingrained culture of fear and mistrust which further drives away those born with magic," Fayleen said seriously.

"Which is why it's the nobles who hate mages the most. They don't like it when something threatens their perceived superiority. You know, that was one of your easier tangents."

Tapping the side of her head, Fayleen said, "I work very hard to maintain my disguise. It's amazing what people let slip when they think you're an idiot."

Eirian shook her head and touched Fayleen's arm, saying, "I don't think you're an idiot. I want you to stay here with me."

Covering her hand, Fayleen smiled sadly and replied, "I want to stay. There's no reason I couldn't, but Baenlin has forbidden it, and I'm nothing but a pest to him. Unlike you, he would squash me if I defied him. He wants you to feel alone and isolated."

"I hope he realizes that once I go through with the coronation, there's little chance I'll ever return to Riane. I'm more likely to have my throat slit in my sleep if things go badly. What Baenlin wants from me is the same as what my council plans."

"And what is that?"

"To sit quietly on the throne and do what I'm told. I'll marry and bed a man of their choosing to produce lots of little heirs. Except Baenlin would have it be him alone. Mages make more mages, and he believes that the more powerful the parents, the more powerful the children." Eirian took a deep breath, asking, "And who is a more powerful choice than me?"

With a squeeze of Eirian's hand, Fayleen uncrossed her legs and swung them around to stand. Going to a plant with some unopened buds, she plucked one and returned to Eirian, holding it out in her palm.

Fayleen murmured, "They say that's why so few human mages are born outside of Riane. Magical bloodlines have fled mistrust, taking sanctuary in the city. It's why questions of your parentage exist. It's not normal for a mage with so much power to be born in the wild."

"According to the records, I'm not the first mage of my bloodline," Eirian replied.

Taking the offered flower bud, she twirled it around in her fingers and smiled as the petals unfurled into an open bloom.

"True, but you're the first in your direct bloodline in generations. No one knows the history of your mother."

Eirian tucked the bloom in behind her ear and stood, smoothing out her skirts as she snapped, "My mother was not a mage."

"I'm sorry, Ree. I know you don't enjoy talking about your mother."

"Don't worry about it, Fay," she dismissed the conversation.

"Ree."

Offering a hand to Fayleen, Eirian smiled and said, "I wish you could defy Baenlin, but I understand why you don't."

Taking the offered hand, Fayleen noticed Eirian remained without the ring that showed which order she belonged to. "Ree, is there something going on?"

Shaking her head with a faint smile, Eirian drew Fayleen in beside her and tucked her hand under her arm. "Nothing is going on except the usual political posturing. Will you take a walk with me?"

"I'd enjoy that."

"I thought we could head up to the inner ramparts and admire the view. We can pretend to be courtiers, maybe giggle a bit. I don't giggle enough anymore. My ladies don't understand me, and can you imagine my guards giggling?"

Signaling to her guards, Eirian started a slow pace along the pathway, with Fayleen beside her. Gabe approached them, his unreadable eyes flickering over Fayleen before he focused on Eirian.

"Are you ready to leave, Your Highness?"

"It's such a lovely day, and I'd like to enjoy my free time, so we're taking a walk on the ramparts."

Gabe saluted and turned to signal the other guards scattered through the garden. Surrounding the two women, the men remained silent. Passing through the arch in the wall, Eirian glanced over her shoulder at the thriving life and mourned leaving it behind. Fayleen could sense the nervousness of those observing them, and watched Eirian's cheeks twitch as she did her best to ignore the reactions. Aware of her discomfort, Gabe led them to the closest doorway that would take them to the top of the wall.

Fayleen kept a hand to the stone as she said, "It's so different from Riane."

"Yes, it is. Amath is a military base. I think the people of Riane forget what it is like to live in fear of invasion."

"That's true."

Her hands grasped the battlement, and Eirian looked out, saying, "When I was little, I used to imagine the battles this place has seen. I'd pretend I was a fearsome warrior princess fighting for my people and leading them to a glorious victory."

Leaning over the edge on the other side of the merlon, Fayleen ran her hands over the stone and sighed. "You are a fearsome warrior princess. These old wards are beautiful."

Feeling Fayleen's magic coursing through the stone, Eirian said, "That reminds me, how goes your leatherworking?"

Smiling, Fayleen caressed the stone and ignored the guards with their suspicious stares. "It goes well. I visited the stables to check over your tack to make sure the wards were still good. Haven't done your armor, and strangely, none of your ladies knew what I was talking about. Your captain wouldn't let me go over your guards' gear. He is delicious. Please tell me you're taking advantage of him."

Tossing her head back, Eirian laughed, dismissing Fayleen's comment, and started walking. She did not want to linger on thoughts of taking advantage of Aiden. They entered her mind far too often for her own good.

"I'm good enough at wards to keep my gear in check, but thank you for checking. As for my guards, Fayleen, you know the law." Glancing at the distant woods, Eirian muttered, "They've kept me within the walls for too long. I need to get out!"

"I know the laws, but they're your guards! I admit it's strange seeing you in dresses and constantly surrounded by heavily armed men. Even when Celi and Gal were visiting, you were never so heavily surrounded. Tara and the others aren't overbearing!"

Giggling, Fayleen trailed her hands over the stone as they walked.

"No, Tara and the others are wonderful."

Fayleen added, "Though I'm sure you don't get into as much mischief without your princes... or do you?"

"Shush, sister! Don't talk about such things."

"You haven't told your people about you courting the elven prince? Poor Gal, you've relegated him to a secret. I hear the elves are coming soon. Maybe it's him."

Glancing over her shoulder, Eirian shook her head, muttering, "There are ears everywhere, Fay. They know I'm friends with Celi. I'm not in Riane. I can't have fancies."

Snorting, Fayleen rolled her eyes and exclaimed, "Another reason to come back to Riane! He isn't some fancy. You've been in love with Gal and Celi for years, and the three of you belong together. Are you going to put your love aside to marry some stuffy lord picked out for you by a bunch of old people? Are you allowed to have lovers?"

"At most, they'll let me avoid it for a year or two, but the demands I marry will come. I need to establish myself as the queen, and if I marry too soon, the man might attempt to assert himself as the one in charge. I won't tolerate that. Maybe I won't marry. You won't hear me complain. One person for the rest of my life? No thanks."

Chuckling, she glanced at her guards. The men pretended not to listen in, but they had their orders.

"Oh, I don't know. Marriage might not be so bad. Everett is rather delightful. I've always enjoyed seeing him. I wouldn't object to being stuck in his bed or your captain's. Of course, there are similarities between them."

"Fayleen!"

Exasperated, Eirian shook her head, sighing at Fayleen's laughter. From the top of the wall, they could hear things from all around. The clang of the castle smithy was the loudest, and Eirian leaned against the stone to peer at the building. Smoke billowed, telling her the fires were running. Looking down, she watched a group of guards rushing along towards the training grounds, their heads bowed as they discussed something.

Eirian smiled at Fayleen, taking in how she stood, running her fingers over the stone. Silent and contemplative, they continued to walk along the wall. A wind was picking up, and Eirian glanced at the pennants on their poles. Her hair was loose, the messy brown locks catching in the breeze and making her wish they were short again each time they drifted in front of her eyes.

"What do you think all that shouting is about?" Fayleen broke the silence.

"Sounds like the guards' training area. Let's keep walking. We'll look down on it soon. Most likely competitive training, you know how it can get."

"That I do. All too well."

Making a sound of agreement, Eirian kept walking, and Fayleen laughed. Feeling the thrum of magic, they looked over the side at the training grounds and the guards joined them. They gasped at the sight of Baenlin in the square, a training sword in his hand while off-duty guards lined up to have a go. Eirian pulled back from the wall, running a hand through her hair, not noticing the flower fall out from where she had placed it behind her ear. Continuing to watch, Fayleen let out a whooping cheer when Baenlin had another guard hitting the ground.

"We should go back," Eirian said.

"But it looks like the show is getting more exciting!"

"Fay."

Fayleen glanced over, pouting as she added, "I mean, he's scary, and I know he'd never give me the time of day, but he's a fine thing to look at."

Closing her eyes, Eirian asked, "Did you know he was going to play with the guards?"

"No, if I had, I'd be watching from closer instead of spending time with you."

"Honestly, Fayleen!"

"What?" Fayleen huffed. "I admire a nice show when it's on, and you used to enjoy it too. We shared quarters for years, and I know how often you didn't return at night to sleep. Especially after a day of training with Rylee."

Several guards chuckled, glancing at Eirian knowingly, and she knew the comments would reach Aiden. Stepping closer to Eirian, Gabe remained stony as he rubbed the hilt of his sword and watched the other guards leaning over the edge. Fayleen whooped again, clearly the only one happy to see the guards easily defeated by Baenlin.

"Your Highness, I spotted the captain down there," he said and shook his head, hand still on his sword.

"What Aiden does on his downtime is his decision. If he takes part in that mess, that is his choice. He has the power to stop it if he wants. I know those men down there will obey his orders."

She had not thought his expression could get colder, but he proved her wrong as he growled. "You should stop it."

Taking a deep breath, Eirian stepped to the edge of the wall and leaned out to look. Things were getting rowdy, the men of the various guard troops becoming incensed as Baenlin kept putting down their comrades. Gabe was correct about her needing to stop it. Eirian ran through her options without paying attention to what her eyes were observing. Silence falling distracted her, and she realized Aiden had stepped into the ring. His back was to the wall where they were watching, meaning he had not noticed them.

Covering her mouth with her hand, Eirian pulled back and looked at Gabe as she furiously demanded, "What does he think he's doing?"

Gabe shrugged, dark eyes remaining tuned to the scene and replied, "As you said, it's his choice. He's the best we have."

Fayleen snorted. "No, he isn't. She is. You should be down there, Ree!"

Pulling her power around her, Eirian moved along the wall to a spot Baenlin would see her. Leaning between the merlons, she allowed the magic to flow towards him. He froze, and she saw him glance up at her before Aiden advanced. Like the rest who had attempted to take Baenlin on, Aiden found himself flat on the ground. Baenlin held the tip of the wooden sword to Aiden's throat and a boot on his chest.

Aiden's weapon was out of reach, and his arm ached from the force of the strike that had disarmed him. The backs of his legs were sore after Baenlin had knocked his feet out from under him in a blur of motion he had not seen coming. Noticing that Baenlin was not looking at him, Aiden tilted his head to follow his opponent's stare. He saw Eirian watching from the wall with her hand flung out towards them.

"Impressive, Captain, you lasted the longest," he said.

"Is that supposed to be a compliment?" Aiden grunted.

Glancing down at Aiden beneath his foot, Baenlin smirked and did not move. "She's furious with me and more than a little angry with you. Can you feel it? The strength of her rage is positively spectacular."

Frowning, Aiden realized it was not his heart pounding in his ears, but the increasingly familiar beat of magic. He tasted Eirian's anger and the desire to destroy an enemy, the emotion finding a match with his. It felt like it belonged to him. Mixed in with the rage was an overwhelming urge to protect that surprised him. Almost as palatable as her magic was Baenlin's pleasure. It tasted of the joy of a good fight and the undeniable bloodlust of a warrior.

He realized the bloodlust was not only coming from Baenlin. Eirian's magic sung with it or to it; Aiden could not be sure. Startled at what he was feeling, Aiden lifted his hands and, with one, pushed at the leg holding him down while the other grabbed the wooden sword at his throat. Baenlin let him struggle out from under him. His smirk remained as Eirian's magic sent his weapon spinning to the ground out of reach, and he held his hands out in a challenging gesture.

Aiden looked at the stunned faces of the other guards as he got to his feet and asked, "Why does it feel so different? Why does she feel like that?"

"It feels different because you're in the crosshairs of two of the most powerful mages alive. You've never been so close to barely restrained power. Magic responds to the emotions of mages. It feeds urges in us and those around us," Baenlin replied.

Aiden did not know what to say. Baenlin did not look at him, his eyes remaining locked on Eirian's face.

He continued, "She's a true warrior. Can you feel her desire to destroy me? It is glorious. I've watched her grow over the years, watched her become so much more than what she is letting herself be. You don't know what walks among you."

"You want her to come down and fight you."

"Always. I've seen Eirian fight, truly fight. She took to the dance as one born to the red. Few can beat her when she picks up a blade, but it's because she lets them just like she lets you. Her restraint during training with you is another way of destroying her potential. This place will destroy her, and she'll let it. She's going to roll over and let you break her, and you won't even realize what you've done."

"Are you sure you have the right woman? I've trained with her for months, and she's decent, but she doesn't move like you. I'd be able to tell if she was holding back." Aiden scoffed, but the seeds of doubt remained.

He did not want to think about what else Baenlin had said. The thought that he would somehow break Eirian bothered Aiden. Especially when he knew what Cameron and others were planning. Baenlin glanced at him and slowly smiled. He saw the doubt, and it was exactly what he wanted.

"You don't know how much she hides from you. If she didn't, you wouldn't stand a chance. Though I doubt you'd complain about being on your back beneath her. I know I wouldn't, and others certainly haven't."

Eyes wide with confusion, Aiden looked at Eirian and felt the doubt grow. Her hand was no longer outstretched, and her fury was dimming. Beside her, he could see Fayleen and the solemn form of Gabe. They appeared to be arguing, though he could not hear what they were saying. Spread along the wall, her other guards were staring at Eirian. Looking around the yard, Aiden could tell the magic had affected many, fear and bloodlust showing on more faces than he was comfortable seeing it on.

Aiden shook his head and pleaded. "Please stop before someone is hurt. I'd beg her, but you're the one beside me. Warrior to warrior, I'm asking you not to let this get out of hand. You've won. You've proven you're better than us. You've shown me she's hiding."

"I am better than all of you, except, perhaps, her."

Licking his lips, Baenlin shifted in the sand towards Aiden, and almost instantly, the furious feel of Eirian's magic returned like the shock of a clap of thunder.

"She wants to play. It seems she's a little protective of you, Captain. I suppose you are her type, even if you aren't one of us. With one exception, Eirian's lovers are always reds."

He tossed his hands in the air and looked up at Eirian before dropping to a knee and bowing. Feeling the magic retreat, Aiden remained and hoped she would stop responding to Baenlin's challenge.

"Well, I have to protect her, and that includes from herself. She can't come down to play with you. The men are already on edge. The last thing any of us want is for something to happen that would send them over. Unless that is exactly what you want. You want her to fight you so that she's forced to reveal herself."

Baenlin smiled and said, "You'd make a good red."

"Eirian, don't do this!" Fayleen tugged at her arm. "He's goading you. You're feeding them your bloodlust, and I know what happens when you do that."

"I hate to say it, but she's right," Gabe said, and he looked worried, the expression strange on his face.

Breathing slowly, Eirian shook her head. "What you're saying is true, but Baenlin knew I was here, and he'd have hurt Aiden to prove a point to me."

"If you go down there and spar with him in this mood, then you'll reveal to all these men what you can do. You don't have the control that he does, and your emotions will cause a riot. Baenlin will feed them on purpose to make them fear you. Then what? Think about it, Ree! You've hidden the truth from them, and is this how you want them to find out?"

Arching an eyebrow, Gabe glanced at the other guards. "We've seen the princess spar with the captain. She wouldn't last any longer than the rest of us."

Fayleen gave him a dark look and said, "No, you haven't. You've seen Eirian pretending for the sake of your delicate sensitivities. All because she doesn't think you can handle her."

The men looked at Eirian curiously, and she pulled away from the wall, taking her eyes off the scene below, where Aiden knelt beside Baenlin. "I need to get off this wall and away from here."

Before they could react, she pushed past, walking so fast she was almost running back the way they had ambled. Struggling to catch up, Fayleen kept close enough to talk.

"Where do you want to go?"

With a shake of her head, Eirian shoved through the door to stumble down the stairs. She took them two at a time in her hurry. Unwilling to upset her further, Fayleen did not speak again. The confused guards followed the women as they returned to the garden. With each step Eirian took, plants forced their way out between the stones covering the ground, leaving a path behind her.

"Fayleen, I need you to keep them out," Eirian said.

The guards protested, and Fayleen stood in the doorway to stop them from following. "Believe me, you don't want to go in there."

A wave of relief came from Eirian as she hurried away, and Fayleen glanced over her shoulder. She saw Eirian heading to the center of the garden with her hands out, trailing over plants. Turning around to watch in fascination, Fayleen forgot about the men when the flood of magic hit her, and she raised wards to contain it. Everything grew, vines covering the walls spilling over the edges while flowers appeared. Bushes grew taller and broader while the trees were more prominent, their limbs reaching for Eirian instead of the sky.

"What is she doing?" Gabe whispered in awe.

"She's venting. She couldn't risk confronting the archmage, so all that pent-up magic must go somewhere. This is a safe outlet for her and everyone else."

Kip asked, "Can all mages do that?"

Fayleen shook her head, hair drifting over her face. The short blonde tresses were longer than before as Eirian's magic caused them to grow.

"No."

"If you can't do that, what do you do?"

"I work leather. Depending on our inclinations, we all have something we do. Yellow mages like me are crafters, leatherworkers, masons, smiths, carvers, and such."

They continued to watch the storm of life growing in the garden as Eirian worked through her emotions. Sighing sadly, Fayleen suspected there was a lot more to her outpouring than simply Baenlin's challenge. She had seen the way Eirian would glance at Aiden when she thought no one would notice, and she had seen the way he would watch her in return. Using the time to study the guards, Fayleen was pleased to see a mixture of fear and awe.

Fayleen hoped Eirian realized this was a far better thing for people to witness than her attempting to kill Baenlin. People would see the benefits. They would see ways of using her gift to help crops grow or bring life back to the land. It was for the best that they did not know it hardly cost Eirian. Or the reality that she could do it on a scale far more extensive than the garden. It reminded Fayleen of the promise she had made to Eirian when they were children. Spotting the other mages approaching, minus Baenlin, Fayleen stood straight, and the guards swung around with hands going to their hilts.

"I wondered how long it would take you to arrive!" She soothed the guards, saying, "It's okay. They felt her outpouring."

Howell glanced past her at the garden and said, "You call that an outpouring? Now I understand what she meant when she told me she could do anything."

The woman gave Howell a baffled look and asked, "You knew she could do this?"

"She recently told me to assume she could do everything I'd ever heard a purple could do. I've felt a touch of her power, and it's a well that runs deep."

Fayleen explained, "We were on a pleasant walk along the ramparts. That was when we discovered the archmage playing with the off-duty guards. I guess he was feeling a bit bored. We came along as the captain of Eirian's guards thought he'd have a go."

"Say no more. I wondered where Baenlin had gotten to, but it's not my place to question his comings and goings. He's pressured Eirian a lot. Does she need Soren?" Howell asked with concern.

Holding up her hands, Fayleen shook her head and said, "No! No, she's good! I've seen Ree do this before. It's a case of pent-up emotions. She'll feed the garden, and the gardeners won't know what hit them."

"Baenlin is coming," Soren said.

"Stop him!"

Running to meet him, Soren stopped Baenlin before he got close enough for the others to hear what was being said. They felt the calming effects of his magic wrapping around them like a warm blanket, and Fayleen struggled to fight back the yawn she had the sudden urge for. It influenced the guards, and cringing, Fayleen looked at Eirian, wondering if she felt it inside her tempest. Whatever Soren said had little effect on Baenlin, and he resumed his path towards them. Realizing he intended to confront Eirian, Fayleen stretched her arms out to either side of the arch. Her fingertips touched the stone, and her magic flowed into them, warding the space against entry.

"Do not test me, girl," Baenlin growled and met her gaze.

"You're not going in there. I know I'm nothing to you, but Ree is everything to me. Right now, you're the last person she wants to see."

"I could force my way through."

"You could try, and it would hurt. I'd make it cost you. Maybe that would be enough to protect Ree. I doubt Howell would lift a finger to help you right now."

Gabe pointed at Eirian, causing everyone else to pause and look. She was standing a short distance away with her arms crossed and her eyes staring at them coldly. Along with the foliage, her hair had grown, the dark brown tresses tumbling over her shoulders. Behind her, the garden was a wild jumble of plants and vines crept along the pavement. The change in Fayleen's stance allowed Baenlin the opportunity to see what had happened, his eyes wide with shock.

"Let him pass, sister," Eirian said, sounding fed up. "I'll hear what he has to say."

"Are you sure?" Fayleen asked, hesitant to let her ward drop.

"Please, Fay. Master Howell, could you take those blues with you and check on the guards? I don't know what state the archmage left them in."

Howell signaled to the two blue mages, and they slipped away, leaving the more powerful duo to face each other in silence. Dropping her wards, Fayleen waved to show he could go through before she returned her hands to each side of the arch. Fayleen raised her magic to deter people from wanting to go in. Meeting the eyes of the silent guards, she shrugged.

"He won't hurt her, don't worry."

Following Eirian into the middle, Baenlin could not stop looking around at the thriving greenery. Splashes of color filled every space available, the dizzying scents from countless blooms permeating the air. Dropping onto a stone bench, Eirian ignored the creeping foliage and rested her elbows on her knees while covering her face. Reaching out, Baenlin touched the trunk of a tree and felt the thrum of her power before snatching his hand back.

"We knew you could do this on a small scale… but this? None of us knew you could do this."

"I'm surprised. I didn't think I was that good at keeping it secret in the beginning, and you were always watching."

Swiping away the vines creeping over the bench opposite hers, Baenlin sat and stared at Eirian. "The grand mage couldn't do this."

"I know. There's no point denying it's not even a fraction of my power. I can do this without trying. I imagine it makes your desire to drag me back to Riane all the greater," she said and looked at him, fingertips digging into her cheeks.

"You're right. It also confuses me."

"Why?"

"This ability should make you more green than red, but you're a terrible healer."

She gave him a wry smile and sat up straight, replying, "That's true. Look, Archmage, I know what you want. I also know you're stubborn, so you can't comprehend why I don't think the same way as you."

"No, I don't." Frowning, Baenlin flicked a creeping vine and asked, "Can you control this?"

The look Baenlin kept giving the persistent vine made Eirian wonder if anyone else had ever seen him so befuddled by a plant.

"When I want to. Right now, it's feeding off my presence, and when I go away, everything will be normal again. I mean, the growth will remain, but they'll just be plants."

"You are magnificent."

"Thank you. You do like to flatter me in one breath, then insult me in the next."

Shrugging in agreement, Baenlin spared a glance at the watching guards on the other side of Fayleen's ward. He regretted that the ward prevented him from encouraging them to look away.

"I only tell you truths. You're a fool, magnificent, but still a fool. So much power, so much potential, and you want to be the Queen of Insignificance."

Eirian replied, "From birth, I've been told what my duty in life is. I know my studies would have been different if we'd known the grand mage would fail in my lifetime. I don't want to be the queen, but I also don't want to be the grand mage. If I must be something, then I'll be what I've spent my life preparing to be."

"How can you not want to be a ruler?"

"I'm not ambitious like you, like my cousin, like so many others who want to use me. Maybe I'm the biggest fool the gods created, but I'm not completely naive. You want me to be the grand mage, to be the queen to your king. You have the wrong purple for that goal. Tessa is the one you want, and she is far more suited to it than I am."

Baenlin slid off the bench and moved towards Eirian, kneeling at her feet. "You don't know how much your power affects me. From the day they brought you to Riane, I felt your magic. All mages would fall at your feet if you so desired it. Why do you think it drew my nephew to you from the moment he met you?"

"Celi is my friend. We understand each other." There was more to it, but she could never utter the words out loud to Baenlin.

"Celiaen feels your magic the same way I do. The way you make us feel is addictive."

"I won't return to Riane. Not unless what you're convinced of happens."

Placing his hands on her knees, Baenlin leaned in to look up at her face. "If you leave it until then, you'll come crawling. If you're lucky, Mayve might still be with us, but if not, then the grand mage will be your rival. Tessa knows she is the second choice. If you come with me, I would be your ally."

"As opposed to what? My enemy?"

"I'm the only one capable of defying a grand mage. You'd need me to protect you, and that would come at an enormous cost," Baenlin answered.

His gaze slid down over her, and she understood his message. Carefully pushing his hands away, Eirian shook her head. She hated that so many people assumed she was at odds with Tessa. No one knew the truth, and it was better that way.

"Well, it's a good thing we won't need to worry about that. Riane is not the only sanctuary for me."

Grabbing her, Baenlin pulled Eirian down towards him, and she squeaked, not expecting it. With her back pressed to the bench, her nostrils flared nervously as he stared at her darkly.

"No matter where you run, they'll use you. Do you think your fate would be different in Ensaycal? I know Paienven. I suspect Celiaen has told you many a thing about his father."

"Yes."

"I'll make you a deal. We're both honorable most of the time, so we can trust each other to stick to it."

A smirk slowly formed, and Eirian was uncomfortable with the gleam of triumph in his eyes. Whatever he was offering, she doubted it would be good.

Baenlin continued, "You'll stay here and go through with becoming the Queen of Endara. However, if you fail at remaining the queen, you will return to Riane."

"How—"

"I won't interfere, and I'll leave tomorrow. Though I'll regret missing the celebrations, I was looking forward to dancing with you."

Eirian searched his eyes for a hint that he was lying. "That's what I said I'd do."

"Hush, I haven't given you the conditions. You won't ask for help from Riane while you rule. If you flee Endara, if you try to take refuge somewhere other than Riane, I'll find you, and I'll drag you back kicking and screaming. You say your place is here while I say your place is there. Therefore, you must be in one or the other."

"You can't expect me to never leave Endara? What if, powers forbid, we go to war?"

Baenlin arched a brow and said mockingly, "I know what they require of you as the queen, or have you forgotten who my sister is? I wouldn't hunt you for being at war. Unless you ask me to, and you may very well do so."

Looking towards the arch where Fayleen remained with her guards, Eirian sighed. "You have a deal. Maybe one day, when I'm old and about to die, I'll return to Riane just to rub it in your face."

Snaking a hand up, Baenlin buried it in her hair and pulled Eirian to him, purring, "Just in case you're right."

Surprised, Eirian did not struggle when he kissed her. The hand in her hair did not cause enough discomfort to distract from the swirl of his magic. It was a feeling she had not enjoyed in months, a reminder of the pleasures that mages only found with each other. Pleasures that Eirian had forsaken for duty. When Baenlin let go, she slid back against the bench and stared at him in a mixture of shock and frustration as he got to his feet.

"And to make you squirm."

Turning his back on her, Baenlin walked off without another word. Eirian saw the desperately worried Fayleen sent her as he summoned her to follow. Not moving from her spot, Eirian rubbed her face tiredly and wondered what she had agreed to.

ELEVEN

"And what do you call this variety?"

"It's a willow bottlebrush, Prince Galameyvin."

The creamy off-white flower fascinated him, and Galameyvin flashed a thankful smile at the duine accompanying him. Stroking fingers over the bristles of the blossom, he wished Eirian was there with him. He could picture her wandering through the sprawling gardens surrounding the gleaming castle of Ashendon and delighting in all the collections. Sighing, Galameyvin dropped his hand away from the tree and turned to stare out over the meticulously laid-out space. Next to him, the gray-haired duine kept his hands grasped behind his back, waiting in silence.

"You can talk to me, Liam. You don't need to stand there quietly until I ask you a question," Galameyvin said.

Clearing his throat, Liam shifted and replied, "I'm sorry, Your Highness, I'm not sure what you want me to say."

"Tell me about yourself." Studying him, Galameyvin added, "This is our first time together, and while my minders change daily, I'd like to get to know you."

"I… well… may I… oh, Your Highness! Thank the powers."

"It's okay, Liam, you can go."

Smiling at the new arrival, Galameyvin bowed. "Good morning, Prince Emlyn. I wasn't expecting your company today."

Thankful for the escape offered to him, Liam quickly spun on his heel and hurried off. Watching him go, the two princes did not speak, but Emlyn chuckled at the disappointed look on Galameyvin's face.

Shrugging, he turned to Emlyn and smiled. "Come to save me from boredom?"

Emlyn inclined his head and replied, "I enjoy picking your mind."

"You're not the only one." Galameyvin chuckled, looking around cautiously. "I'm never sure when Lady Saoirse might swoop in to question me further."

"Let me put you at ease. Our dear Saoirse is with the others preparing to leave."

"Leave?"

"Yes."

There was a gleam in Emlyn's eyes that seemed familiar to Galameyvin, but he could not place it. It told him he was being toyed with, which was not something he was used to. He was accustomed to being one of the most powerful mages in the room. Since arriving in Telmia, Galameyvin had found himself frequently outmatched. Emlyn, in particular, constantly gave him the feeling that he already knew what was going to happen.

Moving away from the row of bottlebrush trees, Galameyvin let the path guide him through the garden. At his side, Emlyn carefully avoided touching anything. It was an odd trait that Galameyvin had noticed about him. While all the other daoine were casual about touching each other, Emlyn maintained a distance. His father was not so reserved, and whenever Galameyvin saw Neriwyn surrounded by his people, it reminded him of Celiaen.

"You're thinking about him again," Emlyn murmured.

"How?"

"Do you need to ask?"

Galameyvin sighed. "No, I suppose not."

Waving at the gardens, Emlyn said, "Sometimes people do things for selfish reasons. Yes, they hurt immensely, but one day, the hurt will fade, and we'll understand it needed to happen. The pain helps us find our way."

"The only time Celiaen behaves selfishly is when it involves Eirian."

"Tell me about her."

Eyeing him sideways, Galameyvin replied, "You ask that every time we meet. Why the fascination with Eirian?"

"She is important, more important than you can imagine. It makes me curious about her."

"Who is leaving, and why?"

"Haven't you worked that out yet?"

"King Neriwyn is sending people to Endara," Galameyvin suggested.

Chuckling, Emlyn agreed. "Yes, he is. I told you, Eirian is important. She needs to be warned of the fight that is coming."

"I don't suppose I can go with them?"

"No, not yet, but I'm sure you'll get your chance. Now, tell me about how she can make a garden grow. What's her favorite flower?"

Pausing, Galameyvin frowned. "I haven't mentioned her ability to make plants grow."

Holding his gaze, Emlyn arched a brow, and Galameyvin continued to wait. He was confident he had continued to keep that aspect of Eirian's power a secret. It was something they had all promised to do soon after they met her. Protecting Eirian was second nature to Galameyvin, and he would not willingly betray her trust.

"Yes, you did," Emlyn said. "The other day in Tharen's garden."

Confused for a moment, Galameyvin rubbed his forehead and sighed. Magic whispered around them, gentle and coaxing, until he remembered the conversation with Emlyn. The details were vague, but Galameyvin recalled telling him about Eirian's power. It left him frustrated and angry over his actions.

"Yes, I did, didn't I. Eirian can make anything grow with no effort. When she wants to, she can turn a street into a meadow of wildflowers just by breathing. I've never met another who could do that, not in Riane."

"There are some here in Telmia who can do it, including my father, though it takes effort for most. We're sending one with the delegation to Endara. A young healer called Muireann."

"Sometimes, I think Eirian should have been a healer," he murmured.

Emlyn asked, "Why is that?"

"She makes you feel alive. I know it sounds like a strange way to describe someone, but it's the only way I can. Her magic is living, somehow. It's a vibrant energy that fills you and makes everything... more? When she grows plants, they don't face the sun."

"They face her?"

"Like she is the sun."

"Perhaps she is, in a way. I understand why you feel she should have been a healer, but I suspect not being a healer serves a purpose."

Looking at the sky, Galameyvin sighed. As wonderful as spending time in Telmia and learning more about the daoine was, he wanted to be home with the people he loved. With Eirian, with Celiaen, with his family and friends. Sunlight caught his golden curls, and Emlyn frowned at the sight. Glancing at him, Galameyvin noticed the regret in his eyes and wondered what caused it. His magic whispered around him, telling him that Emlyn was grieving, and the strength of his emotions tugged at Galameyvin's need to help.

"Is there anything you wish to talk about, Your Highness?"

Fingers toying with the corner of his coat, Emlyn's stare locked on something in the distance. Galameyvin looked at the pale green fabric and noticed the embroidery. Everything the Telmians wore was colorful and decorated, but not what he considered ornate. Instead, they preferred simple lines, layering the wispy spider silk to create illusions. Of everything Galameyvin had seen embroidered on their clothes, it was the first time he had spotted the unmistakable figures gracing Emlyn.

"Ree's favorite flower is a dandelion," he whispered.

Emlyn glanced down at the dandelions embroidered along the hem of his coat and smiled. It carried a hint of knowing, suggesting that he was privy to a secret Galameyvin was clueless of. He was not sure he wanted to know.

"Dandelions are like decisions. One decision leads to hundreds of consequences that drift out in the breeze. Some of those consequences will stick, and others will not, but like each seed, they become part of the past."

"She likens them to life. Most people call them weeds, but not her."

"Tell me about her smile when you give her one."

Galameyvin closed his eyes, imagining Eirian. She had a thousand smiles, and he knew them all. He could picture them as clearly as he could every part of her.

"Pure. Happy. Excited. Innocent. Her eyes shine with it."

"Why?"

"Because they make her happy, but when someone she loves gives her one, it's better than if she had picked it herself," Galameyvin answered. "The world could be an inferno, but time would stop to let you tuck a dandelion behind Eirian's ear and watch her smile."

"Would you?" Emlyn queried.

"Would I what?"

"Ignore an inferno to make her smile."

He knew he would let the inferno consume them for another moment with her. Swallowing, Galameyvin nodded slowly.

"Yes. Another moment, another touch, just one more beat of our hearts. I would let the world burn to be with her."

"Never hesitate to do it. It could end the inferno." Emlyn gave him a lopsided smile and added, "But no one can stop time. They can only glimpse the variations like dandelion seeds in the wind."

Staring at him, Galameyvin was uncertain about how to respond. He decided Emlyn was the most peculiar person he had ever met, even for a duine. From the moment he arrived in Telmia, Galameyvin had found his expectations of the daoine challenged. It was difficult to know if he should take things seriously or not, from moment to moment. Feasts could last days, daoine fluttering in and out like butterflies among the flowers. They exchanged magic as frequently as kisses, the brushes across mind and skin hard to resist.

"If someone could glimpse the variations, as you say, could they tell me if—"

"One day," Emlyn said quickly.

"You don't know what I was going to ask."

"I'm sorry. Yes, one day, you'll go home with the ones you love."

"That's not—"

"Isn't it?"

Taking a deep breath, Galameyvin gave up on his question. Pushing his irritation aside, he resumed his stroll through the gardens with Emlyn. The knowing smirk on his face made Galameyvin want to growl, but he kept his emotions under control. He reminded himself that he was a blue, and his self-control was unrivaled. It had to be, especially when dealing with Celiaen and Eirian.

Gaze drifting over the garden, Galameyvin pondered how many varieties of plants there were. It was something he wanted to find out and make notes of to tell Eirian. He had spent time in many fine gardens, but none of them compared to these. The only time Galameyvin had seen greenery more vibrant was when Eirian grew it. There were so many colors that he was unsure if they all had names, and he knew every aspect of the place would fascinate Eirian.

Waving at a cluster of people, Emlyn commented, "The heart is an interesting thing, but I'm sure you know that."

"Indeed."

"Sometimes, what the heart wants is the right thing, even if the mind disagrees. Love doesn't have to be logical."

"I'm not sure I understand your point," he said.

"Things aren't always what they seem."

Glancing at the sky, Galameyvin sighed. "I know better than to trust thoughts or emotions. As we know, they're not immune to manipulation."

"And you are a master of that."

"I'm a blue. It's what I do. I thought I was one of the best, but since coming here, I question that."

Emlyn said, "People fall in and out of love every day. That's normal. But some people belong together, always, no matter what comes between them. You look at them and know there is nowhere else you should be but by their side. The heart knows this, even if the mind argues otherwise. Even if everything seems to conspire against them."

"If it was so easy to defy the mind, I'd walk away right now and go to Eirian."

"And do what?"

"Run far away."

"And Celiaen?"

"Yes." Galameyvin pinched the bridge of his nose and muttered, "But we can't. Eirian has responsibilities to Endara, and Celiaen has his."

"Not just Endara, but everyone, everywhere. There is a darkness coming, and she must stand against it. That's why my father is sending an envoy to Amath to meet with her. War is coming, and she must be there for it," Emlyn informed him.

Looking at the ground, Galameyvin scuffed the toe of his boot against the pavers. From the moment he arrived in Telmia, he had heard their whispers about the darkness coming, but he dreaded the prospect of Eirian facing war. Not because of some fear it might hurt her, but because he was one of the few people alive who knew what she was capable of. The danger Eirian could present if circumstances pushed her. He was the only one who had ever stood a chance of stopping her.

"If that is true, then I should be with her."

"Yes, but not yet."

"You don't understand!" Galameyvin snarled.

His hand shot out, and Emlyn gripped Galameyvin's arm tightly. Instinctively reaching for his magic, Galameyvin prepared to force him to let go, but Emlyn shook his head. The look on his face was eerily similar to the one Eirian would wear when she was not in the mood to tolerate his attempts to use his power on her. Flinching at the thought, Galameyvin scolded himself for letting his emotions cloud his perception.

"I understand far better than you do," Emlyn said quietly. "Far better than you could. You need to remain here for now, but you'll be with her again soon."

"Emlyn," a man said. "That's enough."

"I thought you were busy with Faolan and the others, father."

Turning to look at Neriwyn, Galameyvin frowned. He had heard no one approaching or felt the ripple of magic that now surrounded them. It was a familiar magic, the simmering rage of a warrior. Sometimes, if he closed his eyes, Galameyvin could imagine it was Celiaen's magic. King Neriwyn reminded him of Celiaen, but Galameyvin dismissed it as more wishful thinking brought about by his homesickness.

Neriwyn winked at Galameyvin, dark eyes gleaming with mischief, and said, "I was. Now I'm not. How are you today, Your Highness?"

Bowing, Galameyvin replied, "I'm well, Your Majesty, and yourself?"

"I'm in the mood to spend some time in the arena. Would you care to join me?"

Releasing Galameyvin's arm, Emlyn stepped back with a sigh. He gave Neriwyn an annoyed look, but said nothing. Glancing at his waist, Galameyvin regretted leaving his swords in his chamber and shrugged at Neriwyn.

"I'm afraid I'm woefully unarmed and outmatched."

Placing a hand on Galameyvin's elbow, Neriwyn chuckled. "Don't worry, I'll go easy on you. You're far too pretty to damage in a fight."

Like every other time he had come into contact with Neriwyn, Galameyvin felt a jolt through his magic. He had noticed soon after his arrival that Neriwyn was the sort of person who liked to touch. It unsettled Galameyvin, so he hid his discomfort with a smile and reminded himself that he was used to it. Celiaen and Eirian were the same. They felt a constant need to feel a connection to someone, like a tether in a storm. Allowing Neriwyn to guide him through the gardens, with Emlyn trailing after them silently, Galameyvin did his best to keep his focus on what he had learned.

"His Highness told me you're sending a delegation to Endara," Galameyvin said.

"Sent. The delegation departed not long before I joined you. Lord Faolan is in charge, but I sent Lord Tharen along to keep him in check. They'll negotiate an alliance with Endara."

"Not Lord Vartan?"

Neriwyn laughed. "No, my dear Vartan stays with me. Not all of us are so foolish as to send those most important to us away on diplomatic missions. I'm sure your precious warrior regrets his decision."

Shaking his head, Galameyvin scoffed. "I doubt it. Celiaen is far too stubborn."

"What a surprise," Emlyn muttered.

"Yes, it is a surprise, isn't it, Emlyn?" Neriwyn said over his shoulder.

"I'm sure it will thrill King Nolan to receive a delegation from Telmia. Unfortunately, you're rather reclusive," Galameyvin murmured to avoid the banter between them. "It's unfortunate I couldn't go with them. I would have been invaluable."

Squeezing his elbow, Neriwyn replied, "I require you here. Your king sent you to serve me, and I'm not prepared to release you."

"I would have been able to introduce Lord Faolan—"

"He has no need for your introduction. Prince Celiaen is currently on his way to Amath, and they have met before. As you know."

His heart sunk, and Galameyvin suspected he knew precisely why Celiaen was going to Amath. Glancing away, he attempted to brush aside his jealousy and reminded himself that they had a bond. He had interfered with it enough over the years, and Galameyvin could not blame Celiaen for going to Eirian without him present. It was better that he was in Telmia and far from both of them. If he were far from Eirian, she would finally admit how much she loved Celiaen.

"Oh, sweet boy." Neriwyn sighed.

Emlyn said cautiously, "Father."

Brushing the curls away from Galameyvin's face, Neriwyn lifted his chin and smiled sadly. Meeting his eyes, the grief he saw within them startled Galameyvin. More than grief, there was a desperate longing he understood. He experienced it every time he was apart from Eirian, and now he felt it for Celiaen. It was something he had never felt for Celiaen before. They had always been together as a team. Pressing his lips to Galameyvin's forehead, Neriwyn stroked a thumb across his cheek gently.

"It will all work out."

"Your Majesty," Galameyvin murmured. "Thank you for your concern, but I'm fine."

Neriwyn nodded, but did not release him, and Emlyn coughed. Taking the cue to remove himself from Neriwyn's grasp, Galameyvin stepped back, avoiding the flicker of pain he saw on Neriwyn's face. He did not understand it, and he was not sure he ever wanted to. Galameyvin had learned in his training that the older a person was, the deeper the well of emotional trauma ran, and Neriwyn was ancient.

"Apologies, Prince Galameyvin. I forget myself sometimes, and you remind me of someone I love. Never let jealousy take away the things that matter to you," Neriwyn said quietly. "If allowed to go too long, some rifts become irreparable."

"Sire?"

Coughing again, Emlyn muttered, "Perhaps your sparring session can wait, father. Why don't you go find Vartan?"

"Emlyn."

"Yes, father?"

"Why don't you go find some stones to play with?" Neriwyn growled.

Eyes darting between father and son, Galameyvin pressed his lips together. He had witnessed the affection Neriwyn held for Emlyn, but it was not present as they glared at each other. Reaching for his magic, he stepped between them and placed a hand on each of their arms. It would have little effect on the two daoine, but that did not stop Galameyvin from making an attempt in the hope it would distract them.

Voice calm, Galameyvin said, "You both make excellent suggestions. There's no need to argue. Perhaps it would be for the best if we all go our separate ways and forget this happened."

Chuckling, Neriwyn covered Galameyvin's hand with his own and replied, "Sweet boy, you're not powerful enough to make suggestions to me. Not yet, anyway, but I applaud your attempt."

"It was worth a try."

"Indeed! I imagine few can resist you."

Shaking his head, Emlyn turned away, grumbling, "The stupidity of—"

"Emlyn!"

"Try not to hurt him! You sent your best healer to Endara," he said, and walked away.

Watching Emlyn leave, Galameyvin attempted to pluck his hand from Neriwyn's arm. Raising a brow in amusement, Neriwyn moved it to the crook of his elbow and patted it gently. Galameyvin allowed him to resume leading the way through the gardens towards the arena complex attached to the castle. He did not want to say anything and tread into a conversation he would regret.

Gum trees towered above them, branches entwined, and clusters of bright pink flowers dangled among green leaves. Dark brown bark curled in strips, revealing paler bark beneath. They lined the pathway, gum nuts scattered on the ground. The bright pink blossoms gave way to a softer pink variety that Neriwyn had told Galameyvin they called silver princess. It was another example of a plant he wanted to show Eirian. He imagined her delight.

"Emlyn worries too much."

"Does he have a reason to worry?" Galameyvin murmured in concern.

"We all have a reason to worry."

"He mentioned something about war, but that's not what I meant. Whenever you're near me, Prince Emlyn seems overly concerned."

Neriwyn snorted. "My son worries that my control might slip around you."

"Because I remind you—"

"Yes."

Frowning, Galameyvin asked, "His mother?"

"No, not his mother, but another. Jealousy drove us apart. That is why you must learn to put yours aside. If you can do it, you'll help Celiaen do the same. Two men loving the same woman can end in heartbreak, but it can be so much more when she loves them both in return. Even more so when they also love each other."

"It hardly matters. Eirian will be the Queen of Endara one day, and such a relationship with us could never be."

"She'll be queen by her birthday," Neriwyn informed him. "King Nolan is unwell."

Staring at Neriwyn in shock, Galameyvin did not notice when they crossed under the covered walkways that surrounded the arena. In the distance, he could hear the clash of weapons as warriors trained. The daoine did not experience the same raging bloodlust that the red mages did, but it was close. Galameyvin had noticed a similar layering of wards on the complex to the ones used in Riane, and he appreciated them greatly. However, sometimes the daoine warriors felt more intense than he was used to.

"Poor Ree," he whispered. "I wish I was there to help her."

"She's going to be queen."

Shaking his head, Galameyvin explained, "She looked forward to time with her father. Now you're telling me she won't get it, and war is coming?"

"I'm sorry Eirian didn't get her time with her father. I imagine growing up without a mother and so far from her father was difficult."

"She had us."

Giving Galameyvin a sideways look, Neriwyn agreed. "Yes, she did. Most fortunate for Eirian to have two people who love her so deeply by her side all those years."

"Tell me about this war."

"Athnaral is under the influence of a most insidious enemy. It will twist minds and hearts, turning people on themselves."

"And you expect Eirian to fight this enemy?"

"She won't be alone. We'll all be there." Neriwyn released his hand with a wink and stepped away, saying, "You know Eirian is special."

Galameyvin said, "Eirian is dangerous. I'm the only person who has ever exerted some influence over her, and even then!"

"What about Celiaen?"

"Not the good kind. Together, they're something to fear. Celiaen and Eirian are..."

Neriwyn prompted, "They are what?"

"They're bound. Magically."

"A power bond?"

"Yes," he answered.

Covering his mouth, Galameyvin cursed himself. He did not know why he told Neriwyn about the bond, but he regretted it. The words had come out without thinking, something that rarely happened to him.

"Will it make you feel any better if I told you we were aware of that already?" Neriwyn said.

"You were?"

"Of course, they meant it to be that way."

"They who?"

Waving a hand vaguely, Neriwyn answered, "The gods."

He snorted. "The gods?"

"Is that so hard to believe?"

"Yes, it is. The gods abandoned us long ago. Even your people say that. Why would the gods have anything planned for us if they couldn't bring themselves to remain?"

They stared at each other, and the sad expression on Neriwyn's face confused Galameyvin. Shrugging, Neriwyn looked away and nodded slowly. His eyes drifted over the pillars and arches, the domed roofs covering junctions in the pathways weaving around the arenas. All of it was carefully laid out to layer wards together and contain the magic of the warriors fighting within.

"The gods are not perfect. Quite the opposite, really. They're powerful, terribly flawed beings who didn't understand the responsibility that came with their choices. What happened, happened, and we can't change the past. All we can do is fight for a better future. To find the balance that will work."

"It's not that simple," Galameyvin said.

"No, it's not, but it could be."

"What happened to Queen Shianeni?"

Neriwyn glanced at him, murmuring, "Foresight is a terrible thing. Our queen made her choices, and the consequences are what they are. That's all I want to say. It's better for everyone if no one speaks of her. Which is why I forbid it."

Galameyvin had heard others say the same thing about foresight. It was something people whispered about, a magical gift to be dreaded instead of welcomed. Accepting what Neriwyn said, Galameyvin started walking again. He did not want to spar, and his power was telling him that Neriwyn did not either. Clasping his hands behind his back, Neriwyn matched his stride, watching Galameyvin from the corner of his eye.

"So war with Athnaral?" Galameyvin asked.

"Yes. It's been a long time since Telmia took part in a battle, but we'll be there when we're needed."

"Will you go?"

"I wouldn't miss it. Is it terrible if I admit I look forward to it?"

Studying Neriwyn, Galameyvin replied, "No, I don't think it is. You're a warrior, through and through, your kind lives to fight."

"Some of the worst destruction I've seen on a battlefield hasn't come at the hands of warriors. There is so much more to fighting than swords." Neriwyn said. "Riane fails to teach that now. Once mages fought with their magic directly, they could move the earth beneath their feet, twist the surrounding air, and turn trees against their enemies. They could even turn their minds, twist their perception of what was real."

"What about lightning?"

"The power of a storm is not something just anyone could draw on, but it is possible."

"I've seen it done."

"I don't think I need to guess who you've seen do it."

Shaking his head, Galameyvin demanded, "Why is Eirian so powerful?"

"Because she has to be," Neriwyn spoke gently. "Because if she isn't, we don't stand a chance against the darkness."

He remembered the carnage, and Galameyvin bit his lip. He remembered the withered remains of elves who had attacked Celiaen and suffered at Eirian's hands for their attempt. Blood splattered walls, and screams of agony chased those memories with others. The taste of her rage would never fade. It was not the fury of a warrior, but something else, something that hurt to feel. Galameyvin wondered what a victory against the darkness would cost Eirian.

"Eirian might be a weapon to you, Your Majesty, but she is so much more than that."

Galameyvin remembered her, blood-soaked and naked in a field of flowers, grieving the death she brought. Every kill she made, Eirian felt. He had helped her process afterward many times, holding her hands through her guilt. It took little for Galameyvin to imagine what war might do to her.

"Let me guess, you're not in the mood for this?"

Straddling her with a training sword to her throat, Aiden frowned at Eirian with doubt in his eyes. Baenlin's words repeated themselves at the back of his mind, taunting him. Eirian sighed and shook her head, feeling the sand shift beneath her.

"I'm sorry, Aiden."

Rolling off, he stood before offering Eirian a hand to get up. Glancing over at the watching crowd of guards, Aiden caught the exchange of coins. He noted to have a word with the men when he had the time.

"You haven't been in the mood for weeks. I thought you're supposed to be some great warrior mage, but I've put you on your ass half a dozen times today alone. They overrated your abilities, which doesn't bode well for the quality of warriors in Riane."

Ignoring his jibe, Eirian shook the sand out of her hair, cringing when she thought of the dismay her ladies would express. It was just another thing for them to huff over.

"I don't know why I keep bothering while my mind is a mess," she grumbled.

"Does hitting the ground repeatedly help?"

Glaring at him, Eirian bent over and picked up her training sword from the ground where it had landed when he sent her flying. As frustrated as he was, Aiden did not resist briefly gazing at her in admiration.

"Not really. It just makes it hurt more. The ground is hard when you hit it."

"If you want to land on soft surfaces, then you're sparring in the wrong place. I value my life, Princess, and I know my job. Sometimes I like to pretend you might be capable of holding your own in a fight, but now I doubt it," he said.

Aiden took the weapon from Eirian, giving her a dark look that she was not used to seeing on his face. It made her hesitate, which was what he expected. Her lies were tiresome, and Aiden wanted them to end.

"What do you mean, Aiden?"

"If you aren't honest with us, we can't guard you the way you need to be. I shouldn't count on you defending yourself if things go wrong. No one will think worse of you if you give this up. Well, I will, but I'm the captain of your guard, and you've made it clear you don't listen to me."

Astonished, Eirian struggled to find the words to respond. She understood what Aiden was saying. Her guards thought she could hold her own while they focused on protecting her. If her recent performances in the sparring ring were anything to go by, she could admit she did not blame them for having doubts. Mulling over what Aiden had said reminded Eirian of her early days in Riane. In those years, she had feared the response of her magic to a blade in her hand. Her bloodlust had been a thing she dreaded.

Celiaen had been the one to help her through her fear. Unfortunately, what happened with Baenlin had caused those feelings to resurface, adding to her anxiety. Her memories flashed back to the guards and the effects of her magic on them. Rubbing her forehead, Eirian noticed a scratch along the inside of her forearm and frowned, wondering how it had happened. Stretching her arm out in front of her to get a good look at it, Eirian was pleased it was a surface scrape and nothing she could not hide with long sleeves. Noticing her actions, Aiden came over to examine it.

He grunted. "I suppose your ladies will make a fuss."

"They do like to make a fuss. It is unseemly, after all. A proper lady doesn't do things like this, and we all know I'm a proper lady!"

Winking at Aiden, she smiled and dropped her arm, waiting for him to chuckle like he used to. He did not blink, mouth twisting as a sign he was unimpressed with her attempt.

Sighing in frustration, she said, "Speaking of said ladies."

He signaled to the other guards on duty. "As you wish, ma'am."

Picking her way over the sand, Eirian felt stiff from hitting the ground multiple times.

"Well, at least that's something you can agree with," she muttered. "It's not what I want from you, but I'll take what I can get."

Aiden stiffened, catching her mutterings as he followed her. "Your Highness?"

"Yes, Aiden?"

"Did you want something else?"

Grinding her teeth, Eirian glanced at him. "What do you think? I used to enjoy our banter, but now you scold me and ignore all of my attempts to joke."

"You honestly think things can ever be the same again? After what I felt that day?"

"I want it to be."

He shook his head as they walked across the yard with the rest of her guards around them. Training continued for everyone else. Finally reaching the shadows cast by the wall, Eirian pirouetted to stare at Aiden sadly.

"I've lost count of how many times I've apologized to you."

"I know you're sorry, but that doesn't change what I know, and what I know scares me. To feel such lust for destruction is unnerving, but knowing it came from you? That terrifies me."

"And you don't think it scares me?"

Aiden sighed and said, "I'm trying to balance it with what you did in the garden. And hearing from that man that you've done nothing but lie to us about what you can do? That hurts, and it keeps hurting because you keep lying. You're not the woman I thought you were."

They stared at each other, the other guards watching them warily from a short distance. Eirian threw her hands in the air with an angry stamp of a foot and shook her head, turning her back on him. It was not Aiden she was angry with, but herself. His feelings were understandable, and Eirian knew she deserved them.

"Fine, let's forget it. You're right to be angry with me."

Nodding, Aiden did not bother to argue and gathered his men to accompany her. Eirian's mood was palatable in her magic. A dark cloud surrounded them. It spread, discouraging anyone from daring to approach, and instead caused them to turn away warily. They found one of Nolan's gentlemen waiting to speak to her when Eirian reached her quarters. Barely sparing him a glance, she glared at her ladies and dared them with a look to say anything about her state.

"What can I do for you?"

"Your Highness, it's the King. He's not himself!"

The man sounded distressed, and Eirian finally looked at him, her eyes going wide at the sight of a large bruise forming over his left eye.

"What happened to you?"

The look on his face made her stagger to the table and sit. Eirian stared at him and tried to make sense of the situation, covering her mouth in horror. Bea poured a cup of water, slipping it into Eirian's hands when they fell to her lap. She tightened her fingers around the pottery and waited to hear more from the man. Even the guards look mortified, Aiden sending out two of the men who had come into the chamber with him.

"He seemed fine when he woke. Thomas mentioned how your birthday celebration plans were progressing and that we weren't sure when the Ensaycalan delegation would arrive. After that, he started behaving erratically and cursing King Paienven. It got worse, and he attacked us. He's never done that before. I tried to distract him while the others got out, but he landed a blow on me, as you see."

"Cursing Paienven? How very curious. Do you think it was being reminded of them that set Nolan off?"

He nodded and answered, "He's getting worse."

Dropping her gaze to the cup in her hand, Eirian fearfully wondered if the group from Riane had sped him along. Despite their deal, she knew Baenlin would do anything to get his way. It occurred to Eirian that all Soren needed was a word from him to encourage Nolan towards madness a little quicker. If someone suggested they had done something to Nolan, it would be a step in the direction Baenlin had told Eirian things would go.

People would react badly and quickly focus their rage and fear on her. They would propose Eirian had done it so she could take the throne without having to wait for him to die. Pushing the thoughts aside, Eirian reminded herself of what Howell had said about the other cases of madness. She found solace in believing he would have told her if they had done anything to Nolan.

"Who else knows what happened?"

"The Dukes of Tamantal and Raellwynt, they were present."

His response explained why Brenna was not with the other ladies.

He added, "I imagine they'll convene the council."

"I don't think there's any need for that."

"I overheard Tamantal say that if he continues to get worse, they'll need to move the coronation forward."

Her ladies gasped, and Romana shushed them. Silently, Eirian tightened her grip on the cup as she grew furious with Everett. Logically, his desire to get the change of power over and done with was understandable because it would be better for stability in the long term. She had taken command of the council and performed the monarchs' duties behind closed doors. Eirian did not feel ready to take the throne, and the prospect of being queen sooner made her stomach churn.

"I see."

The gentleman touched his face tentatively, saying, "We hate seeing His Majesty in decline."

Taking a sip, Eirian placed the cup on the table and stood. "I'll come as soon as I'm tidied up because, as you can tell, I hit the ground once or twice while training today."

In the corner, Aiden muttered, "Was more than that."

He received chuckles from the other guards present, and Eirian's eyes narrowed, her anger flaring. The gentleman heard the dismissal in her words and bowed. He slipped out of the room, knowing his duty was to let those at the King's quarters know Eirian would come as soon as possible. She made her way into her chamber as soon as he left, and her ladies followed.

They prepared fresh clothes in silence while Eirian stripped. Bea quickly fetched several washcloths, wetting them so she could wipe away the layer of dirt coating Eirian's skin. Feeling her mood, they did not mention the bright red scrape on Eirian's arm for fear of adding to her upset. None of them wanted to push her temper.

"Could you please have the maids prepare a bath for me tonight?"

Bea wiped over her hair with a cloth, and Eirian cringed at the sand she felt. She knew her head was full of it from hitting the ground in training.

"Yes, my lady."

"It doesn't need to be hot, Bea, don't worry, but I need to wash away all this dirt properly, and cold water will suffice."

Cringing, Bea shuddered at the prospect of a cold bath and silently continued her task. Once satisfied that Eirian was as clean as they could get her, they helped her into a chemise before holding up a pink gown. Eirian dreaded this part. The weight of the skirts swirling around her legs made her feel caged. She had once asked her ladies if they felt the same about wearing gowns, and they had stared at her as they always did, completely perplexed by how different she was to them.

"Your hair is a mess. I'm not sure we should take it from this braid, but we need to do something with it." Romana shook her head, clearly frustrated, and said, "Elke, you're the best at hair. What do you suggest?"

Cringing, Elke held her hands up as she replied, "We might have to undo the braid and brush it out before redoing it. If we use something to cover her shoulders and back, we shouldn't get her gown dirty."

"That's a good idea. We should have done her hair first."

They hurried around, looking for something suitable. Isabella returned with a towel and carefully draped it over Eirian's shoulders before Elke undid the braid. Once the strands were loose, she ran the hairbrush through it a few times, sighing at the sand coming out. Pointing at the damp cloths they had used previously, Elke alternated running the brush through and wiping the hair. Then, turning her quick fingers to divide the hair, she drew them into a tight braid that sat close to Eirian's skull.

"Well, you look respectable, Your Highness," Elke said.

Eirian sighed. "Thank you. I know I can be quite the challenge."

Gathering her skirts, she stood carefully and made her way over to the door. Pulling it open to go through, Eirian shot Aiden a dismissive look, stalking past him to the next door. One of her other guards scrambled to open it before she got there, earning himself a thankful smile from the ladies trailing behind her. The journey provided Eirian with a chance to gather her emotions. When she entered the audience chamber, she had buried her anger beneath the concern of a daughter worried for her ailing father.

Everett stood in front of a window while Marcellus paced back and forth in front of the door to Nolan's private quarters. Brenna was at the table, glancing over books with a worried frown. Several gentlemen were looking fearfully towards the shut door from their positions. Knowing their place was not within the chamber, her ladies and guards remained outside.

"Has he calmed down?" Eirian asked softly.

Marcellus paused mid-stride and shook his head. "We keep hearing him shouting. Is there anything you can do?"

"No."

"Then all we can do is wait for him to exhaust himself."

Turning around, Everett remained leaning against the windowsill and crossed his arms over his chest. "I heard you had another terrible training session."

They cringed at the muffled sound of Nolan shouting, and Eirian walked towards the door. Marcellus grabbed her arm, stopping Eirian before she opened it.

"Don't go in there. He might hurt you."

She pried his fingers from her arm and smiled sadly, murmuring, "I need to. I can't calm him with magic, but maybe he will calm for his daughter."

"Marcellus is right, he might hurt you, and we can't risk it!" Brenna declared, slamming shut the book she was reading.

"Please don't make me pull rank. I'm not in the mood for it." Studying Marcellus's face, Eirian cocked her head to the side and listened to the wordless shouting. "I can look after myself."

Sighing in defeat, Marcellus stepped out of the way and let her go past, saying softly, "It's not the physical harm I fear."

Giving Marcellus a sharp look before she opened the door, Eirian felt a pang of concern as she shut it behind her. The chamber was as empty as she had expected it to be. Everyone had retreated to the furthermost room. Reaching the next door, she took a moment to lean against it, resting her forehead against the wood and waiting to hear more shouting.

Taking a deep breath, Eirian pushed the door open to slip through and called, "Father?"

The smell was terrible, and she blanched, wondering how many times his gentlemen had kept the secret that Nolan had soiled himself in one of his outbursts. Nolan huddled in front of the fireplace, half-dressed, and she took slow steps towards him. Lifting his head, he stared at Eirian in confusion and did not move, but she realized he had been sobbing. It was confronting, and Eirian understood why Marcellus had not wanted her to see him.

"Who are you? What do you want?"

He sounded childlike and terrified. The sound hit Eirian as an arrow to the heart, and she stopped approaching. Crouching to his level, Eirian remained out of reach to avoid making him feel any more fearful.

"Do you know who you are?"

Nolan nodded, hugging his legs closer to himself and whispered, "I'm Prince Nolan."

Swallowing, she bit her lip to stop herself from cursing. "You look upset, Your Highness. Can you tell me what is wrong? Do you know where you are?"

"Someone locked me in my father's chamber, but I don't know why or how I got here. I woke up, and I was alone. I keep shouting, but no one has come. Who are you? Are you my father's lady friend? Mama always makes comments about his lady friends," Nolan said nervously, giving her odd looks.

"I'm not one of his lady friends. My name is Eirian. How old are you?"

"I'm seven, and mama said I'm going away to stay with my uncle to learn, but I don't want to go. She said all princes must do it, and I'm not supposed to be frightened. I'm a prince, and I'm going to be the king one day, like my father."

Carefully getting to her feet, Eirian smiled at him sadly. She needed to leave.

"Can you wait here while I find someone for you? I better not take you with me, because I might get into trouble with the guards. I won't be long, I promise."

He looked hopeful as he asked, "You'll find my mama? Do you promise? I know she is busy since the elves are coming."

"Why are the elves coming?"

"I don't know!" A petulant look crossed Nolan's face that looked strange on an old man. "No one tells me anything! They say I have to get older first."

"I see. Well, I promise I'll be back with your mama. Maybe you can climb into the bed and have a nap while you wait."

"But it's father's bed."

Watching Nolan look at the bed fearfully, she smiled and assured him. "I'm sure you won't get into trouble for having a nap. I could go for a nap myself, but I have to find your mama first."

"You promise you'll come back?"

Nolan looked worried about being left alone, but, nodding in what she hoped was assurance, Eirian kept smiling.

"Of course, I promise. I'll be back with your mama."

Giving Nolan a little curtsy, her heart broke further at the childish grin he gave her in return with tears on his cheeks. Rushing back the way she had come, Eirian was careful not to slam the door behind her before resting her back against it. Her head fell back as she stared blankly at the ceiling. She took a few deep breaths and wiped away her tears before returning to the chamber where the others waited.

Eirian gave Marcellus an upset look and asked, "Did you know he had reverted to his child self?"

"It wouldn't be the first time," he admitted, looking at his feet.

Anguish filled her, and Eirian shook her head, fighting the tears. She did not want to break, not in front of them.

"I left my father huddled on the floor thinking he is a seven-year-old boy locked in his father's chambers by accident. I promised to find his mother!"

"Eirian." Everett pushed away from the window and approached her.

"He's sitting in his filth, and I don't think he realizes! So what are we supposed to do? He's the king, damn it! The king!"

Pulling Eirian into a hug, Everett shared a look with Marcellus over her head as he stroked her back. She took deep breaths to calm herself, fearful of what might happen if her control over her magic slipped.

"Why do you think we didn't want you to go in there? It kills him when he comes back to himself, and he's told what happened. Nolan always asks if you saw it. He doesn't want you to remember him like this. Even in madness, he wants to protect his little girl. We all want to protect you."

"When he was a child, did the elves ever visit?" Eirian asked Marcellus.

"Not that I recall, but he'd been a ward of my father for years before I was born. They visit after every coronation, but other than that, they leave us alone. Why?" Marcellus replied in confusion.

Extracting herself from Everett's hug, Eirian explained, "He said his mama was busy because the elves were coming. Why is he so disturbed by them coming? I don't understand. I've explained I'm a good friend of Prince Celiaen, but he seems so unsettled about it."

Holding his hands out in a confused shrug, Marcellus looked at Everett. "I honestly don't know."

"We have to move the coronation forward. Nolan is getting too unpredictable, and the risk of him having a public episode grows with every day we delay," Everett said.

Exhaling heavily, Eirian did not answer. Instead, she walked over to the table where Brenna remained seated, watching with worried eyes. Glancing over the open pages, Eirian clenched a fist in anger.

"You're preparing to make an official case."

Brenna reached out, touching her arm gently, and said, "We must do what is best for Endara."

"I understand. Please don't think that I don't."

A gentleman hurried over and pulled a chair out from under the table, offering it to Eirian. Smiling briefly at him, she sat and bowed her head, slumping.

Eirian admitted, "I'm not ready, and I hate this. I'm supposed to cool my heels waiting for him to die of old age or some foolish hunting accident."

"You're as ready as you're ever going to be, Eirian. Think of it this way, you're doing it to protect him. Nolan wants this, he knows it has to happen, and he'd ask you to accept it if he could."

Thomas broke his silence to agree. "He knows it very well. I've had to talk Nolan out of falling on his sword. Each morning I fear we'll find him dead by his hand, but he won't let me leave someone in the room."

The nobles gazed at Thomas in horror, and Eirian was thankful that they had kept it from everyone. Frowning at herself for the thought, she started chewing on her bottom lip, earning a swift kick to the foot from Brenna. Eirian could not hold back a giggle because the action felt so out of place. She felt every pair of eyes in the room on her as she covered her mouth. It mortified her, but the laughter kept coming.

"I don't understand why she's laughing." Everett looked at Marcellus and asked, "Did we miss a joke?"

Rubbing his forehead, Marcellus smiled sadly and replied, "It's overwhelming. I've seen it before. She's not laughing about the situation."

"I'm sorry. I didn't mean to laugh. I couldn't help it," Eirian said, and rubbed her face in embarrassment. "What do we do?"

Knowing Eirian would hate his stance, Everett prepared for her reaction as he said, "We don't stop him. Our priority is getting you on the throne. If Nolan did something, we cover it up and say he passed in his sleep."

"What?" Brenna gasped, glancing at Marcellus. "You can't be serious!"

"Beloved, he's right." Marcellus agreed, holding his hands up defensively.

The gentlemen were distressed at the suggestion, but the dukes ignored them, watching Eirian. She stared at the map hanging on the wall, and her expression was unreadable. They felt the swirl of her magic, fueled by her conflicting emotions. Everett closed his eyes while they waited, trying to decipher what he sensed from her. He hated what he had proposed but reminded himself that it was not the time to let his love for his uncle impede doing what was best for Endara.

"Eirian?" Brenna prompted.

"It breaks my heart to agree. Nolan is my father, but Everett and Marcellus are far closer to him, so I know they're not saying it lightly. King Nolan is a proud man, and he wouldn't decide without first considering everything."

Sensing a protest starting again, Eirian held up her hand for silence. "We must respect his wishes. I don't think he could decide on that course of action during one of his episodes. Therefore, it would be the lucid and logical man making it. The version of Nolan that recognizes the consequences of his actions."

"I won't lie. I'm surprised you agree with me."

Everett felt deflated, her response shutting down the fight he had prepared for. Her eyes found his, and he saw the shimmer of tears.

Eirian admitted, "I'm surprised myself. I should scream at you for suggesting it. I should command we do everything we can to stop him. But it's not about me. It's not about any of us."

No one said a thing.

Shaking her head, Eirian continued, "This is about him and his right to decide for himself. Nolan knows the coronation will happen, whether he is dead or alive. So if he wants to end things on his terms, I feel like we're selfish if we stop him."

Guilt filled Everett, and he crossed the space between them in a few quick strides to hug her, murmuring, "I'm sorry, Eirian. We're thinking about Endara, but you're thinking about your father. Nolan wouldn't want to end life in a pile of his shit, not knowing where he was, and no longer recognizing the faces of his loved ones."

Eirian buried her face in his shoulder to sob. Brenna stood and walked over to the pair of them, leaning against the table to stroke Eirian's hair and back gently while meeting Marcellus's steely gaze. He nodded and slipped out of the room, intending to send messages to the rest of the council to bring the coronation forward. It had to be done.

Pausing outside the door, Marcellus crooked his finger at Aiden and summoned him over. Then, holding the door open slightly, he signaled for Aiden to look at Eirian. Guilt crossed Aiden's face, closely followed by an expression Marcellus could not quite read.

"I don't know what's going on, but it must stop. We need to move the coronation forward. I don't care that you're Everett's bastard brother or the man many of my fellows would like to see beside her on the throne. If you can't do your job, then tell me so I can replace you."

Watching the conflict on Aiden's face, Marcellus felt sorry for him. He had been around long enough to recognize the signs of a man in love. It was an almost impossible position to be in.

"I know what my job is, Your Grace, and I do it to the best of my ability. I'll always do what I have to do to protect her." Aiden stepped back and saluted, adding, "Just as I did when we were small."

Marcellus stared at the man who reminded him of his dead friend. Yet, as much as Aiden looked like his father, Marcellus knew he was a very different man. Which was an excellent thing if people like Cameron got their way.

"She doesn't remember you, does she? Does she realize who you are?"

"No, she's never mentioned it. I'm sure she'd have used it against me if she did. I have no desire to remind her. I'd rather she thought I earned this position by skill, not because of the accident of my birth."

"That's a load of shit. You damn well deserve the position and more!" He knew the reasons Everett had chosen Aiden, and Marcellus agreed with them.

Giving him a crooked smile, Aiden shrugged and said, "I'll do my job. As I've always done the jobs given to me."

Satisfied with his answer, Marcellus did not feel there was anything more to say and stepped away. He made his way to the council chambers with his guards following, hoping to find several of the council already there and working. Entering the room, Marcellus saw his hope answered. Assuming the vacant position at the head of the table, he held up a hand and waited for all attention to be on him.

"We need to bring the coronation forward."

Ulric stood, crossing his arms and demanding, "Why? What has happened? Has His Majesty agreed to this?"

"Chancellor, you know I wouldn't be saying this if it wasn't necessary. The King is getting worse. He'd agree to it if he could do so."

The room burst into an uproar while the two men regarded each other coldly. Her hands slammed on the table, and Sabine brought them to silence. She got to her feet, meeting the gaze of each person there.

"I know you expect me to side with the financial interests of the kingdom, and I do. We're throwing Eirian a birthday celebration, and the cost wouldn't be much more to bring the coronation forward to that date."

"You realize the Duke of Raellwynt is telling us the King is declining faster than we thought he would." Another member of the council scolded her, "Have you no respect?"

Sabine narrowed her eyes and snarled. "Don't you dare talk to me about respect! King Nolan is the greatest man I know, and what is happening to him hurts deeply. We can grieve in our own time and in our ways. But, right now, we're in the council chambers of his kingdom, deciding things he needs us to do because he cannot. Do you understand?"

Nodding, Ulric sighed in defeat. "Sabine is right. We have to do our job. Bring the preparations forward to have the coronation on the day of her birthday. Hopefully, we have enough time, considering it's barely a month away."

"We have prepared coronations in less time," Marcellus said.

Ollier replied, "Only during times of war."

Cameron cleared his throat and said, "Aren't we preparing for a war? We've started receiving reports Athnaral is gathering at our border!"

"He's right. We need to have Eirian on the throne and officially in control of Endara. No questions over leadership can remain," another person added.

Sabine drummed her fingers on the table, watching Marcellus like a hawk, and said, "Has Eirian agreed? I can tell by how flustered you are that you've been with his majesty. If you're here without Tamantal, that suggests our princess knows things are bad. Does she know how bad?"

He nodded curtly and answered, "She knows. If Eirian refuses, we have no choice but to crown Everett."

"Does she understand, or are you assuming she understands? Have either of you overprotective brutes thought to sit her down and have the talk?"

The question brought murmurs of discussion around the room as they argued amongst themselves over who they preferred to ascend the throne. Marcellus scratched his head, waiting for them to quieten. Then, leaning back in the chair, he rested one arm on the table and slowly looked around. His gaze had many squirming in their seats, Sabine the only one willing to meet him with her challenging stare.

"I know many of you would prefer the Duke of Tamantal ascend to the throne. He has as strong a claim. His mother was the King Nolan's sister, his grandfather was the previous king. He's the heir you're familiar with, the one you don't doubt the loyalty of. He isn't a mage. Now, don't argue!"

Slamming his hand down hard on the table, Marcellus pushed himself up and leaned over it to point around the room.

"I don't care to hear arguments or lies about this. The fact Eirian is a mage makes everyone uncomfortable. We can't change that, so we must embrace what it could do for Endara. Everett won't take the throne unless she returns to Riane. He adores her, and he will defend her claim. They know what is at stake, believe me. Eirian will accept the crown."

"Besides, from what I heard, they offered her a perfectly valid alternative, and she refused it," Ulric added, refusing to elaborate.

They knew what he meant. Baenlin had made sure of that. Snorting, Marcellus got to his feet and left the table. Pausing halfway to the door, he looked at members of the council.

"You know what must happen. I'll inform Eirian."

Joining his guards outside, Marcellus shook his head, and they fell into step behind him. His absence had been long enough to have him wondering if Eirian would be where he left her. Marcellus decided it might be better if she was not. Stopping partway down the hall from the doors, he took in the mix of guards and sighed. The thought crossed his mind to head to the great hall and find a potent drink to hide in until Everett came looking. Reminding himself that delaying things would not help, Marcellus slipped through the door and ignored the guards.

Eirian was the first to look up. Her face was red and blotchy from crying, and her eyes showed how exhausted she felt.

"I can hazard a guess at what you were doing, and I want you to tell me why I shouldn't be angry."

"Then my news won't shock you," he replied, holding out a hand.

Brenna walked over to take his hand and leaned in to kiss him. They stood for a moment, their foreheads touching while they drew comfort from each other. Nudging Eirian, Everett pulled a disgusted face, hoping she would laugh at him, but she gave him a blank look and blinked. Marcellus draped his arm around Brenna's waist and turned to look at the pair sitting at the table.

"We're bringing the coronation forward to your birthday."

"So soon?" Eirian murmured.

"Sabine pointed out we're already having a celebration."

Resting her head on a hand, Eirian rubbed the back of her neck with the other and asked, "Is that everything?"

Crossing to Eirian, Marcellus crouched in front of her. "Eirian, with everyone here as witnesses, I need you to assure me you'll take the crown. There can be no doubts, no confusion. Either you say yes, or Everett has to."

"I've already said yes. Or so I thought. Is there some confusion?" Eirian frowned at him, head still resting on her hand.

"I'm serious, Eirian. You're about to become the Queen of Endara. Do you accept the crown and everything that comes with the position?"

Everett sat frozen, eyes wide as he stared at her, saying, "Answer him, Eirian."

"Yes, I accept the crown and everything that comes with being the Queen of Endara." Looking over at her father's gentlemen, Eirian asked, "Thomas, was that a simple enough answer? Do any of you have any doubt?"

"Don't be glib. Yes, that was clear enough, and we have enough witnesses. This isn't a game, Eirian. You'll be our queen in just over a month. You can't back out now." Marcellus squeezed her knee and glanced over his shoulder at Brenna.

"I can do it," she responded to his unspoken question.

Cracking her neck, Eirian stretched uncomfortably and said, "We should check on him. Hopefully, he's asleep, and when he wakes, he'll be himself again."

Thomas replied, "Let me. I'll stick my head through the door and see if I can spot him. We've gotten good at this."

"This is terrible. We're behaving like my father is a wild beast we're terrified of."

Nodding, Everett soothed her. "I know. You should rest. Things are going to get hectic with the coronation brought forward."

"If that's the case, could we please organize a hunt? Just a small one. I need to get out of this place for a morning," Eirian pleaded.

"I don't see why not? We can keep it quiet, just us, some guards, a few others. A pleasant ride would be nice."

Struggling to her feet, Eirian realized how sore she was feeling, and it showed. "I guess I hit the ground a few times harder than I thought."

"I have a word of advice for you, Eirian. You and Aiden need to sort out whatever is bothering you. You need to trust the captain of your guards," Marcellus grumbled, directing a frustrated look at Everett.

"He got a closer taste of my powers than he was ready for. That's all. One day Aiden will reconcile what he experienced with the reality that I feel things that aren't exclusive to men," she replied.

The men in the room looked at her in bafflement, and Eirian shrugged, turning to Brenna to ask, "Are you going to join me?"

Brenna smiled faintly, taking a moment to give Marcellus another kiss and ruffle his hair lovingly. "I'll come. We need to discuss your wardrobe for the coronation and the celebrations."

Horrified at the prospect, Eirian cringed. Alerted by the opening door, they watched a tired Thomas join them.

"Nolan is curled up at the end of his bed, asleep."

"Well, that's something. What else can we hope for?" Everett got to his feet and clapped a hand on Marcellus's shoulder. "I think I need a drink. Care to join me?"

Nodding and agreeing with the sentiment, Marcellus spoke to Thomas, "Will you be alright here? If anything happens, send someone to find us straight away."

"Of course, Your Grace, you have my word. We can handle this."

Annoyed, Eirian frowned at the men and snapped, "You will inform me as well."

They bowed, and she scoffed, following Brenna out of the chamber. Her ladies were hovering in the corridors, chattering with courtiers. The moment they saw Eirian, they excused themselves. They gathered around, reminding Eirian of a flock of sparrows over a crumb. Her guards circled them, and she noticed the shift had changed, leaving Merle in charge. When Merle saw her wry smile directed his way, he saluted. Once they reached Eirian's chambers, her ladies began asking questions.

Brenna put her hands on her hips and said, "That's enough! Yes, the coronation is being moved. Doesn't news spread fast among the idle? Now, your lady requires a bath. Food and drink as well. I think it's an evening for wine. Goodness knows I could use a drink."

THIRTEEN

Fingers moving with practiced ease, Eirian tugged the laces through the eyelets set into the leather jerkin and pulled them tight. There was knocking at the door, but she ignored it. Glancing at the window, she shook her head uneasily and finished tying off the laces. Picking up her bracers next, Eirian slipped them over her hands and made sure that the narrow cuffs of her linen shirt sat comfortably beneath the leather. Flexing her thumbs, she checked the reinforced leather was in the correct position to protect her skin from damage while using a bow.

Eirian used her teeth to pull the cords tight and stared into the chest of gear she kept well hidden from her ladies. The desire to flaunt more of their expectations weighed heavily on her mind. She crouched at the chest and shifted the linen cloth covering the twin blades Celiaen had given to her on her sixteenth birthday. Looking at them, Eirian smiled as she remembered how Celiaen had arrived in Riane the day before her birthday, bearing the freshly crafted blades.

Celiaen had beaten her shamelessly in training, making a show of their sparring before he presented them as a gift. Her fingertips rubbed a pommel, feeling the engravings cast into the metal. Eirian pictured how the engravings carried on past the hilt and guard, adding beauty to the weapons whose purpose was anything but beautiful. They were an identical pair and, though Celiaen never mentioned it, she knew they matched the pair of swords he bore.

"Your Highness!" Brenna shouted impatiently. "You're going to be late."

She quickly covered them and shut the chest before running her hand over the timber with a sigh. A touch of Eirian's power reminded the wards of their purpose. Her ladies and everyone else would continue not to notice it. Picking up her belt, she secured it around her waist. With a hand on each knife, Eirian worked wards to prevent anyone from seeing them. Usually, she only wore her knives when giving her guards the slip, but the urge to wear them hunting was undeniable. Once done, Eirian walked to the door and undid the latch, yanking it open to grin at the flustered group of ladies waiting on the other side.

"Good morning!"

"You're already dressed?" Brenna walked around her in a circle, shaking her head at what Eirian was wearing.

"I've been awake for a while. Didn't see the point of waiting for you."

Reaching fingers out, Isabella touched the leather armor in admiration, murmuring, "I haven't seen this in your wardrobe. Where did it come from? The craftsmanship is wonderful."

Eirian glanced at the disapproving expression Brenna wore and smirked faintly. "It was there. Fayleen made it for me."

"Are you sure you wish to let members of the court see you dressed like this? It's hardly appropriate for the future queen," Brenna said.

Making her way over to the wardrobe, Brenna opened the doors. She began rummaging through the garments stored within for something she felt was more suitable.

"Quite sure. We'll be riding in the woods for most of the day. So if anyone has an issue with my clothing, they can learn to keep their mouths shut."

The four younger ladies gasped, looking between Eirian and Brenna fearfully. Growing stress from the approaching coronation had resulted in more than a few fights between the two strong-willed women. Grinding her teeth, Brenna forced herself to say nothing and shut the wardrobe. Eirian stepped around the other ladies, and going through to the next chamber, she saw they had laid out a light breakfast. Pleased to see the kitchen had provided her favorite, Eirian selected a warm pastry and looked at the ladies in amusement.

"You're not coming hunting, are you? You look more suited to a stroll in the city."

Bea looked excited, smoothing hands over her pale-yellow dress, and answered, "My brother is going. I'm looking forward to spending some time with him."

"It's the first official royal hunt in a while, so of course we're coming!" Brenna snapped.

Biting into the pastry, Eirian sighed. Finishing the food quickly, she selected an apple. She devoured it, leaving the core on the table while her companions nibbled daintily at the food in their hands. Then, rubbing her hands on her trousers, Eirian quickly returned to her chamber to fetch her freshly strung bow. It was in her bow quiver, slung over the chair with the quiver full of arrows. Slinging the straps over her head and shoulder, Eirian let the weight settle against her back.

Wide-eyed, her ladies watched her cross the room to the door, her gaze sliding over the guards. Hearing them scramble to follow, Eirian did not bother to slow her pace. Determined to get to the courtyard before it became chaotic, she ignored the greetings of courtiers and nobles as she strode through the corridors of the keep. She caught the flustered whispers of the ladies, and her mouth curled up in a satisfied grin. Eirian hoped a couple of them would decide they did not want to go hunting after all.

Passing through the keep's entrance, it frustrated Eirian to find the courtyard filled with horses as the Master of the Hunt oversaw preparations. The number of horses made her heart sink. It was the last sign she would not get the outing she wanted. Early morning light gave the surrounding walls an ethereal glow that did not help the sense of unease simmering below the surface of her mind as she took in the scene.

Spotting Everett in discussion with another man, Eirian nodded when he saw her, his eyes wide with surprise. She searched through the horses until she spotted her beloved brown gelding. Halcyon stood patiently with a young man clinging to his reins, and approaching them, she held her hands out. Eirian cooed softly as his muzzle touched her skin, the whiskers tickling her palm.

Standing next to Halcyon, Eirian gently ran her hands over his ears and neck, scratching at his favorite spots. It was her chance to check him for any problems as she inspected his legs and tack. While she murmured to Halcyon, the young man stared in awe, his grip on the reins slack. He had never seen a noble take as much care with their mount as Eirian was, and he could not help but admire her. The moment she looked at him, he jolted upright, standing as tall as he could manage with his eyes downcast.

"How has my boy been?"

Stammering, he smiled at the horse and answered, "He's a total gent in the stables, Your Highness!"

"Good boy, Halcyon." Rubbing his neck, Eirian noticed Everett threading his way through the mess of people and horses. "I'm going to need your patience today, my love."

Removing the quivers from her back, Eirian unbuckled the straps and secured them to her saddle while the curious servant watched. Attaching the larger flat bow quiver against Halcyon's flank with the arrow quiver on top, she stepped back to observe the crowd. Hand on her hip, Eirian resisted the urge to touch the knives secured there. When Everett arrived, his eyes took her in.

"This is not what I asked for," she said.

"Morning."

Waving at the surrounding mess, Eirian huffed. "I thought we were going to have a few of us out for a serious hunt, not this big show."

"What did you expect? Nearly everyone has arrived for your coronation. They want to see you in action outside of the court and council. Everyone has their little birds."

Everett stepped up to Halcyon and studied the bow and quivers before glancing at Eirian. He had not seen them since arriving in Amath from the Riane border when he collected her. She focused her attention on her hands as she tugged at her bracers and flexed her wrists, knowing she would not have many options to adjust them once they were riding.

Eirian grumbled, "The day is getting lighter. Anyone not ready to go can either miss out or catch up."

Before Everett could stop her, Eirian slipped her foot into the stirrup, quickly pulling herself into the saddle. Then, holding her hand out for the servant to pass her the reins, Eirian leaned down to make sure the girth was tight enough with her weight settled into the saddle. Understanding he would not get any more conversation out of her, Everett hurried to his horse and signaled for the Master of the Hunt to sound the horn.

Eirian looked over the flurry of activity while ensuring she could draw her bow without obstruction. Her guards mounted, staying at her side as her ladies guided their horses over. Their dresses were a bright collection that contrasted with her dull grays and browns. Shaking her head, Eirian watched the Master of the Hunt give the signal for them to move out and nudged Halcyon into a walk, aiming to be near the lead. The man she had seen talking to Everett appeared beside her, grinning happily.

"Your Highness! Isn't it a beautiful morning?"

"Lord Gallagher, a pleasure. You're right, it is a beautiful morning. What a pity this gaggle of birds ruined the hunt."

His grin faded when Gallagher realized she was serious, and he looked back at his sister, taking in Bea's anxious expression.

Scratching his head, he shrugged and said, "Everyone wants to see you. We're a little jealous of the time Tamantal and Raellwynt get to spend with you. I heard you're good with a sword, but I didn't expect to see you armed with a bow today."

Tossing his head, Halcyon snorted, showing his impatience with the group's slow pace as they wound their way through the outer bailey towards the bridge. Rubbing his neck, Eirian soothed him.

"We're going hunting. What did you expect me to have if not a bow?"

"Nothing, I guess, like the other ladies. I'm not sure why when everyone talks about how different you are."

"Gallagher, are you already putting your foot in it?" Everett said, joining them.

"Of course! You know I'm hopeless," he answered.

She could not help chuckling, and Eirian shook her head at the two men. "I suppose you think you can keep up with me?"

Leaning forward in his saddle, Everett eyed her curiously and replied, "I don't see why not. Are you suggesting we attempt to abandon this lot and race?"

"Are you suggesting I should suggest it?" Eirian challenged, relaxing in the saddle as they crossed the bridge.

People watched them crossing into the city. It was a novelty to see nobility riding out early to go hunting. Tense, the guards guided their horses closer to the two royals, and Everett checked his sword where it hung from his belt. Eirian took in the watching people. The feeling of unease returned, leaving the back of her neck prickling.

Eirian knew the people would get a wash of her power, the magic responding to her emotions despite the iron grip she was exercising over it. However, she was doing her best to keep it under wraps. Glancing down at her belt, Eirian reassured herself that her two knives were there, the wards working well from the lack of attention the short blades had garnered.

"Is everything okay, Your Highness?"

Aiden's voice stirred her from her observation of the crowds. Other riders watched on, and Eirian shook her head at him, offering Everett and Gallagher a faint smile.

She replied quietly, "Sorry, I was away with the clouds."

Gallagher leaned forward in his saddle and asked, "Do you mind if we talk? I have so many questions about Riane."

"Most people have questions, but very few ask. Instead, they prefer to believe what they've been told all their lives."

People shared embarrassed looks, knowing Eirian referred to the many stories surrounding her childhood departure to study with the mages. Rolling his eyes, Everett nudged his horse forward and joined the Master of the Hunt at the front of the column. Staring at his back, Eirian frowned before turning her attention to Gallagher.

"Yes, my lord, please ask some of your questions."

"I've read all mages train in things other than magic to help with their, well, you know."

There was a childlike giddiness to him that made Eirian smile.

"I know, and yes, everyone must have a skill that helps them. It's the mundane side of our power. A warrior is only a warrior if they have the tools to fight. Without those tools, they're just another person. So I guess the easiest order to explain it with is the greens." Eirian paused before she continued. "Magic can only heal so much. They still need ointments, potions, and bandages. Greens spend half their life learning to craft those things as an aide."

They exchanged looks, but no one dared stare at her as intently as Gallagher as he said, "That's incredible. I thought magic was the only thing you needed."

"The greater your power, the less you need to rely on other tools, but the more they encourage you to do so."

Closing her eyes, Eirian felt the shift in the air as they passed through the gate into the open spaces beyond the city. It tempted her to use her magic to read the land. Doing so would give her a clear vision of what they would encounter in the woods. Pushing the idea aside, she returned her focus to Gallagher.

"I'm told they consider you one of the more powerful mages. What are your skills?"

Holding the reins loosely in one hand, Eirian met his gaze and watched as his eyes followed as she dropped her free hand to caress the upper limb of her bow where it sat free of the quiver. It was a slow action, intended to carry the hint of a threat.

"You'll be sorely disappointed to hear I have no great skill outside of fighting."

"So, you're a red? A warrior mage?"

"Something like that, yes," Eirian replied.

Sounding a horn, the Master of the Hunt drew their attention to where he held his horse in check at the front. Nodding to Gallagher, Eirian gathered the reins to prepare for the pace to increase and nudged Halcyon into a canter. Her ears delighted in the sound of hooves pounding over the ground, briefly appreciating the number of riders. There was a soft breeze, and Eirian inhaled deeply, looking at the trees they were approaching.

Gallagher held back, allowing his sister to join him. The other ladies remained a small distance behind, dresses fluttering like colorful flags. They were not the only women among the group, all as brightly colored as the ladies-in-waiting, and many men matched their brightness. Her guards remained close, and she counted them out, calculating the best way to break free of the group to get a good run in. She encouraged Halcyon forward to come up beside Everett.

Eirian said, "This lot is going to frighten off any potential quarry."

Everett looked back at them and shrugged, replying, "The primary concern of this hunt is letting people see you."

"Just be careful, cousin. There is something in the air today."

Startled by her comment, Everett wanted to demand an explanation. They crossed into the shadow of the woods, the trees causing them to slow down and spread out further. It was cooler beneath the canopy of leaves, their shades of green glimmering where the light caught them. Frowning as they trotted along the paths between trunks, Eirian felt the nervous prickle on her skin return. Sensing her tension, Halcyon snorted, tossing his head and causing the horse next to him to dance sideways nervously. Giving her a sharp look, Aiden moved closer and ignored the looks given to him by the nobles.

"Ma'am, something is bothering you."

"It's nothing, Aiden."

Remaining blank-faced to hide his disbelief, Aiden signaled to the other guards and received nods of understanding. Picking up his wordless commands to his men, other guards became more alert.

He muttered, "I watch you, Princess, and I know when you're on edge."

"Don't be silly. It's just disappointment since we won't see any quarry."

Eirian shook her head, smiling at him brightly. She reminded herself if she was genuinely concerned, she could use her magic. It would be nothing to read the land. Cocking his head to the side, Aiden squinted at her.

"I know why you want to hunt. I'm trying, Princess, but some of us know what we're sensing from you, even if the rest of them don't."

Giving him a dark look, Eirian guided her horse towards the Master of the Hunt.

When she came up beside him, Eirian said, "I think we should split the group. Those of us who want a good chase can go one way, while those interested in a pleasant ride can go in another. If we're lucky, their noise will flush out some prey."

"That's good thinking, Your Highness. I'll pass the word. Serious hunters can drop to the back and let the rest go on ahead."

He whistled, calling one of his assistants over. Dropping back to join Everett, Eirian smiled at him.

"We're splitting up so serious hunters can have some sport," she murmured.

"How do you propose we split up?" he said, ducking as a low branch crossed his path.

"We're going to drop to the back of the group and let them continue. It won't be hard to find them again when we're ready."

His jaw clenched for a moment before he conceded, slowing his horse down to allow others to pass them. "You know the guards won't like it."

"Then they can stay with the other party. I want to hunt, not casually ride through the trees, admiring the scenery!" Eirian snapped, ignoring the angry look from Aiden.

They silently watched as several noblemen steadily dropped back through the ranks of riders as they were. Eirian's ladies had not realized what was going on and remained mixed in with the rest of the group. Finally, when there was enough of a gap between the two groups, Eirian turned her horse in a different direction. As they got further from the rest, the woods settled into a quiet thrum, the beat of hooves on the hard ground the only thing out of place.

Holding up a hand, one of Everett's guards signaled for them to stop and dismounted, a hunter joining him. They crouched over something on the forest floor and murmured to each other while the rest of the group waited. Eirian watched their body language from her place and noted the sudden tension between the two men. She dismounted and walked to the crouching men, relaxing her grip on powers. Everett followed her.

"What is it?" Crouching, Eirian looked at the pile of droppings on the ground with a frown and grunted. "It's horse shit. You stopped us for horse shit?"

The guard huffed, looking at his lord when Everett crouched beside Eirian. "Your Grace, what do you think?"

"I'm with Her Highness. It looks like horse shit," Everett answered.

"I told you, there shouldn't be any here," grumbling, the huntsman sat back on his haunches. "Your Highness, Your Grace, I think poachers have been through in the last few hours. Our people haven't started hunting for the coronation feast yet."

Peering at the pile in question, Eirian was hesitant to admit how much time she had spent handling manure when she was younger. "We might be in for a different sort of hunt now. That's not been on the ground for long."

The thought thrilled her, and Eirian glanced at Aiden.

"What are you suggesting?" Everett glanced at the party.

"They might still be in the woods. We should send someone to warn the rest and then see if we can find their trail. I assume you're a half-decent tracker?" she questioned the huntsman and watched the realization appear in his eyes.

"That sounds like a great hunt!" Chuckling, a nobleman slapped his leg in delight and exclaimed, "Bit of the King's justice! We can make an example of the bastards."

Rubbing his nose, Gallagher corrected him, "You mean Queen's justice, don't you, Adalardo?"

Bowing to Eirian, he did not protest the unspoken chastisement. "Exactly what I meant."

"You think we should warn the others?" Another asked.

Everett stood, dusting his hands off, and replied, "Absolutely. We're assuming poachers, but we don't know for sure. It would be better to warn them to keep an eye out. Lorne, this seems like a task for you."

His guard saluted and turned his horse, pushing the animal into a canter back the way they had come. Remounting, they watched the hunter follow the path on foot for a short distance as he looked for further signs. Once he was sure they had a trail to follow, he returned to them. He remounted as well, looking at the group with a frown, before focusing on Eirian.

"What is it?" Eirian prompted.

"The timing seems odd. Why would anyone risk poaching from here with all the preparations about to start? I mean, we've people out here surveying the herds, so it's twice as risky. Plus, I'm sure there are tracks for a least four horses."

Agreeing with his concerns, Eirian stared into the distance with a frown. She glanced at the guards surrounding the group of nobles. They were well-armed, but she wondered how many of them had fought in a forest before. It was not a question she would ask or admit her own experience. Eirian shook her head and shrugged, her action breaking the layer of tension that had settled on the group. The hunter took the lead, guiding them at a steady pace.

"You should let us return you to the castle." Aiden leaned towards her to say, "He's correct. This doesn't seem right."

"I'm glad we agree on something, Aiden. It's an awful coincidence, isn't it?" Eirian murmured, watching him from the corner of her eye.

Aiden stiffened, unprepared for her agreement. "Then let's go back, now, before we go any further."

The prickle over her skin tempted Eirian to go along with him. At the back of her mind, something prompted her to return to the city. Then she noticed the way the noblemen were glancing at her with admiration. Eirian knew she could use the situation to gain their respect. None of them needed to know they were not in danger. Or that she could find their quarry without taking another step.

"I'm sorry, Aiden, but don't worry, I'll make sure nothing happens to your pretty face."

"As you wish, Princess," Aiden muttered. "But it's not my pretty face I'm worried about."

He remained with her, the irritated set of his jaw warning Eirian he would not leave her side. Their progress was slow, the hunter bringing them to a halt every so often so he could double-check they were going the right way. Eirian could feel the building of anticipation among the men and tried her best to keep her eagerness in check. If she let her control slip, she would spoil the hunt. While they waited for the huntsman to return, she shifted to look around.

Eirian felt it coming, and her magic compelled her to reach for her bow moments before men came crashing through the low scrub. Her hold faltered as Eirian pulled an arrow from the quiver and nocked it. The power located a target as she drew back and loosed. Eirian knew it would find its mark. The guards dismounted, engaging with the attackers while the noblemen attempted to surround her. Snarling, Eirian tossed the bow to Gallagher and dove from the saddle. She ducked around the hands that tried to grab her to keep her out of the fray.

"Eirian!" Everett shouted.

Her name drew the attention of the men attacking, and Eirian pulled the knives free, magic surrounding her like a storm cloud. Shocked, the guards swung between protecting her and killing the attackers. Aiden called her name, yelling orders to the men and pushing towards her. Taking advantage of the confusion, a man lunged for Eirian. His swing found nothing as she pirouetted out of his strike and brought her knife up to slice at his arm.

Seeing blood seeping through his sleeve, the man glanced at her in shock, but Eirian kept moving quicker than he could, kicking dirt at him as her next strike found his abdomen. Eirian's instincts warned of another running towards them, magic thrumming while guiding her movements as she brought the blood-covered blade around for a dive at the next man. It was a familiar dance, one she could not help but love. The smell of blood fueled her rage, urging Eirian to surrender, and at the back of her mind, she felt a distant pull again.

Less shocked than his dying companion, her next target threw his sword to the side and armed himself with his knife, crouching in a fighter's stance. He felt the magic rolling off Eirian and knew he did not stand a chance. If she did not get him, the guards would. All he hoped was to cause some damage on his way down.

He snarled. "You bitch!"

Grinning, Eirian made another strike, her blade catching him under his ribs before he defended. It was followed by several more quicker slices, blood welling on each one. She toyed with him, taking delight in dragging out the kill.

"A pity you can't land a blow on a lady. They should've sent real men," she said mockingly.

Opening his mouth to respond, he lost the chance when Eirian lunged, and the blade struck his throat. Her magic told her they had dealt with the rest of the attackers. Pushing her feelings aside, Eirian turned to assess the rest of the group. Knowing they were fine, Eirian ignored the noblemen and paced back to the first man she had struck, crouching next to his dying form as his hands grasped at his stomach. She knew what he saw when he started begging, fear filling his eyes. Eirian stared at him, knives remaining in her hands.

"Who sent you?"

He turned his head, looking at the still forms of his companions. They were all dead, and he knew he was next.

"Do what you want. I'm dying anyway, bitch."

Her lips curled, and Eirian used one of her blades to poke at his gut. It took the edge off the urging of her magic. She slid the tip along the wound, slicing through flesh and muscle while avoiding organs. He fought the urge to scream, agony ripping through him.

She chuckled coldly. "Yes, you are, slowly. It's not a pleasant way to die. You know who I am. Did they tell you what I'm capable of?"

"Your Highness?"

Aiden approached warily, the other guards at his back with weapons still in hand. She shifted, keeping her eyes on the dying man in front of her with a smile.

"Yes, Aiden?"

He took another step closer, the only one allowed to approach. Close behind, Gabe looked eager to join her, but a tight hand on his arm kept him back. Everyone had dismounted, remaining beside their horses nervously. Everett stood between the noblemen and the guards, his sword bloody and eyes wide. She sensed them, their fear of her more potent than their fear of another attack, but the smell of death made her uncaring. Eirian looked at Aiden and cocked her head, waiting for him to speak.

"We should end him quickly," he said.

The prospect of killing the man brought her bloodlust back, and Eirian watched Aiden shudder when he felt it. She licked her lips, imagining what she would do if he relaxed his scruples and joined her.

"Please, Princess."

"I'll end him quickly. After he sings for me."

Turning back to the man, Eirian lifted a knife and smiled slowly. Running a finger along the blade, she let blood coat her finger. Her eyes followed the drops decorating her skin, the whispers singing in her mind.

"They didn't warn you, did they? Well, I'll tell you how this works." Eirian purred. "The quicker you answer my questions, the quicker your pain ends."

Spitting at her, the attacker tried to cling to a semblance of defiance. His defiance became pained sobs when Eirian shrugged and pressed the tip of the blade into the wound on his arm, knowing he could not move out of it with the grip he had on his stomach. It slid under his skin, slicking through it.

"Fuck you, bitch, just kill me."

"You've never encountered a red mage before, have you? As soon as you felt my magic, you knew this attack was screwed. Your masters sent you to die, and you could've run, but you didn't. Makes me wonder what frightens you so much about your masters that you would die for them like this?"

Leaning in, Eirian touched his face with the handle of the knife, digging into his flesh and making him sob. Ignoring the blood as she caressed his cheek, Eirian let her magic flood into him. She heard the gasps of horror behind her when he screamed in pain, her use of her power making him feel everything so much more keenly. Able to feel his heart racing in terror, Eirian used it against him. Each beat increased the pain he endured.

The fear experienced by the rest of the group fed her bloodlust, and she turned it on her victim. Eirian knew she would regret it later, but she wanted to know who would dare attack them like this. After the attack in the alley months earlier, she had suspicions, but she needed them confirmed. Cutting off her power, she removed her hand and the knife.

"Please, just kill me," he begged when he could speak again.

"Who wants me dead?"

"I don't know his name. I didn't talk to him. The boss did," he answered and looked towards the watching men.

A hand lifted pleadingly, and he hoped one of them would intervene. Fear of Eirian meant none of them dared to move.

Clicking her tongue, Eirian shook her head and said, "I believe you. It's hard to lie to me when I can feel the beat of your heart. What did you see?"

"Will you kill me?"

"Yes, I will. What did you see?"

"Athnaralan uniforms."

"And the nightmares?"

The question slipped from her tongue before Eirian could stop it. She was unsure why she asked, but remembering the man in the alley, she figured it was worth it.

"They started after the Athnaralans came, but they never said you were a red mage. Maybe the boss would have turned them down if they had."

Staring at him for a moment longer, Eirian shrugged before quickly driving her knife into his chest. His answer had not surprised her. Instead, it had confirmed her niggling suspicion that something was not right.

"I'm not a red mage. I'm something far worse."

Wiping her blades off on his clothes, she surveyed the bodies. Eirian caught sight of one of her guards on the ground with another kneeling beside him. Her gaze darkened, and she snarled at Aiden when he tried to stop her from approaching. There was a touch of her bloodlust remaining, but the magic knew the fight was over.

"He's gone."

"I've had a bad feeling since I woke. This is my fault! I should've checked."

"You've been trying to keep your secrets." Keeping his grip on her arm tight, Aiden eyed the knives and said, "I didn't spot those."

She slipped them into their sheaths and shut off the wards. "That's because I didn't want you to."

Hearing another approach, Aiden let go of her and stepped back. There was horror in Everett's eyes as he looked between Eirian and the man they had witnessed her kill. Seeing the look on his face made her go cold, and Eirian turned to stare at the other noblemen with varying degrees of fear emanating from them. None of them held a weapon, though Gallagher stood with her bow limply in his grasp.

"Look at me!" Everett commanded. "You tortured that man, and you knew exactly what you were doing."

"Yes."

His face grew ashen, and the enormity of her statement dawned on him. "By the powers, Eirian, you've done it before."

"Maybe it's for the best you realize what I'm capable of. I hadn't planned on telling you like this, though," Eirian replied.

"Or at all, I'd guess."

Looking at Everett sadly, she waved at the watchers and said, "You view me like I'm any other woman. You smile and chuckle at the idea I can swing a sword, and you shake your heads when you see me wearing trousers. You pretend that even though I'm a mage, I'm a harmless little princess. But I'm not, and I never have been. It was a mistake to keep that from you."

"Was it an Athnaralan the last time you had to kill?"

Recalling the man in the alley outside the fighting house, Eirian nodded. "Yes, it was. There have been others, more than I care to admit."

The guards who had charged off into the trees, searching for any more attackers, returned. They dragged the hunter's dead body and the body of an attacker with an arrow in his throat. It confirmed what she already knew. Her aim was perfect. Sighing, Everett rubbed his face and turned to a guard.

"We need to make sure the others are safe. Then we need to get these bodies back to the city and dealt with."

Gallagher approached and crouched beside the body with Eirian's arrow in him, asking, "How did you spot him?"

"I didn't. I felt him. Unfortunately, too late. I let you down and put you in danger with my negligence." Eirian took her bow from him and looked it over before reaching down to pull the arrow from the corpse.

"I don't know how your power works, but can you sense anyone else?"

Taking a deep breath, Eirian closed her eyes and let her magic spread through the woods. She sensed the trees and animals continuing their lives. Reaching the forest edge, Eirian was thankful not to feel the thrum of human life. Pulling back to herself abruptly, it startled Eirian when she felt Aiden's hands holding her steady.

"There is nothing, and the others have left the woods."

"Can all mages do that?" Gallagher asked with a hint of excitement.

"Some can." Leaning on Aiden, Eirian said, "Thank you."

"Are you able to ride?" Everett asked with concern.

Nodding, Eirian glanced at the horses. None of them needed to know the real reason she leaned on Aiden. The touch of his hands provided a tether for her focus, a distraction from the death. Meeting his gaze, Eirian wanted to pull Aiden closer, her magic demanding a different satisfaction. His lips twitched, the gleam in his eyes informing Eirian he knew what she wanted.

She murmured, "I'm fine."

"We should leave a handful of guards here while the rest of us return to the castle. We can send more men to fetch the bodies and cart them back. It's too hard to shift them ourselves," Everett said, and Eirian admired how easily he took command.

"That sounds like the best option." Gallagher agreed.

Pushing away from Aiden, Eirian turned to face the others and watched as they stared at her uncomfortably. "I'm sorry you witnessed this. I recognize that what you saw doesn't make you any more comfortable that I'm a mage."

"Do you think—" Everett spoke.

"We know the reports about Athnaral, and this is not the first time they've attacked me. With that in mind, aren't you glad you know I'm not squeamish about killing someone? If we must go to war, I can do what needs to be done."

They glanced at each other, and Eirian smiled, spotting relief on some faces as they agreed with her statement. Then, turning back to Aiden, she nodded to him, and he saluted.

"Organize the men to remain."

Aiden gathered guards, doling out instructions while Eirian and the others mounted their horses. Cursing herself for failing to use her magic to search the woods at the beginning of the hunt, Eirian slid the bow into the quiver before hauling herself into the saddle. Once they were ready to leave, Aiden remained close, his presence reassuring. There was no excited chatter, the air of anticipation long gone and replaced with a mixture of regret, grief, and horror.

"I'm surprised you aren't furious with me. Everyone here got a good hit of that bloodlust you are so uncomfortable about me having. Plus, you know… the whole holding out on you about what I can do," Eirian murmured.

Aiden clenched his jaw, and she saw his hands tighten on his reins. "You never told me you'd killed."

Arching a brow, she shrugged and answered, "Why would I? I'm not proud of it. I don't like that I enjoy it."

"Knowing you know what it feels like to kill changes everything. I watched you, and I've never seen you move like that in the ring. I've no problem admitting it frightened and gave me pleasure."

"I'm sorry. I shouldn't have kept the truth from you."

Aiden asked, "Could you have killed all of them on your own?"

Swallowing, she nodded in confirmation. There were shouts from ahead, and the guards drew their swords. They relaxed when they saw guards from the castle moving through the trees, and Everett pushed to the front to meet the incoming men.

"We're glad to find you. Everyone else is back at the castle already." The guard saluted and said, "Looks like you found the poachers."

"What happened?" Everett asked.

"The Ensaycalan delegation arrived. They sent us for you and Princess Eirian. The Duke of Raellwynt thought you'd want to return when you found out who was in the group."

Tossing her head up, Eirian demanded, "Who is it?"

"Your Highness, it's Prince Celiaen."

She gasped, the announcement not what she was expecting to hear. Knowing Celiaen was in Amath, Eirian recalled the pull she had felt during the fight and knew it was their bond.

Eirian said, "If you keep going down that path, you'll find the poachers and some of our men keeping watch."

"I'll send one of my men back to the castle with you for a cart," he replied and saluted again, signaling for his troops to get out of the way.

They pushed their horses into a trot, trying to make their way out of the trees as quickly as they could manage. No one spoke. Their minds focused on getting back to the castle. Lost in her thoughts, Eirian felt a seed of suspicion niggling at the back of her mind. She could not help wondering why the elves had arrived on the same day men had attacked her party. Brenna had not been the only one to mention the rumors to her about Paienven setting his sights on Endara, rumors she could not wait to put to rest.

The prospect of seeing Celiaen filled her with excitement. He was precisely the friend she needed. He was not the only one she looked forward to reuniting with. Galameyvin would soothe her worries in a way that only a blue could manage. Casting a look in Aiden's direction, Eirian wondered how he would handle her closeness to the two princes. Aiden caught her glance, and his eyes narrowed in suspicion.

FOURTEEN

Eirian had never encountered her ladies as quiet as they were, trailing behind her to the gardens. When her party had reached the castle, the first group had stared in shock at the blood covering Eirian and half the guards. It was not long before the story of what happened spread, and she felt the horror and awe directed at her. Brenna had been less scandalized than others, a grim set to her face as she attempted to draw Eirian to her quarters to clean up. She had lost to Eirian's desire to see her friends when a hovering messenger revealed Celiaen was waiting in the gardens.

Pausing in the arch, Eirian caught sight of his back and froze. The familiar touch of his power woke hers, the exhaustion that had been closing in vanishing, taking her confusion over him being alone with it. Eirian needed a moment to take in the view of Celiaen with his head tilted back in the sunshine, short dark hair a ruffled mess. With a smile, Eirian turned to her ladies and shook her head.

"Please stay here."

Brenna crossed her arms and said, "No!"

"You can see us. I have fresh guards, and Merle won't let anything happen. But I'd like some privacy to greet my friend," she replied with a nod at the guards.

"He'd understand why we're there."

"No, he wouldn't. The elves don't have the same ridiculous notions of propriety."

Her gaze got darker, and Brenna forced herself to take a deep breath before she let her eyes linger on the dark stain on one of Eirian's sleeves, the reminder making her step back.

"We'll be here watching."

"Thank you, Brenna, that's all I ask."

Eirian turned to the garden and sauntered over to Celiaen, her boots sounding loud against the pathway. She wanted to run and throw herself at him like she would have done anywhere else. He turned to watch her approach, and Celiaen did not smile. It was clear he could tell something had happened. His gaze dropped to her knives before returning to her face as Eirian stood in front of him. They stared at each other silently, magic rejoicing in their reunion like the familiar friends they were.

Finally smiling, Celiaen closed the space between them and wrapped his arms around Eirian, pulling her into a tight hug. It was an effort to keep from falling into his warmth, but she knew they were being watched. Celiaen buried his face in her hair, ignoring the way she stiffened before relaxing into his familiar embrace. Pressing her face to his neck, Eirian let him hold her, his presence bringing her peace. He smelled clean and freshly washed, but soap had not banished the familiar scent of him she found comforting.

"Song of my song," she murmured.

Celiaen answered, "Blade of my blade."

Tightening her hold on him, Eirian forgot about their audience. Her hands gripped the midnight blue silk, and she did not want to let go, even though she knew she had to. She felt Celiaen move, his lips pressing a kiss to her forehead. Tilting her head back slightly, Eirian met his gaze, wishing he had kissed her lips instead.

"Powers, I've missed you, Ree, so very much."

"I missed you too, Celi." Pulling back, Eirian looked him over and chuckled. "You look fancy."

Grinning, Celiaen bowed and said, "Well, I thought I should look my best to meet the Princess of Endara."

Pulling a face, Eirian waved at her clothes and shrugged sheepishly. "My ladies wanted me to clean up before I saw you, but I've missed you so much I couldn't wait."

"What happened? You know you can't lie to me."

He grew serious and reached for her belt, drawing a knife from its sheath. Eirian watched him bring the blade to his nose, taking in the flutter of his eyelids as his power wrapped around them. It whispered to hers over the bond, stirring the feelings she had banished on the ride back.

"They attacked us. I lost one guard and a huntsman. They lost all of theirs. Celi, please control yourself. I'm tired, but the lust is still fresh."

Celiaen offered the knife and let her return it to its place, giving her a knowing look. Sensing something, he looked at the gateway where her ladies stood in a nervous cluster with her guards, watching them. He knew what concerned Eirian and regretted not meeting her in her quarters.

"I felt it, you know, all the way here in the keep. We must have come close to crossing paths, and if we'd gotten here earlier, you wouldn't have gone out. But I felt it. It called me through our bond, and I wanted to get back on my horse and find you."

"I'm glad you didn't. We make a bigger mess together."

"You bring out the worst in me."

Eirian shook her head, clenching her fists. "I don't do it on purpose."

"Ree," he said, but flinched, running a hand through his hair nervously. "We heard your father is abdicating. What is going on here?"

"My father is ill, and his health is failing. So rather than waiting, they passed the rule to me. You arrived in time for my coronation. I'm sure you weren't expecting to attend that when you left Ensaycal. Your coming has caused a fair bit of upset among my council. There are rumors your father wants to invade us."

Turning her back on him, Eirian moved away and stood in front of a flowering bush. She admired the hard work the gardeners had put in to tame the place after her meltdown. Celiaen followed, coming to stand behind her with a hand on her shoulder. His touch was a comfort. It was always a comfort.

"You know I'd never let him do that."

"Why have you come, Celiaen?"

Stiffening at her tone, Celiaen sighed. "It's Athnaral. Our spies send word that King Aeyren is mustering his army to invade Endara."

"Our spies tell a similar story about Ensaycal. Do you know how it makes me appear to my council? I swear the elves would never invade us and that my friendship with their crown prince means something. Then we receive reports that your father is maneuvering his troops." Glancing at him darkly, Eirian watched his shoulders slump.

"I swear to you, we aren't invading. My family has held a treaty with yours for longer than my father has been king. Endara is our ally, and we'd only ever come to your aid."

"So, your army is preparing to come to our rescue if Athnaral invades?"

"On my honor and the bond between us."

Eirian reached out and touched a flower, stroking the silky petals. "And you had nothing to do with the attack today? You know they'll suggest it."

"I'd never harm you. We're mates, and hurting you would harm me. They probably waited for an opportunity, and it was a coincidence we arrived today."

"My people might be less willing to believe you than I am."

Chuckling, Celiaen rubbed her shoulders and glanced at her people, murmuring, "They don't understand our bond. You're to be queen. It's not their place to question you."

Pulling away from him, Eirian walked along the path to sit on a bench. Like a shadow, Celiaen followed her, and she studied the embroidery decorating his coat. Her eyes found the twin swords at his waist. The match for the pair hidden in her chamber.

"Our laws allow for such questioning. The throne is not absolute for me, as it is for your father or Athnaral. The nobles have the power to refuse me. It has happened in the past, and it's not too late for them to give the crown to Everett—"

Interrupting, Celiaen asked, "What did you do?"

"I used my powers to get answers. They witnessed me torture and kill. They didn't appear to like it as much as you do. Even the guards were a bit thrown." Laying back on the bench, she groaned. "I've been hiding from them, and they didn't know what I can do."

There was concern in his dark brown eyes as Celiaen stared at her. He understood how much her actions cost her. It made him regret Galameyvin was in Telmia because of him. Pushing aside his guilt, Celiaen assured himself he could provide any comfort Eirian needed.

"You have no shield. You shouldn't have engaged."

"You forget, Celi, I'm a purple, not a red. I can control it."

"I've been there with you."

"Yes, and it was your blade with mine, your lust feeding mine. If Riane thought I was a danger, they would have assigned me a blue."

Celiaen growled in frustration as he turned his back on her. He remembered the letters from Fayleen, the words that had prompted him to come to Amath.

"Riane wants you back! I know about the grand mage. She was failing before you left, but they had to let you go. The only way they can gain you is for you to refuse your place here or for your people to rebel and cast you down."

"I know. Your uncle is certain those things will happen. He said my people will never accept a mage queen."

"That sounds like something Baenlin would say." Swallowing, Celiaen dropped onto the bench opposite Eirian and said, "Fay wrote to warn me of his plans."

Eirian frowned, turning her head to watch him. The stone was chilly against her cheek, and the rough scratching at her skin banished her desire to sleep.

"Celi, where is Gal? I can't feel him nearby, and I expected him to be waiting with you."

It had been a long time since she had seen Celiaen go so still that they could have carved him from stone. The moment he blinked, the illusion ended, and Eirian watched an emotion flicker through his eyes that she did not recognize.

"He isn't here."

"But he's your blue!" Pushing herself into a seated position, Eirian grew concerned.

"Prince Galameyvin is a servant of Ensaycal. Our king chose him to go to Telmia on a diplomatic mission," he replied softly, glancing away.

Hearing that, Eirian felt gutted and covered her mouth, whispered, "For how long?"

Celiaen did not speak while he debated his response. "There is no way of knowing how long he will be there."

"And you let him go without a fight?"

"Who do you think suggested Gal in the first place?" There was a fury in his voice that surprised Eirian, and it spread through his magic as he added, "I'm the Crown Prince of Ensaycal. Why should I tolerate competition when I can get rid of it?"

"Do you hear yourself, Celiaen? Competition for what? He's the third child of your father's brother. He's not your competition for anything! You're best friends, and you've had him all but banished. I don't understand! I really don't."

Her anger stirred her power like a wave of heat around them, and Celiaen glared at Eirian defiantly, knowing his power was nothing compared to hers. Merle was uncomfortable with the rising magic and led the guards over. A step behind, three elves strode along, and Eirian felt the calming effects of their power before she could order her men to stand down. Eirian welcomed the feeling of serenity they directed at the two of them, knowing she could not afford to fight it off. With a bow, Tynan looked at Celiaen with concern.

"Your Highness's, is everything okay?"

"Just a minor disagreement. You know how we are. How have you been, Tynan?" Eirian answered with a warm smile. "It's been a while."

Tynan returned the smile and said, "I've been well, Ree. I'm surprised, but it is a great honor, and my family is pleased. Gal is tough to replace, but I'm doing my best."

"Yes, Gal is certainly a tough one to replace. If you'd give us a moment more? Thank you, Alyse, Cai."

Nodding to the other two elves, Eirian kept her smile. Her guards bowed respectfully and retreated to the arch, but Tynan glanced between them and shook his head.

Alyse agreed, saying, "We won't leave the garden. We know what happens when you're angry with each other."

Eirian cocked her head to the side, the gleam in her eyes reminding the blues that she could destroy them. "I'm being nice and cooperating with you. I promise we'll be just a moment longer. I should clean up. No doubt they're planning a welcome feast."

Celiaen nodded, and shrugging, Tynan encouraged Alyse and Cai to move away to join the others watching from a distance. The power remained, a soothing cloud keeping their anger from boiling over. Getting to her feet, Eirian held out her hands and stopped Celiaen as he stepped towards her.

"I'm so angry with you, Celiaen."

Her words made him step back in shock, a chill running down his spine, and he felt his anger vanish, allowing anguish to take over. He had known Eirian would be angry with him, but the cold fury he felt radiating from her over the bond was more than he had prepared himself for.

Celiaen pleaded, "Ree, please."

"No, Celiaen. You knew what you were doing, and you knew there'd be consequences."

"You could never have him!" he said defensively. "My father—"

Eirian replied angrily, "I don't care about your father, so don't pretend you did me a favor. I love Gal, and you had him sent away to Telmia!"

She snapped a new bud from a bush and held it out to Celiaen. Hesitantly stepping forward to take the flower from her, his hands covered hers for a moment.

He whispered, "I'm sorry, Ree."

She closed his hands around the bud, and he felt her magic feeding into it. It was warm, invigorating, and the scent of wildflowers wafted through the breeze.

"You're my best friend, and you always will be. But today, I am angry with you."

Watching her walk away, Celiaen glanced down at the vibrant bloom in his hands and sighed regretfully. The bond between them urged him to chase Eirian like it always did, but he pushed it aside, banishing the pull.

He called, "I'll see you later!"

The ladies stared at her expectantly, but Eirian ignored them, pushing past quickly with her head down to hide the tears that clouded her vision. Sharing looks, they fell into step behind her. Her guards followed, several of them casting glances back at Celiaen. Eirian noticed the increased number of guards patrolling the courtyard and the keep despite her mood. Seeing them and the openly fearful stares of courtiers made her reel, giving Merle a wide-eyed look when he met her gaze.

"Bad news travels fast," he said with a shrug, ignoring her unshed tears. "And visiting royalty."

"You'll feel better once we get you cleaned up." Brenna nudged her.

Hurrying from a desire to avoid the stares, Eirian struggled to keep a grip on her emotions and power. There were additional guards at her chambers that Eirian did not recognize. A quick look at Merle told her he was not happy with the situation. Once safely inside, Eirian turned to him, ignoring the gazes directed at her.

"What is going on, Merle?" she demanded. "Those men aren't part of my guard."

Shrugging, Merle pointed over his shoulder and said, "Well, I wasn't there, but the boss man said they attacked you. Something about Athnaral wanting to kill you? I guess that might be something worth being mildly concerned about."

"Are you being sarcastic?" After the day they had gone through, Eirian wondered if she should laugh at Merle.

"No, Your Highness, I would never be so disrespectful." There was a flash of sadness, and Merle continued, "But we lost one of our own today who had dedicated his life to protect you. He was a good man. We wish you'd given the one who killed him a taste of your justice."

Her jaw dropped, and Eirian looked at each man, meeting their eyes before swallowing back the words lingering on her tongue. Giving a shake of her head, she shifted away for a moment before turning back and saluting them. They returned the salute.

"I know. I can't undo what happened. I made a mistake, and he died because of it."

"It's our duty, ma'am. We know what we're signing up for. The captain told us you were something beautiful today. I wish I could've seen it," Sid said, glancing at Merle.

"No, you don't, Sid. What I did—"

Sid cut Eirian off. "We know what you are now, and we respect that. You're one of us. Beneath the finery and titles, you're a fighter who knows what to do. But you're a scary bitch, and I'm not afraid to admit it."

Tobin punched Sid's arm and rolled his eyes, saying, "Apologies ma'am, Sid forgets himself. Though he has a point, and we're glad you're on our side."

"No, Tobin, he's fine. I don't mind. It's the truth," she replied with a smile.

Eirian let Bea take her arm gently to guide her into the next room. As she walked away, she heard Merle scolding Sid and sighed. No one was in the mood for arguments, and Eirian let the ladies fuss over her. Once they removed her clothing, they pushed her into a warm bath, the scent of lavender filling her nose. Relaxing in the water while Isabella sat beside her and watched, Eirian stared at the ceiling.

"Did you kill three men on your own?" she whispered.

"I did."

Solemn, Isabella chewed on her bottom lip and glanced at the others before asking, "What is it like? Killing someone, I mean."

Eirian turned her head and stared in amazement. "You want to know?"

"I do. Sometimes I wonder if I could do it if I had to. Not that I have any sort of training like you do, but that doesn't stop me from thinking about it."

"Honestly, I don't think I'm the right person to ask because I have an advantage. The magic takes away my ability to care. Afterward, I feel immense regret, and I'll take the regret of every one of my kills to the grave."

"But what do you feel?" she pushed.

"Many things, anger, pleasure, the desire to do more. It's hard to explain everything I feel when the magic takes over. It guides my hand, and I can't fight it. I have to go with the flow until things end. When I'm alone, it's easier to control. There's a good reason red mages win wars."

Blushing at the memory of what it was like to draw blood with Celiaen, Eirian turned her face away from her observant lady. She could not let her mind turn to the bond she shared with Celiaen. Isabella shuddered, then reminded Eirian that she was not an idiot.

"But you aren't a red. I know that's what you and the duke claim, but I heard you admit to being a purple when those mages were here. Why lie? Being a red sounds terrible."

"Because I'm far worse than any red. Don't ask anymore, please, Isabella. There are some answers none of you want to know."

"As you wish. I don't understand why the gods would give out powers like that."

"Hush, Isabella, you don't question why the gods do anything. They turned their backs on us, and that's all we need to remember." Brenna came over and placed a hand on Isabella's shoulder, saying, "I sent Romana to clean up, and I think you should go as well. They expect us in the great hall tonight."

Getting to her feet, Isabella curtsied and hurried off. Remaining beside the bath, Brenna stared at Eirian, and she stared back. Sighing, she shook her head and turned to the remaining two ladies.

"You girls can go. Once you're back, I'll sort myself out."

Sliding down, Eirian dunked her head into the water, soaking her hair.

"I hope you don't plan to lecture me," she said when she resurfaced.

Scoffing, Brenna picked up the bar of soap and wet it, putting it to Eirian's hair. "What's the point? You think you know what I'd say, and you hardly ever listen. The council, however."

Eirian sighed and admitted, "I know I shouldn't have done it. I knew I wasn't in danger, but no one else knew those men couldn't hurt me. What they saw was their future queen throwing herself at assailants who wanted to kill her."

"Indeed, I'm glad the group split. Everett told me what you did. Everyone will know by now that you killed three men and tortured one. How are you not a mess?"

Flinching when Brenna caught her scalp with her nails, Eirian lifted her hands from the water and looked at them. She was a mess, but knew how to hide it. Guilt ate at her mind, feeding the whispers clawing at her mind.

"The first time I killed someone, the guilt was overwhelming. It took a dozen blue mages to help me regain control. That was over ten years ago and an execution ordered by the high council."

The movement behind her stilled before Brenna pushed her into the water to rinse her hair. Suspecting she was using it to compile her thoughts, Eirian did not speak. Brenna shoved the soap into her half-open hand and stood, moving away from the bath.

"How many have you killed?"

"You don't want to know the answer. You're already horrified at the thought without knowing the numbers. Hence why I kept it a secret."

"Did you enjoy it?"

Pursing her lips, Eirian finished washing and placed the soap on the side of the bath. The whispers mocked her reluctance to reply, taunting her with how much she enjoyed killing despite the guilt.

"Do you want me to answer honestly or try to make you feel better about the creature you serve?"

Spinning around angrily, Brenna snapped. "You get so high and mighty about defying our expectations. You act as though it's all some conspiracy because you were born a female or a mage or whatever reason you come up with. It isn't! I've seen my husband break down after killing someone. I know what it costs him."

Remaining silent, Eirian let Brenna speak and closed her eyes, listening to every word. The bathwater was becoming chill, but it did not matter. She knew she needed to hear what Brenna had to say if she had any hope of keeping her respect. Opening her eyes again, Eirian tracked Brenna's movements around the chamber.

"You're right. I get high and mighty, and I'm sorry. I'll always be deeply sorry about something, and that will never change. I admit I get defiant because I'm used to a level of freedom that I don't get here, and I can't help but long for it. The expectations placed on me feel like a cage, and it's my nature to rebel."

"The prince has feelings for you, and you for him." Brenna changed the subject, walking away from the bath to fetch some towels.

The observation threw Eirian, and she blinked, asking, "What are you on about?"

Not answering, Brenna placed the towels on the stool and offered her hand to help Eirian out of the bath. Remaining silent while drying off, they did not look at each other and kept to their thoughts. Allowing Brenna to place a heavy robe over her shoulders, Eirian turned her gaze to her bed longingly.

"There is food on the table. I thought you might be hungry."

"Bren—"

"You need to eat. Powers know you're always hungry."

Sighing, Eirian walked over and stared at the food on the plate. Pulling the chair away from the table, she sat and picked at the food slowly, her stomach reminding her that Brenna was correct despite feeling nausea at the thought of eating. While she ate, Brenna took a brush to her hair and started working on the knots.

"Sometimes, Eirian, you forget you don't know everything. You're so confident in yourself that you miss things. I watched you with the prince in the garden, and what I saw… you're more than a friend to him."

"We're friends, that is all!" she protested, hoping Brenna would believe the lie.

"Maybe in your mind, but he thinks otherwise. Why were you angry with him?"

Flinching when Brenna pulled hard on a knot, Eirian fought the urge to pull away from the brush. She had quickly discovered that long hair came with a painful downside. There were always knots to be fought with.

"Celiaen is a red mage, which means he always has a blue assigned to him. His blue has been his cousin since they passed the tests for their orders. Galameyvin is also my friend, and they sent him to Telmia."

"That's a lot of anger about hearing your friend went to Telmia."

Satisfied with Eirian's hair, she put the brush down and sat on the other chair. When Eirian did not respond, Brenna sighed.

"I know I sound like a lecturing old woman, but whatever you have between you, I fear it can't be. You're going to be the Queen of Endara."

"I know. I doubt I'll ever see Gal again. That's why I was angry." Looking at her bed, Eirian said, "I need to rest before I face people."

Seeing how tired Eirian was, Brenna lifted a hand, stroking her wet hair as she murmured, "I wish I could make life simpler for you. Perhaps that tells me I'm overprotective of my children. You never had a mother to be protective of you."

"I had my aunt for a time."

"Yes, you did, but Tegan was a hard woman, and you were so young when you left. Get some rest. I'll keep the others from disturbing you for as long as we can. If you need anything, send for me."

Giving her a motherly smile, Brenna kissed her forehead. "By the way, I've sent your armor and knives for cleaning. So, don't stress about them."

"Thank you, Brenna. For everything."

Waiting until she left the room, Eirian got to her feet and stumbled into the bed. Her head had barely touched the pillow before her eyes shut.

FIFTEEN

"**M**y lady, you need to get up now."

Eirian rolled over, grumbling, "I thought Brenna was going to keep you away for a while. She just left. Didn't you see her?"

Chuckling, Brenna appeared beside the bed and said, "How do you feel?"

"Like I haven't slept at all."

Scrambling out of the mangled blankets, Eirian pulled the robe tight around her and took in the vision of her five ladies dressed in some of their best gowns. They regarded her with a mix of amusement and concern. Rubbing her face to banish the sleep from her eyes, Eirian yawned and covered her mouth sheepishly.

"But admittedly, less exhausted."

"Good. Let's get you dressed. With everyone here, this will be a big gathering, and we should make you look like a queen."

Eirian let the ladies fuss over her without protest. When they finished, she admired their work in the mirror. Her hair was loose, and they placed a delicate diadem atop her head. Brenna had told Eirian it once belonged to her mother and was one of the few things left by the late queen. Glimmering emeralds accented the curl of gold and silver fashioned into vines and leaves as it sat nestled in her hair. They matched the shade of her gown, the deep green fabric trailing behind her as she moved.

When she stepped through to the next room, her guards exchanged looks before ushering the women out. Aiden's absence surprised Eirian, but she did not question Merle about it. She suspected he would show up like he always did. They expected him to be by her side during feasts, and Aiden never failed to meet expectations. As they went, the increased number of guards positioned throughout the keep did not detract from the fact that the corridors were quiet until they reached the great hall.

"Is His Majesty in there?" Eirian paused, looking at the steward in front of the doors.

The man nodded and glared at the six guards, grumbling, "Yes, Your Highness, but at this rate, there'll be more guards than guests!"

Shrugging, Eirian stepped towards the doors, and the guards pushed them open. The sight of the hall filled with people made her pause, and it occurred to Eirian that she had never seen so many people in an enclosed space. Brenna touched her elbow to reassure Eirian, guiding her to the King's table where Nolan conversed with Celiaen. Everett and Marcellus were by his side.

Eirian read the tension in the way they stood, their gazes tracking her progress through the hall. People moved out of her way warily, dipping in bows or curtsies as Eirian passed, voices murmuring greetings she did not respond to. Turning to look at her, Celiaen stared in awe, his reaction making Eirian purse her lips as she shared a glance with Brenna. She dropped into a deep curtsy before Nolan and waited to be acknowledged.

"And here is my lovely daughter. Your Highness, have you met the Princess Eirian?"

Nolan smiled at his only child. Eirian shot a quick look at the two dukes, trying not to frown. Their faces hid their concern, but she noticed the subtle hints that betrayed them. They told her that the men had doubts about Nolan's stability.

She said, "Yes, Your Majesty, Prince Celiaen and I are old friends."

"Indeed, I informed His Majesty that our long-standing friendship would continue to keep our two kingdoms united," Celiaen replied.

Nolan caught sight of the diadem on Eirian's head, and she watched fearfully as confusion flickered over his face. It made her stomach clench with anxiety. When Brenna had brought it out, she had doubted the wisdom of wearing something that had belonged to her mother. The uncomfortable feeling of forgotten memories it stirred had not helped.

"Of course, our alliance." Eirian agreed.

Offering his arm to her, Celiaen bowed and asked, "May I take a stroll with you, Your Highness? If His Majesty doesn't mind, of course."

"Go ahead." Nolan gave his permission.

As Nolan turned to speak to Marcellus, something gleamed in his eyes, and Everett shook his head at Eirian. She allowed Celiaen to slip his arm through hers and guide her away from the table. Unable to shake the concern she felt, Eirian kept glancing over her shoulder at Nolan.

"What happened before I arrived?"

"A few more steps, and we can be sure he won't hear us," Celiaen replied, fingers toying with the fabric of her sleeve. "This is the first time I've seen you in a gown, and your hair has grown. You're so beautiful that I feel as though you've stepped out of one of my dreams, and the illusion will end in a moment."

"Thank you, Celi."

Eirian looked at him, taking in the detailed embroidery of his coat, the red and silver thread a stark contrast to the black fabric. It was like the one he had worn in the garden, but the embroidery was more detailed. A sheen to it told her Celiaen was wearing the fine silk Ensaycal took great pride in producing. She took a step closer, wanting to run her hands over the fabric and draw him close enough to kiss.

She murmured, "You look every bit the prince you are."

"Ree, I—"

A cough nearby reminded them that Eirian was not alone. She glanced at Merle, who raised a brow at her, before looking away indifferently.

"What's wrong?"

Celiaen's eyes were black in the flickering lights as he stared at her knowingly. He asked her a question instead of what he had wanted to say.

"Answer me truthfully, is the King going mad?"

"Hush!" she scolded softly, glancing around nervously and wondering who might have heard his question. "He is ill, increasingly too ill to rule."

"I see. That explains a few things. How are you feeling? You look less worn than earlier. I felt your exhaustion over the bond, and I can tell you haven't been sleeping well. Have your nightmares returned?"

Turning to observe the King's table as they spoke, Eirian leaned against Celiaen for comfort. She was not thinking about what she was doing, her hand stroking the front of his coat. Ignoring his question about her nightmares, Eirian turned the conversation a different route.

"I'm sorry for getting so angry with you, but I hope you can understand."

"Ree—" he started.

His arm slipped around her waist, but stopped short of pulling her closer when Eirian stepped away from him. A sudden commotion at the table where Nolan sat drew their attention. Hurrying back to the table, Eirian could hear Everett trying to calm the King.

"Your Majesty, is everything okay?"

Nolan turned to her, furious as he demanded, "Why are you huddling with that elf bastard, Siani? Don't listen to anything he says. He would destroy us!"

Startled by her mother's name, Eirian felt Celiaen at her back, and she turned to him quickly to ask, "Where is Tynan? We need him now. Or Ianto? Darcie?"

"Tynan won't be far away."

"Don't you dare speak to my wife! Guards! Seize that elf!" Nolan shouted, summoning men to the table who looked between their king and princess in confusion.

"Your Majesty," she spoke calmly to Nolan, hoping he would stop shouting. "Do you know who I am?"

"Don't be stupid! I know who you are. You're my wife!"

"Your Majesty, please," Marcellus said, attempting to distract him.

Nolan pointed at Celiaen. "And you, Your Majesty, can step away from her."

Bowing his head, Celiaen stepped away from Eirian, not wishing to aggravate Nolan further. The distress flooding over the bond made him want to gather her in his arms and shield her. But Celiaen knew he could not protect Eirian from what was happening, no matter how much he wanted to.

"My apologies."

"Bloody elves, you always want what isn't yours! Well, Paienven, you can't have Endara. Not while I live and breathe!"

Tynan slipped between the gathered people, his power sliding over the other mages and wrapping around Nolan like a calming cloak. Close behind him, other blues followed. They were ready to assist as needed, their concern for Eirian clear.

"Everything is okay, Your Majesty," he soothed.

Everett signaled to the guards, and they stepped back nervously to let Tynan take over.

He suggested, "Your Majesty, perhaps you should retire."

"Indeed, that is a good idea. Let's retire. It's been a long evening," Eirian said. "Please, sire, your guests won't mind."

She caught Tynan's gaze for a second and nodded. Using his power to make Nolan more compliant, he stayed beside Eirian. While she grasped one of Nolan's arms, Tynan took the other. The two dukes exchanged whispers before Marcellus assumed the lead, and they guided Nolan away from the watching crowd. They could hear the disbelieving questions shouted at Everett as he attempted to calm everyone down. Celiaen remained, knowing his presence might cause more upset, his eyes tracking their progress.

Safely out of the hall and into one of the smaller hallways, Eirian did her best to remain calm as she glanced at Marcellus. "What happened?"

"He seemed stable. It would have looked strange if he hadn't made an appearance to welcome the prince, and we thought it was better to avoid questions being asked. But, Eirian, you need to go back in there. Make excuses, take command, and pretend something, anything, to distract those people," Marcellus told her.

She knew he was right and sighed. "Tynan?"

"I know. You should have sent for a blue if you wanted to keep this a secret," he replied. "Your Majesty, it's time to get some sleep."

Eirian caught Nolan's wandering gaze, and she thought she saw recognition flare in his eyes. She hoped it was a sign he was coming out of his episode.

Nolan lifted a hand and stroked her face, saying, "Oh, sweet Siani, my darling. I'll keep your secret, I promise. Paienven won't discover what you are. I'll kill him if he does."

Going still, she let Marcellus and Tynan lead him away and stared at the back of them as they left her standing there, surrounded by her guards. When they turned a corner and left her line of vision, Eirian rubbed her face in frustration. Merle stood beside her, arms clasped behind him as he stared off in the direction they had led King Nolan.

"You won't keep that quiet anymore. It might be a blessing," Merle muttered, glancing at her. "I know it isn't my place, but what do you think he meant?"

"I don't know, and right now, it's not important. How could everyone finding out the King is going mad be a blessing?"

Shrugging as he turned and waved at the door to the hall. "Well, until now, the biggest subject was the hunt. Instead, everyone will talk about the news that the King of Endara is crazy. The little tidbit that his daughter tortured and killed a man will get lost in the frenzy of that far more interesting news. Seems like a blessing to me."

Laughing in disbelief, Eirian shook her head at him and commented, "I think you should be in politics."

"I'm a royal guard, and there's enough politics involved in that. The duke is right, though. You need to go in there and make excuses. If you make weak enough ones, it will help keep their minds off your actions. Pick your battles, ma'am."

"I don't think any excuses will cover up what they saw. If the coronation hadn't moved already, I doubt there'd be a choice now." Taking a deep breath, Eirian tugged at her bodice and gave the men a look, asking, "How do I look? Composed enough?"

Merle saluted and bowed, waving at the door as he replied, "You look like a queen. Now be one. We have your back, and the captain is here. Just in case you were missing him."

One of the other guards opened the door for her, and Eirian stepped through, taking in the hall's state. Letting her eyes drift over the crowd, she could see that the number of people had shrunk. Her suspicions told Eirian that they would spread the news about the King. Everett was standing beside Nolan's chair, his voice attempting to rise above the din of chatter. Squaring her shoulders, Eirian strode back to the table, meeting the stares of those who noticed and turned her way.

Stepping between the chairs, Eirian assumed Nolan's spot, the place she knew was hers to take, and held up a hand patiently, waiting for the noise level to drop. Her power filled the hall, helping draw attention towards her and lending the authority Eirian struggled to feel over her nervousness. In the corner of her eye, she saw Celiaen watching with an unreadable look. For a moment, she wondered if she could genuinely count on his support, then quickly banished her doubt. Celiaen would never abandon her, and Eirian knew it.

"I know things have gotten a bit out of hand, but everything is fine now."

"Things aren't fine! The King is mad, and you've been hiding it!" someone in the middle of the crowd shouted.

She stared in the voice's direction and answered, "His Majesty is unwell and has been for quite some time. We have not kept that a secret. Or did you somehow miss the preparations for my coronation?"

There was a ripple of anxious laughter as people agreed she had a point. Eirian realized sticking to the illness line would continue to remind the court that they had been open about Nolan's inability to continue ruling. She shared a look with Everett before gathering her skirts and sitting. They knew it would make a statement no one would miss. Scolding herself, she realized she needed to stop thinking of things as her father's and begin thinking of them as her own. Seeing her sit, people spread, but she could feel the tension remaining.

"He shouldn't have been here," she whispered to Everett.

Nodding in agreement, Everett sighed, "He is still the king, and we couldn't stop him. What could we have done? Order his men to lock him in his room? "

"Couldn't you reason with him?"

"We should have seen the signs."

She huffed, "At least Nolan has given them something else to talk about."

"His Majesty seems to have taken offense at the elves being here. He unraveled after he met them. You should ask the prince if he has any idea what might have occurred between your fathers because I don't know."

Lifting a hand to touch the jewels in her hair, Eirian shook her head. "No, it wasn't just them. Besides, Celi looks nothing like his siblings, let alone his father. That was the first time I'd heard him say my mother's name. She has always been 'your mother' or 'the late queen.' No one ever speaks her name, and then he calls me by it in the grip of madness."

"I've heard stories of his grief when she died. They say he loved her... well, he had to have done. She was no one before she married him."

"What did you say?"

Giving him a sharp look, Eirian thought back to what Nolan had said to her while thinking she was his late wife. Everett summoned a page to fill his cup and sipped the wine.

"I've read accounts about how she arrived one day, and no one knew who she was or where she came from. Your father fell in love. I suppose he could get away with it. He was king by then, and the council was keen to see him wed."

Allowing the page to fill her cup, Eirian stared at Celiaen, who was working his way through the crowd. Taking another sip, she mulled over it, breathing in the heady scent. She wanted to drink heavily and allow the wine to banish her memories of the day.

She finally said, "Yes, he could get away with it. Who would dare tell a king no?"

Everett followed her gaze and frowned. He watched Celiaen speak with Sabine, other council members hovering close. People had witnessed the greeting between Eirian and Celiaen in the garden. Rumors about the two of them were spreading as quickly as the news of her actions in the woods. Shifting his focus, Everett noticed Aiden deep in conversation with Cameron, and his eyes darted to Eirian.

"What do you think?" Cameron asked, nodding in Celiaen's direction. "Were you there?"

Glancing at Celiaen, Aiden replied, "I caught a glimpse, and I don't trust him."

"Careful, my boy, wouldn't want anyone to suggest you're jealous of the Crown Prince of Ensaycal. It would imply you're developing feelings for our queen."

"I'm off duty, Cameron."

Cameron chuckled. "You're never off duty, Aiden. It's not in your nature. Have you introduced yourself to him yet?"

"Not yet, but I'm sure the opportunity will present itself. From what I know, I suspect we won't like each other very much," he muttered. "You didn't answer my earlier question. Did you have any idea that Athnaral planned to kill Eirian?"

"You know it's not that simple, Aiden. We had reports, including ones that suggested they could kill her in an alley at night. What are the chances of that happening? So what reports do we believe and take as serious threats?"

His gaze darkened, and Aiden glared at Eirian. He knew the chances were higher than Cameron believed. It made him wonder if she would tell him if he asked her. There was no doubt in his mind that she had slipped out of the keep far more than they realized. He wanted to know if she had killed other attackers without bothering to inform them of the attempts on her life. Clenching a fist, Aiden shook his head and looked at Cameron.

"I think our soon-to-be queen keeps a lot of secrets."

Clapping a hand to his back, Cameron said, "I can't think of a better man to learn those secrets. You know you have my full support. We just need to give her a few months on the throne before we push."

"She blindsided me today," Aiden admitted. "I underestimated her."

"That was your mistake, Aiden, and something she warned us not to do. I'm disappointed I didn't go on the hunt this morning. It sounds like I would've enjoyed it."

"It was eye-opening, and yes, somewhat enjoyable. Eirian said she could have dealt with all of them alone."

"And she could have."

They turned to look at the woman behind them. She wore mail and leather, a pair of axes secured to her belts among an array of knives, and magic simmered around her. Aiden studied the sword hilts poking over her shoulders before glancing at her short, sandy brown hair and the pointed curl of her ears.

"With one hand tied behind her back and blindfolded," she chuckled and held out a hand, flashing the red band adorning it. "Tara."

Accepting her hand, Cameron replied, "General Cameron. I take it you're familiar with our princess?"

Tara nodded, giving Aiden a curious look while waiting for his name. While he was not as ornately dressed as most nobility, he wore a deep green coat over his armor embroidered with a sword and axe motif. Clean-shaven, the piercing blue eyes gazing at Tara beneath dark brown curls suggested they would miss nothing.

"Aiden Cathasaigh."

She whistled. "The bastard of Tamantal?"

The title made Aiden sigh. He had heard it flung at him in a wide variety of ways, and he was never sure how he felt when it came with a hint of respect, as Tara had addressed him. Chuckling at the look on Aiden's face, Cameron glanced over at the table where Eirian was.

"They've called me that in the past. Now I'm the captain of Princess Eirian's guard," Aiden said.

"I could say a lot of things, but I think I might settle with good luck."

"Very familiar, I gather?" Cameron chuckled.

Lifting her hand, Tara caught the attention of a page and snagged a cup from the tray they carried. Taking a sip, she nodded in Eirian's direction, eyes tracking Celiaen's progress through the room. She expected he would reach them before too long.

"I've known Ree since she was about six, and let me tell you, you're in for some fun." Tara chuckled. "Well, I suppose that depends on your definition of fun. How much has she swindled from you at cards?"

Giving Tara a bemused smirk, Aiden made a note to ask Fionn to play the other elves and attempt to pry information from them. If there was anyone who could ply gossip from a card game without being obvious, it was him.

"Not me, but I suspect she has swindled some unaware commoners."

"Gave you the slip?"

Aiden nodded. "Yes, frequently."

"Yeah, they do that," she replied. "The pair of them think they're so clever, sneaking out using Ree's little tricks. We always knew. They're not as sneaky as they'd like to think. You could say I had a hand in raising both of them."

"Really?" Aiden asked, sharing a look with Cameron.

"Really. Isn't that right, Your Highness?"

Shifting to direct attention to Celiaen, Tara winked. Making a point to turn slowly, Aiden clamped down on his reaction to the magic oozing from him. There was no way he would let on how it made him feel or the thoughts it stirred. He gazed at the dark brown eyes staring at him, noting the flicker of attraction that appeared. Despite what he thought of Celiaen, Aiden felt satisfaction over his response.

Celiaen snorted. "I know better than to agree with you blindly, Tara."

Bowing, Cameron greeted him, "A pleasure to see you again, Prince Celiaen."

"And you, General."

Pointing at Aiden with her cup, Tara said, "Remember the man responsible for capturing those rebels who slipped over the border? The ones King Paienven paid handsomely for."

Looking Aiden over thoughtfully, Celiaen smiled and extended his hand in greeting. He knew the reputation Aiden held and understood why Tara was lurking in the corner talking to him. What baffled him was the dark look on Aiden's face when he returned the gesture. It was coldly disinterested, with a hint of contempt. Feeling the firmness of Aiden's grasp on his hand, Celiaen wondered what it would take to ruffle his demeanor.

"Your work impressed my father," Celiaen told him.

"Thank you, Your Highness. I take all my jobs seriously."

Laughing, Tara slapped Aiden on the back and ignored the looks directed at her. She had recognized the expression on Celiaen's face and knew what it meant. It did not surprise her. Tara knew him well enough to know Aiden was the sort of challenge Celiaen enjoyed.

"Oh, Captain, you are so screwed."

The title surprised Celiaen, and he asked, "Captain? I thought you'd have a higher rank than that."

His eyes drifted to Eirian, and Aiden said, "I'm no longer in the army."

Following his gaze, Celiaen saw Eirian talking to a noblewoman. Listening to Tara's laughter, he watched Eirian look in their direction. Celiaen felt a flash of panic across the bond, accompanied by a mix of other emotions. They allowed him to understand why Tara found the situation amusing. Eyes sliding towards Aiden, Celiaen knew they explained why he had given him such a cold greeting.

"They gave you the captaincy of her guard as a reward?"

Straightening his jacket, Aiden smirked and shared a look with Cameron. He had not considered it a reward previously, not when he knew what they were planning for him.

"I didn't ask for it, but I'm not complaining. Fighting with her every day is a pleasure I can look forward to for the rest of our lives."

"You're outmatched, Captain."

Aiden disagreed, "I'm more than capable of handling you, Your Highness."

"You're welcome to try. I'd love to see how you handle me. Believe me, I wouldn't complain. However, I didn't mean me."

Scoffing, Aiden took several steps, and Cameron crossed his arms. He took in the anger flickering in Celiaen's eyes and knew Aiden had aggravated him on purpose. Beside him, Tara's laughter had died, and she watched in concern. Their reaction to each other had not gone the way she had expected.

"Enjoy the feast, Your Highness. I'd remain and talk, but my place is elsewhere," Aiden said, glancing over his shoulder. "And thank you for your concern, but I think you'll find my princess is happy with how I handle her."

Hand shooting out, Tara grabbed Celiaen's arm and shook her head. Clenching his jaw, Celiaen watched Aiden weave through the crowd until he reached the table. Eirian looked in their direction, worry flickering over the bond, while Aiden moved to stand to the side of her chair, an arm resting on the back. Next to her, Everett waved a hand at the group of people dancing to one side of the room.

"I'm sorry, Celi," Tara murmured, releasing his arm. "I didn't expect that."

"Why would you?"

Cameron said, "Aiden is a very loyal Endaran. His record is exemplary, and his father, the late Earl of Tamantal, ensured his education was complete. There is no one better to protect Her Highness."

Arching a brow, Celiaen replied, "She mentioned that she'd been hiding her abilities. I think you'll find Eirian Altira doesn't need protecting. The good captain is merely a decorative sword."

"I think you'll find he's more than that. Aiden's a Cathasaigh, which means a great deal to many people. As does his position at the side of our future queen. After all, queens need decoration to keep them busy. Have a good evening, Your Highness."

With a bow, Cameron walked away, leaving Celiaen and Tara alone. Sneering, Celiaen crossed his arms and watched Aiden offer a hand to Eirian.

When she took it and allowed him to lead her to join the dancers, Celiaen shifted to look in a different direction.

"I wouldn't worry, Celi."

"Surely you caught what the general was implying?" he muttered. "The captain is a noble bastard with a respected reputation. They have plans for him and Ree, and he knows it."

"Well then, you better prepare to make your case to the Endaran council. Have you learned anything useful?" Tara asked, watching Aiden coax Eirian through a dance.

"Nothing we didn't already know. Men in Athnaralan uniforms hired the attackers. Most of them are aware of Aeyren moving troops but refuse to believe he's a threat."

"I've heard the same. A few believe your father is planning to invade, but you said Ree suggested as much. We better make sure Paienven is aware of what happened. The messengers informing him of King Nolan's abdication will have reached Luina by now."

Celiaen agreed. "He should know Aeyren has ordered attempts on the life of the future Queen of Endara. We should also let him know King Nolan has the madness. Get Tynan to walk through anything he learns with the other blues. We'll make sure his household knows they can call on them."

"It will reassure Ree, and that's what matters."

Turning back, Celiaen watched Aiden catch Eirian when she stumbled. It stirred his jealousy more than if it had been Galameyvin. At least he knew Galameyvin and could trust him with Eirian's heart. Aiden was an outsider.

"Ree is all that matters," he murmured. "Excuse me, Tara, but I wish to dance with my mate. Try to enjoy the feast in between overhearing conversations."

"Celi, you need to get along with the captain."

"Why?"

Tara sighed. "Because if you leave Ree out of it, Aiden is your sort, and I think the two of you have a lot in common. Potentially even be friends."

Before he walked away, Celiaen replied, "You might be right."

SIXTEEN

"Don't do this, Eirian."

Ignoring Everett, she prepared to enter the council chambers. He let out a frustrated groan and grabbed her arm, and the action caused her to swing around to glare at him. Magic swirled around Eirian defensively, and Everett did his best to dismiss the sudden clenching of her fists and the dangerous gleam in her eye.

"I'm telling you, it's a mistake. Don't do it."

"It's been weeks, and news of His Majesty's madness is spreading. Athnaral will soon know, and they'll see it as an opportunity. We need to prepare."

He tightened his grip on her arm. "Or they'll see what you are doing as an act of hostility and invade us out of spite."

"Don't you think they're already planning that? Be realistic, Everett, and look at the evidence. The enemy is coming, and we need to be ready. Either support me or be silent!"

Nodding to the guards at the door, Eirian waited for them to open it before walking into the chamber.

"I hope you know what you're doing," Marcellus said when she sat next to him.

Greeting each person seated around the table and those standing to watch, Eirian rested her arms on the smooth timber to lean forward. "My ladies and lords of the council, war is coming, and we need to prepare for it."

"War is always coming, Your Highness, but it never seems to make it here. What makes you so sure?" a noblewoman responded.

"I imagine by now, they've informed King Aeyren that His Majesty is mad. Even before that, he ordered attacks against me. He'll see us as weak and seek to use that opportunity."

Cameron pushed a pile of papers forward, saying, "I've been mentioning this for a while. Peace does not last! I've received increasing amounts of reports that both Athnaral and Ensaycal are mobilizing and where else—"

"We have the heir to Ensaycal here. What does Prince Celiaen have to say about his father moving his armies?" Sabine said. "Most of our trade is with the elves."

"Prince Celiaen claims they received reports about Athnaral, and Paienven intends to defend us if needed," Eirian replied, noticing the scoffs around the room.

"And we're to believe him?"

Turning towards the young noble who had spoken, Sabine contemplated him. He shifted nervously under the sternness of her gaze.

She replied, "Well, why wouldn't we? The elves aren't stupid. In the long term, they know they should have an independent kingdom between them and Athnaral. There has never been true peace between them, and if they share a border, they'll spend to defend it. If they had to force an all-out war, someone would lose, and I doubt it would be the elves. Can you see humans happily accepting the rule of elves?"

"Riane wouldn't let them do it!"

"Be quiet, Vander!" His father scolded him. "You're here to learn, not argue with those who know better. My apologies, Your Highness."

"It's fine, Kendall. He's right to ask." Eirian sighed and said, "Riane would support the elves. We can't expect non-partisanship from them."

"But you're a mage, the first human mage to rule in generations. Won't they answer your summons if we ask for help?" Ulric asked.

His question threw her, and Eirian sucked her breath in through her teeth, debating what to tell them. Deciding on a variation of the truth, she leaned back in her chair and looked at Everett beside her.

"It's unlikely they'd come to my aid without a steep cost. The grand mage is failing, and they offered me the position. My refusal to set aside my duty here may have made them a little less friendly towards us."

The council broke into an uproar, and Everett loudly slapped a hand against the table. "We don't need Riane! Eirian made the correct choice, and I gave her my full support when she made it. Better the mages stay out of the conflict."

"Mages win wars," Gallagher said. "We have a mage."

"Thank you for the vote of confidence, Earl Jurien, but I alone can't turn a big a tide as we face. I'm good, but I'm not that good." Eirian chuckled.

"You might make them more willing to negotiate."

Leaning forward, Cameron said, "Let's be honest, we have a queen, and there is only one thing Athnaral will demand out of negotiations. I don't know about the rest of you, but I don't fancy serving Eirian up on a platter to those pigs. She'd be a hostage for their king to marry. They would execute most of you and carve up Endara. Then the elves would invade."

"He has a point, my dear cousins."

Hearing the fresh voice behind her, Eirian turned and caught the look that appeared on Everett's face as she moved. "Llewellyn!"

"Sorry I'm late, but it's a long ride from the border, and I took a few detours!" Leaning in, he kissed Eirian's cheek and said, "Leadership looks good on you, little cousin."

"We're glad you made it here in time for the coronation, Duke Onaorbaen." Marcellus offered his hand, asking, "What did you learn?"

"Ah, Marcellus, you know me too well. I saw Athnaralan troops, lots of them. I saw our keeps well manned, but not nearly enough to stop an invasion if they made moves before winter. Which they will!" Llewellyn perched on the edge of the table and looked around.

Scowling at him, Ulric asked, "What are you suggesting we do?"

Eirian half stood, leaning over the table to point at the map carved into the timber. "We increase our numbers along the border for a start. After the coronation, I'll tour the kingdom, and we'll use it as an excuse for having troops on the move. My gut tells me that if they plan to invade, it will be this summer."

"What makes you think that?" Adalardo asked.

"Because it's what she would do," Llewellyn replied with a chuckle. "Everyone will be busy working out which way is which with a new head on the throne, and they won't be looking behind them for the snake in the grass."

Giving Llewellyn an appreciative look, Eirian nodded. "It is what I'd do. There is one catch. I might be friends with Prince Celiaen, but I don't think he has the authority to renew the treaty between Endara and Ensaycal. As we know, King Paienven has required it renewed with each monarch."

"You think Athnaral would hope to catch us before that?" Ulric looked thoughtful. "No, that's not it. You think with the news of the King's madness, he'll also find out that Prince Celiaen is here."

"Yes."

"Every man and his hound can see the way the prince looks at you. Any spy worth their pay will report it."

Eirian leaned further forward and stared at Ulric curiously. "And what do your spies tell you for their pay?"

Uncomfortable with her question, Ulric glanced at the other council members and replied, "You've been friends for a long time with him and his cousin, Prince Galameyvin. Particularly said, cousin. Celiaen targeted you from the first time you were both in Riane. Your Highness, don't you fear that they have cultivated your friendship to conquer Endara?"

"I wouldn't marry Celiaen Kaetiel, and if that's Paienven's plan, I hope he didn't wager on it. Are you asking me if I suspect Athnaral might think it's the plan?"

Watching them realize what she was suggesting was like watching raindrops fall. People started talking among themselves, and Llewellyn chuckled at her amused expression. Cocking her head to the side, she stared at Everett thoughtfully. He spoke to Marcellus behind her back, half slipping from his seat so they could murmur.

"General Cameron, I want you to send the orders to move troops to the border. We'll use the excuse of my tour," she said, and they fell silent.

Cameron saluted with a smile. "You're decisive. I'm glad someone is. My men will leave as soon as possible."

"Thank you." Eirian turned her eyes from him to Llewellyn and instructed, "You'll let them know what you saw."

"If we end up in war, we're all as screwed as you'll be if Aeyren gets his hands on you." Scratching his neck, Llewellyn shrugged, adding, "At least I have a plan if things go wrong."

"And you wonder why we barely consider you a candidate for the throne," Marcellus hissed disapprovingly.

Hopping off the table, he laughed. "Not much choice if these two get themselves killed or captured. I suggest everyone makes escape plans for their families because those of us here in this room are the ones who must die for either side to conquer Endara. Unless our fair princess spreads her legs for the elf. He'll leave us alive."

"That's enough!" Everett slammed his hands on the table and snarled, "Get cleaned up, Llewellyn."

Bowing mockingly, Llewellyn winked at Eirian and said, "My apologies, Your Highness, you know I adore you. I'll clean up and check on my mother and siblings. My sisters will be excited to meet a Prince of Ensaycal, and my mother wants to attend to her brother."

Eirian reached out and caught his hand as he walked past her. "Please tell your mother that I'll see her later when I visit His Majesty."

"She'll be happy to see you." Nodding, Llewellyn started walking once her hand left him.

"I swear by the powers that boy gets wilder every year!" Kendall muttered.

Unimpressed, Eirian stared at him. "Mind your words, the Duke of Onaorbaen is my cousin and the nephew of our king."

"We know Llewellyn is rough around the edges, but he has a point. We need to plan for everything. If there is a war with Athnaral, we can't win, and I suspect Ensaycal will demand a price for saving us. But what if they decide not to? I have grandchildren." Ulric crossed his arms and looked around as he pointed out. "Most of you have a family. If it looks like war won't go our way, perhaps making plans for them is a good idea."

Everett snorted. "I think it's early for suggesting that!"

"No, Everett, it's not. They're right," Eirian said, rubbing her face.

"You're the one who says the elves will honor her friendship with their prince, and you're suggesting we fear the worst?" Sabine replied.

"I'm fairly sure Ensaycal will honor generations of treaties, but many things could happen. It harms no one to prepare a backup plan."

"We need one for you as well," someone said.

Closing her eyes and shaking her head, Eirian pictured Baenlin. She knew they had decided on her backup plan the moment they made their deal.

"I have one."

"And on that note, I think we should call an end to this meeting. Your Highness, I presume your plan was to order the moving of troops?" Marcellus spoke, recognizing that the subject needed to change.

Thankful for his question, she nodded and answered, "It was."

"I don't think anyone disagrees about preparing." Clapping a hand to Ulric's shoulder, Marcellus chuckled. "No, don't start."

Silenced, Ulric shrugged. Knowing the meeting was at an end, the various nobles and small council members began filtering out, bowing, and paying their respects to Eirian as they passed. She remained seated, fingers drumming against the table as she studied the map, nodding to each person. Pushing out of the chair, Eirian leaned forward to run her fingers over the markings denoting the border with Athnaral.

"If I were Aeyren, and I had the superior numbers, I wouldn't push as a single large army or close to the Fingers."

"Why not?" Everett asked, moving around the table.

She pointed, saying, "Too easy to get trapped against Onaorbaen. Then there's the weather. Winter comes earlier up there."

"You're suggesting they'd divide, knowing we'd have to do the same."

"Yes, Marcellus, that's right. If Aeyren drew us northwards towards the Fingers, he could send men through to cut us off and move on Amath. He takes the city, and we're left divided and easy pickings until the elves arrive to do whatever they decide to do. If we're trapped in the north for winter, he has months to solidify control over the south."

Cameron nodded and asked, "You don't think he might try something else?"

"They've tried everything before. What do you think Aeyren might do? Bypass Amath and take everywhere else? Trying to hold the primary locations in Endara would spread him thin, and Paienven would destroy him. Hold Amath, and you split Endara."

Everett stepped back and commented, "We've done this before. Athnaral goes crawling back, scolded by Ensaycal, while Endara picks up the tattered pieces. Life continues. What has changed? That's the question we need to answer."

"I have." They turned to look at her, and Eirian shrugged. "Don't lie, you've all thought it. I'm the first queen to take the throne in three hundred years and the first mage in a thousand."

"The world doesn't revolve around you, Eirian," Everett said.

Spreading her hands, Eirian replied, "I don't want it to, but from where I'm standing, it sure seems like it does. We know the gods abandoned us, but we don't know what they put into play before moving on. My existence feels like a game they planned a long time ago."

"You've thought about it a lot, have you?" Cameron asked in amusement.

"I owe it to everyone to prepare for everything, every possibility. We don't have the luxury of being complacent, and it's certainly not my nature!" She scowled at her skirts, then glanced at the door, stating, "Now I'm going to eat before I see my father."

Everett touched her arm. "Do you think it's a good idea? Aunt Amira will take over."

"As is her right. My coronation is in nine days, and I need to focus on that. It'll be for the best if she is supervising Nolan. We should allow Amira to take him to Onaorbaen."

The men gaped at her, and Eirian sighed, making her way out, not wanting to discuss the suggestion. Slipping through the door while they burst into conversation, she met the blank gaze of Gabe with a faint smile. The guards quickly fell into step with her, their ever-present weapons giving Eirian a sense of safety. Since the attack, the guards had increased their vigilance, and she felt stifled by their constant hovering, but she did not argue with them.

"Gabe, anything to report?" Eirian asked as they strode through the keep.

"More people have arrived for your coronation. Did you get what you wanted?" Gabe inquired, glancing at her sideways.

Smiling, she nodded. "Indeed, I did. No one opposed me."

"Perhaps you made too much sense to argue with?"

"Or they've had their reports and know that we can't ignore it?" Eirian chuckled. "Has anyone requested an audience with me today that you know of?"

Gabe pointed to a door. "Not that I know of, but ask your ladies."

Startled, she stared at the door in surprise before glancing at him. "Don't tell anyone I wasn't paying attention."

"Your mind has a lot to deal with, ma'am. That's why we're here."

Letting a guard open the door, Eirian prepared herself for what was on the other side. She suspected Brenna would lecture her about the decision to call a council meeting. Walking through, she saw Brenna sorting through stacks of paper on the table. The other ladies sat watching, their hands full of fabric. Glancing up as Eirian approached, they murmured their greetings, knowing that she was more interested in what Brenna was doing. Eirian picked up a paper, reading it with arched brows.

"What is all of this?"

Brenna straightened, hands on her hips as she stretched her back. "They cleaned out His Majesty's chambers and had everything brought here. There are letters, petitions, documents. It's a mess. You need to arrange for a secretary. There are a lot of things you need to consider, including the council."

"I don't intend to change any of the positions in the court. Those men and women have served my father well. The kingdom is in an excellent position."

"You'll need to appoint more ladies. I heard the party from Onaorbaen had arrived. Your aunt will expect her eldest daughter to join your household," Brenna said as she shuffled through documents.

Smiling, Eirian stilled her hands and took the papers. "Ask Ulric to appoint a secretary as soon as possible. Now, have you noticed anything in this mess that you feel needs attention?"

Shuffling through a pile, Brenna pulled out a folded letter with a broken seal and handed it to Eirian. "It's Paienven's seal. I presume they gave it to His Majesty when the prince arrived."

"Have you read it?" Holding it in her hands, Eirian frowned.

"No."

Walking over to the window, Eirian perched on the ledge and leaned her back against the arch of stone, taking pleasure in the cool against her spine. Looking at the city, her eyes went to the distance beyond, and she wondered if it would look the same in a year. Shaking her head, Eirian turned her focus back to the letter in her hands, rubbing a thumb on the broken wax seal before she unfolded it. The writing was familiar, Paienven's elegant script filling the parchment. She skimmed through the initial formal greetings with a bemused smirk before she reached the part she was interested in. Greedily reading the assurances she needed, Eirian rested her head back on the stone and looked at Brenna.

"He's given Celiaen authority to renegotiate the treaty, but it will depend on his final approval. It specifies with Nolan, but I'm sure we can make it work."

"You can't officially begin until after your coronation, but I imagine you can convince the prince to give you anything," Brenna replied.

"True, but I can tell Ulric to prepare for it," Eirian said, lowering the letter. "It's rather odd that he'd provide this before he was aware there was a coronation occurring."

Romana carefully set her work aside and got to her feet, saying, "I'll arrange some lunch now you're here. Bea can come with me."

"Thank you. I meant to ask, but this distracted me."

Smiling at the ladies, Eirian was thankful that someone remembered food. Turning her attention back to the letter in her hand, Eirian grew pale as she took in what else he had written. Covering her mouth, she stared at the page in anger and wondered if Celiaen was aware of what Paienven had proposed. Dropping her hand, Eirian made herself take slow, deep breaths to calm down, her power simmering. Finishing the letter, she folded it and slipped it into a pocket.

Hopping off the ledge, Eirian crossed to a guard and said, "Jack, I want you to locate Prince Celiaen and bring him to me."

"Your Highness?" Brenna asked.

Jack saluted without waiting for further commands and left.

Eirian told the curious women. "I need to speak to Celi."

Brenna laid out some documents waiting for her to return to the table. She pointed at them, hoping Eirian would lean in close.

She whispered, "Let me see the letter."

"No."

"Do we need to worry?"

Pursing her lips, Eirian let out a slow breath and answered, "I don't know. Let me talk to him."

Touching her hand gently, Brenna met her eyes with concern. "I know you'll send us out, but I can stay if you need me."

"I might be mad at him, and we'll probably argue, but I trust him."

"I rather like him."

Smiling faintly, Eirian sat and started going through the stacks of paper, hoping to use them as a distraction. Her two ladies continued working, knowing better than to get involved. Brenna stared at Eirian thoughtfully between sorting documents. Silence filled the chamber, and the guards were unwilling to chat amongst themselves. Romana and Bea returned, food following closely at their heels. Forced to make room, Brenna carefully shifted the piles so they could put the trays down.

They had barely begun eating when a heavy knock on the door caused them to turn. Eirian knew who it was. The whisper of his magic was as familiar as her own. She nodded, and the guards opened the door. Jack stepped through and saluted before moving out of the way for Celiaen to enter. Sighing, Eirian looked at Brenna and nodded. She gathered the other ladies and ushered them out of the chamber.

"I need you to leave."

Meeting Gabe's steel gaze, Eirian knew he would not argue. Celiaen cocked his head to the side and kept out of the way of the departing people. When the room was empty, he turned his dark eyes to Eirian and crossed his arms.

With a smile, he said, "You wanted me."

"Indeed."

Putting her food down, Eirian wiped her hands off on a cloth before drawing the letter from her pocket. His eyes took in what she was holding, realization appearing on his face.

"I wondered when you'd receive that."

"Do you know what your father wrote in this letter?"

"I do."

"Damn it!" Eirian crumpled the letter angrily and threw it at him, demanding, "Why?"

Uncrossing his arms, Celiaen ran a hand through his short hair and sighed heavily. "I wish you weren't so completely clueless. Your attention has always been for Gal, even though I'm the one by your side. Even though we're mates!"

"Celi—"

"When we met, you were this headstrong girl that my father ordered me to befriend. Once I felt your power and how it made me feel, I didn't mind so much and could see the advantage of being your friend. Eventually, that stopped mattering."

"I suspected it was something like that, but you're right. Over the years, it stopped mattering because you were always there for me. That doesn't explain this. What happened?"

"You grew up and became a beautiful woman with a keen mind and a wicked sense of humor while remaining every bit as headstrong. Every time I left Riane, you grew more, and when I came back, I couldn't help falling in love with you."

Slumping, Celiaen looked at the window sadly, ignoring her stare. Eirian said nothing. She suspected he had more to add.

Celiaen sighed and said, "So yes, out of jealousy, I suggested to my father that he send Gal to Telmia. I thought you might finally realize the truth if he wasn't around. Then I told him I wanted to marry you."

Eirian remained silent and sat staring at him. She felt like there was a sudden gulf between them and thought back over the years, over the time they had spent together, and tried to remember if she had noticed anything. Her mind recalled every look and touch, the way his hands would linger when Celiaen sparred with her, every little gift he gave her. Days spent training and exploring, nights curled up next to each other under the stars. Things Eirian had dismissed as displays of friendship because she did not think he felt otherwise.

Covering her face, Eirian shook her head and waited for Celiaen to speak. She did not want to say anything when she could not trust what would come out of her mouth. He walked over to the table and glanced at the piles of paper and the half-eaten food. Sitting next to her, he considered how Eirian would react to what he planned to say.

"Paienven told me he'd make the proposal, but I wasn't to expect approval. He suggested the best I could hope for is that you might take me to bed in a few years after you married and produced an heir," he said bitterly.

Insult flickered across her face, and Eirian replied, "Celi, I don't... what do you expect me to say? You're my best friend. We've shared the blade, taken lives together, and we have an incomplete but unbreakable mate bond."

"Yes, we do."

"I've watched you take men and women to bed. If you feel what you claim, why would you parade your conquests in front of me? You never, not once, made me suspect you felt this way. I didn't think you felt for me—"

"You mean, while you and Gal made eyes at each other, leaving me out in the cold? I wouldn't have said no if you had invited me to join the two of you. What about the women and men you took to your bed when we weren't in Riane? Rylee?"

"What about them? You weren't there!"

Celiaen snarled. "I can't forget there is an unbreakable bond between us! You can't imagine what I wanted to do to you that day or the days before and after. We are mates!"

"It was the magic that made you want that," Eirian said softly, her voice filled with certainty.

Barking out a laugh, he gave her a doubtful look. "You don't believe that any more than I do. You're a purple. You know magic takes what we feel. There would be no bond if you didn't love me."

Pushing the memory from her mind before it fueled her power, Eirian closed her eyes and tried to focus. She had to keep her emotions and magic under control.

"What your father proposed, it would never work. I don't think my people would accept a half-blood. Everyone would see it as Ensaycal taking over, and Athnaral would retaliate."

"Don't make excuses! At least do me the decency and tell me it's simply that you wouldn't have me. Would you accept Gal if it was him?"

She hesitated before replying, "No, I wouldn't. We know our duty. As your father suggested, maybe I might have been free to love him one day, but I could never marry him. If I have any, my children must be completely human. Endara is a human kingdom."

"You are ever the creature of duty, my noble Eirian, the Queen of Self-sacrifice. Does it make you feel good?"

Something bitter in the way Celiaen spoke made her open her eyes. Watching him push food around on the tray, Eirian got to her feet and walked over to the window. Looking out at the city, she slumped against the stone and shook her head.

"No, it doesn't. I want other things, but we're born with our part to play, and I accept mine. I could have refused the crown and left, but the guilt of abandoning my duty would've plagued me for the rest of my days. I could've let the high council put their chains on me, binding me to a worse fate. I chose this."

"You think the high council a worse fate than here?" Celiaen asked in surprise.

"More power doesn't mean more freedom. Celi, you can love me until I die, but I wouldn't marry you or Gal, and now, I couldn't."

"You suggest there are different reasons for couldn't and wouldn't."

She chewed her bottom lip and stared out the window. "That's because there is. I wouldn't marry you because I doubt my people would ever accept it. Athnaral certainly wouldn't, and it would put Endara in more danger."

"Ree, what aren't you telling me?"

The scrape of the chair on the floor caused Eirian to glance at Celiaen as he approached.

"I made a deal with Baenlin."

"What sort of deal? My uncle is a master of manipulation."

Chuckling, she shrugged and said, "You aren't wrong. You know they want me to become the grand mage? There were lots of threats, suggestions Endara would revolt against me, and I kept refusing."

Eirian chose to not tell him of the charming and flirtatious side of his uncle. His jealousy did not need any additional excuses. She had seen the way he looked at Aiden, especially when they sparred.

"In the end, to get him to back off, I agreed to a deal. I knew what he wanted from me before I made the deal. I'm not always clueless."

Celiaen grabbed her wrist, forcing her to face him, and demanded, "Ree, what did you do?"

"I have to be queen or return to Riane. I can't ask for help from the high council. If I do, I'll pay a steep price. If I'm forced from the throne, Baenlin will hunt me. If I try to run away, he'll hunt me. It would be the greatest hunt in history, and the longer I fled him, the greater his pleasure in the pursuit would be."

Her words sunk in. Eirian felt his fury, the rising of his magic causing hers to flare in response. It woke the bond between them, and Eirian closed her eyes, breathing deeply to maintain control. She sensed Cai on the other side of the door, their concern a frustrating taste on the tip of her tongue. Cai was not the only mage outside. The others were there beyond the wards they had raised around the room.

The grip on her wrist tightened, and Celiaen's hand on the back of her neck caused her to open her eyes. Eirian found his face hovering over hers so closely that she thought he was going to kiss her. She wanted him to. Their closeness brought back the memory of the day they bonded, the ghost feeling of Celiaen's lips on her skin making her shudder.

"He can try, but you're mine. You'll always be mine, and I am yours."

"Celi—"

"Shut up, Ree. Do you remember how it felt when we created this?"

Celiaen stroked the inside of her wrist, feeling the memory at the forefront of her mind. Her hand slid over the silk of his coat, fingers digging into his back as Eirian let him pull her closer. Magic swirled around them, tugging at the bond and urging them together. She wanted to drag him to her bed, where they could lose themselves in the power binding them and forget the world outside existed.

His lips brushed against hers, Celiaen whispering, "I will never stop wanting you."

"Celi, step away from Ree!" Cai shouted and startled them.

The guards were behind Cai, hands gripping their swords and expressions suggesting they would draw on him. With them stood several of Celiaen's companions, the mages equally concerned.

Celiaen chuckled. "We're only talking."

"No, you're not. You're barely in control. Trained killers are everywhere, and if you two can't control yourselves, what do you think will happen?" Tara reminded them.

She had seen enough of what they could do together to feel a pang of fear. The last thing she wanted to contemplate was what might happen if they lost control in the middle of the keep.

"Tara is right, Celi, please," Eirian whispered.

Growling, Celiaen let go of her and stepped back, allowing Eirian to stumble to her feet. "I will present my father's proposal. We'll see what your council says."

Shaking her head, Eirian stepped past him and approached Cai, meeting their concerned gaze for a moment before passing them on her way to the door.

"You can't stop me from doing it. I'm the Crown Prince of Ensaycal, and this would unite our kingdoms stronger than any treaty."

Pausing in the doorway, Eirian did not look at him. If she looked at Celiaen, she would either kill him or kiss him.

"You're right. But if you value us, you'll look for that grain of sense I know exists in your fool head and let it prevail."

Brenna was waiting outside the door for her, eyes wide with fear as she asked, "Your Highness, what happened? We felt... I don't know how to explain it."

"I'm sorry, Brenna. It got a little out of hand. Now, I'm overdue to visit my father."

"Are you sure that's a good idea?"

Nodding, Eirian smoothed her skirt to help her focus and ignore the pull of Celiaen's power behind her. She needed to put distance between them before her control slipped, and she surrendered to the bond's demands to be completed.

"Anything is a better idea than staying here right now."

Sighing, Brenna nodded and shot a furious look at the door as she started after Eirian. The other ladies attempted to chat among themselves, remaining a few steps behind. Eirian felt the anger lingering on her guards, but Gabe surprised her with concern in the looks he directed at her. Swallowing back unease, Eirian rubbed her arms and reminded herself that she needed to be composed before facing her aunt.

When they reached Nolan's quarters, it threw Eirian to see Everett's guards. Passing into the audience chamber, she heard the laughter and chatter from the next room. She paused and let the feeling of pleasure from the reunion beyond the doors fill her, the palatable joy chasing away her lingering anger. Before Eirian entered the room, the door opened and a tall woman came through, shutting it behind her.

Crossing her arms, she stared at Eirian sternly and instructed, "Let me get a good look. It's been a long time since I saw you."

"Your Grace." Eirian bowed slightly, smiling at the warm tone of the demands.

"I mean it, turn around and let me see you."

Making a motion with her finger, Amira arched a brow. Giggling, Eirian complied and turned in a circle slowly. She caught sight of Brenna watching in amusement. Satisfied with what she saw, Amira pulled Eirian into a hug before turning to Brenna.

"You've been working hard on turning her into a lady, but it should be easier with both of us. We need to sit and talk."

"Aunt Amira, is that necessary?" Frowning, Eirian felt defensive of the woman she counted as a confidant.

Huffing, Amira shook her head and replied, "Brenna knows what I mean. Now, young lady, I hear you've taken to leadership like a duck to water. Your father is proud of you."

Pursing her lips, Eirian was uncertain if the tone suggested a compliment or not and muttered, "It's what I was born to do. Is he?"

"Yes, he is. You should have summoned me."

"We wanted it kept quiet as long as possible for the sake of the kingdom," Brenna explained. "We even kept it from Eirian until she had settled in."

"Well, it's done now. Come in and meet the rest of your family. It's about time you did," Amira said.

She walked back to the door to open it, the laughter from within louder with the barrier broken. Following, Eirian smiled at the sight of Everett and Llewellyn tickling a young girl. Nolan watched on in amusement as twin boys attempted to defend their sister. He looked like the man from her memories, the broad smile showing a fatherly benevolence he reserved for the people in the room.

When Nolan saw her watching, he held out his hand, and Eirian slipped through the people to take it, wrapping her arms around him tightly. She heard his breath hitch before he hugged her back, resting his cheek on her head. It was like the dreams Eirian had as a child. When she longed for the warmth of a family, the feeling of being home and belonging somewhere. Eirian clung to it. The desire to hold it close drove her. She swore she would never forget what it felt like, even when she was utterly alone.

SEVENTEEN

The fabric layers felt more restricting than usual. Eirian shifted uncomfortably as Brenna and Amira stood back, discussing the heavy gown with the team of seamstresses. Glancing at her reflection in the looking glass propped against the wall in front of her, she struggled to recognize the woman staring back. Rich crimson silk encased her, and beneath it were layers of linen to give the skirt more support and form. Slightly off the shoulder and edged with gold and purple, the neckline was shallow, so she could wear the heavy gold links of her predecessors.

Gold and purple embroidery covered the bodice, trailing onto the bias-cut skirt. They represented each of the regions of Endara in painstakingly detailed embroidery. A split in the skirt revealed a dark purple silk underskirt that matched the back lacing. Fitted sleeves ended above her elbow and fell in a pleated drape with the edging done in purple. Further gold embroidering showed the crowned rearing horse, which was the emblem of her family. Along the edges, the hemming and embroidery were the same as on the bottom of the skirt. Underneath, the same purple silk was used to line the sleeves.

"It's spectacular work for the time we gave your team," Brenna told them. "It's perfect. You should be very proud of your hard work."

Frowning, Amira could not argue, and walked around Eirian. "It is outstanding work. This cut suits her beautifully, and I suggest we have more gowns done in this style in the future. We'll store this for when she marries. What about the one for the vigil?"

The seamstress beamed and clapped her hands, summoning her assistants. "Help Her Highness out of the gown and into the next. Be careful!"

Eirian sighed as the women unlaced the gown and gathered the skirts to lift it over her head. There was barely a moment to breathe before they slid more fabric over her. The bone-white dress was a stark contrast to the one for her coronation. It was a lot lighter, and Eirian was thankful she could move comfortably in it. She would spend a night kneeling and sitting in it. Pleased, Amira stood in front of her niece with her arms crossed and a smile.

"Lovely, I like this one. It gives Eirian an air of lightness."

"It's much more comfortable than the coronation gown," Eirian said, tugging at the skirt. "I doubt I could last the night in that one."

Giving her a knowing look, Amira commented, "The throne is hardly comfortable, so you'll have to get used to being uncomfortable for the rest of your life."

"I don't understand why I need a special gown for my vigil. It seems a waste."

Brenna replied, "It is symbolic. At dusk, we lock you in the tomb to present yourself to your ancestors unadorned by any finery. Once, it was completely naked, but that had to change after a coronation in winter, and the prince in question nearly died of the cold. The plain white is to symbolize your prover-bial nakedness and the purity of your intent."

She huffed. "Yes, I know. My point is, I've plenty of plain white garments I could wear. We didn't need to have a special gown made."

"Don't worry, we'll have it dyed and adjusted for you to wear again. I know you don't enjoy having excessive amounts of dresses to choose from, but you realize you're about to become queen, and they expect you to always look the part."

"I don't understand your dislike of gowns. You're a lovely young woman, and you should want to look your best!" Amira declared.

"Please remain still, Your Highness," the seamstress muttered.

Striding over to where the assistants had folded up the coronation gown to transport for final adjustments, Amira stroked the silk. "Pity we can't produce silk as fine as Ensaycal. It's so lovely."

The seamstress fussed over the dress, sticking pins where she felt it needed adjustments and discussing it with her senior assistants. While she stood patiently, Eirian watched Amira pace around the chamber. In the days since her family had arrived in the city, they had disrupted the routine she had estab-lished. Eirian found it frustrating, and she could tell Brenna and her other ladies agreed.

Standing beside Eirian, Brenna gave her a concerned look and asked, "Are you well?"

"I'm reaching the end of my patience. You know me." Smiling faintly, Eirian tilted her head towards the door, muttering, "I constantly hope for a way out of tedium."

"Is the council expecting you today?"

Shaking her head, Eirian was glad when the seamstress stepped away and summoned her assistants to remove the gown. When her ladies fetched a dress for her to wear, Eirian protested despite the opposition she would receive from Amira.

"I'm training today. It's been days, and I won't neglect it."

Amira crossed her arms, glaring as she said, "You can't be serious! It's time to stop playing games and behave like a queen."

Anxious, the seamstress and her team gathered their things and hurried out of the chamber. Looking between Eirian, Brenna, and Amira, the ladies hovered at the wardrobe, waiting for confirmation. Eirian crossed her arms, glaring at her.

"Yes, I'm about to be queen, but I'm not some pretty little figurehead. Besides, my training with the blade has nothing to do with my royal status and everything to do with being a mage." Seeing Amira about to argue, Eirian threw her hands in the air and continued, "Honestly! I don't know where you get these ideas from. Should I worry Athnaral is trying to invade us by aligning our way of thinking with theirs?"

"What man is going to want a woman who can beat him in a fight?"

Eirian went still, and the look she gave Amira was cold enough to freeze a river. "Ladies, my training garbs, please, and my armor."

Brenna remained quiet while she supervised the ladies dressing Eirian. Glancing at where the chest sat, unconsciously ignored by everyone, Eirian pursed her lips.

"I think people need to realize I don't take orders. I won't lead from a distance."

"What do you mean?" Brenna asked in confusion.

Satisfied they had finished dressing her, Eirian took a few quick strides to the chest. She crouched, touching it to drop the wards. Her ladies gasped, their reactions making Eirian snort in amusement. Opening the lid, Eirian unwrapped the twin blades in their scabbards and withdrew them, placing them on the floor. Letting her hands linger on them for a moment, she turned back to the chest and removed her sword belt.

Holding it in one hand, Eirian burrowed into the bottom of the remaining items. She found where she had hidden the purple band depicting her order. Pulling it out, Eirian slipped it onto the middle finger of her left hand and closed her fist, staring at the ring. Her ladies were quiet as she closed the chest and placed the belt on it before adding the swords. Brenna crossed over and picked up the belt, unbuckling it with practiced ease, while Eirian stood.

"Let me help you."

Arching an eyebrow, Eirian did not protest and instead looked at Amira. "Before you berate me, remember this. The more you push, the more likely I am to disagree. And let me assure you, I will have the final say."

Brenna finished buckling the belt and lifted each scabbard, securing them in their spots while trying her best not to turn and look at Amira.

"These are mage crafted, aren't they?" Brenna asked, glancing at Eirian.

"They were a gift from Celiaen."

"You should talk to him. He seeks you every day."

Scoffing, Amira said, "I heard what he was threatening to do. If you're determined to be in charge, you need to establish that you won't tolerate his behavior."

"He'd never abandon Endara to Athnaral. It's all bluster. You're right, Brenna. I should see him. I overreacted because it was a shock." Checking she could draw the swords, Eirian smiled and said, "I should resume wearing these every day to remind people I'm not defenseless."

Elke chuckled. "I don't think anyone would ever think you're defenseless."

Nodding in agreement, Eirian rolled her shoulders and turned to the door. "As always, you ladies are free to do whatever you want or need to do. Unless any of you are thinking of taking up my offer?"

"I talked to my brother, and he thought it was a wonderful idea." Bea looked nervously at Amira, mumbling, "I'd like to learn, especially after what happened."

The other ladies looked at her in surprise.

"Come with me today, and we can talk to a Master of Arms about who would be best to train with. I'm terrible at it, or I'd teach you."

Eirian did not wait for Bea to catch up, and the other ladies trailed behind. In the audience chamber, her guards waited, and she saw the flicker of shock on their faces when they took in the weapons hanging at her side. Aiden looked her over with his head cocked to the side and nodded in approval as he matched her stride. Catching his eyes dropping again, gaze lingering on the knives at the small of her back, Eirian smirked.

"If you'd said something, I would've accommodated you. You might have beaten me a few times."

"If you want to try me with two, I won't stop you, though I'm probably a little rusty." Eirian winked at him as she stepped into the corridor and added, "And, Captain, stop deluding yourself. I let you win."

Aiden rolled his eyes and the other guards chuckled. "I'm not the one deluding themselves, Princess."

"Bea would like to learn. Can you suggest a teacher?"

"Good, they should all learn." He glanced at Bea pensively and said, "Merle would be good. He has sisters and more patience than I do. I'm surprised you don't want to do it."

Her lips twitched, and Eirian shrugged as she replied, "She'd end up running away in tears and never come back."

"You say it like it's happened before."

"That's because it has."

Cringing, Aiden did not respond to her statement and changed the subject. "Have you looked over my suggestions for the tour?"

Before she could reply, a messenger came running towards them and stumbled to a halt when he faced the guards. Glancing through them until he spotted Eirian, he bowed and waited for permission to speak. Amira and Brenna were slightly behind the group and pushed the guards out of the way to stand behind Eirian.

"Yes?" Eirian prompted.

"Your Highness, you need to come. Athnaral has arrived," he told her.

The announcement startled everyone, and Eirian said, "What do you mean Athnaral has arrived?"

"A delegation rode through the gates, and they've gone straight to the throne room. Chancellor Ulric, Chamberlain Wendel, and Justiciar Ollier are receiving audiences today, but the ambassador won't speak to them. He is demanding King Nolan, and they sent me to get you."

Understanding the underlying message regarding her father, Eirian pursed her lips. "Well, that's unexpected. I better find out what this is about. Have they sent for the dukes?"

The messenger shook his head and answered, "I don't know, Your Highness. I was the first one sent."

"Eirian, change first. You want to make a good impression," Amira said, reaching out and touching her arm.

"Let the Athnaralan envoy see me like this."

Eirian smirked, signaling to the guards to start forward again. Word had spread fast, people in the hallways giving Eirian and her companions worried looks as they passed them. Aiden guided the group toward the private entrance, but she shook her head and turned towards the main door with a wide grin.

"Are you sure?"

They all looked surprised.

"I enjoy making an entrance. I'll stride through the room and let them have plenty of time to watch me and wonder. Knowing the councilors, they'll get some enjoyment out of it. Ulric does like it when people squirm."

"You could do with more guards to make an impression," Aiden suggested with a chuckle.

She shook her head. "No, you're enough. I don't want them to think I need a lot of burly men to protect me. Powers know it's not true. I keep you for decoration."

They reached the entrance, and the crowd turned to look in surprise. Moving out of the way, they watched Eirian stride through the great doors with a disdainful look on her face, the feeling of her magic radiating like an oncoming storm. The throne room had a clear path down the middle marked out by different colored stones engraved with the noble families' arms. Guards stood between the long tapestries that lined the walls and along the edges of the crowd, their attention never wavering.

Looking forward, Eirian saw the three councilors seated at the bottom of the dais where the throne resided. Her gaze met each of them, and the looks on their faces told Eirian they understood what she was doing. Everett and Llewellyn were there, standing behind the men and watching their cousin in curiosity as Eirian strode through the watching people who dropped into bows as she went past. The realization struck the diplomat, and he turned, his furious expression melting away to shock.

Eirian looked him over and was pleased she was taller. "So Athnaral has sent us a delegation! Aren't you the lucky one?"

"Your Highness," Ulric said cautiously.

"This changes nothing! You can bring out dukes, you can parade this woman around, but I demand to speak to your king!" Sneering, the ambassador looked away from Eirian.

"I'll be the queen in a few days. I'm sure you can bring yourself to speak to me."

Shrugging, Eirian walked up to the throne and sat as her guards surrounded the dais. Aiden assumed his place behind her, leaning against the seat with a hand on the hilt of his sword. He toyed with it, watching the Athnaralans coldly.

"You are not the queen yet."

Everett laughed. "She's been the queen for a while now."

"My business is with the legitimate King of Endara."

Leaning towards him, Eirian propped her elbows on her knees and laced her fingers under her chin, saying, "That's unfortunate. King Nolan is unavailable, and if the soon-to-be legitimate queen isn't good enough? Well then, you'll have to turn around and return to your king. Of course, he doesn't seem to be a fan of failure, but maybe that's the impression I got from the various men he paid to kill me. Do you want to return to your king and admit you failed to speak to the ruler of Endara?"

Blanching, he looked away, and Eirian watched the tick in his cheek as he contemplated her words. "I know nothing about any assassination attempts, but I doubt His Majesty would do such a thing."

"Oh, I'm sure he wouldn't!" Eirian kept staring at him. "Does it matter if you speak to me? By the time you're back in Athnaral, I'll be the legitimate queen."

"Athnaral does not recognize your right to the throne."

People gasped at the declaration, and Llewellyn laughed, clapping his hands. "Well, it's a good thing we're in Endara, and we recognize her right to the throne. Besides, she's got more balls than most men."

"Maybe that's what has King Aeyren all uppity!" Everett chuckled.

A ripple of laughter spread through the watching crowd, and leaning back against the stone, Eirian held up her hands. She saw what the dukes were attempting to do.

"Now, boys, the size of my balls is irrelevant. Do you have a name? I'm afraid I missed the introductions," Eirian said.

"I'm Ambassador Darrell."

"Well, Ambassador Darrell of Athnaral, I'm Eirian Altira, daughter of King Nolan Altira of Endara. I'm his only child, which means I'm the first in line to the throne by Endaran law. My people recognize my blood right; hence we're preparing for my coronation."

Ulric said, "That's right."

Eirian continued, "There's nothing you could say or threaten to convince us to allow you to see His Majesty. You're more than welcome to return to Athnaral, but if it's not pressing, I invite you to remain until the coronation. After that, there will be no reason not to reveal why you're here."

"Ensaycal recognizes Princess Eirian's right to the Endaran throne," Celiaen spoke loudly.

He stood at the other end of the room with Tynan and his other companions, causing Darrell to turn. At Celiaen's side, Tara looked bored, a hand on the haft of an axe.

"But of course, we don't impose our laws on our neighbors."

"Thank you, Your Highness. As ever, our alliance with the great elven empire is a blessing," Eirian responded.

The councilors glanced back at her, and Eirian winked at them. Ollier returned the wink, and she chuckled, getting to her feet. Eirian looked at Celiaen, taking in how his eyes widened when he saw his gifts hanging at her waist. Buoyed by the other mages, her magic filled the throne room, and those unaccustomed to her displays of power flinched at the feel. Turning back to Eirian, Darrell tried to look unimpressed, crossing his arms as Eirian stepped towards him.

"So, it's true then?"

She cocked her head to the side and said, "I'm not sure what you refer to."

"You're a puppet for the elves!"

His accusation made Eirian laugh. She was not the only one.

"I'm no one's puppet, least of all the elves," Eirian replied, shaking her head vehemently.

Celiaen covered his heart and gave her a sad look as he said, "Your words cut me deep. I was excited to find out you were my puppet."

Rolling her eyes, Eirian turned to her advisors. "I'm sorry we interrupted your work, my dear councilors. Unfortunately, the ambassador has wasted his time and ours."

Ulric bowed and smiled, commenting, "I'm sure he didn't intend to waste our time, Your Highness."

Turning back around, Eirian smiled at Darrell. "Have a safe journey home. When you see Aeyren, thank him for the workouts. I rather enjoyed playing with the men he sent to kill me."

"Are you dismissing me?" Darrell gasped.

"Why yes, yes I am. You don't want to speak to me, so it appears we're at an impasse, and I don't fancy wasting any more time on you. Decide right now. Will you talk to me, or are you going home? Because I'm about to walk out."

Stepping around him, Eirian waited a moment for her guards to follow before she started towards the main doors. Darrell watched her go and glanced at the smiling dukes and the blank-faced councilors before sighing.

"Fine."

Eirian did not turn around, a triumphant smirk curling her lips as she paused in her stride. From the corner of her eye, Eirian watched Celiaen move through the edges of the crowd while Aiden let out a low chuckle.

"You're going to have to be more specific."

"I'll speak with you. However, I suggest we take it somewhere else."

Everett said, "That might be for the best. We can move this to an audience chamber and allow these good councilors to get on with their work."

Following Everett, Darrell signaled for his men. Llewellyn waited for Eirian to join him before making their way into the smaller chamber connected to the throne room. Aiden let the ladies through, but stopped Celiaen. He crossed his arms in frustration, tilting his head towards Tynan.

"We should be in there. Whatever the ambassador has to say might affect Ensaycal. Or what if it upset Eirian? Tynan can calm her."

"Fine, but I'm watching you!" Aiden stepped out of the way and let the two elves into the chamber.

Giving Aiden a sideways look, Celiaen winked and said cheekily, "You can watch me all you like, Captain. I don't mind where your eyes go."

Perching on the edge of the table, Eirian watched Darrell pace around the room nervously and noted his demeanor had changed once they were behind closed doors. She cocked her finger at Celiaen, and he crossed the room, leaning against the table beside her.

She murmured, "What do you think?"

"I'm not sure. It could be anything. I'm pleased to see you wearing your band." His eyes dropped to the swords, and Celiaen purred, "And my gifts."

"Not now, Celi, we'll talk after."

"You have our undivided attention, Ambassador Darrell," Llewellyn said, and sat on a chair, legs stretched out in front of him.

"I'm waiting, but my patience is not unlimited. You agreed to this discussion. Now talk before I walk!" Eirian sensed the frustration coming from her cousins.

Reaching into the pouch on his belt, Darrell withdrew sealed papers and offered them to Everett. "I have the documents to support what I'm informing you of."

"Excellent. Get on with it," Everett replied, taking the papers and passing them to Eirian.

"There has been a tentative peace between Athnaral and Endara for years, and while we don't particularly wish for it to end, we will invade if forced to."

He paused, expecting them to say something.

When no one spoke, Darrell continued, "Our laws don't recognize the right of the female line to inherit a throne. King Aeyren, however, can see the potential of the situation. He proposes we unite our two kingdoms as they should have been generations ago."

Snorting, Llewellyn looked at Everett and said, "You owe me twenty."

"Your Grace, this is not the time." Eirian scolded. "What exactly is your king proposing."

"That you marry him. Endara would become part of the empire, and you'd rightfully be the Queen of Endara and Athnaral. Your children would rule over all humans."

His words confirmed their suspicions, and Eirian glanced at Celiaen when his hand brushed against her leg. Even though she knew her answer, Eirian felt she needed to let Darrell think she was considering the offer. Bringing herself to ask for further confirmation of what they already knew, she looked at Darrell.

"And if I refuse his proposal? Will Aeyren declare war on Endara and invade us? Does he forget we have an alliance with the Ensaycal? Our alliance has defeated Athnaral time and time again."

"If you refuse him and insist on being crowned queen, he'll feel forced to invade. We don't recognize the legitimacy of your claim, and we would overthrow a false monarch."

Furious, Celiaen took a deep breath and looked at Tynan, watching from the corner of the room. Eirian's hand touched his, a gentle reminder to control his temper.

He demanded, "Who does your king think he is to declare the laws of another kingdom wrong? This is Endara, and Endaran laws allow for women to inherit. It is not Athnaral, and Aeyren cannot dictate who can take this throne."

"He is the rightful king to all humans."

"Not these humans!"

Darrell crossed his arms and said, "You would say that when you want this land for your empire."

"Enough!" Eirian growled and looked at the two men. "Endara has no desire to be invaded. We're proud to be independent. While we don't have the military numbers that either of your kingdoms possesses, we're an important middle ground. If we didn't exist, you lot would never stop fighting. We facilitate trade between you. Trade that provides a lot of coin for many people, including your kings."

"So, you don't deny the Crown Prince has proposed the same thing?" Darrell accused.

"If he has, his reasoning and offer differ from that of your king. My answer is the same. No."

Everett shook his head and explained, "The entire council must approve her marriage, and we'd never agree to your offer. Endara is independent for a reason. Our ancestors had no desire to fall under the yoke of Athnaral. The elves have supported us over the years because they recognize our independence benefits them. It's a pity Athnaral continues to deny the truth."

Sighing, Eirian dropped a hand and touched the hilt of a sword for reassurance. "You'll return to your king. Tell him I refuse, and he'll order his troops to invade my kingdom. War won't end well for any of us, and I'd rather negotiate other options that won't result in thousands of lives lost."

"Believe me, I don't want to see those lives lost, either. Can I be candid?" Darrell's shoulders slumped, and Eirian cocked her head to the side, waiting for him to continue. "I agree with you. We have no right to make demands. Your laws are your laws, and our laws end at the border. Things have worked the way they are for generations. Who are we to change that?"

Eirian answered, "I'm pleased to hear that, Ambassador. Unfortunately, your king disagrees."

He glanced around the room, gaze lingering on his men as he said, "Not that long ago, I'd have argued that he agreed. Things have changed recently, and some days, I… we wonder what is going on. Aeyren used to be a good man, and now it's like a shadow shrouds him. Only those approved by his closest advisers can see him."

Blinking once, Eirian did not let anyone see how his words troubled her. She remembered what the man in the alley had claimed and what the attacker in the wood had echoed. Shadows and madness kept popping up, and Eirian did not know what to make of it. Whatever it meant, she could not let it distract her from the conversation at hand.

"It wasn't recently he first sent men to kill me."

There was a flicker of anger in Eirian's magic, and Tynan took a warning step towards her. He remembered what she had done to the Athnaralans who had ambushed them years before. Eyes darting to Celiaen, Tynan could tell he recalled the same things.

"I know nothing about that. Such a decision would be behind closed doors, and only Aeyren's most trusted are likely to be in on it. It's not something I approve of. I'm a diplomat, Princess Eirian. We look at more peaceful options like you suggest."

Nodding, Eirian stepped over to Darrell and offered her hand. "There's a coronation happening, that means celebrations. Take the time to enjoy the freedoms Endarans take for granted. We can explore other viable options for you to take back to your king."

He replied appreciatively, "Thank you, Your Highness. I'll do that. It's a long ride between Mirrenel and Amath, and we could use the rest. I have a question for you. Is it true that King Nolan has the madness?"

No one answered, and the looks on their faces told Darrell everything. Understanding the implications of them acknowledging it, Darrell did not press the matter further. He glanced at his boots in dismay. Even though they were on opposite sides, he respected King Nolan. Everyone knew the Altira family were fair rulers. The way Endara continued to grow and prosper under their leadership was enviable. Meeting Eirian's gaze, he nodded slightly and knew she understood.

"I'll take these fine men and see them settled into their quarters," Amira said.

"Thank you, that would be wonderful." Crossing to the side door, Eirian gave Darrell a smile. "I like you right now, Ambassador, don't risk angering me."

"I'll keep that in mind, Your Highness, and I'll do my best," he replied with a soft chuckle. "It's unfortunate I can't promise the same for my king."

Exiting the room, her cousins and the two elves followed Eirian, with her ladies and guards bringing up the rear. The corridor outside was almost empty, a few guards dotted at critical points. They observed the group head around a corner before focusing on watching the second group emerge from the room.

Eirian turned to her companions and said, "I don't know if that could've gone better. Everett, will you let the council know? Take this letter, read it to confirm what the ambassador told us, and present it to them. We were right to start preparations."

"What are you going to do?" Llewellyn asked.

She smiled, inclining her head towards Celiaen. "I'm going to go beat his ass."

Arching his brows, Celiaen smirked, asking, "When have you ever managed that?"

Chuckling, the two dukes exchanged amused looks.

Everett said, "Don't get hurt and don't damage him. We'll talk to the council. Do you want us to mention the possibility of sending a counteroffer?"

"Yes, that's a good idea. We can see what ideas arise before we meet with Darrell. If someone can comb through records for previous treaties with Athnaral, we could use precedence."

Llewellyn grunted. "Good idea."

Shaking her head, Eirian walked away, her guards and ladies striding after her, but then she stopped and pivoted to look at her cousins. "What state is His Majesty in today?"

"Not a good one," Everett replied.

"I understand, and I won't visit. Thank you." Hesitating, Eirian glanced at Celiaen and frowned.

"I'll follow shortly. I need a few words with your cousins," he told her.

His response made Eirian nod and stride off.

"Better chase after her, Princeling." Llewellyn wriggled his brows at Celiaen and cackled. "Don't want to leave Her Majesty waiting for an ass to kick."

Rolling his eyes, Celiaen glanced over his shoulder at the retreating group. "You should look at past treaties with my father. There might be something you can use."

"Not just a pretty princeling. Tell me, are your blades the twins to hers? I can spot mage work a mile away, and it's rare to see four identical hilts. You all like to have your little flair imprinted on your signature weapons."

Everett looked confused and asked, "What are you on about, Llewellyn?"

"You're correct. They're a set of four identical blades. I had them crafted for us to celebrate her birthday and our friendship. Understand this, I'd do anything for Eirian." Giving them a hard stare, Celiaen turned and strode in the direction Eirian had gone, with Tynan close on his heels.

"I'm still confused, Llewellyn. What were you on about with the swords?" Everett watched the retreating elves and asked, "How do you know so much about mage weapons?"

There was a twitch in his cheek as Llewellyn answered, "I have a lot of business with the elves. If you want to be effective in your dealings with them, you pick up on things. He's very much in love with our little cousin, and that makes him a concern. How much influence does Celiaen have over her?"

"What do you mean?"

"I mean, if she doesn't marry Celiaen, we need to encourage him to leave and never come back. He needs to go once the coronation is over, and we sort the treaty renewal. There can be no question as to the paternity of her children. Not if we want the next coronation to go smoothly."

"I've seen what Paienven proposes, and it makes sense. If it made her happy and benefited Endara, we could encourage her to say yes. There's no guarantee their children would have the long lives of the elves," Everett said.

Shaking his head, Llewellyn ran a hand through his hair, replying, "It's not about happiness, cousin, you know that. We are royalty. It is all about duty. My mother's making a list of matches for me because she says I'm getting old and need to hurry and make some heirs. I think she's hoping Gallagher's sweet little sister will catch my eye."

"Bea is a nice girl."

"I'm royal, and the council has to approve. You'll be next, probably sooner than me. The council won't want to let Eirian marry for a little while, but they need to guarantee heirs, and you and I are the logical targets."

Cringing, Everett said, "Eirian isn't a young woman, and if she weren't a mage, they'd have matched her up years ago. She's the least likely person I know to have a husband influencing her."

"Isn't that the truth!" Llewellyn laughed.

"She'd make the poor man know his place."

They fell silent, each thinking about the future. Around them, the bustle and noise of the castle continued, the footsteps of Eirian and her companions long since faded.

Taking a breath, Everett continued, "I love Endara, and the needs of the kingdom will always come first. Right now, I think we need to consider the long-term possibilities of being bound to the elven throne. Athnaral may or may not attack this time. But if Eirian is the queen, they'll be frothing at the bit to put her down. We've always been able to count on Ensaycal to come to our aid, so what is one more assurance?"

"Are you suggesting we should encourage the council to accept Celiaen's proposal? I see what you're saying. We'd never have to worry about Ensaycal defending our borders with elven royal blood on the throne."

"Exactly."

"You aren't the first to suggest it. Others can see the long-term potential, and they know the council would never approve it without both of us agreeing first." Sucking a breath through his teeth, Llewellyn screwed up his face and grumbled, "We'd need Marcellus to agree as well."

Frowning, Everett rubbed his hands against his trousers and shifted his feet, glancing at his guards. "It would be hard to sell it to the people."

"Do you think so? Our people know the elves come to our rescue when Athnaral threatens. They know Ensaycal is their primary source of trade, and our culture is far more in line with the elves than Athnaral. There's no conflict between our two kingdoms, and our people cross the border freely. I have elves who call my lands home. People flow back and forth over the border."

Llewellyn took a breath before he continued, and Everett let him talk.

"I like the elves. I have many friends among them and probably a bastard or two. I like the prince. He's a good man, a feared warrior, and highly respected. There's something between Eirian and Celiaen, and there will be more, eventually. If she marries another, there will always be the question hanging over the heads of her children, and questions of legitimacy lead to civil war."

Everett shook his head at Llewellyn. He could not argue with what was being said.

"It's just you and me right now. If Eirian doesn't marry the prince, he needs to leave. I don't have the same relationship with Eirian that you do," Llewellyn said.

"You want me to talk to her. We need to convince her to marry Celiaen or to banish him from her life."

"Yes. Now, we need to speak to people. Or did I distract you from the matter of Athnaral?"

"No, I haven't forgotten. We should get on," Everett said as Llewellyn walked away.

Llewellyn halted and looked at him to add, "By the way, has anyone spoken to you about your brother?"

Shuddering at the idea, Everett replied, "Aiden knows his duty."

"I'm saying, and I'm not the only one who has suggested it. He's a suitable match for Eirian." Holding up his hands defensively, Llewellyn grinned and said, "One piece of paper with a signature. That's all the bastard son of the late Earl of Tamantal needs to become a suitable candidate to marry the Queen of Endara. There are enough council members considering it. Powers know he's one of the few who could handle her, and I think Aiden would embrace the challenge."

"Did you hear Gallagher made noises?"

"Oh, good grief, she'd chew him up and spit him out before he could even touch her!" Tossing his head back, Llewellyn laughed as they started walking.

EIGHTEEN

They sat opposite each other with the table between them, and books spread over the surface. Library staff hovered, ready to jump at the slightest command. Newly assigned to Eirian, a young man chosen by Ulric was at another table, with quills and ink spread around him. Papers laid out, ready for anything she might direct him to record. He watched Eirian like a hawk, wanting to familiarize himself with her mannerisms as quickly as possible.

Scattered around the library, her ladies worked on other tasks. The bright sunlight filtered in the windows, providing light as they combed through books. Eirian loved the library. It was nothing like the libraries in Riane, and she enjoyed the openness of the space. Massive rows of shelving housed books, while lower rows of shelves provided homes to rolls of parchment. The library staff carefully categorized and monitored everything.

"I don't understand why you asked me to help," Tynan said as he leaned back in the chair and stretched out, glancing around at the quietly working women.

Eirian did not look up from the book and replied, "I had an ulterior motive."

"You haven't gotten to the motive yet, and I'm bored. Plus, you specifically called on me while Celi was busy with your council. That suggests you don't want him involved."

Shutting the book he had been looking at, Tynan slid it out of the way. He reached for an apple from the tray of food balanced precariously on the edge of the table.

"I'm spending tomorrow preparing for a night alone locked in a tomb, then the day after that, they're going to stick a crown on my head. I have no more time to ask you or for us to do it."

Frowning at Eirian's words, he glanced at the ladies with their heads bowed. "I don't exist to come at your call."

"I know. Honestly, I don't know if I want to risk it, but it would be better for everyone if Nolan was there. We don't need him to be, but it would be better." Eirian rubbed her face warily and said, "I know it's a long shot, but if we can buy him a few days for the coronation."

"You know what you're asking? I'm not sure I have the power to do such a thing, even if I agreed. It would only be temporary, and when it wore off... Ree, you shouldn't be considering this. Everyone would understand if he wasn't there."

Lifting her eyes from the book, Eirian stared at him sadly. "You're right. I didn't say it would benefit the nobility. What if the benefit was for Nolan and me? The dignity of ending his reign knowing what was going on. I'd like to give that to him. Maybe I want to remember him as he was."

Sighing, Tynan crossed his arms on the table and laid his head down on it. "You know, I can't argue with that sentiment, but it doesn't matter if I don't have the strength to pull it off."

"Don't worry about the power. Remember, I can channel."

"Have you channeled for someone other than Celi, Gal, and Fay?"

Shrugging, Eirian shut her book and said to the staff, "Thank you, I'm done for today."

Her ladies took it as a cue to finish what they were doing and began packing away their work. Waiting while the librarians removed the books from the tables to return to their designated homes on the shelves, Eirian stared at the row of windows. Tynan watched her thoughtfully, head resting on his crossed arms, with his chin digging into his wrist.

"I've channeled for them, yes, but Riane ensured there were others. They didn't skim over my training."

"You're close, and channeling for them is second nature. Say I do this. Are you comfortable sharing with me? We might be friends, but we're not that close."

Rubbing her hand on the smooth timber of the table, Eirian did not look at him. "It's unlikely you'll be unassigned from Celi, even if Gal comes back from Telmia. You've been part of his group for longer than me."

"That's true. You realize you and Celi will never be the same once you're the queen, and we leave here with a completed treaty. You might see each other formally every few years with some great excuse, but you could never be what you were before. Not unless you accept his proposal." Tynan lifted his head and looked towards her ladies, wondering how much they knew.

"I know. I want to try this if we can. If you aren't willing to do it yourself, would you walk me through it, or should I ask Alyse?"

"You don't have the right inclinations to do it. If we do this, Nolan needs to be lucid for me to anchor him there."

Pursing her lips, Eirian looked away from the window and faced him, saying, "I understand. No lucid, no go. If he is, we can give him a choice. Will you do it for me?"

"I need you to consider my next question. How would your council react if they found out and disapproved? It wouldn't be a good start to your reign to have your council questioning your willingness to manipulate minds with magic to get what you want."

"I'd like to think they have formed enough of an idea of what sort of person I am to know it's not something I'd normally condone. I assure you, I've considered everything. That I'm asking you to do this means I've concluded it's a valid path of action, and I want to take it."

Brenna approached and rested a hand on Eirian's shoulder, gently asking, "Are you going to do it? If not, you should get on with relaxing."

Tynan sighed and looked at Brenna to say, "It's up to me. Tell you what, Ree. We can go now to see if your father is himself. If he isn't, then that's it, but if he is, we can talk and find out how he feels about the matter."

Nodding, Eirian pushed the chair back from the table to get to her feet. Following suit, her ladies stood and waited for her to start towards the door. Perking up, the guards stirred themselves from around the library. Once she stepped away from the table, Tynan scrambled to his feet, bowing his head in thanks to the quiet staff before joining Brenna. They mirrored Eirian's silent thoughtfulness as they shadowed her through the corridors.

Guards outside Nolan's quarters saluted when they approached and opened the door. Eirian hated seeing the audience chamber empty. She could tell it bothered the guards to see the constant flow of people trickle to nothing. They had rerouted everything through the council. Once she returned from her tour and took them over, councilors, nobility, and petitioners would refill the chambers. Giving thanks that the next room would not be so empty, she turned to the next set of doors and paused.

"We don't have to do this," Tynan said as he stood beside her, sensing her reluctance. "You could go in there, find out if he is lucid, spend time with him and enjoy it. I can turn around and walk out of here."

Eirian shook her head and glanced at him. "It's not that. No one wants to see someone so vital decline this way. These almost empty rooms feel wrong.

I feel the anger of his household. They're so loyal to him, and it hurts them. They love him."

"If only humans went as we do. It would be easier to say goodbye."

"Elves aren't exempt from madness. In some ways, I'm thankful this isn't Riane. You know their policy." Taking a deep breath, Eirian reached for the door then said, "Then again, there might be something to it."

Cringing, Tynan reached out and grabbed her hand, causing Eirian to shake her head at the guards when they made a step towards them.

He pleaded, "Don't do this. I don't think you'll forgive yourself for the fallout when it wears off."

"Let me worry about forgiving myself. What is a little more guilt? Just worry about what you need to do if he is able and willing to agree. Nothing else is your concern."

Tynan released her hand and recoiled at the coldness that came over her. It felt like being thrown into an icy lake. He had experienced the backwash from Celiaen and Galameyvin more than a few times, but it never stopped being a shock. Like all blues, Tynan thrived on the emotions of those around him, but it was only the most disciplined of people that could shut him out. He watched Eirian's face as she opened the door and went through to the next chamber. There was a tense set to her jaw and shoulders, and she turned a blank look towards the gentlemen. Thomas bowed with a sad smile and nod of affirmation.

He said, "He's himself, but he didn't want us hovering. The last time I checked, he was going through some old books. The Dowager hasn't been yet."

"Thank you, Thomas." Eirian turned to her ladies and guards. "Just Tynan, unless I call for you. No one is to interrupt us for anything."

Nodding, Brenna crossed her arms and cocked her eyebrow at the quiet guards, daring Fionn to disagree. "We understand. Good luck."

Sighing, Eirian crossed quickly to the next door and opened it enough to slip through. Catching it with his hand, Tynan followed her into the room he had seen multiple times. They had called on him and the other blues to calm Nolan during episodes more than he liked to remember. He was uncertain if Eirian knew how many times and Tynan would not tell her.

Nolan was at his desk between two open windows, the light and fresh air helping chase the memories of soiled sheets and sickness away. In front of him, a stack of books with nothing written on the bindings sat, and his hand rested on them, the bent fingers stroking the cover of the top one distractedly. He did not turn to look at them, and Eirian walked over, placing a hand gently on his shoulder while stroking his head with the other.

"Hello, father." She kissed his cheek softly.

"My sweet girl, you shouldn't be visiting me. You have little time for yourself. They tell me your vigil is tomorrow." Nolan grasped her hand where it rested on his shoulder and squeezed it, smiling at her as he said, "You'll be fine. I know it seems like an inconvenience, sitting in a tomb for a night, but no one will know if you curl up on the floor and go to sleep. I certainly did."

Pulling over a chair, Tynan chuckled at the thought, and Nolan glanced at him as he asked, "You don't think the ancestors know?"

"You're a mage. What do you think? I'm sure there are libraries dedicated to that question in Riane."

Shrugging, Eirian sat on the chair and tilted her head to look at the stack of books. "I'm not concerned about being up all night. It wouldn't be the first time or the worst place I've done it.

"I'm proud of you. You'll be a good queen, and Endara will continue to flourish under your rule. I know I'm not supposed to be told much because of my condition, but Thomas tells me. I suspect he does it so I can know it's okay."

There was a finality in his eyes that unsettled Eirian.

"I have excellent support. You trained them well, and I wish you could've trained me." Eirian swallowed and said, "Father, there is something important that I need to ask. I hope you can understand all my unspoken reasons for it."

Nolan stared at her, eyes squinting as he replied, "I can try but forgive me if I'm not as shrewd as I used to be. It gets harder to think every day."

Tynan watched the hesitation that flickered over Eirian's face before she pushed on with her decision.

"Working together, Tynan and I can give you a few days without the madness. It's not a fix, and it's not something we could do again, which is why I haven't brought it up before. It's temporary, and when it wears off, you'll be worse than before. But it would give you time for the ceremony."

"How long would it last?"

"Most likely three days, maybe four, if you're lucky. But there will be a crash in your health afterward," Tynan answered, and Eirian shot him a look.

"What exactly is it? How does it work?"

Nolan looked at Tynan, a hint of authority in his gaze, and he saw the similarities between father and daughter. Leaning on the back of Eirian's chair, Tynan knew he needed to be honest.

"I'll use my power to build a barricade around your mind. I can't undo the damage or change things, so I can only do it if you are lucid. It may take more magic than I have, and Eirian will open hers to me to draw from."

"Is she at risk if you do this?"

"No, father, there is no risk to me," she assured him.

"Her mind will be open to me, and I'll know things about her that others do not," Tynan responded.

There was a flash of fear on Nolan's face. "Will my mind be open like that?"

Shaking his head, Tynan said reassuringly, "No, it doesn't work like that. I can't see into minds like you're thinking, but when two mages share power in this manner, it opens them up to each other. Eirian will know things about me that others do not. As the years go by, she won't be willing to do this for exactly the reason you think."

Nolan rubbed his arms and looked between them before resting his gaze on Eirian to say, "You don't need to do this for me. I understand why you want to, and I'd make the same offer in your position. By the powers, I want to say yes. A few days without the madness, and I can say goodbye. Of course, I want to say yes."

"I'm not offering it just for you," Eirian murmured.

"I know. You're doing it for yourself, for Everett, for your aunt and cousins. For the council. You want everyone to have that finality, and I understand. Despite our years apart, you are very much my daughter. Riane could never change that." Nolan took hold of Eirian's hands and leaned forward to stare deeply into her eyes, telling her. "You made the right decision about both of them."

Blinking back tears, Eirian shook her head. "What do you mean?"

"Saying no to marrying your elf prince and the King of Athnaral. You need to be the queen only you can be. I know the council will go back and forth over the issue. They'll have concerns about your age, but be firm and say no, not until you're ready. Just…"

They waited for Nolan to continue.

"Just push the boys into marriage and make sure you have heirs. You don't have to marry. You could be the queen and trust Everett to provide you with an heir. At least you wouldn't die in childbirth," he said hoarsely.

"Like my mother."

Nolan nodded solemnly and said, "Yes, like your mother. They encouraged me to marry again and have more children, but I loved her so much I couldn't do it. Once you love someone as I did her, you can't disrespect another by making them compete with the memory. No woman would've been happy knowing they couldn't compare to her, and no one deserves that."

Bowing her head, Eirian hid her emotions behind the curtain of hair that hung around her face, but she knew Tynan felt them. It was more for her father's benefit.

"I'm sorry I killed her."

"You didn't kill her, Eirian. I've never blamed you."

"Then you are a better person than I am."

"One day, my darling girl, you'll understand. I hope when that day comes, you'll forgive yourself. What happened was beyond your control. Your mother gave everything to you."

Uncomfortable listening to their conversation, Tynan shuffled his feet and said, "If we're going to go ahead, we should get on with it."

Nolan nodded. "We can't tell how long this will last, and if we delay, I might lose myself before you have a chance."

"You agree?" Wanting absolute confirmation, Tynan focused solely on Nolan.

"Yes, I agree. Do you understand that if it goes wrong and Eirian is hurt, I'll kill you?"

Ignoring the threat, Tynan glanced at the door and pursed his lips. He grabbed the stool beside the bed and brought it over, signaling Eirian to move her chair away from Nolan. Sitting between them, Tynan rubbed his hands together and leaned towards Nolan. Behind him, he sensed Eirian shuffling closer, and her power bordered on overwhelming. Nolan stiffened, and Tynan watched him stare in amazement. Tynan knew what he saw. He had seen it so many times. The way the magic surrounded Eirian, the sheen of it glittering across her skin, gave her an ethereal appearance.

"What do you need me to do?" Nolan asked.

Lifting his hands, Tynan said, "I need you to lean back in the chair and let it support you. You're going to want to fight me. Your mind will try to reject my presence. Don't touch Eirian."

Curious, his eyes flickered to Tynan. "Why?"

"Because it will take control on my part to feed my power to Tynan and not overwhelm him. He needs precision, and unfortunately, I've got a habit of being less than precise," Eirian explained and half-smiled, shrugging. "I'm working on it."

Tynan admitted, "Ten of me wouldn't come close to her power. You have an incredible daughter. Now, I'm going to put my hands on either side of your face. Ree, you know what you're doing."

Taking a deep breath, Tynan lifted his hands and placed them on either side of Nolan's face. Shuffling behind him, Eirian was careful not to touch anything but Tynan, and placed her hands on his shoulders. Closing her eyes, she swallowed before focusing on the flow of her magic and nothing else. She felt more than heard his gasp and the swirl of his power in response as he focused on Nolan.

Eirian divided her focus between holding back her mind and maintaining a steady flow of magic. The longer they shared magic, the harder it would be to keep Tynan out. At the end of the link, Eirian sensed Nolan. An image of him standing at the bottom of a well reached her. When Tynan pulled back from Nolan, she was unprepared for his power losing its focus and did not have time to brace for it. She felt Tynan's magic flood back across the link between them before she could stop it.

Nolan stared at the two mages with their eyes closed and heads tilted back, power filling the surrounding air. He felt calm and suspected that it resulted from the magic. Desperately wanting to touch them, Nolan kept his hands balled in his lap and told himself it was a bad idea. The question of how far the reach of their power went made him cast a look toward the door warily. There was an expectation that at any moment, someone would come crashing through the door, demanding to know what was going on.

Returning his focus to the mages, Nolan frowned at the euphoric look on Tynan's face and its contrast to the strange look on Eirian's. It was hard to tell if it was serenity or anxiety, and it left Nolan wondering what was going on in their minds. A glance at the windows at the position of the sun told him it had taken a lot longer than it had felt like.

"I don't know what's happening, but I think you need to stop."

He felt foolish speaking to them when he was unsure if they could hear him inside their bubble of power. His voice must have been enough, because Eirian dropped her hands, and in her hurry to get away from Tynan, she fell off the chair. Chest heaving, Eirian battled to calm her breathing while sitting on the floor a short distance away. Tynan remained perched on the stool, his eyes closed and breathing calmer.

Looking between them, Nolan stood and approached Eirian, offering his hand to help her from the floor. Staring at him, she nodded and grabbed it, allowing him to hoist her up. Nolan did not let go of her hand, hanging on to it until he was sure Eirian would not fall over.

"Thank you," she rasped.

Nolan looked around for a jug of water. "Are you alright? Did it work?"

Watching him pour a cup of water for her, Eirian chewed on her top lip anxiously. "I don't know. Do you feel like it did?"

Offering her the cup, Nolan turned his gaze to Tynan and noticed he had opened his eyes to watch Eirian. There was anger smoldering in his stare.

"I think so. It was bizarre. I could've sworn I was in a pit, and there was a wall being built around me, but I didn't feel trapped."

"It worked." Tynan sounded as dry as Eirian had, and Nolan went to pour a second cup when Eirian finished.

"Here."

"Who knows? Damn it, Ree, who knows?" Tynan snarled.

"Gal, Tara, Fay, Alyse." She knew exactly what he was referring to and added, "I thought all of you knew, to be honest."

Looking back and forth between them, Nolan muttered, "I don't think I want to know what you're talking about."

There was fury in his voice when Tynan said, "If anyone else found out, it would endanger both of you! There is a bloody good reason they're forbidden."

"You think I don't know that? It wasn't like we planned it... or maybe Celi did!" Shaking her head, Eirian scolded herself. "It's wrong of me to suggest it because he'd never purposefully endanger either of us like that."

"Not with a clear head, he wouldn't, and you didn't have a clear head when the two of you did what you did. You're human! Do you realize how much it's going to affect him when you die? It could kill him!"

Making noises, Nolan scratched his head, grumbling, "I don't want to hear this. Are you sure it worked? Will I be myself for the coronation?"

"I'm sorry, Your Majesty. Yes, it worked. I can feel my wall surrounding your mind, and I'll know when it comes down. Hopefully, I'll have enough warning to prepare us for the crash. Enjoy the time you have." Staggering to his feet, Tynan felt the mental exhaustion of what he had done creeping in.

Eirian could tell, and she said, "Go eat and rest. Even with my power helping, that took a lot out of you. I can't express how grateful I am. Thank you so very much, Tynan."

Nodding, Tynan passed them on his way to the door, and Nolan bowed his head in thanks. He could not express how he felt about the time Tynan had given him.

"I know. You owe me, and one day I will collect."

Eirian paced over to a window when the door clicked shut and leaned against the ledge, looking out over the castle grounds. "Did you know two mages can bind their magic together so tightly it's impossible to break without death? It's not easily done. It requires an almost complete loss of control and an existing emotional bond."

"No, I didn't, but I imagine it's a well-kept secret. Is that what Tynan was talking about? Are you and Prince Celiaen bound in this manner? How did it happen?"

Stretching his arms, Nolan felt better than he could remember feeling in a long time. He waited for Eirian to reply to his questions.

"They attacked us. It wasn't the first or last time, but perhaps the most savage. We'd slipped off on our own, and they were after him, rebels who thought they could hurt the king by killing his heir. Of course, they didn't count on me," Eirian said bitterly.

"What do you mean?"

"I have a terrible bloodlust and enough power to send an army of red mages into a frenzy, let alone just one. It's not like Celiaen lacks in power either. The result is always a complete mess, but we know how to cover it up, and his companions know to keep their mouths shut. I imagine Aiden and his men would do the same after they helped me dispose of the bodies of those I'd brutally butchered."

"You could say it's part of their job," he told her.

Eirian glanced over her shoulder at him sadly and reminded Nolan of her mother. "I don't suppose you expected to learn that about your daughter. I lost control, which caused Celiaen to do the same and then, surrounded by blood and blades, we found our magic bound."

Shaking his head in disbelief, Nolan knew he could not understand and asked, "But you turned down his marriage proposal?"

"Yes, I did. I suppose it's an odd decision when a magical binding is a much more permanent marriage. It's why I know the elves would never abandon us to Athnaral. If I could undo it, I would. Tynan was right. My death will wreak havoc on Celiaen. Thankfully, he's powerful enough that it shouldn't kill him."

"That's why it's forbidden? Because it can kill you if you're not strong enough?"

She nodded and covered her face, asking, "Have you killed someone?"

"Yes."

"And you're not surprised I have?"

Unsure how he should answer, Nolan crossed to the window and leaned on the ledge next to her. "I'm relieved. You understand the price, and that will help you as queen. Even more so if we end up at war with Athnaral. So many young noblemen play at being warriors without spilling blood or understanding the price."

"So I've discovered."

"They don their shiny armor and buckle their fancy belts with ornate weapons that have never parried a strike intended to kill them. They parade around at tourneys with crowds screaming their names, and they declare they're the greatest swordsmen in the kingdom."

"And they never understand. During the attack in the woods, none drew a blade to join in. They huddled and stared, except for Everett. I know he has seen combat, and so has Llewellyn. War scares me," Eirian admitted.

"It should. It breaks my heart that it must be you facing the reality of war. Perhaps it is a circle coming back around."

"What do you mean?"

He pursed his lips and frowned, glancing back at his desk and the books. "It's something forgotten and lost in the ages, but it was a queen who originally united our kingdom. Everyone remembers the king who founded Amath, but it was his mother who founded Endara."

Turning to stare at Nolan in amazement, Eirian waved at him, asking, "Why hasn't anyone told me?"

"There aren't many records of it. If indeed there were many. I've studied the history of our kingdom extensively over the years, and there are few references. It was during what they call the dark times. Over generations, she's forgotten, and we credit everything to him."

"I've heard of the dark times before and thought it another name for the mage wars. I wonder what happened. I suppose only the daoine would remember." Eirian noticed a fearful look on her father's face at her words and said, "Not that it matters anymore. Thank you for telling me. Perhaps she's the reason Athnaral has such restrictive laws about women."

Nolan chuckled and patted her shoulder. "I expect their laws came about because of strong, ferocious women like you."

"What was my mother like? You don't talk about her, and we might never have the chance again."

Pulling away, Nolan turned to the window and stared out at the tumble of stone walls and rooftops. "She was strong and determined. I'd never change my love for her, but I wish she'd come into my life sooner. Unfortunately, things happen as the gods destine them."

Eirian nodded, saying, "The gods abandoned us long ago, but their stones still roll."

"Your mother used to say the gods had plans. She was beautiful. You often look like her. I see her in your expressions, the way you smile when you are happy, and your joyful laugh." Nolan glanced at her and saw how Eirian stared at him like she was trying to memorize everything about the moment. "I don't regret agreeing to this short reprieve. No matter what happens, never forget that. I don't regret it at all."

"Why don't you talk about her more?"

He closed his eyes and sighed. "Because it hurts, and I didn't want to remind us of what we lost. Tegan tried to be a mother to you, raising you with Everett until it became obvious you were magical. I was always closer to her, but that didn't stop Amira from trying to take you."

Pushing away from the window, Eirian ran a hand through her hair and realized she was starving. "I'm going to ask Brenna to organize some food. Is there anything you'd like?"

"I'd like to go for a walk. Are you sure you're not drained from helping Tynan?" Nolan asked in concern.

"I wish I could say I was. I need to eat, but I always do. It's normal for mages. Being a mage isn't a bad thing… until you have as much power as I do. It's not fair the gods have given me so much magic."

"Eirian, your power…" Nolan shook his head, admitting, "There have been mages in our family in the past, and what we did to them, it's not something we can be proud of."

Her mouth hung open as his words sunk in, her hands balling into fists. "Are you saying our forefathers killed their children if they had magic?"

"Childhood illnesses or accidents. I can't say if any of them would've been as powerful as you, but maybe you're powerful for a reason. Maybe you're to be the light in the darkness, the flaming sword that battles the shadows."

"It sounds like you know something about my future."

Eirian doubted what he said was a coincidence. Not with everything else she had picked up from other people. The whispers clambered at her mind, demanding she listen to them. Sometimes she caught hints of warnings among the noise, assuring her she was right to pay attention to what people said about nightmares and shadows.

Nolan turned to stare at her and said, "Maybe it's the madness, but I've dreamed of such darkness. Sometimes Siani is there, pointing at a figure bathed in light. The figure is you, but it's not you as you are now. You're different. It's hard to explain. The darkness makes me feel such fear, but you banish it."

"How do I banish it?" she asked, cocking her head to the side.

Thinking hard, Nolan tried to recall. "I can't say. It's behind Tynan's wall."

"You can feel the wall?"

"I do when I try to remember the dreams."

Eirian felt cold, saying, "Don't think about it anymore, please. Do not, whatever you feel or think, press that wall. I think we should change the subject. I need to eat. I'll get my ladies to fetch something, and then we can go to the gardens."

"You're upset by this, Eirian." Nolan held out his arms as an invitation, taking a step towards her. "I'm sorry."

"How about a picnic in the garden, and I can show you something beautiful?"

Dropping his arms, Nolan murmured, "That sounds lovely. I haven't been in the garden for a long time. Could you send Thomas in?"

Flinching at the sadness in his tone, Eirian met his gaze and stepped in to hug him. "I'm sorry too. I feel like there's something else going on."

"With me?"

As Eirian rested her head on his shoulder, it reminded Nolan of the little girl she used to be. He stroked her hair gently.

"With the world. There has always been something present in the corner of my eye that I can never quite see. The hint of memories that aren't mine."

"I'm not sure I understand what you mean, Eirian."

She pulled back and said, "That's just it. Neither do I. But something feels wrong, and it has for long enough that it's feeling normal. Creeping shadows, and nightmares, and madness."

Reaching out, Nolan took hold of her hands and peered at Eirian's face, eyes searching for something he knew not. He understood what she spoke of, and Nolan wished he could tell Eirian what he knew. But there were some oaths he could not forsake.

Instead, he said, "Eirian, the world has always been a dark place. Sometimes I think it's why the gods left. They saw the dark flaw in their creations, and rather than destroy everything to start again, they left us to our faults. All we can do is try to stay on top of our darkness and help those around us do the same. We can't control the actions of others, only ourselves."

"But as sovereign—"

"Who we are as a sovereign of Endara is not who we are as individuals. Having the crown placed on your head does not mean you stop being Eirian, the woman. It means you also become Eirian, the queen. You need to learn to be both. Decisions you make as the queen will not be the decisions you'd make as an individual. What is best for the kingdom isn't always what you'd choose."

"I'm not sure I can be completely separate in my decisions."

Nolan chuckled. "For a long time, you won't be. That's why we have councils. Everyone will have an opinion on what is best for the kingdom, and our job is to listen, then find a solution that works. Compromise is the key."

"I'm getting the hang of compromise, but they don't always make it easy," Eirian grumbled.

Nolan smiled and said, "No, they don't."

Walking toward the door, Eirian turned around and looked at him. Age and illness had robbed Nolan of his vitality, and gray peppered his brown hair. His gentlemen had been keeping him trimmed, only a slight shadow of facial hair showing. There were hints of the man he had been, and Eirian remembered Nolan holding her on his shoulders when she was little. Eirian shook her head and gave him a smile before opening the door to leave.

"His Majesty would like some help, please, Thomas. We're going to have a picnic in the garden," she said, ignoring the concern on their faces.

Thomas nodded, and with the other gentlemen following, joined Nolan in his chamber. Brenna crossed her arms and glanced at the door, waiting for Eirian to say something else. Sitting on a chair, Eirian stared at her hands thoughtfully and sighed.

Brenna asked, "A picnic?"

"Yes, Brenna, a picnic. This is only temporary, and I want to enjoy my time with my father. Is it so wrong I want to have some positive memories of him, and not just the ones of him failing?"

Taken aback by the grief on Eirian's face, Brenna blinked in realization. "That's the real reason for this. It's got nothing to do with the coronation, does it?"

"The gardeners are going to hate me, but I want him to see the beautiful things I can do with my magic. Is there something we can do to reward them for the extra work they have to put in? Perhaps a bonus pay?"

"Eirian!"

She ignored Brenna's frustrated hand gestures and glanced at the window, muttering, "It's later in the day than I thought. I'm surprised Amira isn't here demanding to know what was going on."

"She came, and the guards wouldn't let her in. You'll hear about it from her later. They explained you were having some private time with your father while you could, and that put a dampener on her attitude." Romana replied.

Eirian nodded her thanks. "She's going to be a pain in my ass. The sooner she returns to Onaorbaen, the better. I think we can agree on that."

"She's ambitious. I suspect your father knew, and it's why he allowed her to marry the Earl of Onaorbaen. You know she's pushing Llewellyn to ask your brother to consider a marriage with you, Bea," Brenna said.

Bea shrugged. "I know, Gallagher told me. He's not sure about it. Besides, I'm a lady-in-waiting, and the decision is in the hands of the council."

"Only if you agree to it. You can say no," Elke muttered. "If the duke asked for my hand, it would thrill my father. He has enough of us to consider."

Shaking her head, Brenna told them, "Amira wants Bea because she presumes Bea is young enough to be shaped into what Amira believes her son needs. I know this because we think of these things as mothers."

Romana glanced sideways and muttered, "Besides, the duke isn't interested in Bea."

"My father suggested I never marry," Eirian said softly, and her words had the ladies staring at her in shock. "I can understand his reasoning for it."

"Just because your mother died in childbirth doesn't mean you will."

Looking at Brenna, Eirian smiled sadly and said, "Is it worth the risk? Everett and Llewellyn can provide me with ample heirs. I've never been particularly interested in being married, so I'd be happy not to."

NINETEEN

The dress fit perfectly, which surprised Eirian. She had expected it to be looser, as some days, despite her need to eat, she could barely stomach food. Sliding her hands over the linen, Eirian appreciated the coolness of the fabric and glanced at the thick wool cloak laid out on her bed. It was a warm day, but the tomb was always cold, and the night was long. Elke finished dragging the brush through her hair and wove it into a tight braid to keep it tidy.

"Are you sure you've eaten enough?" Brenna nagged, holding a slice of bread in her hand. "You won't get another chance until tomorrow morning."

"Eating doesn't work like that. I can't keep stuffing food down now and hope I won't get hungry later. If I eat any more, I think I might be sick!"

Shaking her head, Eirian continued stroking the fabric of her skirt nervously. She had stayed up late, spending as much time as she could with Nolan. It had helped, distracting Eirian from the impending ceremonies and allowing her to sleep in. Her ladies had spent more time than usual scrubbing and washing Eirian before dressing her. Brenna had admitted it was because she could not bathe before the coronation ceremony.

Passing the bread to Romana, Brenna stilled Eirian's hands and said encouragingly, "It's okay to be nervous."

"I presume no one has changed anything from the last time I checked?"

Looking at her weapons, Eirian itched to take at least a knife with her. Following her gaze, Brenna shook her head.

"You know you can't."

"I don't need them, but they're a reassuring presence sometimes. Besides, with the number of guards surrounding the tombs, if anyone gets through them and in with me... well, they'll probably be glad I'm unarmed."

The ladies were uncomfortable with the implications of her words. Eirian ignored the change in mood and paced towards the door. Before she reached it, she turned around and strode back again, her nerves making her impatient. Nodding to Romana, Brenna watched her hurry to the door and slip through it.

"Where is she going?" Bea asked curiously.

"To find out if it's time to move before Her Highness drives herself to distraction. It shouldn't be too much longer," Brenna answered.

She looked at the food tray and picked up a piece of cheese, nibbling at it. Eirian stopped at her weapon stand and selected a knife, drawing it from the sheath. Holding it in front of her face, she examined the blade.

"I should get these seen before we leave. The sheaves could do with oiling. Swords as well."

"I'll organize it when the festivities are over. Can't imagine much work will happen in the castle for a day or two. Not with the celebration feasts or the tourney. All smiths will be busy tending to the competitors."

A flicker of jealousy passed over Eirian's face, and she slid the knife home angrily. "I don't understand why I'm not allowed to compete. Everett and Llewellyn can, and if it were my father presiding, I could have."

"It's about fairness, and you understand that. No one wants to come against you in the arena out of fear of hurting or insulting you. Even if you weren't the queen, I suspect they'd be reluctant because of your magic. Everyone now knows you're handy in a fight," Brenna replied, ignoring the petulant look on Eirian's face.

Huffing, she crossed her arms and walked to the door again, muttering, "I'm fed up with this wait."

"We couldn't tell," Isabella commented sarcastically.

Bea waved at a chair and hoped she would not get her head bitten off as she suggested, "Why don't you sit. I can massage your shoulders while we wait. It might help keep you distracted and calm."

Arching her brows, Eirian uncrossed her arms and approached the chair, dropping onto it. Receiving a nod of approval from Brenna, Bea confidently began working on her shoulders while they waited. Groaning in appreciation, Eirian could not deny that Bea's idea had been a good one and enjoyed the massage while she watched the door eagerly.

"Who taught you?" Eirian asked.

"My mother did. She claims it's a useful tool in marriage."

"Really?" Elke looked curious.

Nodding, Bea smirked. "She said she used it to get out of more than a few visits from my father when she wasn't in the mood. Of course, I'm sure it wouldn't always work, but you never know."

Snorting, Brenna gave them a look that spoke of experience. "Hot baths with lots of lavender and a massage works wonders for Marcellus."

"I'm sure a hilt to the back of the head would work, with half the effort required by hot baths, lavender, and massages. Or saying no, like we do in Riane," Eirian muttered. "I mustn't give you enough work to do. You're always thinking about men and marriage."

"Not all of us can afford the luxury of not needing marriage. I'm one of many children, and the greatest thing going for my prospects is being your lady-in-waiting. Romana is the same. Our father will probably consider the first offers to come our way," Elke said, rolling her eyes at Isabella.

Nodding, Isabella agreed. "I have fewer siblings, but the same deal. You know you need to take some interest in our prospects. We're your ladies, and you have the final say. Nobles and wealthier men with aspirations will want to court us to get closer to you."

"I'm aware of all that. Just… sometimes it seems… Can't you pick a man, tell me who, and I'll give a royal decree so you can have him?"

"Well, if you're offering men like that, I'll gladly have the Duke of Tamantal. Everett is a fine, fine man!" Isabella giggled, covering her mouth.

Laughing, Bea squeezed Eirian's shoulders tightly and said, "I'll take the Prince of Ensaycal. You don't want him, but I won't say no."

Freezing, Eirian felt a pang of jealousy and met Brenna's knowing stare as she said, "I'm afraid Prince Celiaen is not mine to command."

The ladies stopped laughing when the door opened and Romana entered. Behind her, Everett and Llewellyn stood in the audience chamber. A faint blush to Romana's cheeks had Brenna's eyes narrowing suspiciously. Standing, Eirian walked through to the room full of men. She watched how her cousins stared before they bowed and the guards followed suit.

She met Aiden's gaze, and he smiled faintly while his eyes drifted over her. It was a smile Eirian recognized. A smile that made her wish there was not a mountain between them, made of rank and propriety. Or a room full of people preventing her from challenging him to show her exactly what his smile meant. Touching Everett and Llewellyn's arms, she gave them a nervous smile.

"It's time," Everett said.

He wanted to hug her, but did not dare. Kissing Eirian's cheek lightly, Llewellyn admired her.

"You look beautiful."

Eirian stared at Llewellyn and sighed before looking over at the guards. Aiden stood at the forefront with his hand clapped over his chest in salute. His eyes no longer held the same desire. They were shuttered, aware of the surrounding people. She wondered if he would take her away if she asked. Celiaen would not hesitate. All Eirian had to do was say the word.

She muttered, "I suppose we should get on with this."

Nodding, the dukes led her to the door and went through first. On the other side were additional guards and several council members, who bowed and saluted when Eirian appeared. For a moment, she faltered. Eirian had expected Nolan to be there. The group escorted her through the castle to the entrance, where more people waited with the horses.

Standing at the top of the stairs leading to the courtyard, Eirian swallowed nervously as she looked down over them. Dressed in their finery, the bright colors separated the nobility from the servants. On the guards, exposed sections of mail gleamed in the sunlight. They stared at Eirian as she stared at them, the air of expectation making her nervousness increase.

"Your Highness." Ulric was the first to set foot on the stairs and bow as he told her, "We're waiting for you."

Taking a deep breath, Eirian stepped down, carefully avoiding her skirts. "Thank you, Chancellor. I'm ready."

He offered Eirian his arm, and she took it, allowing him to lead her to her beloved horse. Halcyon stood patiently, unfazed by the tension.

Bowing his head in close, Ulric murmured, "Your father is at the tombs. He wanted some time alone before you arrived. I heard you spent the better part of the night with him. He has made an incredible recovery."

"No, he hasn't. Tynan brought him a brief window of time. That is all it is, a moment of clarity to say goodbye." Running her hands over Halcyon's neck, Eirian smiled at and scratched his favorite spot behind his ear. "I know what we did and the consequences of it. When I say Nolan can say his goodbyes, I mean it."

"I'm an old man, My Queen. Give me more credit. What you've done is give everyone a chance for closure instead of a dragged-out smattering of opportunities that might pass as quickly as they come. I know something about what mages can do, and I know what sort of person you are. I'm proud to be the chancellor who's seeing in the dawn of your reign."

Taking the reins from the servant, Ulric held the horse steady. Carefully checking the tack out of habit, Eirian knew everyone was waiting for her to mount. Nodding to Ulric, she let her shoulders slump and turned to the servant.

"I might need one of those steps if I want to get up there without ruining my dress."

Aiden stepped up beside her and offered his hands. "I'll help you up. It's part of my job."

"Thank you, Aiden," she said, and chuckled. "We talked about this, and I should probably practice mounting with a dress on."

Helping her up, he was careful not to touch her more than needed. Aware of the people watching, Aiden tried to distract himself from the suggestions his mind was providing. The white dress clung to Eirian's body, doing nothing to hide her figure. When she had walked out of her chamber, he had wanted nothing more than to drag her back in.

"It would be a good idea," Aiden muttered, his hand squeezing her leg in reassurance. "But I'd hate to stop being useful."

Ulric handed Eirian the reins with an amused smile and bowed his head before going to his horse. Brenna stepped over to Eirian and helped her settle her skirts comfortably.

"We aren't far away if you need anything."

"I know. Stop worrying, Brenna. Everything is going to be fine."

Playing with Halcyon's mane while she waited for everyone else to mount, Eirian looked around thoughtfully. She felt magic everywhere, but her eyes could not locate the elves. Celiaen had insisted his company spread themselves along the route to the tombs as an extra precaution. Eirian let her magic flow out and touch the unseen elf, sensing the startled reaction with a smile. Once everyone had mounted, they gave a signal.

The procession filed out of the gate in a previously decided order. Everett and Llewellyn flanked Eirian with her ladies not far behind. Above them, standards fluttered in the breeze, carried by serious youths from lesser noble families. Winding through the grounds of the castle was the straightforward part. Those remaining behind watched from windows or the walkways atop the wall. When they crossed the bridge, Eirian glimpsed the crowds.

As much as she tried not to let it daunt her, she struggled to stop her anxiety from rising. Nolan had assured her it was customary to feel intimidated by the sight of the crowds. Even in her years in Riane, Eirian had never seen so many people gathered in one place. Her magic felt all of it, the beating of hearts a deafening sound that only she could hear. Counting the beat, Eirian clung to their drum to stop her power from being overwhelmed. It was a coping mechanism she had learned with Galameyvin's help.

Young children lined the front of the crowd, many waving little flags made by some crafty person who saw the chance to earn coin off doting parents. Giving small nods and smiles to the people as they passed, Eirian reminded herself that the morrow would be more significant. Many people would continue to work, passing on this trip through the city. It was the return trip that was important. It was their chance to see Eirian in her coronation gown, on her way to have the crown placed on her head. It marked the beginning of a few days of rest to attend feasts and tournaments to mark the celebrations.

Llewellyn leaned forward in the saddle and said, "You're doing well. Just keep acknowledging that you see them and don't stop smiling. This is a joyous occasion."

"I'm taking over leadership from my unwell father. I don't see the joyousness in the situation," she replied, her smile not matching her tone.

"It doesn't matter to them who rules so long as things remain good. They'll remember your father by saying they not only survived but thrived under his rule. That is what you want them to say when your heir makes this ride."

Shaking her head slightly, Eirian glanced at Llewellyn out of the corner of her eye. "My father never led them into war. That's what they'll remember. I'll be the queen who caused a war."

He sat upright and met Everett's gaze behind her back. Everett did not smile, his mind a constant whirl of possibilities as he switched his focus between the lines of guards and the woman they protected. He could not stop worrying that something might happen. Llewellyn's carefree manner frustrated him, and the constant thrum of Eirian's power was an irritation. Turning his stare to Eirian, Everett watched her head tilt back suddenly and felt the flare of her magic as her stance grew tense.

"Eirian?" he said cautiously.

Her head whipped around, eyes wide as she replied, "I don't recognize them."

"Recognize who?"

"There are strange mages here. I'm not sure where, but I can feel them."

There was a flicker of fear in her eyes, and Everett grew concerned, signaling for a guard to approach.

Eirian told him, "They're powerful. I can't tell how many, and they might not be in the city."

Nodding, Everett said to the guard, "Tell the men to be wary of any mages they don't recognize and get word to the elves."

The guard saluted before wheeling his horse around to push back along the line. Llewellyn had one hand on his sword, eyes scanning the crowd.

"Let's continue and do our best to pretend everything is fine. Your pretty prince will know about them."

"If I know, he knows. There's no malice that I can feel. It's just magic," Eirian muttered, sensing Celiaen's concern over the bond.

"Focus on your task, Eirian, because whatever may come of it isn't your concern. That's what we're for. If we need a big, bad mage to back us up, we have Celiaen," Everett said, sharing a look with Aiden.

Knowing she could not argue with them, Eirian forced a smile and resisted the urge to probe further with her magic. She felt the press of the strange powers against hers, a little testing of strength here and there. The familiar flares of magic from the elves scattered throughout the city felt closer to her than the strangers.

Unaware anything was amiss, the common folk watched them pass, cheering here and there. Eirian heard her name shouted occasionally and always turned in the direction it came from to acknowledge them. The confines of the city opened as they approached one of the oldest parts of Amath. Her ancestors had hollowed the ground when they built the keep, using the same stone that made the city's foundations to build a house for the dead. They rarely visited, and the most life it saw was at each coronation when the heir came to spend a night asking for guidance.

Soldiers lined the pathway from the wall to the green hill, flags fluttering from the top. Statues stood in the gardens around the tomb. Cold stone depicted armored men with swords or books, and the occasional woman with a crown, children at her feet. Tiny purple flowers grew throughout the grass. Dandelions accompanied them, the bright yellow flowers making Eirian feel a touch of happiness. Towering trees shaded the waiting crowd. The occasional flowering bush gave a burst of color and fragrance to an otherwise sober place.

Eirian spotted Nolan first as the guards broke away from in front of her. He stood there, the fine clothes he wore hanging loosely on him despite the efforts made by his gentlemen to hide his weight loss. A brush of familiar magic drew her gaze to Celiaen, and she welcomed the sight of him. Held carefully in his hand was a single dandelion flower, a reminder that he knew what she liked.

Tynan stood at his side, his focus flickering between Eirian and her father, a perpetual frown creasing his brow. Smiling tensely, Celiaen gave her a bow and turned to Marcellus as he stepped out to take hold of Halcyon's reins. Everett was there, offering a hand to help her dismount, and Eirian took a deep breath before she turned to face the gathered people.

"Who comes seeking the guidance of the ancestors?" An old man Eirian had never seen before stood at the tomb entrance, his voice drawing all attention to him.

Stepping past Everett and Marcellus, Eirian held her head high and replied, "I do."

"What is your claim to their wisdom?"

There was something about him that made her skin crawl. A pull at her power that reminded Eirian of the strange man in the alley the night she had killed the assassin.

"I am Eirian Altira, firstborn of Nolan Altira V. I am the rightful heir to the kingdom of Endara. My claim is one of blood."

They had made Eirian practice her response until she was sure she would never forget it.

"Do you understand why you have come?"

"I seek the knowledge of my ancestors so that they may guide me as I offer myself to my kingdom."

He stared at Eirian, eyes a piercing shade of blue that caused her to think of Aiden. The stare lasted long enough to make Eirian drop her gaze before he finally bowed. Holding an arm out towards the shadows beyond the doorway, the man smiled. Eirian thought she recognized the smile, but the memory slipped from her grasp like they always did.

"Welcome, Eirian Altira. Step forth and find the wisdom you seek."

Seeing Nolan nod, Eirian followed the old man into the tomb and closed her eyes for a moment to adjust to the darkness. Torches lit the narrow corridors, casting dancing shadows over the stone of the walls. Rustling fabric and muffled footsteps behind her told Eirian that others had followed. The old man did not glance back until they stepped into the large chamber with its alcoves of stone coffins holding the kings and queens of the past.

It was her first time in the chamber, and Eirian wondered which stone container held her mother's remains. As though he sensed what she was thinking, Nolan touched her arm gently, and Eirian whirled around to face him.

"Nothing in here can hurt you. It'll be a long night, but no one will know if you fall asleep to pass the time."

"Are you saying the dead won't speak, and they won't impart some profound wisdom that will help me become a great queen?" she asked with a smile.

"Well, they didn't speak to me, but I wouldn't put it past you to have the magic to make them." Nolan chuckled.

"I think command of the dead is beyond Her Highness," Celiaen said, joining them.

He glanced around the tomb and lifted a hand to tuck the dandelion behind Eirian's ear, thumb brushing against her cheek. Eirian turned her face into his hand, but Celiaen dropped it away before she could kiss his palm.

"Not to alarm you when you can't do anything about it, but I know you sensed them. Were you expecting a Telmian delegation?"

Eirian watched Nolan go white and frowned as she murmured, "So that's why they felt unfamiliar. Why would the daoine come here?"

Celiaen shrugged and admitted, "I only know it's them because I've felt their power before. It's intoxicating. You must be careful, Ree. In here, you're a little sheltered, but tomorrow will be a unique situation."

"Won't… you know… help both of us?"

"I don't know. It could make it worse. I'll try to speak to the delegation and ask them to restrain themselves. Hopefully, they'll respect the situation. While I'm a prince and a powerful mage, I'm neither my father nor the high council." Celiaen glanced at the nobles wandering the tomb and said, "Be on guard and try to get some rest. I'll join a watch late tonight."

"Thank you, Celi."

Grasping Celiaen's hand, Eirian bowed her head and let him press his forehead to hers. It was a familiar action, one that provided her with comfort. She wanted to cling to him and curl into his arms, but people were watching them.

"You are the blade of my blade, dear heart, and I'm not complete without you fighting by my side," he murmured.

Celiaen released her hand before she replied, stepping back and nodding to Nolan. Chuckling softly, Nolan shook his head as Celiaen walked away.

"I'm never sure how to feel about elves. He's older than me, but he behaves as though he's of an age with you. I can't say much about his words of affection."

Frowning, Eirian watched Brenna approach with her cloak. She could not recall the first time they had exchanged their words of endearment. It was something they had always said to each other.

Brenna said, "I'd forgotten how chilly this place is."

"I hadn't," Amira grumbled.

Llewellyn and Everett trailed behind her.

"Celiaen told us about the daoine," Everett said.

Amira's eyes settled on the dandelion behind Eirian's ear, and she made her disapproval clear. "Where did that weed come from?"

Brushing her fingertips over the flower, Eirian smiled. "A gift from Celiaen. He knows how much I like them."

"It looks ridiculous and inappropriate."

Eirian turned to Everett to say, "Try to find out what you can about the daoine. Tell Brenna everything you learn, so she can tell me in the morning. Whatever you do, don't aggravate them!"

"We're dealing with it, Eirian," he replied.

Giving each of them a look, Eirian shook her head in frustration. "Keep them away from my father."

A flicker of relief crossed Nolan's face, and he said, "When I return to the keep, I'll remain in my quarters. Amira can keep me company and continue helping sort my belongings ahead of my relocation."

"Are you sure?" Everett asked.

"Yes, I am. My time has ended. I give my kingdom to Eirian and you boys. Endara is your responsibility, and I trust you'll always endeavor to do the best thing for her, even if it doesn't seem like it's the right thing. I'm eternally sorry for any missteps I made as the madness dug its fingers into my mind."

"Uncle—"

Nolan placed a hand on his nephews' backs and inclined his head towards Eirian, silencing what Everett had planned to say. "Guide her, protect her, make her think twice, and never let her fool you. Eirian is my daughter. She's very headstrong, and she knows her duty. Remind her to carve a moment for herself to forget the duty and find happiness."

Crossing her arms, Eirian tucked her hands into her sleeves and huffed. "Father."

Nolan smiled sadly at her, thinking about how the flower made her look like a girl. "Indulge your father. I know what's coming. Let me speak while I can. Ruling a kingdom isn't a solitary role, so you must be able to share the burden, Eirian, and share it with the right people."

Eirian stared at him.

"These two fine men are your blood, and I hope they'll never betray you. They know this land, the people, and the same duty you do. It is to them you must delegate because the burden is too great for one person alone."

"Like you delegated to my father," Everett muttered.

"You must work together. I know it'll be hard for you, Llewellyn, but you'll need to spend more time in Amath. Eirian needs to count on you for support."

Llewellyn grinned and said, "She can always count on us."

Nolan smiled patiently and continued, "You need to keep your disagreements private. It will be years before the entire council will respect her, but they already respect the two of you. Well, Everett, at least."

Narrowing his eyes at Amira, Llewellyn watched her back down on her protests.

"Indulge me. I want to see the three of you hug." Chuckling, Nolan winked at Amira and said, "Stop scowling, Amira."

Unable to resist the urge to giggle, Eirian slung her arms around Everett and Llewellyn, pulling them into a hug. They responded and stood together, heads touching, while the others watched. Everett planted a light kiss on Eirian's cheek before stepping back to stand beside Nolan. Llewellyn cocked an eyebrow at Nolan and kissed her other cheek, keeping his arm slung around her shoulder.

"Happy, old man?"

Still chuckling, Nolan nodded and said, "That I am. I want the three of you to do that often and remember you are family. Llewellyn, you might have brothers and sisters, but she doesn't. All she has is the two of you."

The caretaker appeared again, saying, "It's time we leave our young queen to her solitude."

Swallowing the lump that formed in her throat, Eirian looked at each of them nervously. "Remember what I said about the visitors."

"You sound frightened of them," Everett said in surprise.

"I am. If we're careful, they'll leave peacefully." Shaking her head, Eirian stepped back and took the cloak from Brenna. "I'll see you on the morrow."

"We'll be here at dawn for you."

Brenna touched her arm lightly before she walked away to join Marcellus, where he stood talking to Celiaen. Meeting Celiaen's gaze across the tomb, Eirian nodded once. Nolan extended his hand and waited for her to place her own in his grasp. They stood there, holding hands at a distance before Nolan let go and turned away to let Amira guide him out of the tomb. His departure signaled to the others milling around that it was time to leave.

Eirian watched them file out through the narrow corridors. The strange old man stood inside the doorway, watching her with a peculiar expression. Eirian felt the memories lingering out of reach again. Something at the back of her mind told her she knew the caretaker. Staring at him, Eirian thought she glimpsed black lines at his throat.

"I hope you find your answers," he told her.

"As do I, but I doubt they'll come from the bones of the dead."

He grinned, and Eirian was sure she had seen it before. On a younger face, in a different place, adorned with the blood of the slain.

"I wouldn't discount the dead. They guard their secrets close and can surprise you. Remember, no mortal can step through the doorway until the light of the dawning sun touches it. You might think this is a silly formality before they crown you, but the dead know."

Looking at the shadows, the stone, and the stillness, Eirian frowned. "What do you mean?"

"Good luck, darling."

His words shocked Eirian, and she stared, speechless, as he turned his back and vanished into the dark. It took her a moment to adjust to the almost complete stillness of the tomb, the flickering shadows cast by the torches the only movement remaining. Looking around, Eirian rubbed her arms and roamed. Placing the cloak on the ground in the light, she folded it into a neat bundle, smoothing her hands over the creases.

Eirian crouched and laid her hands on the rough surface of the stone covering the floor. Her power flowed out and through the tomb, providing her with the layout. She sensed sparks of life in the dirt, earth-dwelling creatures that did not care for the human sentiment placed on the monument. She felt the hollows containing generations of dead Altira's.

The faint traces of magical warding in the chamber drew Eirian's attention. Pushing herself up, Eirian dusted her hands off and started into the chamber's darker recesses. Stopping in front of the furthest alcove, she peered at the arch and struggled to make out any words carved into the stone, feeling the faint thrum of ancient wards. Chewing her bottom lip, Eirian turned around to look at the one opposite and spotted words that were worn by time.

Making her way along, Eirian recounted the names from memory. She froze when she reached the tomb where her mother lay waiting for Nolan to join her. Glancing back the way she had come, she frowned, wondering who lay in the first spot. Turning her focus back to her mother, Eirian stepped into the alcove and ran her hands over the stone coffin, feeling all the groves of engraving with her fingertips.

"I'm sorry, mother."

Leaning over the coffin, Eirian rested her forehead against the cold stone and felt her power brush against a hint of magic within. Jolting upright, she left her hands on the lid and frowned, closing her eyes to focus on what she felt. The remnants came from the bones within. There was a familiarity to them that made Eirian question if it was a hint of her power left behind.

Questions filled her mind, and Eirian longed for a green to theorize with as she stood in the flickering light. Nolan's words about her ancestors killing mages born to their bloodline came to the forefront of her memories. Eirian made her way back through the chamber, touching each coffin, hoping she would feel something similar that would tell her they had carried a mage within them. There were no traces of anything that felt like her mother did.

Eirian stood before the oldest alcoves again, arms crossed as she frowned into the darkness. Turning her focus to the ancient king's tomb, Eirian hesitantly stepped into the darkness surrounding his coffin and placed her hands on it. Feeling traces of magic remaining on the bones, she gasped. There were wards worked into the stone, and the whispers in her mind told her to leave them be.

"I don't understand this."

Shaking her head, Eirian turned to the last space. There were wards present that she had already sensed. She stepped up to the stone coffin, her hands recognizing a distinct feeling to the stone. Even though her eyes could not see them, her fingers found words carved around the outside. Not quite willing to invade the space enclosed, she walked around the outside, trying to make sense of the writing. They formed no words or symbols that she recognized.

Returning to the head of the coffin, Eirian took a deep breath and rested her hands flat on the stone. Her power found the wards, the old magic within them flaring bright in her mind. Determined, she pushed past them carefully, despite the whispers warning her not to, and felt the magic that lingered, as it had on her mother and the old king.

"So, you're the heir."

The whisper of a voice startled her, and Eirian spun around, looking for the source. A shadowy figure of a woman stood at the entrance, the flickering light from the torches reflecting through her. Eirian stared, her eyes wide in shock and magic recoiling from the presence. Chuckling, the shadow woman glided towards the coffin, Eirian shuffling out of the way quickly.

"Don't you have anything to say, child?"

Shaking her head, Eirian cleared her throat and asked, "What are you?"

"I'm one of your ancestors."

"The ancestors are real?"

Smiling patiently, the form shrugged. "I can't attest to all the dead, but some of us are. You're the first to disturb me."

"Who are you? I found no name on this tomb, and I recounted everyone else. Why do some of you feel of magic still?"

Eirian dug her fingernails into her arms to help keep her magic focused, the strange presence making it react differently. The whispers mocked her, dragging claws along the edge of her mind. She suspected they were punishing her for ignoring their warning.

"My son did his best to hide the truth about me, my mother, and even himself. I imagine you feel magic because they had magic or had been affected by it after death."

"My mother didn't have magic."

The woman laughed and said, "Didn't she? I thought she was magic. She was life until you took her place, though that has little to do with the Altira's. The Altira line all but bred magic out, except for those carefully smuggled into Riane. My son made sure of that."

"I don't understand."

"I suppose you wouldn't. Your father went against the unspoken family rule to destroy offspring born with magic, though he had his instructions. It was hard initially, but my son found the right combination would eventually produce an heir with no power. Or with power weak enough that they could bind it without repercussions. He even chose nobles to rule Endara based on their lack of magical blood."

Slumping against the wall, Eirian understood.

"We're not good people, are we?"

"We're a bloodline chased by shadows. We're the children of death. My mother was the force that pulled Endara together against the darkness. She was the one who led us here across lands you don't know to exist. We left our home, the twin cities that gave their names to these lands. Mages ruled everything then, waging war like there was no tomorrow because of fear and distrust fed by the darkness."

Eirian said, "The mage wars."

"It was the dark days when the gods turned on each other, and madness descended on the world. She made a great sacrifice to help banish the dark. I helped forge Riane and bound the mages of these lands to common laws to protect the non-magical. My son feared the past, feared what part his blood played, and turned his focus to a mundane war with Athnaral. He planted the seeds for what the elven nations would become."

"And now none of us remember it as anything but ancient times gone by. What is the darkness you speak of?"

She evaded the question. "You're the first to disturb me, and I'm surprised my son isn't awake. He would be furious you exist."

"What was your mother's name? What happened to her?" Eirian pressed, hoping for an answer.

The lights flickered, and the spirit cocked her head, looking over her shoulder at the tomb of her son. "Her name is your own. Your mother gave it to you out of twisted sentiment. I'm a ghost now, a remnant of magic bound to my bones. Perhaps my purpose was to wait for you to come."

"Why?"

"You feel like life, and goodness, blood, and death. You were born to be power, but another is the Altira. Your mother meddled with things. She took what was his and gave it to you. You must beware."

"Beware of what? How can I feel like all those things? What do you mean, the Altira? How could my mother meddle?"

"Life and death are the cycles of existence. They are the greatest balance there is. To save all life, we must sacrifice life in balance."

"What do you mean? These riddles tell me nothing!"

Frustrated, Eirian pushed away from the wall and stepped towards the shadowy figure. Her magic flared in response to her anger.

"When the time comes that you need to understand, you will. You're the heir to more than you realize. You are the heir to life."

"Did they destroy the darkness you fought?"

"No, we can't destroy her. We speak of monsters lurking, fear the shadows, and tell stories to make ourselves tremble. Those monsters waiting beyond the veil of death for life to free them. Things come to us naturally, but we never question the origin or the meaning. No one asks why."

Eirian knew what the spirit spoke of. It was the shadows in the corner of her vision, the memories that she could never grasp. The nightmares which woke her in distress, but she could not recall. The glimpses of wings and fangs, feathers and scales, of strange people out of reach.

"You know of what I speak."

"Yes," Eirian said faintly.

"It's a strange thing, isn't it? We'll not talk again, but I doubt I'm the last spirit bound to their bones that you will encounter. You must heed our words and let them guide you."

A strange gleam surrounded the figure. Eirian felt coldness wash over her, unwittingly retreating until her back hit the wall. Fear gripped her, the whispers warning her he was coming.

"Why do I suspect I won't remember this?"

"Because you won't until you need to. I'm sorry for what you must do when the time comes and the sacrifices you'll make. It will be worth it. You'll be reborn, and it will right the balance."

The woman smiled coldly, and Eirian felt a strange power sweep her away into darkness. Arms caught her, carefully placing her on the ground. In the shadows, blue eyes glanced at the dead woman. Keeping his arms around her, he did not move.

"Lord Death," the spirit said.

He brushed a hand over Eirian's forehead and murmured, "Sleep well, darling."

TWENTY

Her entire body ached, and the way someone was shaking her arm was not helping the throbbing of her head. Eirian opened her eyes with a groan and stared at Brenna's concerned face before pushing herself up off the wall. Glancing about, Eirian spotted her cloak in Elke's hands and wondered why she had not stirred when they pulled it off her.

"You picked an odd spot to fall asleep, Your Highness." Offering a hand, Brenna frowned at the alcove and said, "I expected you to fall asleep next to your mother. What happened? Why and how are there dandelions everywhere?"

Rubbing her face, Eirian stopped with her hands on her cheeks and peered at Brenna in confusion before looking around the tomb. Her eyes darted from one clump of dandelion to the next, baffled by their presence.

She muttered, "I don't know."

"What do you mean, you don't know?"

The question made the younger ladies huddle closer together, uncomfortable being in the tomb. Gripping the offered hand, Eirian struggled stiffly to her feet and groaned when it felt like every joint protested. Snorting, Brenna helped steady her and looked at the ladies pointedly.

"I remember coming here, and I remember everyone leaving. Then I was keeping myself busy and feeling the bones—"

Brenna looked horrified and dropped her arm, saying, "Excuse me? Feeling the bones?"

Waving a hand, Eirian scowled. "With my magic! I was investigating a theory I had. By the powers, what do you take me for?"

"Can all mages do that?"

Her shoulders dropped, and Eirian felt a moment of befuddlement. "You know what? I don't know. I didn't know I could do it. It started because I read the land to learn the layout. When I did that, I detected old wards and other lingering remains of magic. So, I started reading the coffins and discovered I could feel the bones. No, that's not quite right. I can feel remains of magic or the lack of it."

"It's disturbing to think that long after I'm dead, a mage could come along and feel my bones with magic."

"I doubt you have anything to worry about, Brenna."

Stepping away from Eirian, Brenna looked around, her brow furrowing, and said, "Let's get you out of here so we can prepare you for your coronation."

"I still don't know what happened during the night. I'm not joking. It's like I passed out suddenly, and then you were waking me. I don't even remember making it back to this alcove," Eirian admitted.

Turning around, she stared at the oldest coffin in the tomb, taking in the bright yellow flowers that were now growing around it. Her headache worsened with Eirian's attempts to remember.

"Perhaps the ancestors shared their wisdom with you," said the old man.

He stood at the other end of the chamber, and Eirian glanced at him. Something about him continued to leave her troubled. Her magic reacted to his presence in ways that Eirian was not used to. When he looked at her, the whispers became more like screams.

"The dead are dead. Besides, if they could impart some knowledge to me, shouldn't I remember? What would be the point if I didn't remember? No, there's a ward here that I disturbed, and the magical backlash knocked me out. That explains why I don't remember." Eirian waved at the dandelions and added, "It also explains why I lost a little control and turned this tomb into a garden."

The ladies stared at him, eyes wide with a hint of fear, but he ignored them, his focus entirely on Eirian. "You'll remember what you need to remember when the occasion calls for it. Don't dismiss the dead. You may be a mage, but even the wisest of mages knows when to ask others for their knowledge."

Eirian shook her head, scoffing. "Indeed. Well, let's go because today is a day I can't be late to."

Allowing the other women to gather around her, Eirian glanced at him over her shoulder as they walked the length of the chamber to the single door. He remained still, arms crossed and a strange smile on his face, while the flickering torches cast eerie shadows that did not seem to touch him. For a moment, she saw another face beneath. One she recognized, but blinking banished the illusion, and scowling Eirian resolved to pay no more attention to the caretaker.

The doorway into the tomb was lit with the faint glow of sunrise, but Brenna guided the group into a small room set a few paces back. It was mostly empty except for barrels of oil and spare torches. They had propped a broom against the wall, and glancing around, Eirian saw a pile of dirt in the corner. The remaining item occupying space was a chair. Romana gave it a disgruntled look before taking the cloak from Elke and draping it over it.

"Bea, tell Aiden he can bring the dress in now." Brenna scowled and sighed, telling Eirian, "He wanted to see you with his own eyes as soon as possible."

"That doesn't surprise me."

Rubbing her head, Eirian hoped the headache would vanish before too long. The sound of heavy boots made them turn to observe Aiden maneuver through the doorway with a box in his arms. Bea stood behind him, watching in concern while keeping out of his way, as Aiden placed it as far from the barrels as he could manage. Straightening, he turned to Eirian and strode over to look her in the eyes. While Aiden inspected Eirian, her ladies opened the box, sorting out what they needed.

"You survived the night, then?" Glancing her over, Aiden frowned and said, "I know your cues. I can tell you have a headache."

Eirian smiled, commenting, "Sometimes you're a little too observant, Aiden."

Aiden shrugged, a smile tugging at the corners of his mouth. "It's my job. I'm sworn to you for life, and you can bet I'm going to know everything. You tell me I'm too observant, and I remind you I call it being dutiful."

Shooing him out, Brenna rolled her eyes, saying, "And now we need to prepare her. Knock on the door when everyone arrives."

"At least feed her before you start."

He hovered in the doorway, watching Eirian thoughtfully before Brenna shut the door in his face. Holding out a carefully wrapped package, Romana grinned.

"I convinced the kitchen to make your favorites early enough to bring them. There was a bit of complaining, but they did it."

"Don't lie. They were more than happy to make them for her," Elke said, laughing while she tucked a hairbrush into her belt.

Unwrapping the bundle, Eirian inhaled the sweet smell of berries. The scent reminded her she was hungry, despite her nerves. Devouring the pastry, she gave Romana a thankful look.

"This is a welcome breakfast. I suppose that's something positive about passing out. I missed the boredom and hunger."

"I remembered water as well. Personally, I'd rather wine, but I didn't think it was appropriate."

Romana passed a full flask to Eirian. Lifting several washcloths, Bea waited for her to have a drink before holding them out so she could tip some water onto them. Eirian let her ladies fuss over her when she finished the last pastry. Closing her eyes, Eirian smelled peppermint and felt a hand dabbing oil on her temples and neck. The scent filled her nostrils, and she hoped it would help with the pounding of her head.

A tugging at her back as fingers undid laces told Eirian they were preparing to remove the white gown. The air was cool against her skin as she stood naked, and the wet washcloths did not help. Working quickly, the ladies cleaned off any dirt before assisting her into fresh undergarments.

"Why does the sight of that dress fill me with so much apprehension?" Elke murmured as she hovered beside Eirian.

Brenna supervised Romana and Isabella as they lifted the luxurious red gown from the box after removing the layers of linen protecting it.

"Me too," Eirian said.

Brenna examined the dress while the women held it up, then gave a nod of approval. Carefully bringing it over, they helped Eirian into it. Once it was on and laced, Elke pulled the brush from her belt and freed Eirian's hair from the braid. Shaking her head, she pointed at the chair, and Bea carefully brought it over, rearranging the cloak. Sitting, Eirian smiled in amusement at the happy little noises Elke made. Winces followed the smile as Elke's quick-moving fingers drew the strands back into a high braid.

"No, don't do that! It will end up being uncomfortable with the crown on. If you do low side plaits, it will keep her hair out of her face and leave the bulk of it loose. She looks better with her hair down," Bea said.

Everyone glanced at her in surprise, and Bea smiled brightly.

She added, "Plus, Eirian has a headache, and this isn't helping. You're good with hair, Elke, but your braids are tight."

"Thank you, Bea, that's good thinking," Eirian murmured.

Her words cut short any arguments the other ladies might have made. Sighing, Elke undid the braid and started again. She drew the hair into lower plaits on either side of Eirian's head and down behind her ears until they joined beneath the mass of brown hair. Stepping back when finished, she crossed her arms and gave Bea a dark look.

Elke grumbled, "How about that?"

"I think it looks good," Isabella said.

Nodding, Romana winked at Bea and admitted, "I think I'd find that comfortable if I was wearing a crown."

Cocking a brow at the niggling women, Eirian bowed her head slightly. "Thank you, Elke. I'm sure it looks wonderful. Your work always does."

There was a knock on the door, and Brenna called, "Is it time?"

"Well, if it's not time, then I don't know why all these people have arrived," Aiden answered sarcastically.

Eirian froze in the chair, eyes darting from one lady to the next. She felt the overwhelming weight of responsibility hit. Closing her eyes, Eirian took several deep breaths before rising to her feet as gracefully as possible. As she crossed the room, the rustle of fabric was loud in her ears, and Eirian barely noticed Brenna open the door to let her through.

Aiden clapped a hand to his chest and saluted, his eyes unreadable when they met hers. Holding his gaze, Eirian wished he would say something to distract her from everything. She did not care what he said; anything would do. Even a simple touch would help her break from the spiral of thoughts threatening to take over. When Aiden did not speak, she turned to face the sunlit entrance to the tomb, listening to the sounds of people and horses waiting outside.

"You can do this."

Turning to Aiden standing behind her, Eirian swallowed and replied, "I know I can, but right now, I don't feel it."

"It's too late to back out now. I have faith in you. We all do. Forget everything else, and remember, you have people believing in you. Just you, exactly as you are," Aiden told her.

"Sometimes you surprise me, Aiden. I'm not sure being a guard is your real calling."

"It led me to you. What better calling could I have than serving my queen?"

"Yet sometimes you hate it. For a while, I thought I'd have to dismiss you because of your attitude toward aspects of my magic."

"I know, and there will be many more such times in the future. We aren't always going to agree, but you know what? I don't need to agree with you to protect you, and I know you have my back as I have yours."

"That's true," Eirian said.

Aiden leaned in closer to murmur, "Besides, training with you is so much more fun when we're angry with each other."

Her breath caught at the look Aiden gave her, making Eirian glad her ladies were still in the room. Rubbing her hands on the silk skirt, she felt the rise of the threads where she encountered the embroidery and focused on it, hoping he would not spot flush of her cheeks. It was the distraction she needed. Her thoughts spiraled in a different direction, no less dangerous than the negativity and doubt that had her stomach clenching with anxiety.

"Thank you, Aiden. I know being a royal guard limits possibilities in your life, but if you ever wish to leave your post, I won't prevent you. Just say the word."

He chuckled, glancing at the ladies as they came out. It was one of those times when Aiden was thankful Eirian did not seem to remember him. He was even grateful she remained clueless about what some council members plotted.

"You would have to reward me well. Perhaps a title."

Looking at Brenna, Eirian took a deep breath and told her, "I'm ready. Well, as ready as I'm ever going to be."

It took effort not to blink repeatedly and shade her eyes when Eirian stepped out into the light, leaving the cool darkness of the tomb behind her. Guards and nobles dropped to a knee, their lowered heads giving her a moment to adjust without feeling embarrassed. Everett and Llewellyn stood beside Halcyon, the horse decorated with a half sheet caparison. They had embroidered the black fabric in silver with the Altira family's arms. A wide breast band matched it, equally embroidered in silver thread.

As she approached her cousins, no one spoke, allowing the two men to assist her into the saddle. Brenna carefully arranged her skirts, the train of the red dress partially covering the caparison. Handing Eirian the reins, Everett touched her hand lightly to reassure her. Sweeping her gaze over the mounted people, Eirian noted that either the current head or their immediate heir represented every single noble family. Banners fluttered on poles handled by standard-bearers, matching pairs ready to fall into line behind Eirian.

Signaling they were ready, Llewellyn dipped his head and waved for Eirian to proceed. An air of anticipation hung heavily over the group, and she felt her magic responding to it. It made the hairs on the back of her neck stand, her skin feeling like it had insects crawling all over it, and Eirian hated the sensation. Refusing to look over her shoulder at the tomb, Eirian could sense the staring eyes of the odd caretaker and the niggling suspicion he was more than he seemed returned.

Pouring her focus into the journey, Eirian watched Halcyon's flickering ears and listened to the beat of his hooves on the stone pavement as they approached the gate. High above, the watchtower guards sounded horns to tell the people she had entered the city. They would give those at the keep time to prepare for her arrival. When Eirian saw the people lining the roads, she realized the reason behind her power reacting the way it was. It was a struggle to not stare in blatant shock.

"Just keep breathing and smiling," Everett said, breaking the silence.

"I've never seen so many people."

"It's a big day."

Eirian did not glance at him and replied, "You don't know what it's doing to me. I wasn't taught how to control my magic around massive jubilant crowds."

"Well, try not to turn them into a bloodthirsty horde, and we'll get through this in one piece!" Llewellyn laughed.

Scoffing at herself for not thinking of it sooner, Eirian grinned and looked at the crowd. Focusing on the feelings coming from the people, Eirian worked to separate them, pulling on the threads that felt most like joy.

"I think I can do one better than a bloodthirsty horde. Thank you for the idea, and I hope it works," she said.

Everett asked in concern, "What are you doing? Eirian?"

"Trust me, it'll feel good. I haven't done it on a scale like this, but it should work."

Drawing on the joy, Eirian let it chase away her anxiety and spread out through her magic into the crowd. It was a skill she had kept quiet. The similarities to her ability to feed the bloodlust made her fear the high council's reactions. The cheering progressively grew as she channeled their joy back. It gave her a rush utterly different from the bloodlust.

She felt her magic hit the other mages, and their confusion as joy filled them. None of them was strong enough to stop her influence. There was laughing and cheering among the procession. No one was exempt from her power. Eirian smiled, the pounding headache washed away by the joy. Horses tossed their heads, experiencing the magic as intensely as their riders, and it made them pick up their hooves, prancing along.

"How have you done this?" Llewellyn questioned, his voice filled with wonder.

"It's their joy. I enhanced it. On the plus side, if anyone was going to attack us, they can't now."

"Can you always do this?"

Eirian shook her head and said, "No, not like this. I mean, the bloodlust I can, but this is different."

"You won't exhaust yourself?"

"It takes a great deal to exhaust me. I've focused my magic on a positive feeling and let go. It's hard to explain, but basically, my magic is happy, so anyone feeling it is happy, and I have an extensive reach."

The keep loomed ahead, drawing Eirian's gaze to the soldiers lining the walls as the magic hit them, and they displayed signs of joy and excitement. Once Halcyon's hooves touched the bridge, Eirian made herself rein in her power. Inside the castle grounds, it became easier to control. She looked at the amazement and fear directed at her by the surrounding people.

"I'm not sure I liked that," Everett muttered.

"Why not?" Eirian asked.

He shook his head. "I felt so extraordinarily overjoyed that I don't think I could have lifted a finger to defend myself."

"I agree. It might be useful in battle, though. You could make the enemy feel overwhelmingly happy to let us kill them!" Llewellyn commented.

Horrified at the suggestion, Eirian told him, "It doesn't work like that. I can't differentiate between theirs and ours."

"Not even with practice?"

"No! Absolutely not. I have limits."

As they got closer to the keep, Eirian realized she had forgotten about the Telmians. The brush of their magic against hers grew stronger with every stride Halcyon took, and Eirian could tell they were doing their best to shield themselves. She barely sensed the elves beneath the feel of the strangers. Their magic was not what Eirian was used to, but it had a sense of similarity.

"Quick, tell me, why are the daoine here? They slipped my mind."

Eirian peeked over each shoulder at her cousins. They looked disturbed by the reminder of the visitors.

"They're here to mark the occasion," Everett answered.

Chewing on her bottom lip, Eirian hesitated before asking, "Did an elf come with them?"

"None that I saw. Why?"

The moment of hope Eirian had allowed herself went as quickly as it came.

"It's not important," she said, and her heart sunk. "So long as we behave, nothing should happen. Perhaps Athnaral will misconstrue their presence, and we can benefit."

The last gate into the courtyard loomed ahead, and the trio fell silent. A light breeze tugged at her hair, and Eirian glanced up. Barely a cloud broke the sea of blue sky, the sun creeping higher. Noting the warmth, Eirian was glad it was early in the day. Stable staff were in the shadows, ready to run out and take control of the horses once the procession halted. As the next highest-ranking nobles after Everett and Llewellyn, Marcellus and Gallagher stood at the closed doors to the keep, awaiting her approach.

Accepting Llewellyn's help to dismount, Eirian faced the steps and made her way up. Marcellus stared at her, and she did not smile, coming to a halt before the doors. Gallagher was beaming with a hand on the sword attached to his belt. Smoothing her hands over her skirt nervously, Eirian waited for the two noblemen to open the door, watching the guards out of the corner of her eye as they stared in fascination. Someone signaled, and Marcellus bowed his head slightly. Together, they pushed open the heavy wooden doors to allow her to enter.

Members of the household occupied every available space, hoping to see Eirian as she passed. Walking ahead of her, Marcellus and Gallagher pushed open the doors and allowed Eirian her first sight of the packed throne room. Eirian's guards lined the pathway down the center, each of them smiling proudly. There was an empty spot close to the throne for Aiden.

Nolan stood waiting, his eyes locked on Eirian as she walked steadily towards him. Behind him, the crown rested on the throne, waiting for the moment Nolan would place it on her head. There was a proud look on his face when Eirian reached the dais and carefully knelt before him. The racing beat of her heart and the rustle of her skirts were loud in her ears. Her nervousness had returned. The brief reprise she had clawed out of the crowds' joy vanished.

The boom of Nolan's voice over her head made Eirian even more thankful for what Tynan had done.

"We gather to bear witness to the passing of the crown from the old to the new. Today Eirian Altira, daughter of King Nolan Altira, comes before you to lay claim to the throne of Endara by right of blood and with the ancestors' blessing. I ask you, are there any who would contest her claim?"

Eirian bit her lip, filled with fear and hope that someone might protest. Every person who had the right to speak had assured her they supported her completely. Still, the doubt returned the moment the chance came. She sighed softly and glanced at Nolan without raising her head when no one said anything. His eyes roamed over the crowd, fierce and challenging.

"Eirian Altira, do you come of your own choice?" Nolan asked.

"I come here freely."

"And are you willing to swear the oath that binds you to Endara?"

Flinching when she heard the slight waver in his voice, Eirian glanced at him and said, "Yes, I am willing."

Nolan continued, "Before the people of Endara, do you swear to govern in a fair and just manner, under the law?"

"I swear so."

"Do you swear to uphold the laws of Endara, to live by them as all others must?"

"I swear so."

"Do you swear to protect Endara from those who would destroy it, no matter the cost?"

"I swear so."

"Do you swear to honor and uphold the traditions of Endara as set forth by the ancestors?"

"I swear so."

"People of Endara, do you accept Eirian's oath?"

The crowd responded enthusiastically, "We do."

"In return, do you swear to serve her to the best of your abilities and under the law?"

"We swear so."

"May none forswear the oaths given here!" Nolan declared.

His feet moved from her line of sight, and Eirian knew he had gone to the throne to pick up the crown. She lifted her head and met his gaze while Nolan held the crown high over her. There was a hint of sadness in his eyes, and she frowned, knowing he would be the only one to see it. Letting his hands descend, Nolan placed the crown on her head and stepped back.

The weight was more than Eirian expected. She desperately wanted to adjust it on her head to a more comfortable position. Nolan returned to the throne and retrieved the heavy gold links inlaid with stones and engraved with all the Endaran families' arms. Giving Eirian a moment to prepare, he carefully draped it around her neck, fingers trembling as he did up the clasps at the back to secure it. The weight was greater than the crown, the gold cold against her skin.

"By the powers, so it shall be. Rise, Queen Eirian I."

Glad she had practiced going from kneeling to standing in dresses, Eirian managed the movement gracefully and took the hand Nolan offered her. He led her to the throne, and she sat, resting her hands in her lap with her shoulders squared and head held high. Turning to the room, Nolan looked at the crowd.

"Hail, Queen Eirian."

One by one, the people dropped to a knee, bowing before her. Nolan nodded, watching them before he took a few steps to the bottom of the dais and turned, joining the rest on one knee. A pang of anguish at the sight of her father kneeling before her struck Eirian, and she wanted to scold him. Eyes sweeping over the crowd, Eirian felt a sense of loss, as though she had held on to an expectation that it would not go ahead at all.

Everett was the first to rise, stepping over to Nolan and giving him a hand. There was a flash of love in the look Nolan gave Everett, and Eirian envied their closeness. As everyone rose, she allowed herself a moment to take in the circle of isolation surrounding her. Her guards took their places, Aiden's eyes catching hers as he moved. Eirian knew what it meant. From that moment on, nothing would be the same.

Catching sight of Celiaen, she met his gaze and saw the defeat in his eyes. He had closed off the link between them, only the barest connection remaining. It felt strange, having him so close and not feeling his magic as effortlessly as her own, but Eirian understood why he had done it. Understanding did not change the anguish the feeling caused her, and she wanted to run to him. She wanted to feel the calm that his touch gave her, the tether Celiaen provided.

Appearing from the shadows, Ulric strode towards the throne with a small carved timber box. Bowing at the bottom of the dais, he presented it before stepping up and opening the lid to reveal the thick gold ring with the royal seal. Goldsmiths had adjusted it to fit her, and Eirian held out her left hand so the ring could be slipped onto her finger. He held her hand briefly and kissed the ring. Smiling faintly, Ulric stepped back to stand beside Nolan.

As Everett walked towards her, Eirian prepared herself for the next part. Each head of a noble family would approach and kneel before her. They would kiss the ring and swear fealty on behalf of their house. It was to remind Eirian that she sat on the throne by their grace. She was there because they let her be, and they could take back what they gave just as fast. Everett's lips curled up into a smirk as he kissed the ring on her finger and met her stare with a wink.

"I, Everett Altira, Duke of Tamantal, pledge my continuing loyalty, and that of my people, to the throne of Endara and Queen Eirian Altira."

Nodding once to show acceptance of his oath, Eirian replied, "The crown thanks you for your continued loyalty."

It was like a training drill, repeating the same sequence over and over. Some swearing allegiance to Eirian had barely spoken a sentence to her in the past. Some because they spent little time in Amath. Others because they begrudgingly accepted her, either because of their preference for Everett or their dislike of her magic. By the time they finished, Eirian's head was pounding, the tendrils of her headache digging in. Faintly she heard bells being rung throughout the city and was thankful for what it meant.

Once the last of the nobility had done their part, Everett shouted, "All hail Queen Eirian!"

TWENTY-ONE

Once out of sight in a hallway, Eirian rubbed her face and let her shoulders slump. She had endured the ceremony, the pledges, the greetings, and now it was over. Feeling arms wrap around her, she uncovered her eyes and saw the concerned look on Nolan's face. He had escorted her from the throne room, Ulric accompanying them into the silence and calm.

"You did well."

"I don't know how I feel." Eirian lifted a hand to touch the crown and said, "It feels strange."

Nolan replied, "Yes, it does. I remember my coronation. My father died first, and Marcellus's father placed the crown on my head. It's different in that situation. People recognized me as the king from the moment my father passed on, and my coronation was more of a formality than a formal exchange of power."

"I wish it had been that way for us."

"We can't change what has happened, my sweet girl. You're the queen now, and you'll be magnificent. I've never been prouder of you, and it was my greatest honor to place the crown on your head."

"Father…"

Glancing at Ulric, Nolan sighed and said, "Your ladies will join us soon, and you'll have a short amount of time for yourself. Then the feasting begins."

Making a noise, Eirian grumbled, "My head is pounding. I don't know how I will make it through the feast. Do I have to stay for the entirety?"

"Didn't you sleep at all?" Ulric asked, giving her a funny look.

"Sort of, but that's a story for another time. How do you feel, father?"

"Like a proud old man. I won't attend the feast, but I'm sure you'll forgive me for that."

"I understand." She touched his arm softly. "You can rest now."

Frowning, Ulric nodded at the door, telling her, "I'd better return to the fray and play my part as your chancellor. The daoine delegation wishes to have an audience with you at the first available opportunity."

"I understand. Make the arrangements. We need them gone from Endara as soon as possible. It won't be private, and I insist on the dukes, Prince Celiaen, and Tynan. The prince has dealt with Telmia before and hopefully will guide us through any mistakes."

"They concern you a great deal, don't they?" Ulric asked Nolan.

There was an odd note in Nolan's voice when he answered, "The daoine don't mix with humans and barely interact with the elves. I think we're right to have some concerns."

"I think it's worth asking why they would show up now, of all the times they could have picked."

He turned on his heel and slipped through the door into the throne room, leaving them with the guards. Hearing the noise of multiple people approaching, Eirian turned to see who it was. Brenna and the other ladies-in-waiting rounded the corner to the corridor and dipped into curtsies when they drew close. Close behind them, Amira followed to escort Nolan to his chambers to rest. Pulling Eirian into a hug again, Nolan murmured in her ear.

"Beware the daoine, don't let them close, and remember to dance with your prince."

Gripping his back, Eirian inhaled the scent of him and wished it did not feel like he was saying goodbye. "I'll see you in the morning before the tourney."

"I hope so." Kissing her cheek, Nolan turned to Amira and said, "Such a lovely young lady to help an old fool back to his bed."

Amira rolled her eyes and chuckled. "Cheeky old man."

Watching them amble away, arm in arm, Eirian sighed. "How long do I have?"

"An hour. Two at the most. We'll return to your quarters and let you rest for as long as we can. Isabella will prepare some more peppermint oil and tea for you if you still have that headache. I'm sure Bea will help with one of her massages," Brenna replied.

Brenna had no smiles for any of them, her eyes skipping from one person to the next and giving each of them a stern look. Merle appeared at the end of the corridor and waved at them.

"If we go now, most people are lingering in the throne room or out in the courtyard. The Telmians are quite the distraction even during a coronation."

"Well then, they've made themselves useful. My head is pounding, so a massage, tea, and oil sound very welcoming right now," Eirian said.

"Did you notice them in the room?" Bea asked curiously. "I didn't. Not that I was looking."

Elke snorted. "I saw them last night. They're something else. Can they shapeshift?"

"Regardless of what you might think, I don't know everything about magic, and I have met no daoine previously. I need them kept away from me as much as possible. I mean it. Aiden, do you understand?" Eirian said, and stared at Aiden as he strode along in front.

Aiden did not look at her. "I understand. We'll do our best to keep them away, but it won't always be possible. Besides, you can't avoid them completely. They might take insult."

Groaning, Eirian balled one hand into a fist and replied, "You're right. All we can do is hope they leave as suddenly as they appeared and do no harm in the meantime."

Merle's prediction had been correct, and hardly anyone lingered in the corridors. The lack of people made it easier for the group to reach their destination quickly. When they got to the heavily guarded hall outside her quarters, it surprised Eirian to see Celiaen standing outside her door with Tynan. There was a worried look on Tynan's face, and her heart plummeted, suspecting she knew why.

"Aiden, would you come in with me and His Highness? The rest of you can wait outside. We won't take long."

"Are you sure?" Brenna asked tentatively. "I can come in."

Pushing the door open, Aiden gave Celiaen a calculating look before turning to Eirian and saying, "Of course, Your Majesty."

Waiting for the two elves to enter, Eirian followed them. Once they were through, Aiden shut the door. He kept out of the way, knowing from the looks on the faces of the two elves that they were not there with good news.

She murmured, "It's my father, isn't it?"

Tynan nodded and told her, "Ree, if he makes it through tomorrow…"

"Thank you, Tynan. We knew this would happen. Can you please tell him? He needs to know if he doesn't already." Not looking at him, Eirian said, "I'm glad we did it. The brief time I got to spend with him meant the world to me."

"I know. I'll wait outside for you to finish speaking to Celi before I leave to see your father. I presume the Lady Amira is with him?"

"She is."

Hearing the door open and shut again, Eirian glanced at Celiaen. Moving to stand next to her, Celiaen reached for her hand and lifted it, staring at the gold ring. With a crooked smile, he kissed the amethyst band on the finger next to it, and her eyes narrowed at the challenging look he gave Aiden.

"Your father is hiding something," Celiaen murmured.

Frowning, Eirian plucked her hand from his grasp and crossed her arms. "I'm sure he has many secrets, but why are you suddenly concerned?"

Running a hand through his hair, Celiaen said, "Just for a moment, try not to be argumentative. I spoke to the Telmians, and they're not here for the sake of it. King Neriwyn sent them to meet you. I quote, 'King Nolan knows why our king sent us, even if we don't.' Sounds like a secret to me."

"How could my father have had dealings with them? The daoine have never visited."

"According to your records, but Eirian, it wouldn't be hard for them to slip in and out of the city unnoticed. You do it."

Covering her mouth, Eirian closed her eyes and shook her head. It was more than she wanted to deal with at that moment. She was tired, her head throbbed with pain, and all she wanted to do was crawl into her bed and sleep. Preferably with both of the men watching her. Their arms holding her would do more to banish her headache and anxiety than any soothing oils or tea could.

"If it's true, why hasn't he said anything to warn me? They don't leave Telmia for any little reason."

"You're hardly little, even without a secret kept by your father. Tynan knows, and I asked him to see what he could learn from Nolan."

"No one can know. But I said those same words to Everett when Baenlin came, and it seems common knowledge that they offered me the grand mage position."

Celiaen chuckled. "I suspect my uncle had his hand in that. I was expecting Baenlin to storm through the doors shouting about higher callings when your father asked if anyone contested your claim."

"Or were you hoping that anyone would contest it and the delay would make me rethink my decision and decide that it was better if I didn't become the queen? You can't fool me, Celi. You hoped I'd change my mind."

"I love you, Ree, but I accept your decision, even if it means I might never have you."

"If?" Eirian raised a brow.

Glancing at Aiden, Celiaen gave her an unreadable look and said, "That is a question to ask your cousins. Be careful around the daoine. Whatever they want from you won't be a small thing."

"I plan to avoid them as much as politely possible. The Telmians want to meet with me. I told Ulric to arrange it, and I'd like you and Tynan to be there. You know them better than we do." She touched the crown and told him, "I'm going to rest before the feast."

"I know you have a headache. I read it in your magic before you arrived. I'd offer to help you with it, but I know what your answer would be. What happened in the tomb?"

Guiding Celiaen to the door, Eirian met his gaze, muttering, "I don't know. I found old remnants of magic, and I must have disturbed a ward that knocked me out."

"That would have to be a powerful ward to knock you out."

"It's over and done with."

Before Aiden opened the door, Celiaen spun and kissed her, lingering until she lifted a hand to push him away. It was a reluctant attempt at a shove, Eirian's fingers stroking the silk covering his chest. Their bond called her, no longer walled off as it had been during the ceremony. The contact between them banished her headache, and she wanted to curl up in the safety of his arms. He was home, and the words were on the tip of her tongue. Whispers across her mind urged her to tell him, but she refused.

Celiaen brushed his lips over her ear and murmured, "Whenever I get the chance to remind you how much I love you, I'll take it. Even if it makes you cranky. I like it when you're mad at me."

Letting him walk out, Eirian sighed and met Aiden's concerned gaze. "He drives me crazy, Aiden, but I trust him with my life more than anyone else. Even you."

"I won't pretend I'm not insulted. Or that I understand what is between you. However, I won't hesitate to kill the prince if he tries to do you harm," Aiden said, and prepared to open the door. "You need rest. I'll let your ladies in."

"Thank you, Aiden."

Eirian smiled at him, shoulders slumping. Aiden paused, turning to look at Eirian standing in her coronation gown with the crown of Endara on her head. Smiling slowly, he met her gaze again, and what she saw in his eyes made Eirian blush. Crossing the space, he caught her hand and lifted it, placing a kiss on the back. He wanted to reassure her about Nolan, but bit his tongue. As much as Aiden longed to tell her it was safe to break down in front of him and provide Eirian with the comfort she needed, he knew he could not.

"Don't worry, Your Majesty, I'll claim a dance tonight as thanks. After all, dancing is another type of sparring, and I've proven I'm better at it than you."

Giving her a wink, Aiden opened the door to let her ladies in and slipped through, leaving Eirian alone. He might not be allowed to comfort her, but he could rile her anger just enough to give her something to cling to. Gathering the other guards outside, he intended to issue orders, but Merle held up a hand and gave Aiden an amused look.

"Captain, I think you need to go clean up and prepare for the feast."

"That's right." Fionn laughed. "You sat outside that fucking tomb all night. Go have a bath and wash off the long-dead scent."

Crossing his arms, Aiden growled. "Are you asking for a flogging, Fionn?"

"No, sir, not me."

Glancing between them, Gabe muttered, "Merle and Fionn have this under control, Captain. You need some rest before the feast. We know you'll be in attendance and off duty."

"What are you trying to say?" Aiden demanded defensively.

"That it's easier to remain at the Queen's side when you look like a noble rather than a guard. No one will question when you swoop in to save her from strangling someone."

Merle agreed. "Gabe is right. I've got this. I'm your second-in-command for a reason, Aiden. She's not going anywhere until it's time to join the feast. Just go."

"If anything—"

"Go!"

Directing a last look at his men, Aiden turned and strode away. The castle was a hive of activity, and the people everywhere waited for the great hall to be opened for the feast. Aiden and his men had moved into quarters within the keep ahead of the coronation. Their rooms were close to the monarchs' chambers to be nearer to Eirian. It was better than the barracks they had been living in. As he reached their section, the sight of Celiaen leaning against the door to the guards' quarters surprised Aiden.

"I've been waiting for you," Celiaen said.

Sighing, Aiden glared and waited for Celiaen to move away from the door. Smiling, Celiaen stood straight, tugging at the blue silk coat he was wearing. The action made Aiden frustrated, reminding him of every time he had caught Eirian casually touching Celiaen. He had noticed many times that certain textures drew her. It made Aiden wonder if Eirian would be as casual in handling him if he wore silk all the time.

"What do you want?" he demanded.

Celiaen made a show of licking his lips and letting his eyes drift over Aiden. A smug smirk betraying that part of his intention was to unsettle him. Aiden did not dismiss it entirely, giving Celiaen a similar examination. It was hard to resist imagining the reaction he would receive if he grabbed a handful of silk and dragged Celiaen through the door. Celiaen's smirk faltered, seeing a flicker of desire cross Aiden's face.

"I can think of many things, Captain."

Aiden forced a blank expression and said, "What do you want from me?"

"Again, I can think of many things." Cocking his head to the side, Celiaen added, "But I'm here about Ree."

"Are you going to threaten me, Your Highness?"

"No. It's about the Telmian visitors. Ree is on the back foot today, emotionally, so I'm asking you to protect her."

Frowning, Aiden knew Celiaen did not mean protection with a sword. He thought about the news Tynan had given her and the emotions she would have experienced constantly from the moment she woke. During the ceremony, the look on Eirian's face when she had sat alone on the throne to receive oaths had been one of resignation. It had made him want to grab her hand and promise she was not alone.

"I understand." Aiden glanced away before looking back to say, "You're not the only one who cares about her."

The comment had Celiaen chuckling, and he closed the gap between them. It was the first time they had stood so close, and Aiden noted he was slightly taller than Celiaen. Something that made Aiden gloat a little as he stared into his dark eyes. Lifting a hand, Celiaen stroked his cheek and cocked his head to the side. He expected Aiden to jolt away from his touch and hid his surprise when he did not.

"Let me one thing clear, Captain, there is no competition between us. I know some of the council would like to see you legitimized and married to Ree, but that won't happen."

"She turned you down, Princeling. Going over her head to sway the council your way won't win you any favors."

"We'll see about that." Celiaen tugged at a stray curl behind Aiden's ear and told him, "But a word of advice, Captain, before you let your feelings get the better of you."

Aiden's eyes narrowed.

"You're our type."

"Our type?" he asked, even though he knew what the answer would be. "What do you mean by that?"

"Ree and I have the same taste in lovers, and you, dear Captain—"

"Would have made a good red," Aiden said. "I've heard that before. From someone else who told me I'm her type. You're right, Your Highness. There's no competition between us. I could have both of you if I wanted. Now, I need to prepare for the feast. Unlike you, I have a queen to escort."

Jealousy coursed through Celiaen, and he allowed Aiden to push open the door. It made him forget what he had asked of Aiden. Waiting until he had vanished through it, Celiaen pressed a hand to the timber and worked a ward into the frame to discourage anyone from leaving through it. Smirking as he walked away, he brushed his mind against the bond to Eirian as a gentle reminder. She brushed back, letting Celiaen feel the tendrils of pain from her headache and, through them, a flicker of her loneliness.

"What have you been doing?" Tara asked, slipping in beside him.

"Just paying someone a visit. Have you been following me?"

"No, but I had a feeling." She snorted. "What did you do to the captain?"

"How did you?"

"Celi, I raised you, and I know how you think. You were with Tynan and Ree, but now you're not. I saw Tynan on his way to attend King Nolan. He mentioned Ree has a headache, so Lydia has gone to see her."

Celiaen regretted not having a green accompany him to see Eirian when he felt her pain. Ashamed by his neglect, he looked away and avoided Tara's concerned stare. Her hand squeezed his shoulder, reminding him she was not going anywhere.

"I felt the need to see the captain."

"To tell him to stay away from the one person he can't stay away from?"

"No, to ask him to protect her," Celiaen replied.

Tara laughed, squeezing his shoulder again. They wandered the halls aimlessly while they talked, Alyse on the other side of Tara. People avoided them, the arrivals from Telmia far more intriguing to the nobles of Endara than the elves.

"That was a good thing you did for Ree," Alyse told him. "It's really quite peculiar, but Aiden seems to have an anchoring effect for her like you and Gal do."

His eyes darted in her direction, and Celiaen asked, "How do you know that?"

"I sense the shift in Ree's emotions when they come into contact. It's the same. She's emotionally invested in Aiden, Celi, and you can't change that any more than you can change the fact she loves Gal."

Grunting, Celiaen remained silent. Beside him, Tara gave Alyse a concerned look, but she smiled in response. Her magic blanketed the two red mages, a calming influence discouraging them from arguing. Celiaen knew she was not as powerful as Galameyvin or Tynan. Rather than shut her out, he let Alyse affect him. It was soothing, and they kept going, waiting for the bells to be rung ahead of the feast.

They wandered until they found themselves in the library. With the excitement of the coronation and feast, the chambers were silent, even the staff absent. Afternoon light filtered through the windows, illuminating the rows of books that dominated the space. Finding a table in a nook beside a window, the elves sat themselves down. Alyse fished a pack of cards from a pocket, setting about dealing a game to keep them occupied while they waited.

"Oh, good, I found you," Tynan said as he joined them. "I don't have good news."

"How long?" Celiaen asked, knowing what he referred to.

Tynan cringed, replying, "Mid-morning if he's lucky. Do I tell Ree?"

"No, don't tell her. She knows it's coming and that it'll be tomorrow. If you tell Ree a more specific timeframe, she'll want to be there for it."

Agreeing with Celiaen, Alyse said, "Ree doesn't need to see that. Better to tell her after."

"Alright, I won't tell her. Nolan and Amira know, but I doubt either of them would say anything to her about it. He wants to protect Ree."

Celiaen studied him. "I don't suppose you found out anything related to the daoine?"

"Nothing except they frighten him. He's definitely hiding something, and the sensation increases when they're mentioned. Honestly, I expected my wall to last longer, and I feel that their arrival has exasperated his situation," he told them.

Puzzled, Tara glanced between the two blues before saying, "Lord Faolan doesn't leave Telmia for just anything."

Deciding to reveal information he had picked up over the bond, Celiaen murmured, "Something is bothering Ree. I don't know what, I haven't asked, but it's there. Sometimes it feels like she is watching everyone and waiting for... I don't know what. I just feel it over the bond, like a shadow following her."

"They crowned her the Queen of Endara this morning, Celi. It's probably just that. She is under a lot of pressure. Something you should understand better than anyone," Alyse said.

"It's not, and Gal would say the same thing."

Tynan shrugged at Alyse and commented, "None of us is as in tune to her as they are. I couldn't tell the difference any more than you could."

"I think her nightmares are back," Celiaen said.

Freezing, the three of them stared at him before exchanging worried looks. All of them knew the trouble Eirian's nightmares could cause. Most of the time, the dreams were nothing more than a disruption to her sleep. Sometimes something in them triggered her to lose control of her magic. They could do little about it except pay attention, and Tara considered taking Aiden aside for a chat. He and his men deserved to be prepared for what might happen.

They heard the bells chiming, a sound that echoed through the hallways of the keep. Taking their time to pack up the cards and leave the table, the elves remained silent. Celiaen knew Eirian would not be there for some time and felt no rush to go to the hall. As they went, he contemplated approaching the various nobles he needed to speak to. Every chance he got to work on convincing council members to agree to his proposal, he took, and the feast would be no exception. With all the effort he had been putting in, Celiaen could not help wondering if it would please Paienven.

By the time they entered, the hall was bursting with people. Noblewomen in their gowns fluttered through the crowd like butterflies, many of the men equally extravagant. They made Celiaen feel subdued in comparison. Detailed embroidery offset the midnight blue silk of his coat, all of it focused around the triple sword emblem of his family. It was longer than the jackets preferred by the Endarans. Mages chose the design to give the appearance of elegance while hiding weapons.

"It's her birthday tomorrow," Tara commented, plucking a glass of wine from a tray as a server went past. "You going to give her your gift?"

Thinking of the rings tucked away in a pocket, Celiaen sighed, "I'll give it to her when it's right."

"Good luck with…"

Tara's voice trailed off, and Celiaen turned to look at her, noticing the rest of the hall had gone quiet. He saw Eirian, the vibrant red of her coronation gown making her look like a splash of blood across the rainbow of other colors. No one else wore red, the color reserved for the monarch during a coronation. Aiden was at her side, dressed as finely as the rest of the nobles. The sight made Celiaen frown, wondering why he had not felt his ward break. Sensing his jealousy, Alyse and Tynan placed hands on his shoulders, magic reminding him to stay calm.

"Celi," Tara said. "It's his job as her captain."

"It should be me," he muttered in frustration.

The three of them exchanged looks, ignoring the clench of Celiaen's jaw when he saw Aiden take Eirian's arm to guide her towards a group of nobles. Keeping his hand on Celiaen's shoulder, Tynan noticed one of Eirian's guards had joined them. Gabe stood next to Tara, his arms crossed, and a bored look as he watched the crowd. Something about him set them on edge, and a smug gleam in his eyes when he shifted to look at Celiaen told them he was aware of it.

"Evening, Your Highness. Enjoying the festivities?"

Celiaen shrugged, replying, "The view just improved immensely."

"Yes, it did. They're so perfectly matched, almost as though the gods intended it." Gabe chuckled. "Though I'm sure you'd argue otherwise. Jealousy is such an ugly thing. You really should be careful about letting it get the better of you."

Before he could respond, Gabe walked away, leaving Celiaen with a baffled expression. Next to him, Tara sneered in confusion while Alyse and Tynan exchanged looks. Shrugging off Tynan's hand, Celiaen started forward to cross the hall and join Eirian. Aiden saw him coming, his fingers curling around Eirian's elbow to draw her attention. Celiaen caught the look directed his way by Aiden as he leaned in and whispered something in Eirian's ear.

"Your Majesty," Celiaen said warmly.

Turning to smile at him, Eirian extended her hand so Celiaen could make a formal display of acknowledging the seal adorning her finger. Placing a kiss on her knuckles, he let his lips linger against her skin, slightly longer than necessary, magic tugging at the bond. Eirian gazed at him, a brow raised in amusement. Marcellus, clearing his throat, disrupted the moment, and Celiaen released her hand.

"Prince Celiaen, I'm pleased to see you," she told him.

"And I, you. Always."

Her eyes drifted over the crowd before coming back to him, and Eirian asked, "Have you seen the Telmians? They're not here."

"No, I can't say I have. Now that you're here, they'll start serving food. Before that happens, would you grace me with a dance?"

"Celi."

"Ree."

"There's no music yet," Eirian argued.

Holding out his hand for her to take, Celiaen asked, "When have we ever needed music?"

"I'll remember you said that."

Sighing, she placed her hand in his and smiled. Crossing his arms, Aiden watched Celiaen draw her into the middle of the room. People moved away, creating a space for them to dance. Alerted to what they were doing, the musicians hurried to gather their instruments. Everyone was aware of Eirian's lack of dancing talent, but Celiaen had a way of making up for it. Ladies shouldered their way to the front of the crowd, whispering to each other about what they would do if they had Celiaen dancing with them.

Marcellus watched them, chuckling. "How does he do it?"

"He's had practice," Alyse commented. "She's always been a terrible dancer."

Catching the dark look on Aiden's face, Celiaen kept smiling and guided Eirian through the steps like he had countless times before. He had seen her dance with others, but the only time she truly relaxed was when he was leading her. It was one of the few things Celiaen excelled at over Galameyvin. Pulling her close, he kept a hand on Eirian's waist and leaned in to brush his lips over her ear.

"You belong in red," he breathed the words. "But as much as I enjoy seeing you draped in silk from Ensaycal, I'd rather see you laid out on it."

"Celi!"

Chuckling, Celiaen spun her away, controlling the action carefully. It would be easy to let her stumble if his concentration slipped too far. He had never let her fall, and he never would. Keeping his hands steady, he watched her lips curl in delight when he caught her again. Drawing Eirian back, Celiaen went for her other ear.

"You're breathtaking, Ree. They could dress you in rags, and I'd still think you the most beautiful person in the world."

She blushed, turning her face away to mutter, "Flattering me won't change my mind."

"I don't need to flatter you to change your mind. All I need is time alone with just the two of us, uninter—"

"I hope you don't mind me interrupting," Aiden said and chuckled, cutting into the dance. "My Queen."

Allowing Aiden to take her hand from Celiaen, Eirian caught the anger flaring over the bond. Directing a smile at him, Eirian inclined her head and silently bid him walk away. Clenching his jaw, Celiaen bowed and backed away, refusing to give Aiden the pleasure of saying anything. He felt Eirian's relief over the bond and her thanks for not engaging in a jealous exchange.

"That was unnecessary, Captain," Eirian told him.

Ignoring the stares of the court, Aiden held her as carefully as Celiaen had. They had danced before, and Eirian trusted him not to let her stumble. He had seen how she relaxed into Celiaen's hold, and Aiden planned to reach that level of trust. There was a hint of amusement in his eyes as he glanced in Celiaen's direction.

Aiden murmured, "I disagree. It was vital."

"I didn't require the assistance of my guards."

His fingers dug into her hip, and Aiden pulled her as close as he could get away with while the eyes of the court were on them. Eirian held his gaze, feeling the stroke of his fingers when his grasp loosened. The pressure was a constant motion, never skipping a beat while Aiden guided her through the dance. Around them, others were dancing, following the lead of their queen. With the news Tynan had delivered, Aiden was determined to do what she needed to keep her distracted.

"I'm your captain, Eirian. I know when you need me," he told her, voice low. "He might have taken the first dance."

Bringing her to a halt, Aiden smirked, and Eirian inhaled sharply when he ran his hand along her side. Out of the corner of her eye, she took in the intricate red and purple embroidery on the cuff of his sleeve. It was not the first time Eirian had noticed Aiden's clothing matched her, and she wondered who was responsible for it.

"But I know which of us will escort you back to your chamber tonight."

Catching her hand, Aiden lifted it to his lips and kissed it, his breath making her skin tingle as he lingered. Leading Eirian away from the dancers to the head table, he watched his men move with them. They mixed with the nobles, keeping close enough to defend Eirian if needed, but not so near that she could not interact with those seeking her time. At the table, Celiaen conversed with Llewellyn and Everett, their gazes tracking Eirian's approach.

"Having fun, Eirian?" Llewellyn asked with a laugh. "You're a terrible dancer. Has anyone told you that recently?"

Allowing Aiden to pull the chair out for her, Eirian sat with a faint smile. She caught Celiaen's gaze, staring at him before she answered Llewellyn.

"I don't need anyone to tell me. I'm quite aware of how terrible I am."

Remaining behind her chair, Aiden surveyed his men and noticed Gabe watching a servant intently. She did not look any different to the rest of them, hands grasping the tray she carried tightly. When she approached the table, Gabe intercepted her quietly, eyes darting to Aiden. He said something to her that Aiden did not catch, and she nodded, turning around to walk back the way she came. Gabe went with her, and for a moment, Aiden considered following. The thought faded as quickly as it came. Whatever it was, he knew Gabe could handle it. His only concern was Eirian.

"Ma'am, do you need anything?" he asked quietly.

Eirian did not look at him, her focus on the dukes beside her as she replied, "Since you're determined to protect me, make sure I don't drink more than a glass of wine."

Standing straight, Aiden chuckled and caught Everett glaring at him. "As you command, Your Majesty. We wouldn't want you to drink too much and suffer a lapse of judgment."

TWENTY-TWO

The sun beat down unforgivably on those who had arrived too late to secure a spot in the stands. They had hoisted massive panels of bleached cloth, connected by ropes and poles to provide shade to those patrons lucky enough to get a seat. The crowd was a constant shift of cheering people waving little flags showing the coat of arms of their preferred fighters, purchased from vendors hovering around the entrances, along with people keen to make some coins by selling their cooked goods or watered-down alcohol. Lurking in shadows, savvy men and women exchanged money, betting on various fighters.

Seated comfortably, Eirian watched the hustle of people at the furthest end of the field at the fighter's tents. Rounds of the melee between guards and soldiers had occupied the morning. The soldiers won two out of three victories. Despite the ban on steel blades, there had been several injuries, and one guard had died after an unlucky blow to his head. It was the one-on-one fighting that was the principal attraction for most people.

"If I disguise myself somehow, do you think I could take part in the archery competition tomorrow morning?" Eirian glanced at Brenna.

Giving her a blank look, Brenna replied, "We've been through this already. You can't compete. Disguise or not, you're not allowed."

"It's not fair, it's my birthday, and it's only archery."

"Goodness' sake, Your Majesty, you sound like a whining child. You're twenty-six today. Behave like it!" Brenna scolded, glancing at the nobles seated in the stands to either side. "Do you think it's a good look for your subjects to see?"

Eirian lifted her hand and waved to the people watching, muttering, "I think a good look for my subjects to see is a queen that can protect them."

"You're frustrated because Prince Celiaen is taking part."

"It's hardly a fair fight for whoever draws him. Is Marcellus entering?"

Frowning at the mention of her husband, Brenna huffed. "I told him tournaments are a young man's game. Llewellyn goaded him about his age, and now Marcellus feels he has a point to prove. He paid them to rig it so he gets Llewellyn."

Chuckling, Eirian shared a look with Aiden hovering in the box's corner, where he could easily watch the fights and her at the same time. "What about you, Captain? Didn't you wish to enter? Remind everyone of who's on top?"

"I don't need to prove myself capable. I put Your Majesty on your ass nearly every day. That should be enough proof for you of who is on top." Aiden chuckled and added, "Knowing my luck, I'd have drawn the prince."

"I'd enjoy watching that."

Aiden looked down at the two men who had walked into the arena, hauberks glinting in the sunlight where their tabards did not cover them. They uncovered their heads, tucking helms under their arms. He recognized one as a member of the palace guard, and the other was a younger son of a noble. Sighing, Aiden shook his head as they saluted Eirian and waited for the signal to begin.

"I doubt Prince Celiaen would be as quick as the archmage in putting me down. He'd make a show of it and enjoy every moment. Before we leave on your tour, you need to establish who is in command if war happens. If you don't, you might find you have squabbling lords confusing the troops."

"We have the general and his staff. He's in charge," Eirian replied. "I'll cede to his greater experience."

"Do you think all of your nobles will follow your example?"

Brenna said, "Marcellus has a great deal of respect for General Cameron."

"No, Aiden has a point. There can be no doubt who is leading the army. What made you bring this up?" Shifting in her chair, Eirian slung an arm over the back and watched Aiden instead of the duelists.

Aiden waved at the fighters, saying, "Watching these young noblemen prance around like they're the greatest fighters in the land. Watching better fighters throw the round because they fear the repercussions of disarming a nobleman."

His words made Eirian feel fresh guilt over her lies. "I didn't want this tournament, Aiden, you know that. You also know I'd rather the fights didn't get thrown, but I can't do anything about it. I can't change a system of thinking overnight, though I wish I could."

They fell silent and observed the guard easily defeat the inexperienced young noble. Eirian leaned forward, studying the men as they moved, and shook her head in frustration. Shifting, Aiden watched and enjoyed how her eyes took in every move of the combatants below. He suspected Eirian knew what moves they would make before they happened. She caught him watching and raised a brow questioningly.

Mouth curling in a smirk, Aiden smoothed a hand over the top of his leg and watched her gaze drop. His fingers stroking his trousers reminded Eirian of his hands on her waist the night before, and her breath hitched. Thoughts turning to memories of dancing with him. Her cheeks flushed, and Eirian looked away, the sound of Aiden's soft chuckle making her blush more obvious. Watching the exchange, Brenna shook her head. She turned to a hovering servant, summoning them with a crook of her finger.

"I think we need some wine and something to eat," she said.

A man cleared his throat at the back of the box as the servant slipped past, and Aiden stood straight, causing Eirian to turn around and look. Receiving a nod from Eirian, the new arrival bowed.

"The chancellor is waiting to speak to you, Your Majesty."

"I was expecting him," Eirian replied.

Frowning, Aiden kept his gaze on the space behind Eirian, asking Ulric, "Is it about the visitors?"

"Yes, it is," Ulric said.

He stepped into the box, bowing slightly to Eirian's back while Brenna watched him. Aiden gave him a nod, stance relaxing.

"I've arranged an audience with the Telmians. They agreed to your terms."

"Good. When? Did they have any protests?"

Not glancing at him, Eirian kept her gaze on the fighters, her eyes tracking their every move. Staring at Aiden thoughtfully, Ulric inclined his head.

"No protests. They seemed to think if they concede to this, you'll speak more later without the entourage."

Startled, Eirian turned around to look at him. "That's implying they intend to stay."

"I'm afraid so, Your Majesty. I don't think you're going to be free of them as quickly as you'd like. As we'd all like. We need to find out why they're here."

Brenna commented, "You'll have to meet with them on their terms. They might agree to Celiaen attending."

"We need them gone, so if that's what it will take," Eirian muttered.

Aiden snorted in amusement. "I suggest using a different tone while talking to them."

Shaking her head, Eirian turned back to look at the field, noticing it was empty. "I don't like this. When are we meeting? Did they mention why they didn't attend last night?"

"I asked, and they said they didn't want to distract from your moment more than they already had."

Eirian studied Ulric, noting the carefully maintained blank expression. "How polite of them. When, Chancellor?"

"Soon, now, in fact, and I've already sent messengers to the dukes and Prince Celiaen. They agreed to meet under your conditions, but it was their idea to meet here. People will see but not hear. An audience will hopefully discourage them from doing anything," Ulric said.

He moved out of the way as servants brought in trays of food.

Chuckling, Aiden added, "Good thinking. It'll discourage Her Majesty from doing anything if they anger her."

Giving him a faint smile, Ulric nodded. Eirian sneered at Aiden, and he arched a brow at her, smirking.

Ulric said, "I arranged for more chairs. Where are your ladies?"

"It's a tournament, and they're young women. Where do you think they are?" Brenna laughed. "They have favors to give, hearts to flutter."

"For the best, we don't need them around the daoine. We'll need more food. I'd say no more wine, but that would be impolite." Leaning forward in her chair, Eirian watched as one of her guards entered the arena and asked, "Is that Fionn?"

"Indeed," Aiden muttered. "Like several of the others, he felt compelled to display that you have the best men protecting you."

Brenna ordered the servants to fetch more food and wine before looking outside. Spotting the three dukes walking in their direction, Marcellus in the middle, Brenna smiled happily. Despite their age, she felt proud watching Marcellus and knowing he was still a fierce fighter. He was the first up the narrow stairs, leaning in to kiss her while the two younger men whistled. Giggling, Brenna shook her head and slung her arms around his neck to kiss him a second time.

"You still have it, old man!" Llewellyn came up behind them and gave Marcellus a light shove, commenting, "Everett and I should be so lucky."

Letting Marcellus keep an arm around her waist, Brenna gave Llewellyn a look over her shoulder as they stepped into the box. "Yes, you should."

Arching a brow, Ulric glanced over at the three men and said, "Your Graces. We're waiting for Prince Celiaen and Tynan. The Telmians should be with us soon."

Everett glanced at the food and picked something out, sitting on the chair next to Eirian. "Having fun?"

"Not really," Eirian replied, taking in his armor. "Are you?"

"More than you, I expect. It's a lot of waiting around in tents until they call your match. I'm currently hoping I haven't drawn an elf. I'd like to make it to the next round."

Laughing, Llewellyn poured himself a mug of wine and walked to the rail, staring out at the arena. "I don't mind drawing one of them so long as it's not the lover prince. It wouldn't be the first time I've fought a mage. At least we don't have to worry about having our asses kicked by you, Eirian. Besides, Everett doesn't want to embarrass his—"

Aiden cleared his throat and gave him a warning look, saying, "I don't think I can bring in any more guards. How many daoine are coming to this meeting?"

"Three of them. Most are simply entourage." Ulric remained in his spot and explained, "Their leader is Lord Faolan. Lady Saoirse and Lord Tharen will accompany him. I know little about the Telmian court, but I think Lord Faolan is equivalent to a duke of sorts, and the lady is his sister. The other lord is the silent and observant kind. I imagine the formidable sort as well."

Eirian admitted, "I wish I'd read more about them in Riane, but I didn't think it necessary. Wasn't I wrong? I'll have some wine, but water it down, please. I don't want it going to my head."

Hearing heavy footsteps on the stairs behind the curtain, they turned to see Celiaen and Tynan slip in. Tynan was ashen, his gaze going straight to Eirian. Dressed for the arena like the dukes were, Celiaen wore his mail and a midnight blue tabard emblazoned with the triple sword emblem of Ensaycal. At his waist, his twin blades hung, and Eirian glanced at them, wishing hers were hanging at her side. Their gaze met, and she read the concern in his eyes.

"Your Majesty," Celiaen said and bowed, giving her cousins an equally concerned look.

Nodding, Eirian smiled faintly and replied, "Your Highness, you're only half-dressed. Are you sure you're prepared?"

He did not get to answer as servants began bringing in more chairs so everyone could sit. Additional trays of food followed, and the servants carefully balanced them on the small table. Once done, most of the servants left except for two. They stood at either end of the table, watching for any signals. Frowning, Eirian shook her head and looked at Brenna.

Tynan sighed and turned to the servants to say, "It's alright. I'll serve them."

"Thank you, Tynan!" Celiaen sounded surprised as he sat on the other side of Eirian, taking the spot before Llewellyn had a chance.

"It's the daoine. I doubt whatever is said is something we want to be repeated." Leaning against the rail beside the table, Tynan added, "And we know servants talk."

Nose flaring, Eirian turned to look at the curtains as she felt the prickle of their power approaching. "Celi, who is Lord Faolan exactly?"

"A man who is close to King Neriwyn, part of his inner circle. He's the one who leaves Telmia when needed, and I've met him before. They call him the loyal wolf."

Hearing footsteps on the stairs silenced them. One of Eirian's guards held back the curtain, allowing the trio of Telmian nobility to enter. Eirian stared, getting her first look at them. She understood why they caused a fuss, their ethereal beauty making her breath catch. Eirian wondered if they seemed more beautiful because she was a mage.

The first thing she could think of to describe them was that someone had poured moonlight over their skin. Magic surrounded them like a mist, betraying nothing of the people who wielded it. It was familiar and stirred something in her memories that made Eirian frown. She did not want those thoughts plaguing her while she met the daoine. Forcing herself to look away, Eirian met Tynan's gaze and sought his calm, letting it wash over her.

A man with deep red hair bowed and drew her attention, saying, "Thank you for seeing us, Your Majesty. I am Lord Faolan, this is my sister Lady Saoirse, and Lord Tharen."

Offering Faolan her hand, Eirian tried not to flinch when he took it, the contact increasing the whisper of memories at the edge of her mind. The press of his magic forced her to meet his green eyes, and Eirian noticed the curiosity in their depths.

"I won't pretend I'm not surprised and unsettled by your presence in my kingdom, Lord Faolan."

He let go of her hand and glanced at the seats to ask, "May we sit?"

"Of course, you're my guests. We have food and wine. Entertainment if you feel inclined to watch them fight."

Eirian waved at the table before pointing at the scene of two men swinging swords at each other. Tharen stared at her while Saoirse sat near Brenna.

Saoirse smiled at Eirian and commented, "You're dying to tell us to get on with business, but you know we must go through the formalities."

"I try to be polite," Eirian replied. "You're free to ignore them."

She did not return the smile, her eyes taking in the way the mess of deep auburn curls tumbled over Saoirse's shoulders like a curtain of old blood. It was a stark contrast to the silvery hue of her skin. A flicker of a memory hit her, Eirian recalling those same curls draped across her chest while she stroked them. Celiaen cleared his throat and Eirian looked away from Saoirse, thankful for the distraction.

"Her Majesty can be rather direct," Celiaen said.

"No doubt a trait she got from her father," Faolan replied, and there was something sad in his eyes when he glanced at Eirian.

"I wouldn't know." Eirian held his stare.

Faolan turned to Tynan. "I think I'd like some wine before we begin."

Shifting her focus to Tharen, Eirian thought it looked like someone had forgotten to add color to him after they had dunked him in moonshine. His hair was silvery gray, and his eyes reminded her of river stones. There was a sharpness to his gaze as Tharen studied each of the people seated around the box that suggested he would not miss a thing. Tynan offered her a mug of wine, and Eirian shook her head in refusal, showing him the drink beside her.

"Our king sent us to broker a treaty with you." The words had them staring at Faolan in shock.

"Why?" Llewellyn was the first to speak, his question earning him a sharp look from his cousins.

"I can't tell you everything. That's between your queen and my king. What I can tell you is something is coming that has King Neriwyn fearful for the future, and he wishes to help prevent the worst from happening."

"I don't suppose you could tell us what it is?"

Eirian hushed her cousins before they could speak. Both men were unhappy with how Faolan had dismissed Llewellyn's question.

"After the gods vanished, there was a void of power, and the darkness took advantage. I thought we had vanquished it in the last war, but perhaps I was wrong."

"My father tells stories of the great madness. He repeats the stories as they were told to him by those who fought the darkness. A time of war and death, when mages fought mages, and great cities fell. No one is sure of the truth to them." Celiaen glanced at Eirian and continued. "It's an era we've forgotten. Not even Riane teaches of it."

"Your great grandfather was a good man and a powerful mage. I remember they kept him from the fight after it claimed his older brother." Inclining his head to Celiaen, Faolan held a hand to his chest in respect.

Eirian stared in shock and asked, "Forgive me, but how old you are? I know it is said the daoine are immortal, but I never thought it was the truth."

"Age does not touch us. I remember the gods, and I remember the death and destruction that came when they turned their backs on us. We were the first, and perhaps we'll be the last," Faolan told them.

"Brother, you know our laws," Saoirse muttered, receiving looks. "I'm sorry, Queen Eirian. We'll answer what we can. What you did yesterday was rather impressive for a human."

Cocking her head, Eirian stared at Saoirse. She ignored the feelings of discomfort from her cousins at the mention of her manipulation of the crowd. Dismissed also her curiosity at the way Saoirse stirred fragments of memory. It was not the time to dwell on those thoughts.

She said, "I understand the realities of the law. Thank you for your praise, Lady Saoirse. My dear Dukes of Onaorbaen and Tamantal were not so impressed."

"On the contrary, it impressed me, but for us non-magical folk, it's rather daunting to find our emotions changed and on such a large scale," Llewellyn told them.

Silence fell on the group, and Eirian turned, looking at the arena. When she turned back, her gaze went to Celiaen first before facing Faolan.

"You said a treaty brings you here. Did your king send emissaries to Athnaral? And what about Riane? It has been a long time since he interacted with the high council."

"You're the only one who matters in the face of what is coming," Faolan said simply.

Marcellus scowled, letting go of Brenna's hand to point at each of the daoine. "Why is Eirian the only one who matters?"

Tharen scoffed and answered, "Your little Queen is far more powerful than she knows."

Sipping her wine, Eirian stared at Tharen. "No doubt I am. Why does my power matter that much?"

Tharen stared back at her, his arms crossed. "You can answer that yourself. You know what you're capable of."

"That's true, and I also know the cost. I wouldn't say it's worth the advantage."

"In desperate times, you'll take desperate measures."

She admitted, "Let's hope that times never get that desperate."

Everett cleared his throat, and Eirian turned to him, ending the staring between her and Tharen. They waited patiently for him to speak.

"I'm not sure I'm following. We're on the verge of war with Athnaral, but it's almost as though you're implying there's another war. Please correct me if I'm wrong."

"Our king believes Athnaral to be a symptom of the bigger issue. There is much happening that you're clueless about," Faolan replied.

"So you claim."

Standing, Faolan walked over to the table and plucked a piece of fruit from a tray. "I may not tell you more than I have."

"Forgive me, Lord Faolan, but you haven't exactly told us anything," Brenna muttered.

He bit into the fruit and replied, "Are you sure of that? Anything else I can say can only be told to Queen Eirian. I'm bound by oaths to my king."

Furious, Brenna snapped, "I'm a most trusted confidant to the Queen."

There was a hint of condescension in the look Faolan gave Brenna before finishing his fruit and turning back to Eirian. "I'm sorry about your father. The human mind is such a fragile thing, so easily influenced by madness."

"That is an interesting choice of words. Influenced," Llewellyn said. "Are you attempting to imply something? The former king began his descent into madness before Her Majesty returned from her studies in Riane."

He arched his brow and shared a look with his fellow dukes.

"I don't mean to imply Her Majesty had anything to do with it. In fact, I know she did not. King Nolan has been a victim of circumstance."

Digging her nails into her palm, Eirian felt a twinge of fear and stared at the three daoine with as blank an expression as she could manage. She recalled everything that she had picked up on and suspected a link to why they were there.

Eirian said, "I'm sure you didn't mean to imply it. I'm aware some people mutter such accusations, but no one will say it to my face."

Breaking his silence, Ulric held up a hand and said, "Since you say you can't talk about certain things with anyone but our queen, can you at least tell us on what terms your king would offer an alliance?"

"Telmia will come to your aid in the war." Faolan glanced sideways at Tharen and continued, "In return, Eirian Altira has to play the part the gods assigned her."

Everett looked incredulous, standing to point at each daoine in frustration. "This feels like a game! You can't tell us this, or you can't tell us that, but you'll bring the might of Telmia to our aid. All in return for Eirian doing something in the future that you can't define."

"I'm sorry, but he has a point," Celiaen spoke softly, avoiding the amused stare of Faolan. "I'm sure my father would agree."

"Don't worry, little prince, our king has no designs on your beloved. She is quite forbidden to us." Tharen laughed drily, shaking his head.

Celiaen stiffened, and Eirian reached out, touching his arm gently to bring his focus to her. They regarded each other briefly before Celiaen turned back to Tharen.

"That's not what I meant. You're talking in riddles, and it won't win you any favor."

"What makes you so sure they're riddles to her?" Saoirse asked.

"I know her better than anyone!"

Shaking Eirian's hand from his arm, Celiaen's magic flared, and Tynan took a step towards him. They could ill afford him influencing Eirian or the surrounding crowds.

Saoirse smiled, saying, "Do you? We know a lot about Eirian. All thanks to someone who knows her just as well as you do. If not better."

"What does she mean?" Llewellyn asked Eirian.

Eirian met Saoirse's amused green eyes and smiled coldly. She knew precisely what Saoirse was speaking of. As did Celiaen.

"Galameyvin wouldn't tell what he knew of me willingly to anyone. Either you used your powers to trick him into speaking, or you hoped to cause angst to Celiaen and me."

When Saoirse laughed, Eirian wanted to cover her ears to block out the sound. It added to the press of memories at the edge of her mind. Eirian hated the feeling. She had always hated it.

"You're correct. Galameyvin doesn't willingly tell his secrets. He is, however, happy to sing your praises and, in doing so, tells us more than he realizes. We can easily read your magic, and it tells us many things," Saoirse informed her.

"What do you get from me?" Celiaen asked angrily.

"You taste of blood, fury, and death. Typical for your kind," Faolan answered. "But it doesn't hide your unwavering devotion to her."

Slumping back in his chair, Celiaen gave Eirian a fearful look and asked, "And the Queen?"

A reserved look chased away Saoirse's amusement. "She is the balance between life and death. Her power is unique. When I close my eyes and breathe in her magic, I see fields of flowers in a perpetual cycle of life. They bloom, wither, and die. They are reborn to flower once more."

"As much as I enjoy the insights into Queen Eirian and her magic, we're here to discuss other matters. Besides, some of these men have duels to take part in," Ulric commented and held his mug out to Tynan.

"What would you rather discuss?" Tharen asked.

"I must tell you it will be difficult for us to accept a treaty with such vague terms."

"I don't understand what is vague about the terms?" Faolan replied and frowned at Ulric.

Eirian could tell it was taking Ulric a lot of effort not to stare in disbelief at Faolan, and she could not help the faint smile that his expression caused.

Ulric patiently said, "I'm sorry, but how can you say you're not purposefully vague? I know most of us haven't dealt with your kind before, so perhaps this is your way."

"We give you aid, and in return, Queen Eirian does what she has to do." Tharen snapped, "How could we make it any plainer?"

Marcellus sighed. "It's the whole Queen Eirian doing her part that is a little vague. What exactly is her part?"

"She'll lead all of us, united against the darkness." Shaking her head, Saoirse tucked a red curl behind an ear before pointing a delicate finger at Eirian and saying, "She is the Altira. The mage who can command all magic."

Pushing himself off the rail in his corner, Aiden stood behind Eirian. "Forgive me, but surely there are more qualified people who could lead the fight against this unverified foe?"

Faolan responded, "You don't understand. It has to be her because she is the Altira. There is a lot of power in certain bloodlines. The three most powerful bloodlines are the ruling families of Endara, Ensaycal, and Telmia. That's why those families are in charge. They're not like everyone else."

"I have to rule Endara, defeat Athnaral if we go to war, and then wait to see if we go to war against something else?" Eirian held her hands out and muttered, "I can do that. My choices are the Queen of Endara or the grand mage."

"You can't be the grand mage! They declared in the beginning that no Altira could serve as the grand mage. The Altira who founded Riane made the law." Saoirse froze, covering her mouth and murmured, "I'm sorry, I shouldn't have said that."

They stared at her, a range of emotions on their faces. Holding up a hand, Celiaen shook his head and stood.

"That's not the founding story they teach us. A unified group of mages felt magic users needed a safe city to learn, grow, and be the land's ultimate law. They believed that by withdrawing mages from the kingdoms to Riane, they could prevent the mage wars from happening again."

"Yes, that's correct. An Altira mage led them and established the high council before returning to the kingdom she founded. Altira mages are powerful. You could say the most powerful," Faolan explained.

Eirian felt like they had struck her with a heavy blow, covering her face. She sensed everyone looking at her, and she shook her head, face still covered. Everett's hand on her arm caused Eirian to remove her hands to give him a look of understanding.

"My father told me that for generations, they killed any mage born of the Altira family when they showed signs of magic. Just quietly dealt with and accidents and illness blamed. Forgotten and the shame of it kept secret within the family," Eirian whispered.

"What?" Brenna gasped.

She continued, "He believed they took some children out of the city and gave them away. It's unlikely I'm the only mage with Altira blood."

Horrified, Everett and Llewellyn stared at each other, and Llewellyn spoke, "I'd never harm a child of mine because they had magic."

"My father intended to end the practice. He might not have told me, but he felt I needed to know. If what you're saying about the power of the Altira bloodline is true, it explains it."

Saoirse had tears in her eyes, and she blinked, wiping them away. "I can't imagine such cruelty. I knew your ancestor who founded Riane. She was a powerful woman whose purpose was to protect her people. All she wanted was for her son to have a chance at life, a chance to have his children born into sanity, and she would've given her life for it. She was there when her mother did exactly that to end the war."

"I don't think they killed all the children. Maybe the odd one where they had the stomach to do it." Looking at each person present, Eirian swallowed her disgust and said, "Unless you have some magical way of finding others, we'll never know for sure."

Tharen agreed. "And it doesn't change the fact you must rule here until your time comes."

"I'll do my best to start drafting a treaty with what you have provided. With your permission, Your Majesty?" Ulric murmured.

She nodded, watching him turn and make his way through the curtain at the back. His frustration with the daoine had been apparent, and Eirian did not envy the task ahead of him. Marcellus stood, looking at his fellow combatants.

He reminded them. "We should get back to our tents. It won't be long before they call our matches."

Understanding that their time with Eirian was up, Faolan bowed as Saoirse rose from her seat and joined him, Tharen following slowly.

Faolan commented, "I hope we speak again soon, Your Majesty."

"We will. You've made it clear you have more to tell me. However, it will have to wait until after the tournament has ended," Eirian replied, and inclined her head to them.

"By the way, I'm sorry about your father. I hope that the time you brought him provided some closure. At least you could say goodbye," Saoirse said.

Eirian looked at Tynan, aghast. "He crashed?"

While she stared at Tynan, the three daoine slipped out of the box, leaving only a lingering trace of their magic behind them. Brenna narrowed her eyes at their backs, suspicious of their motives. Beside her, Marcellus watched the other three armored men as they looked at each other with the occasional glance at Eirian. Returning to his corner, Aiden crossed his arms and waited. He knew his chance to speak his thoughts would come.

"I didn't want to tell you before you met them," he said.

Holding his hands out pleadingly, Tynan hoped she would not grow furious. Eirian slumped in her seat and rubbed her face.

"You warned me it was coming, but he seemed fine when I visited this morning."

Crossing to her and ignoring the looks from the others, Tynan knelt. He took her hands in his own to share his soothing calm.

"I know. You were holding onto a fragment of hope that it wouldn't happen. He was a good man."

Breathing in the taste of his power, Eirian stared at him. "Were you there?"

"Yes, I felt it coming. I prepared Nolan and did what I could to make the descent gentler. Your aunt is watching over him, and I left Osric with her. I'm sorry, Ree. He loves you, and he is so proud of you. We did the right thing."

Celiaen clapped a hand on Tynan's shoulder, saying, "He's right, Ree. What you did gave your father closure. It gave all of you peace. I'd make the same choice."

Everett and Llewellyn made sounds of agreement and placed a hand each on her shoulders.

Leaning down to kiss her cheek, Everett said, "Thank you for doing it. I don't know what it cost you, and I don't want to know. That's between the two of you and your magic. I know you wouldn't have done it if it posed a risk, and that's all I need to know."

"Indeed. I was glad to say goodbye to my uncle. I know mother enjoyed her time with her brother. They had much to discuss and to make up for. As siblings do." Llewellyn was the first to step away from Eirian, crossing to stand at the curtains.

Kissing his wife, Marcellus winked, telling her, "Your favor is in my pocket, and you better cheer loudly."

"Don't lose," Brenna said and placed a hand on his cheek tenderly, smiling.

"Right boys, let's leave these lovely ladies to their spectating."

Giving Eirian a lingering look and keeping what he wanted to say to himself, Celiaen turned to Marcellus. "You realize I'm older than you?"

Laughing, Marcellus clapped a hand on Celiaen's back. "Son, you act like a boy."

Squeezing Eirian's shoulder as he left her, Everett shook his head at the two men in front of him. Watching them go, Eirian looked at the empty chairs before turning to Tynan, where he crouched in front of her. Tynan searched her gaze, looking for something he could not name before letting go of her hands and pushing himself to his feet.

"Tynan, I need a favor." Her words stopped him before the curtains.

He answered, "Don't you think you've asked more favors of me than you have a right to?"

"You're right, but this is simple. Could you write to the high council? Inform them that having spent time here with me, you feel they must assign me a blue," Eirian said seriously.

Swallowing back his shock, Tynan pursed his lips and replied, "You realize what you're asking? If I write such a letter, it suggests I fear you might do some harm."

"Even though I should have one anyway, and they withheld in the hope I make a mistake and am forced back to Riane? Nothing is stopping you from informing them about what you learned from the daoine."

"Why can't you do it?"

Scratching her head, Eirian glanced at Aiden. He arched a brow at her look.

She admitted, "I'm not allowed to ask Riane for help. That information is strictly confidential."

Tynan scoffed. "Requesting a blue is hardly asking for help."

"I don't think certain parties would see it that way, and I can't risk the consequences. Please, would you do it?" Eirian pleaded.

"I can write, but I won't promise anything. Why do you think you need a blue?"

Pulling a face, she muttered, "You know what I'm capable of. I have red tenancies, and we're facing a war. You can't tell me you don't see the problem?"

Hearing his name called, Tynan nodded in agreement before he slipped through the curtain. "I'll write your letter and express my concerns about the potential for issues in the event of a war. War is dangerous for a mage like you."

The box felt empty with everyone else gone, and Brenna rose to her feet, walking to the table to look over the barely touched food. "I don't like them."

"Unfortunately, I have a feeling we'll see more of them than we hoped. They aren't what I was expecting. I guess I was expecting them to be more... I don't know, something." Eirian joined Brenna at the table and perused the food to select something to eat.

"Magical?" Aiden suggested.

They looked at Aiden and he shrugged.

"They seemed to glow." Brenna agreed.

"Moonshine," Eirian told them.

"Yes," Aiden replied. "I bet they're like moonshine and will slip through your fingers quicker than you can grab them."

When Eirian returned to her chair, Aiden noticed Brenna had her back to them. Taking the seat next to her, he leaned in close, head bowed.

"Are you okay?" he asked softly.

Her eyes darted in his direction while Eirian half-heartedly picked at her food. She knew his question had nothing to do with the daoine and everything to do with Nolan. There was worry in his gaze, genuine concern that made her wish they were alone in a room with wine and a fire. A safe space to let her grief show.

"I'm fine, Aiden."

Aware no one could see him do it, Aiden placed a hand on her knee, feeling her tense through the layers of linen that covered her. Fingers stroking gently, he stared out at the arena until he felt her hand cover his. Eirian squeezed it, and he peeked at her. She knew what he was offering, the reminder that she was not alone.

She mumbled, "Thank you."

Turning his hand around, Aiden held hers tightly while they rested on her lap.

TWENTY-THREE

Galameyvin watched the daoine flutter around the courtyard, swaths of transparent silk draped over them. Music was louder than the chatter of voices, and he was thankful for it. Lazing back on a pile of cushions, he swirled the wine around in his glass and watched Neriwyn prowling through his people like a predator on the hunt. There was something about him that Galameyvin found fascinating.

The shift of fabric above him caused Galameyvin to glance up and watch a large damselfly work its way through the shade. Lifting his drink to sip, he chuckled when it landed on the cushions beside him and felt the flare of magic that heralded a duine transforming between their forms. A hand stroking across his leg made Galameyvin shift to look at the naked woman stretched out, black curls like a cloud around her head.

"Why are you sitting here all alone, sweet prince?" She purred, hand lingering on his thigh. "It's remiss of us to leave you unattended."

"Thank you for the offer, but I'm not interested," Galameyvin said, then took another sip of his wine.

She pouted, leaning in as her fingers shifted closer to his crotch. Galameyvin caught her wrist and removed her hand from his leg, giving her an unimpressed look. The response made her sigh and lay back on the cushions. He wanted her to leave, but the sight of Neriwyn closer to his position distracted Galameyvin from the woman beside him. Catching where his gaze went, she giggled.

"I see why you're not interested in me. You have ambitions for something a little more dangerous." Bringing her hand to her chest, she dragged a nail over her breasts and added, "It's understandable. He's the finest of us. No one can resist his charms."

Not responding, Galameyvin decided Neriwyn reminded him of Celiaen on bonfire nights when he would search among the crowds for Eirian. It was not a fast search, and there was no desperate flurry. It was the confident prowl of a hunter who knew where to find their prey and felt no need to hurry. The whole thing was a game intended to drag out the anticipation of capture. Sweeping his eyes around the walled garden, Galameyvin wondered where Vartan was or if Neriwyn had his sights set on someone else.

Plucking the glass from his grasp, the woman murmured, "He rarely strays from Lord Vartan. You should forget your ambitions. If you like, I can help you."

"Is it true that your king and queen shared Lord Vartan?" he asked curiously.

She froze, gazing at him with dark eyes and lips parted in shock. Galameyvin knew he was broaching on territory the daoine avoided. The longer he remained in Ashendon, the more he questioned the strangeness of Telmia. Sometimes it was like a haze lingered over the city, a fog of forgetfulness and forbidden subjects. Galameyvin wanted to know more about Queen Shianeni and what had happened to her.

"You shouldn't ask those questions. They're forbidden, as you know. Though, they'll certainly gain you his attention, but not in the way you want."

Curious, Galameyvin leaned towards her and gripped her chin. His magic was a soft cloud around them, soothing and encouraging. Force was not what he needed in this situation. Lips parting, the duine smiled, and the slightly out-of-focus glaze to her eyes told Galameyvin she was not resisting. His actions trod a fine line of consent, but he was willing to proceed as long as she let him. It was simply an encouragement, and she could push his magic away with her own the moment she wanted to.

"If you answer my questions, I'll let you have what you want," Galameyvin said, his voice carrying a hint of his power.

He hated that his time in Telmia had made him willing to trade himself for information. It made him question the limits he would go to get what he wanted. There was only one thing Galameyvin truly wanted, and he could not have it while he was among the daoine pretending to be a diplomat.

"I'd be happy to answer your questions, sweet prince."

He smiled, asking, "Did your king and queen share Lord Vartan?"

"Yes. Why is it so important?"

"Because I want—"

"You dream of the possibility where a king and queen can be with each other and share another," Neriwyn said, his voice cold. "Now, I'm not sure what manners they teach you in Riane, but it's not polite to manipulate someone at a feast."

Releasing the woman and plucking his drink from her hand, Galameyvin flopped back on his cushions to smirk at Neriwyn. Shaking, she shot an angry look at him before rising to her feet and bowing. Brushing a hand over her hair, Neriwyn signaled for her to leave, and she gladly hurried off. He regarded Galameyvin sprawled out in front of him, a glass of wine in his grasp. Sunlight caught the gold curls framing his face, and Galameyvin hoped it would influence Neriwyn as it had previously.

"Apologies, Your Majesty, I didn't intend to be rude."

Dropping to his knees, Neriwyn crawled over to lie on his side next to Galameyvin. Stretching out, he located the bottle of wine and unstoppered it, taking a swing. It was a rich blackberry wine that carried a hint of tartness. Neriwyn kept a note of what wines Galameyvin had taken to, making sure they were always available to him. He showed a preference for the less common berry wines that the daoine produced, but Neriwyn could not fault him for it. They were wonderful wines, and Neriwyn had many bottles of them stored in his private cellar.

"You wanted my attention, Galameyvin, but are you sure you can handle it?"

Galameyvin swirled the wine in his glass and replied, "Who said I wanted your attention, Your Majesty?"

Defiance gleamed in Galameyvin's eyes while he sipped from the glass. He had half wanted Neriwyn's attention, but he knew better than to admit it outright. There was one thing he knew about warriors like Neriwyn, and it was that they enjoyed toying with their prey. It was an aspect of their nature Galameyvin had learned to turn to his advantage.

"If you didn't want my attention, why put on a display that would attract it?" Neriwyn asked, propping his head up with his hand.

"I wanted to ask questions. She could have cast my influence off if she wanted, but she didn't."

"You wanted to ask questions you couldn't get answers to without your influence. Questions that skirt the edge of what I allow. My people know it's forbidden, and I've made it clear to you previously."

There was little friendliness in Neriwyn's voice, leaving him wondering if he had made too big a miscalculation. He was often told his willingness to use his power to sway things his way was questionable. Galameyvin mulled over his decision and stared at the fluttering panels of silk above them, taking a sip of the wine. It was too late to take back what he had done. All he could do was take responsibility and play to Neriwyn's amiable nature. If he was lucky, it would work.

"I suppose you're right," he admitted. "It's difficult to resist using my influence to get my way. It was the hardest lesson to learn as a child."

"It's an important lesson to learn. Just because you have the power and ability to do something does not mean you may do it. But, unfortunately, too many have suffered because of the choices made by powerful people to satisfy their desires."

Eyes sliding in Neriwyn's direction, Galameyvin said, "I suppose you're old enough to have seen it happen thousands of times over."

Neriwyn stared at Galameyvin sadly, a thumb flicking the stopper from the bottle of wine again so he could take another swig. Sensing the shift in emotions from mild anger to grief, Galameyvin lowered his glass to face Neriwyn. The sadness crept through Galameyvin's magic, driving him to sit up and reach out, cupping Neriwyn's cheek. Even though he knew it would not affect Neriwyn, he tried to share his calm.

His cheek was warm beneath Galameyvin's palm, bordering on feverish. He had noticed it before, the heat that radiated from Neriwyn. Focusing on it, Galameyvin attempted to draw it into his magic, weaving it through the calm he was trying to share. Aware of what he was trying to do, Neriwyn let himself feel it for a change. The understanding, the sorrow, the warmth, the calm. Everything that Galameyvin was pouring into his power.

"I'm sorry. My actions have caused you distress, and it wasn't my intention."

Covering Galameyvin's hand with his own, Neriwyn replied, "I know all too well the unforeseen consequences of a choice made without regard. You're still so young, sweet boy, but you'll understand when you're older."

"Perhaps not so well as you," he commented.

"Or perhaps, better than I ever could."

"I'm not sure about that. Unfortunately, I'm not blessed with a lifespan like yours."

"No, but you have something I don't. Mortality. It gives you a perspective I can't appreciate the same way."

Chuckling, Neriwyn turned to kiss the palm of Galameyvin's hand. The grief remained, and Galameyvin felt like the weight of it was in that kiss. It was not the playful action he had imagined while alone. Swallowing nervously, he looked out at the daoine drifting around the garden. They would come and go, fluttering between piles of cushions and chambers, plucking food from tables scattered around the space. All of them would lose a sense of time, not that time mattered to them.

"I thought you might like to know that Lord Faolan and his company arrived in Endara," Neriwyn informed him.

At the mention of Endara, Galameyvin's thoughts went to Eirian and Celiaen. Fingers flexing inadvertently, Neriwyn's chuckle reminded him that his hand was still on his face. Attempting to pull free, it confused Galameyvin when he would not release him. Bringing himself to meet Neriwyn's gaze, the intensity there was enough to leave Galameyvin fearful of drowning in a battle he was not strong enough to fight.

"Which of them do you miss more?"

Galameyvin stammered, "They are—"

"No, don't answer. It would be a lie to put one name before the other when you miss them equally, with the whole of your heart. I understand how that feels. The excruciating pain of being separated from those you belong with," he murmured.

"Is she okay?"

"Eirian is a newly crowned queen facing a war. She is well but under strain."

"You told me Celiaen was there. He'll hold her together. He always has. It's better when it's both of us, but he'll manage alone. Alone with Eirian and no me is what he wanted."

Slipping his fingers between Galameyvin's, Neriwyn drew the hands from his face and curled them so he could kiss their combined knuckles. It almost felt like a challenge, but Galameyvin could not decide if it was for his benefit or Neriwyn's. He did his best not to respond, but it was difficult when he had spent months imagining what it would be like to be the focus of Neriwyn's attention. The thought sent guilt lancing through him, a voice reminding him of Eirian, and it was enough to bring himself under control again.

"If you, and they, had taken the time to sit down and speak honestly about your feelings for each other, things would have taken a different path."

"Speaking from experience?" Galameyvin inquired.

Groaning, Neriwyn released his hand and rolled over onto his back with his eyes shut. People avoided their little nook in the wall, flitting past it on their way to other things as though there was nothing to see. Galameyvin could not decide if they were unwilling to disturb Neriwyn, or if he had told them to stay away. He envied the daoine ability to speak to each other with their minds. A few times, he thought he heard the whisper of their voices during intimacy. It was when his mind and magic were most vulnerable and open to their influence, despite his attempts to protect himself.

"Yes, speaking from experience. Open and honest communication is one of the most important aspects of a relationship. If you don't have that, it becomes all too easy for the relationship to break down."

"I'm a blue. I should have facilitated the communication you speak of, but I let my personal feelings get in the way. You're right that we could've taken a different path. One that would've seen all three of us refuse our royal positions and remain in Riane." Watching the flutter of Neriwyn's lashes, Galameyvin murmured, "I suspect you prefer the fact we didn't."

Guilt flashed through Neriwyn's magic, a brief tensing of his jaw and the shift of his shoulders confirming to Galameyvin that his suspicions were true. He awaited the reasoning Neriwyn would provide, preparing arguments in his mind for why those reasons were wrong.

"I should say no, but for our war to be successful, she needs to be the Queen of Endara."

A touch of his magic removed the glass of wine to a safe spot, and Galameyvin shuffled closer to Neriwyn. Chuckling, he opened his eyes to stare at Galameyvin, a hint of amusement flickering in their depths. Then, with a smirk, Galameyvin straddled him, placing his hands on each side of Neriwyn's head so he could lean down easier. He felt the strange jolt through his magic that he always felt when he touched Neriwyn. It bordered on painful but not so severe Galameyvin could not push it aside and dismiss its presence.

"Eirian doesn't need to be the Queen of Endara to unite Ensaycal, Telmia, and Endara in a war against Athnaral and the darkness," he said.

Folding his hands beneath his head, Neriwyn arched a brow and replied, "I wish I could say you were right. But, unfortunately, you're not. You're picturing her rising as some uncrowned leader of armies, using her raw power to force us all together. While she could do that, it's not the easiest path. Nor is it one in which King Paienven willingly comes to the table."

"My uncle respects power."

"Paienven respects his power, not those more powerful than he is. If he didn't control Eirian, he'd see her as a threat."

Scowling, Galameyvin admitted, "You're right. If Celi and I had walked away from Ensaycal and his control, he would not cooperate. He'd let Endara fall to spite us."

Turning his head, Neriwyn kissed the inside of Galameyvin's wrist, murmuring, "Precisely. This way, he thinks he has a chance at controlling the Endaran throne through Celiaen. This way, he cooperates. The darkness will drive men to throw themselves to their own deaths, wave after wave of soldiers fighting until none of them remains."

"When it's over, I'm going to leave the service of my king. Eirian needs a blue, and no blue can manage her as I can."

Moving faster than Galameyvin expected, Neriwyn buried a hand in his hair and pulled his face down. Anger burned in his eyes, creeping through his magic like a fog. The control over it he demonstrated left Galameyvin breathless. He wondered what it would be like to witness Neriwyn in battle. Celiaen and Eirian were beautiful in their rage, but they were nothing in comparison. Neriwyn would make killing look beautiful, and Galameyvin wanted to watch it.

"What have you done?" he said, power woven through his voice.

"I don't know what you're talking about."

"You would dare lie to me?"

He wanted to lie about it, and Galameyvin ran through his options before deciding on what to say. The look on Neriwyn's face suggested there would be no mercy for him if he was not honest about his actions. It irritated him to have to admit what he had done to Eirian when he had told no one else. Protecting her was the most important thing, and if Riane had known what was going on inside Eirian's head, it would not have gone well.

Galameyvin huffed. "She lets me in. I'm the only one she lets in. Ree thinks she can hide it from me, but I know what thoughts have lingered in her mind."

Snarling, Neriwyn pushed him over and rolled to pin Galameyvin down. Knowing he was outmatched, Galameyvin did not fight back. He had spent enough years sparring with more powerful warriors to know when offering submission was the safest route to take. Finding out what Neriwyn would do to him if he did not answer any of his questions was not something Galameyvin wanted.

"What did you do?"

"She wanted to kill herself, and I couldn't let that happen! Would you tell me I did the wrong thing?" he answered.

Shaking his head, Neriwyn sighed. "No, I would not. Why?"

"Ree fears her magic and what she is capable of. Sometimes, she'll linger on her fear, and her thoughts spiral, leaving her wanting to destroy herself. In her nightmares, the ones she remembers, Ree envisions killing those she loves."

"An understandable fear."

"Whenever the spiral began, and I was in Riane, I'd slip between the cracks in her shields and sway her from those thoughts," Galameyvin admitted with a hint of pride. "Eirian Altira is powerful, and much like you, if she doesn't want someone to touch her, they don't."

"You admit she's more powerful than you. So how do you find your way in?"

"How do you think? You know when we are most vulnerable."

Lowering his face to Galameyvin's, Neriwyn murmured, "It takes a certain kind of mage to do that. To maintain enough control over their own mind and magic during intimacy that they can manipulate another. I had not thought you capable of it, but clearly, I was wrong."

He shrugged, replying, "I love her, and I want to see her grow old and die peacefully in her sleep. Preferably in my arms. Not by her own hand from self-loathing, and certainly not by execution because Riane feared what she might do."

"I suspect you'd try to find the cracks in my shields, given a chance."

"Is that a challenge?"

Chuckling, Neriwyn brushed his lips against Galameyvin's and whispered, "I don't recommend you try."

It was a tempting idea, one Galameyvin had considered repeatedly from the first time he met Neriwyn. Lifting his head, so he was nose to nose with Neriwyn, Galameyvin smirked. The heat radiating from him was almost too much when combined with the warmth of the day. What slight breeze there had been earlier had died down, leaving the air almost stifling. Galameyvin could not decide if it was because of the thrum of emotions expressed by the surrounding daoine, or the promise of rain at some point.

"Are you sure I haven't already done so? I know how to manage cocky warriors like you, sire. Especially ones so powerful they're constantly overconfident."

Neriwyn growled, kissing Galameyvin. He sensed desperation and urgency, a possessiveness that shocked him. It seeped through his magic, driving Galameyvin to return the kiss with the same hunger Neriwyn felt. Hands freed, he buried them in Neriwyn's hair, clinging to him and tugging at the silky black strands. Hearing Neriwyn whimper, Galameyvin smirked against his lips.

Running one hand down Neriwyn's back, Galameyvin tugged at the spider silk shirt he wore until it was high enough to expose skin. He suspected that, like Eirian, someone could easily sway Neriwyn with the right touch. Galameyvin's fingers traced patterns along his spine, and Neriwyn hissed when they slipped to his side.

"You're playing with fire, sweet prince," Neriwyn murmured.

Nuzzling Neriwyn's cheek, Galameyvin replied, "I'm not as sweet as you think."

"I see that."

"And I'm adept at handling fire," he whispered in Neriwyn's ear before nipping at the lobe.

Neriwyn chuckled, magic curling around them, and said mockingly, "Now who's overconfident?"

"Having calmed storms with a kiss, I think my confidence has been earned."

"I've been looking for you, father," Emlyn said louder than necessary. "I didn't expect to find you toying with Prince Galameyvin."

Galameyvin watched regret flicker through Neriwyn's eyes and suspected Emlyn was there to bring an end to their game. He did not remove his hands, hoping that Neriwyn would tell Emlyn to leave. Instead, his fingers continued to stroke Neriwyn's side, a gentle tease to keep him distracted. Lips twitching, the hint of a smirk betrayed to Neriwyn what Galameyvin intended. It was a game to Galameyvin, and Neriwyn knew he could ill-afford to indulge in it. No matter how much he wanted to.

Not looking at Emlyn, Neriwyn answered, "I think you'll find I'm the one being toyed with."

Emlyn gazed at them in annoyance. "Either way, you're needed elsewhere."

"You should go, Your Majesty. You have a kingdom to rule, and I know how much work that requires," Galameyvin said.

"I can feel you trying to find my cracks, sweet prince, and I commend your efforts."

Magic pulled Galameyvin down, away from Neriwyn, and he grunted in surprise. It held him there, a reminder that Neriwyn was that much more powerful than he was. Stroking Galameyvin's face tenderly, Neriwyn brushed a stray gold curl away from his eyes and smiled. A finger tapped against his nose, making Galameyvin chuckle. Then, winking at him, Neriwyn rolled off and got to his feet quickly among the cushions.

"The banksia grove," Emlyn informed Neriwyn when he came to stand next to him.

"The usual place then." Glancing over his shoulder at Galameyvin, Neriwyn chuckled, "You need to improve your strategy if you think you're going to get the better of me."

Released from the magic, he smirked and folded his arms beneath his head. Tempted to taunt Neriwyn further, Galameyvin sensed something had shifted in his power that left him curious. Watching Neriwyn stride off, he waited for the magic to release him. It came once he was out of sight. Left alone with Emlyn, Galameyvin waved at the cushions around him and wriggled his brows. While Neriwyn was every bit the warrior, Emlyn was a curious man he desperately wanted to understand.

"Since you sent my enjoyment elsewhere, would you like to sit with me instead?"

Emlyn froze, staring wide-eyed at Galameyvin. Blinking rapidly, he shook his head and turned to look at the feasting daoine. He was aware of the fascination he inspired in Galameyvin, but had no interest in allowing him a chance to investigate. What time Emlyn spent with him was when he was in control of himself. Surrounded by daoine taking pleasure in each other, Galameyvin's magic showed the effects their influence had on him.

"I think not. You're not my type, Your Highness. I doubt either of us would find much pleasure in the other. Enjoy the feast. I'm sure you can find many willing partners."

Waiting until Emlyn had slipped through the crowd, Galameyvin scrambled to his feet and looked for the easiest way out of the walled garden. He spotted a break in the wall a little further along and hurried to it before anyone could think to approach him. Curiosity drove him, Galameyvin focusing on the map of the gardens he had memorized. The banksia grove Emlyn had mentioned was on the far side, and it was not a short walk to reach it.

Galameyvin ignored everything except the pathways beneath his feet with his magic wrapped around him. He did not know what drew Neriwyn away so quickly, but if it had anything to do with the impending war with the darkness, he wanted to find out. If it could help Eirian, he needed to know. There was no way he would let the meddling of the ancient people risk her life.

Glancing at a marker, Galameyvin knew he was close to the grove. It was a part of the garden he had spent little time in. They were a favorite tree of Eirian's, and memories of her laughter while harvesting seeds from the pods made him long to run to her. Galameyvin moved slowly through the trees, applying wards to himself, careful not to make a sound. He heard the murmur of voices, Neriwyn's loud laughter causing him to halt. Doubt struck, and taking a step back, he considered what he was doing.

A flash of black and white caught his eye, Galameyvin turning to watch a pair of wagtails darting between the branches of the trees. There were several pairs in the gardens, the bold birds unafraid of making their presence known. It was enough of a distraction to allow Galameyvin to focus on what he was doing. Running through the potential repercussions if they caught him listening to conversations not meant for him to hear, he turned and walked away.

The voice at the back of Galameyvin's mind reminded him of his concerns for Eirian. Stopping when he reached the path again, he stared ahead at the next section of the garden and tightened his hands into fists. He knew the chances that Neriwyn's meeting had anything to do with Eirian were slim, but something urged him not to take the risk. Hearing the sudden snap of a beak nearby, Galameyvin jolted when one wagtail flashed past him.

Watching it dance on the ground with an insect caught in its beak made him smile. The birds were endemic in Ensaycal and Riane, their presence welcomed by all the gardeners Galameyvin had ever encountered. He had spent hours lying in the sun, watching Eirian grow things with a wagtail companion. Her magic attracted all manner of critters when she used it to create instead of destroy. While she made flowers bloom, Celiaen would find the insects she summoned and feed the wagtails, enamored by their bold attitudes.

"I wondered where you had gotten to, Your Highness."

Continuing to watch the wagtails dart around, their tails bobbing as they moved, Galameyvin did not look at the man approaching him. He did not know what to think of his arrival, but suspected it meant Neriwyn had been aware of his attempt to follow. Standing beside him with his hands clasped behind his back, the duine joined him in watching the birds dance, black and white feathers gleaming in the sunlight.

"I thought I would go for a walk." Then, eyes sliding in his direction, Galameyvin added, "I know I'm not supposed to wander alone. However, I received news earlier that left me craving some solitude to think. I'm sure His Majesty tells you everything, Lord Vartan."

Vartan chuckled. "I'd like to think so. Would I be correct in assuming the news was about Queen Eirian?"

"How did you guess?"

"Does it bother you she's a queen now?" he asked gently.

"Yes. And no. I worry about Ree constantly. She's capable, but…"

"I understand." Dark eyes turned to the sky, and Vartan said, "I worry about Neri all the time. You and I have much in common, Galameyvin. We are both in love with an inferno contained only by chains of duty."

Crossing his arms, Galameyvin nodded in agreement. It was a fitting description for Eirian and Neriwyn. Celiaen as well, if he let his thoughts drift to him. They were raging fires, caged by the roles thrust upon them by others. They each shouldered their burdens instead of allowing someone else to be chained. Not because they wanted the power, but because they felt they owed everyone else.

"It breaks my heart to be here."

"I wish I could offer you some assurance that it won't be long until you are free to leave. But, unfortunately, I can't tell you when we'll leave to fight the darkness."

Digging his fingers into his arm, Galameyvin let a sliver of anger slip through his calm. Vartan turned slightly, studying him before inclining his head in the track's direction through the banksia grove.

"He knows."

"I figured as much."

"I'm glad I caught you before you invoked his anger."

"Actually, I changed my mind before you got here." Smirking, Galameyvin commented, "I worked out it was probably not a good idea. I've pushed enough boundaries today that I shouldn't try my luck."

Inhaling sharply, Vartan asked, "Do I want to know what you've done?"

"I'm sure His Majesty will let you know all about it."

"You should rejoin the others."

Shaking his head, Galameyvin said, "I don't want to. I'm no longer in the mood for that sort of entertainment. What interest I had vanished when something interrupted my efforts."

Eyes narrowing, Vartan studied him with a faint smirk. He had been busy attending to other matters and had not taken part in the feast. It took little effort to work out how Galameyvin had known to find Neriwyn in the banksia grove.

"Should I be jealous?" he asked.

"Are you ever?" Galameyvin countered.

"You don't need me to answer that."

Sighing, he agreed. "No, I don't. I try not to be jealous, but I can't help it."

Waving at the garden, Vartan said, "Walk with me."

"Any particular reason?"

"Consider it an opportunity to ask your questions safely. Neri need not find out. If I can give you the advice to help you find happiness with the ones you love, then I'll do it. Even if it makes my king angry with me."

Speechless over the opportunity presented to him, Galameyvin matched Vartan's stride as he started along a pathway. Neither of them said a word until they were far enough away from the grove that Vartan felt confident Neriwyn would not stumble upon them talking.

"I know you've asked about my relationship with my king and queen. The answer is yes." Eyes downcast, Vartan murmured, "Until she left, and took a piece of my heart with her. Both of them had others as well, but I was the only one they shared."

"How?"

"Communication. Knowing what function each person fills in the relationship. Not letting jealousy rule our thoughts. Sometimes it's only through exploring other options that you understand the things you desire most were right there the whole time. You learn to work together, balancing strengths and weaknesses to make the whole stronger."

Thinking about Eirian and Celiaen, Galameyvin understood what he meant. People had commented for years that they were better together as a team. It was something that came easily to them, and he wondered if it had been that way for Vartan.

"Sometimes it's second nature."

Vartan nodded slowly, replying, "It can be. That doesn't change the fact it still needs to be worked on. You can't just toddle along and expect everything to be effortless. Any lasting relationship requires work. There'll be fights, days when you can't stand the sight of each other, but you can work it through. If you want to."

"I wish I could say Endarans were as open as Telmians," Galameyvin admitted. "Maybe in Riane, we could have built a relationship like you had, but not in Endara. Celi wants to marry Ree, and I'm okay with that. I don't see it happening, but I'm okay with it."

"Are you okay with it because you believe it won't happen?"

"Maybe."

Chuckling, Vartan gave him an amused look and said, "Don't worry, I don't think it will, either. With the war coming, there are bigger things to be concerned about."

"Even if there wasn't a war coming, I believe their marriage would cause one. Athnaral wouldn't take kindly to a half-elf on the Endaran throne."

"Well," Vartan murmured and leaned towards Galameyvin. "Running away is always an option. There are plenty of remote places in Telmia where a trio of lovers could vanish and wait to be forgotten."

Smiling faintly at the thought, Galameyvin stared at the garden. He would hold on to the idea until the end of the war.

TWENTY-FOUR

Standing in a private audience chamber, Eirian cast a look at Cameron across the table from her. He crossed his arms tightly over his chest as he regarded Darrell and did not return the gaze directed at him.

Cameron said, "I sincerely hope you can talk sense into your king, Ambassador Darrell. We don't want to go to war with Athnaral, but my army is ready to defend our kingdom."

"Ambassador Darrell understands the situation," Eirian spoke gently.

There was a hint of despair on his face as Darrell glanced at the others of his party. "I hope my news regarding the Telmians will help His Majesty change his mind. He's a proud man, however, proud and determined. He'll regard your refusal of his offer as an insult."

"You've told us he might seize on any reason to proceed with the war. Let's hope Aeyren sees sense when you tell him there is now a treaty between Endara and Telmia. Surely the prospect of the united forces of Endara, Ensaycal, and Telmia would make him think twice," Everett said.

"If he were the man he once was, none of this would be happening. But, should things go bad for my men and me, do you hold to your offer of refuge?" Darrell looked at his boots, scuffing the toe against the floor and added, "If we could escape, that is."

"You're a good man, Ambassador. Your loyalty to your people is commendable. We have no issue with Athnaral, and we don't wish for war. So you're welcome to return here," Eirian replied.

She shared a look with Ulric. He handed over the sealed letters they had prepared for King Aeyren. Accepting the letters, Darrell slipped them into the secured pocket on the inside of his jerkin.

"Thank you for your hospitality. I hope what little information my men and I could give your people was useful."

Offering Darrell her hand, Eirian smiled warmly when he reached out and clasped it, the corner of the table between them. She observed the dance of discomfort in his eyes as her magic wrapped around him. The power flowed through him and reminded Darrell of how much she was capable of.

Eirian's smile faded, and she said, "I'm glad you could take the time to gain perspective."

"Perspective. Yes, I appreciate a healthy dose of it." Darrell agreed, waiting for her to let go of his hand. "I hope my next perspective of Endara is not across a battlefield."

"That is not a perspective you wish to see. Tell Aeyren I'll do whatever I have to and that there is an awful lot I can do."

Letting his hand drop, Eirian stepped back, and her smile returned. The warmth had faded entirely to leave behind a look that he could only describe as predatory. It made him bow, and Darrell shuffled back to the illusion of safety his men provided.

"I understand. You know Aeyren will do the same."

"Everyone will do what they must do to win. No hard feelings right, it's only war," Llewellyn said.

He chuckled darkly from where he leaned against the wall next to the door, his heavily armed presence serving as a warning. Everett gave him a frustrated look, but it made no difference to Llewellyn.

"Before I leave, I need to say one last thing. Not as an ambassador, but as one who has witnessed what his master does to things that displease him. Don't let Aeyren get his hands on Queen Eirian." Sighing, Darrell turned and gave his men a warning look, adding, "None of us will repeat my words to anyone. You're a good person, Your Majesty. I hope you'll be a far better queen than Aeyren has been king."

"Don't worry, we'll kill Aeyren before he can put his hands on her!" Everett declared.

Rolling her eyes, Eirian bowed her head to Darrell and silently permitted him to leave. The four Endarans around the table watched the gaggle of diplomats file out through the door, past the smirking Llewellyn as he remained leaning against the wall. When the door shut, Llewellyn walked over to stand next to Cameron.

"What do you think?" Eirian asked.

"The poor man is dead. Aeyren will have his head," Cameron muttered, sharing a look with Llewellyn.

"I agree. They're going back to their death. Every report we have received in recent years suggests Aeyren is an unforgiving man. Possibly, they were dead the moment he assigned them this task," Llewellyn replied with a shrug.

Sighing, Eirian glanced at Ulric and Everett. "He honestly wouldn't have expected us to agree to his requests, would he?"

Pursing his lips, Ulric stared into space contemplatively, answering. "I'd like to say no. There's the possibility Aeyren expected your feminine nature would incline you to say yes as an easy option to avoid death. Of course, there's also the option that he is, to quote several reports, deranged."

"Aeyren knew there wasn't an option available to you that wouldn't result in war. If you'd agreed to marry him, Paienven would march on Amath. It wouldn't have been a matter of a prince scorned. Celiaen's feelings would mean nothing compared to his father's anger at generations of treaties being thrown in his face," Llewellyn said.

"I feel like we can link it to why the daoine are here with their talk about darkness, madness, and wars. Perhaps this ancient foe Neriwyn fears has taken over Athnaral," Eirian said.

Placing her hands on the table, Eirian leaned over it and stared at the map from the Athnaralans that showed what route they would take. Scoffing, Everett shifted on the edge of the table and turned to look at the map as well.

He asked, "You don't believe them, do you, Eirian?"

She met his eyes, the shade of brown a reflection of her own, and replied, "I do. I'm not entirely sure why, but little things here and there…"

"What do you mean?"

"I don't know, but random comments and observations from people have all been lingering in my mind. They're about darkness and shadows. It started before the daoine arrived. Even my father told me he thought I was the light in the darkness."

"Your father is mad," Ulric murmured, tugging at the hem of his left sleeve.

Glancing at him, Eirian disagreed. "It was after what Tynan did. Nolan was in his right mind when he told me. I have to meet with Lord Faolan alone. We need to know what he'll tell me. If this potential war with Athnaral is part of something bigger, we need Riane on board. I'm only one mage, and as powerful as I am, I'm not enough."

"If something else is going on, surely Riane would be aware?" Cameron asked, sharing another look with Llewellyn.

"They know something is going on."

Rubbing his chin, Llewellyn scratched at the stubble that cast a shadow on his face. He grunted, and Eirian looked at him.

He said, "You're going to think I'm crazy, but I think Eirian is right. I've heard whispers. People vanishing, others found dead for no apparent reason or found having killed themselves and their families. Lots of people are going mad. I hadn't paid them much heed, thinking they were nothing other than rumors, but from now on, I will. We all should."

"There have been reports," Ulric admitted. "But they're mostly dismissed."

Cameron grunted. "Might be time to stop dismissing them. If we collate the reports, we can try to see the links."

Eirian murmured, "It's madness, like creeping shadows at the edge of your mind. Memories that torment by never being remembered. Sights unseen in the corner of your eye. A whisper of your deepest fears and darkest thoughts."

Touching a hand to the hilt of his sword for reassurance, Llewellyn turned to Everett and said, "I hope you can make more sense of that than I can."

Holding his hands up defensively, Everett pulled a face and replied, "Don't bring me into this. You're the one who agreed with her."

"Is everything completed for His Majesty leaving?" Ulric asked Llewellyn.

"Yes, it is. My mother likes to be organized. I half wish she'd remain a little longer, but she wants to get Nolan settled before he gets worse."

Glancing at her hands, Eirian bit her bottom lip, saying, "I'm going to spend some time with him when we're done. Your mother has been feeding him herbal remedies with the guidance of Lydia that keep him calmer."

Clearing his throat, Cameron saluted Eirian. "Please excuse me, ma'am, but if I'm no longer needed?"

"Of course, General, you're a busy man." Eirian inclined her head, adding, "Ulric, you're welcome to leave as well."

Bowing, Ulric murmured, "Thank you, Your Majesty."

Left with her cousins, Eirian expected Llewellyn to inform her he was going. But they pulled out chairs on either side of the table, seating themselves. Looking between them, she frowned, suspicious of the severe looks on their faces.

"Eirian, we need to warn you," Everett spoke first, refusing to meet her stare.

"Warn me about what?"

Leaning back in the chair, Llewellyn crossed his arms over his chest. "The council is calling a meeting before you depart on your tour. Some think your refusal of Prince Celiaen's offer of marriage was hasty. They feel your union would offer greater security for the future."

She snarled, replying, "That's ridiculous! We can't have a half-blood on the throne. The people wouldn't accept it."

"Are you sure about that? Elves and humans cross the border daily. They mix, fall in love, marry, and have lovely little half-blood children."

"Everett?"

Turning her gaze to him, Eirian arched an eyebrow expectantly. She considered him more sensible than Llewellyn. Everett's eyes darted between them.

Llewellyn continued, "You can't deny Celiaen loves you and would do anything for you. Imagine when he's the King of Ensaycal. His legitimate children by his beloved first wife are on the throne of Endara. He'd do anything to protect your legacy together."

"Enough, Llewellyn! I want to hear what Everett has to say."

He looked startled at her harsh tone and held up his hands in concession.

Sighing, Everett said, "I've heard both sides repeatedly. You say you don't feel the same way towards Celiaen, but I don't believe it. It would please me if you could have happiness. We all deserve some happiness. While the two sides argue, I feel like I'm the only one reminding everyone that you don't want to marry him."

"Do you agree with either side?"

"I agree with both, and in all honesty, I was the one who suggested we reconsider the offer. Because I see the logic in what Llewellyn is saying. Ensaycal would come to our defense every time because their royal family would also be ours."

Llewellyn grunted. "Keep going."

"However, I also agree with sentiments that suggest your marriage to Celiaen would be akin to surrendering Endara to Ensaycal. Llewellyn raised a valid concern over your relationship with the prince. If you married another, and Celiaen remained around, people would raise questions about the father of your children. Such questions lead to civil war," Everett told her.

Eirian was still. Her eyes locked on her hands, and the two rings adorning her fingers that were a reminder of her duties. She felt her freedom to choose for herself slipping away. They waited for her to respond, and she finally looked up.

She replied, "I'm surprised by you, Everett. I believe it's more important for the two of you to marry first. Everett, you're my heir until I have children. Being a mage doesn't exclude me from the dangers of being a woman in child-birth."

"Are you suggesting what I think you are?" Llewellyn asked in surprise.

"Yes, I am. The two of you can produce far more heirs than I can and with less risk," Eirian told him. "It's a matter of state. The two of you will marry. The sooner, the better."

Crossing his arms, Everett stared at her and said, "I don't agree with you, Eirian."

There was a coldness in the look Eirian gave him, and she replied, "That's fine. I don't care if you agree with me. This is coming from your queen, not your cousin. If I die in childbirth, I'm dead, and there is no coming back from that. If your wife dies, you can marry again and keep going. I'll inform the council that my marriage is off the table. At least until after we have dealt with Athnaral. I'll also tell them your marriages are of the highest priority."

"Yes, Your Majesty." Everett bowed stiffly, glancing at Llewellyn, who was smirking and said, "I don't see why you look amused."

Llewellyn continued to smirk and told him, "I've no problem with settling down. I have my eye on a nice young lady, and if my queen orders it, I'll approach her father. Everyone calls me the wild one, and I've played on it for years, but I know my duty. If neither of you has children, the throne goes to mine. One of us needs to be responsible."

"May I ask who? Does she know?" Curious, Eirian smiled faintly.

"She's one of your ladies. I know my mother likes Gallagher's sister, but she's too young for me. Lady Romana is the one I have my eye on. Her father is a good man, a practical man, and she takes after him in that regard." Shrugging, Llewellyn turned to the door and added, "If we've said all we need to, then I'd best see my mother."

Nodding, Eirian pushed the chair back and stood, hands still on the table. "Romana is a smart and sensible woman. She'll make you an excellent match. Unless Everett has anything that he wants to say?"

"I've got nothing!" Everett declared with a shake of his head.

"Excellent. I'm going to see my father for what may be the last time." Stepping away from the table, Eirian passed Llewellyn on her way to the door and gave him a wink. "I won't mention anything to Romana."

Inclining his head, Llewellyn opened the door. "Thank you, much appreciated."

Snorting, Eirian slipped through the door and faced the hardened stare of Gabe, who was leaning against the wall with his foot resting on the stone. Dotted along the hall, the rest of his squad watched either end of the corridor. His eyes followed Llewellyn as he left, snapping back to Eirian when Llewellyn passed around a corner. Staring back at Gabe for a moment, Eirian arched an eyebrow and waited while he slowly pushed away from the wall.

"Where to, boss lady?"

"I'm going to visit my father."

Eirian glanced over her shoulder at Everett before she started walking as he remained seated at the table, staring into space. Falling into step beside her while his men joined them, Gabe did not look bothered by her decision.

"The boss man said he had something for you. He'll bring it when he comes back onto rotation."

She was curious, gaze flickering towards him while they walked. "Did he say what?"

"No."

Watching courtiers scurry away, Eirian frowned before turning to him to ask, "Have you heard anything concerning?"

"I hear many things. You need to be more specific."

Resuming her stride, Eirian waited until they were in an empty corridor closer to Nolan's quarters to say, "Just anything. Even if it seems like people jumping at shadows."

"That's oddly specific without being specific," Kip said in amusement. "Yet I get what you mean."

"Kip, you're a twisted thinker," Gabe muttered.

Kip replied, "Not as twisted as you. I've heard things. People seem to have had an awful lot of nightmares recently. Men whisper to their friends over their mugs in taverns about shadows chasing them in the night and fear enough to make them piss the bed."

Hitting his arm, Wade snapped, "Don't forget who you're talking to!"

"Oh, shove it, Wade. Do you think she cares? I behave myself when the prim and proper ones are around. But when they're not, she's one of us." Returning the friendly blow, Kip grinned at Eirian when she glanced back at them.

"Have any of you had these nightmares?"

"Not that I know. We can ask around if you want us to. All quiet like, wouldn't want to make anyone feel concerned."

Eirian held Gabe's gaze and saw a flicker of amusement. "Gabe, you know something, don't you?"

Scoffing, he cast a glare at his men and replied, "I hear what they hear, ma'am. We'll keep our ears open and let you know if we learn anything."

A few guards patrolled the hallway outside Nolan's quarters, and Eirian knew there would only be a handful of gentlemen in the chambers. The rooms felt strange. They had packed away his belongings and loaded them on a wagon to travel to Onaorbaen. Taking a moment to look over the bare room and the bored gentlemen playing a game of dice at the table, Eirian tried to imagine the buzz of activity that would return to it. She suspected that to her, they would always be her father's quarters and never her own.

"Your Majesty." Thomas greeted her. "He's calm."

Giving a smile of thanks, Eirian paused and asked, "What sort of mood is he in?"

"He was an expectant father earlier. Kept on telling me he was looking forward to the birth of his first child and asking what I thought it might be."

"Did you tell him a girl?"

He chuckled sadly. "I did."

Making her mind up, Eirian turned and unbuckled her belt, handing the swords to Gabe. "Just in case."

Not waiting for a response, Eirian went through. The room was bare, and Nolan paced in front of the hearth, his hands clasped behind his back. Shutting the door, Eirian leaned against it, her hands trapped between the wood and her body as they remained, gripping the knob tightly. Nolan stopped pacing and looked at her, his face lighting up with an overjoyed expression.

"Siani!" Nolan held his hands out to her, and Eirian's heart plummeted at his use of her mother's name. "Where were you? I've been so worried."

"I'm sorry. I've been dealing with some issues," she replied.

Remaining at the door, Eirian sighed and contemplated how to handle his state. Frowning, Nolan looked concerned.

"Is everything okay? Is it the baby? They haven't found you, have they? They can't take you back. You're my wife, and you're pregnant with my child. You left for a damn good reason, even if you couldn't tell anyone."

"I'm fine, and the baby is fine. Who do you fear taking me away?"

Curious about what he had said, Eirian chewed her bottom lip and glanced at the door from the corner of her eye. It crossed her mind to quash her curiosity and walk away, but she could not leave without knowing more. Shaking his head, Nolan turned to stare at the stack of wood.

"You know who. Are you sure they don't know where to find you?"

The words tasted strange as she said, "Humor me, Nolan, who do we fear?"

"Your people. Why are you asking me this, Siani?"

"Who are my people?" she asked, tendrils of dread filling her. "Please, I need to be sure you remember. You must remember, it's important."

Nolan spun around and pointed at her angrily, each motion of his hand emphasizing his words as they reached her ears. "I'll never forget! You're duine, and no one can ever know. Too much is at stake, not just Endara."

Eirian's jaw dropped as she stared at Nolan in complete shock. It took her a few moments to speak again, a sick feeling settling in her gut. Nolan resumed his pacing, ignoring the expression on Eirian's face.

"I'm pleased you haven't forgotten. You're right. It's important no one ever finds out."

Wanting nothing more than to cover her ears and forget everything, she focused on remaining upright. It felt like Nolan had pulled the ground out from beneath her. Eirian promised herself she could break down later, but she had to extract more information from him. On the other side of the room, the windows were uncovered. Eirian stared out at the sky, tracing the outlines of the white clouds with her gaze. Counting the beat of his boots against the floor, she let the silence settle while she waited for Nolan to collect his thoughts.

He finally spoke. "I know, Siani. I understand everything is at stake. You've made clear how important it is to keep this secret. You know I love you even though you came to me because you had to. Because you needed to marry me and have my child for the sake of destiny. Prophecy may have brought you here, but I want to think you remain out of some affection for me."

"Of course, I do. You're a wonderful man, Nolan."

It felt wrong, prying information from Nolan by pretending to be her dead mother, but Eirian could not help herself. His revelation had left her desperate to know more. If he had kept this big a secret from them her entire life, what else did he know that might affect her. Pausing mid-stride, Nolan glanced at her fearfully.

"What do we do if your prediction comes true?"

Eirian said, "There are so many possibilities. Which one do you worry about most?"

Rubbing his face, Nolan frowned and looked at the windows. While she waited for his answer, Eirian dug her nails into the wood of the door. She promised herself that as soon as she had heard the answer, she would leave.

He told her, "I fear your death. I love you so much, and our child should have her mother. I know you said it's important that I let the mages of Riane raise her, but I fear they could never teach her the things you could."

"You're right, a child needs their mother, but there's nothing we can do to change what will happen." She had her answer, and unwilling to hear more, Eirian found the smooth doorknob. "I'm sorry. Never forget I love you."

"Siani! Don't leave me. I'll always keep my promises to you, I swear it. I'll take the truth to my grave!" Moving towards her, Nolan was desperate and pleaded. "What am I supposed to do when the darkness comes if you aren't here to guide us? Our daughter will need you."

Pulling the door open, Eirian did not hesitate as she stepped backward through it, wanting to escape from Nolan's words as they burned into her memory. She had to hold herself together until she was somewhere safe.

"Goodbye, father. I'm so sorry, so deeply sorry."

Quickly shutting the door behind her, Eirian did not look at the people in the audience room. Nolan started banging against the wood on the other side, shouting her mother's name. Thomas walked over quickly, locking the door with a distressed look. Accepting her belt and weapons from Gabe, Eirian ignored the stares.

"The herbs have worn off, and he's getting agitated. He thought I was my mother, so it made things worse. Sorry, Thomas," Eirian said.

"I'll prepare more and try to get him to take it. It's been an honor to serve."

Bowing, Thomas did not question why she hurried to leave. He saw her distress and sympathized. They all understood how she felt.

Eirian murmured, "Thank you. I'm forever grateful for the dedication and loyalty you have given my father."

Not waiting for a response, Eirian hurried through the door and into the next room. Her guards formed a bubble of safety around her. All of them could tell the visit had upset Eirian. Gabe held the door open, sharing a look with the other guards.

He said, "Your Majesty?"

"I need some time alone, so I'm going to the garden, and I don't want to be disturbed. If you can't fucking manage it, find someone who can."

Keeping her face down and her pace brisk, Eirian wanted to reach her little sanctuary before her emotions overwhelmed the tight grip that she had on them. The guards followed without a word. No one dared approach between their expressions and the magic emanating from Eirian. Flinching when the sunlight blinded her, she ignored the bustle and hurried to the garden. A handful of courtiers were strolling the pathways, but as soon as they saw Eirian, they bowed and left, unwilling to disturb her. Remaining at the arch, Gabe sent three of his men around to guard the other break in the wall.

"Do you think we should tell someone?" Kip asked.

He craned his neck around the edge of the wall and watched Eirian huddle on a bench, covering her face with her hands. Kip was not the only one observing in concern.

Shrugging, Gabe inspected his fingernails and said, "Tell who? The dukes? Her ladies? The prince? She's upset about her father, so she'll cry and probably make the garden go crazy. Then she'll dust herself off, regain composure, and everything will be fine."

"Aren't you in the least bit curious about what exactly upset her?"

"No, that's not our job. The only ones of us that need to worry about that are the captain and Merle."

Kip said, "Maybe we should tell the captain? You know what he ordered."

Lifting his gaze from his hand, Gabe stared at Kip and arched a brow slowly. He knew Aiden would be there in a heartbeat if they told him. The thought to do so had occurred to him, but Gabe figured it might be something Eirian needed to process alone.

"You want to disturb the captain for this? Make him think you can't handle her when she's having a private moment? Just stand there and watch for anyone wanting to disturb her, and we'll continue behaving as though you can handle this job."

"Don't pretend you're any less worried when she's like this. Just because you're one of her favorites," Jack grumbled.

"Do you know why she likes me, Jack? I understand what she is. I respect the killer hidden under her smiles, and she knows it. The captain understands as well. That's why I'm in charge of this squad, and not any of you."

Crossing his arms, Jack scoffed. "We all respect her as a fellow warrior. I'm proud to serve her, knowing she's as capable as she is. Our queen isn't some fainting lass."

A strange smile curled Gabe's lips, and he looked amused. "I said nothing about respecting her as a warrior. She's a fine warrior who'll always have our back, and I sure wouldn't want to meet her in a battle. The part I respect is the part I wouldn't want to meet in a dark alleyway."

"We know you do the dirty work for the captain."

"And I'm good at it, but believe me, I'm not as good as her. She needs me more than she needs you because I understand what she feels when she wants to drag a knife through someone."

Refusing to engage any further with the men he commanded, Gabe stepped into the arch and leaned against the cold stone, the wall casting a shadow on his face. He watched the explosion of life surrounding Eirian. It fascinated him that it was not just the plants, but everything else. The faint buzz of insect life carried in the air, the noise underlying the call of birds appearing. The intoxicating scent of wildflowers drifting on the breeze.

Eirian was unsure how long she had been sitting there on the bench with her face in her hands. Her thighs hurt from the dig of her elbows while she chased her thoughts in an endless loop. It still felt like someone had pulled the floor out from under her, and Eirian could not quite regain her balance. The whispers clambered for attention, suggesting they knew the truth.

Nolan's words kept repeating in her mind. The horror at finding out about her mother's origin left Eirian nauseated. It made her realize that all the suggestions regarding her blood status were correct. Every comment made that she was not as human as she seemed came back. Memories accompanied the stories of how her mother had come from nowhere, working her way into the court and her father's life.

"Damn it. Damn them both!"

Dropping her hands, Eirian looked around the garden at the creeping growth fed by her power and felt fresh resentment towards her magic. It all made sense, the whole reason she was so powerful. Her capacity for destruction and creation on a large scale. The reason she could do things no other mage in Riane was capable of. Eirian suspected it was the truth behind why Nolan never spoke of her mother. It was easier to remain silent, to make her a taboo subject than risk slipping and revealing her secrets.

Eirian sighed heavily, glancing towards where she could see the shadowy form of Gabe watching her. While he kept the world from invading her solitude, Eirian wondered how she would keep her secret. She accepted that knowing was better. It meant there was time to prepare before her lack of aging grew obvious. Thoughts played out about what would have happened if she had never found out, and the truth revealed itself in later years.

For all her cousins' suggestions that the people would not be against a half-blood ruler, Eirian knew she was the wrong kind. A half-elf was plausible, especially if it bound the two kingdoms closer than any treaty could, but the daoine were something else entirely. Eirian stared at the two rings adorning her left hand. The royal seal was a weight dragging her down with the knowledge it did not belong on her hand. Neither of them did, and Eirian struggled against the urge to pull them off and throw them away.

She could not abdicate, though she had the desire to march into the council chambers and do so. It would cause chaos and do far more harm than good. Eirian was not sure on what grounds she could argue for it. Baenlin's words that she was making a mistake echoed in her memory, and Eirian wondered what he would say when the truth eventually came out. Celiaen would accept it. She doubted anything could budge his loyalty to her, and it was something she would always be thankful for.

Her mother had to be the reason King Neriwyn sent a delegation. What Celiaen had shared with her about something between Nolan and Neriwyn made sense. Siani had not been as free of Telmia as she had led her husband to believe. Eirian wondered if Neriwyn had chosen Siani specifically for the task. If her mother had been the perfect woman to give birth to an Altira with more magic than she knew what to do with. She could not risk asking the delegation, and Neriwyn was the last person she wanted to face.

Footsteps made Eirian lift her head, and she glared at Gabe. He ignored her expression and sat on the bench opposite, creeping vines covering the pavement between them. Gabe glanced down as a tendril got too close to his boots and, with a slight sneer, lifted his toe and pressed down on the bright green creeper. Scowling, Eirian remained silent, knowing he would not have approached without a good reason. Leaning on one arm, Gabe drew a knife from his belt to twirl it around in his fingers.

"The first time I killed someone, I was seven. I wasn't born in a slum, and my parents didn't work in a grand castle. They were farmers, raised sheep. My mother and sisters would spend their days spinning the wool, while my father and brothers would tend to the farm."

She waited for him to say more. Nearby, a wagtail danced on the path, snatching an insect from a branch.

"Us smaller children would look after the gardens and orchard, tend to the chickens and the dairy cow. It was a good life, we knew our duty from birth, and there was always food on the table even if sometimes it wasn't great food."

"What happened?"

Gabe shrugged, balancing the knife carefully on two fingers. "I went with one of my older brothers and our eldest sister to town. She was courting the butcher's boy but didn't like the walk on her own. Our parents thought it was a suitable match and encouraged it."

"Of course."

"While she was in the shop visiting him, my brother got into a fight with some other boys, and one of them struck him with a knife. There was blood, and it enraged me. I pulled the knife out of my brother and ran after the boy who did it, getting him in the gut as he turned because his mate shouted out a warning."

"Did your brother live?"

"He did. A mage healer lived in the area, and my parents traded for his services. It wasn't a terrible wound, but it went bad. He took the blame, claimed it was self-defense. The other boy went for him first, and he feared for his own life. Didn't mean to kill him, he said. So for a long time, he kept my secret."

Eirian glanced at the wall and asked, "What changed?"

"I did. I stood over that bigger boy with a bloody knife in my hand and watched him die. All I could think was how good it felt, how human blood smelled different somehow to the blood of the livestock I had watched and helped kill."

"Yes, it does."

Gabe arched a brow, and Eirian shrugged.

"I started watching people, watching them move, listening to them, collecting secrets. I'd watch the local soldiers train, run errands, and in return, they taught me. My family figured it was acceptable if it was the path for me. My brother, though, he knew deep down it was more than that."

Gabe pointed the knife at her, his grip on the hilt loose. Her eyes dropped to the blade and Eirian sighed.

"I understand."

"Occasionally, someone would turn up dead in a dark spot, the drunkard who beat his wife and kids, or the pretty young widow who poisoned her husband because she was seeing another man. I'm always picky about my victims, but I wasn't careful enough, and my brother caught me."

"Did he turn you in?"

"He did. The garrison captain saw my potential, this fourteen-year-old murderer he had locked away in a dungeon. He didn't hang me like the entire town, including my family, was demanding," Gabe said.

"Why not?"

She was curious, his story distracting Eirian from the chaos in her mind. Glancing around the garden, Gabe could tell her magic was settling, the growth decreasing.

"Because he knew men like me are useful to your sort. We're the ones you send to do your dirty work and bury your secrets. To do that sort of work, you need to take some pleasure in killing. It's not like fighting in a battle. You don't want your target to see you coming. A throat slit in the shadows, some poison in their wine, a carefully orchestrated accident."

"How did you end up in my service?"

He smiled and replied, "The captain. He knew my reputation because I'm the best. Said he was putting together a troop of guards for the future queen. I wasn't interested. Then he said you were a mage. Mages fascinate me. The stories of the ferocious warrior mages using magic to help them become perfect killers. So, I agreed to become the one responsible for doing your dirty work."

Frowning, Eirian wondered if he had already killed on her behalf without her ever knowing. She decided not to ask.

"Do you regret the decision?"

"No, and I don't think I ever will!" Gabe laughed.

It was the first time Eirian could recall hearing the sound, but there was a familiarity to it she could not place. One that tugged at the frustrating memories she could never reach.

"See, it's an even greater pleasure to serve you now that I know."

"What do you know?"

Gabe leaned forward, the knife still in his hand, and said, "That you love it as much as I do. Of course, you must be careful to hide it, but that's okay, I understand. All these people surrounding you, none of them know that part of you like I do. Except for the captain, but that's because he's the same as us."

Eirian looked down at the vine trapped beneath his boot, giving him a funny look. She considered asking Gabe to kill her, but banished the thought like she did every time.

Eirian asked, "What brought this on, Gabe?"

"You needed a distraction from what's bothering you. I don't pretend to know what it is. I want you to know I'll take care of the Athnaralan king if you want it done. I'm sure your dukes have considered it, but you need to hear from someone it's an option."

"If Aiden thought it was an option, would he have given you the order already?" Eirian shook her head and muttered, "Perhaps it's better if I don't know."

His brow arched, and Gabe sat back upright, resting the knife on the flat of his hand where she could reach it. The thought of asking him to kill her crossed her mind again, and Eirian dismissed it. As much as she hated her existence, she had a duty to her people.

"Would it make you feel better if I gave you the details? I watched you with those men in the woods, so I know you like knives. It was beautiful, the way it was so easy to you, and the fact the blood didn't turn you off. You can inflict pain without batting an eyelid, and that makes me want to sneak out with you to find someone to kill."

"Do you think that's appropriate to say to me, Gabe? I'm your queen." Her eyes rested on the knife he held towards her.

"Is the way you look at the captain when he's got you on your back beneath him appropriate?" Gabe asked with a chuckle.

Eirian stiffened, blushing as she said, "I don't... there's nothing to see."

"We know what we're seeing. The darkness you asked about earlier? People in conflict with themselves are at the most risk. Others might not notice, but I see the things in the shadows. Whatever it is, whatever is going on, it feeds on conflict, on negative emotions. I don't fear it. I own my darkness."

Watching Gabe sheath the knife and get to his feet, Eirian realized what he was saying. She bit her lip, considering his words.

"You think things are going to get dangerous everywhere, not just the battlefield we may find ourselves on."

"I think you need to ask if there has been an increase in violence. Not only towards each other either, but towards animals as well, because killing animals is a good way to tie over any bloodlusts." There was a knowing look in his eye as he commented, "But you know that. It's why you used to sneak out alone."

"Thank you, Gabe."

"Of course. If you ever want to sneak out and find some enjoyment, I always keep my ear to the ground. I can't think of anything I could wish for more than to kill someone deserving with you."

Disturbed, Eirian squashed the spark of excitement she felt at the prospect. "Well, you might get your chance if we find ourselves at war."

The look Gabe gave her felt strangely familiar, and he said, "That's not the same thing. The offer is always there. However, I think it best you go inside before anyone questions your absence."

Eirian glanced down at the vines on the ground as Gabe walked away. She frowned, noticing the way they had withered. Brushing the thought aside, Eirian followed him out of the garden.

TWENTY-FIVE

E irian marveled at the craftsmanship, running her hands over the polished metal links, and took pleasure in the way they sat locked together closely. It had surprised her when Aiden presented the mail haubergeon, the gift completely unexpected. She had never mentioned using it in Riane, and it had been years since Eirian had bothered with it.

"I hope this doesn't take me too long to adjust to," she admitted, looking at Aiden from under her lashes.

"We'll try to get in as much training as possible," Aiden said from the other side of the table and glanced at Brenna hovering to Eirian's right. "Of course, you could always wear it all the time. It's not the norm for anyone other than guards, but I think you can get away with it."

Eager to try on the haubergeon, Eirian unbuckled her belt and placed her swords on the table. Aiden reached out and touched the hilts, rubbing his thumb over the engravings. He knew who had given them to Eirian, and he looked forward to getting his hands on one to have a new set forged for her.

Humming, Eirian mused. "Yes, I could do that. Would help me adjust to the weight."

Moving to assist her, Brenna shook her head, muttering, "You're going to start a trend. I've noticed several young ladies of the court strutting around in trousers."

"Nothing wrong with that. It's the common practice in most places."

Rolling her shoulders as the mail settled onto them, Eirian lifted her arms to test the weight. It was not as light as the mage-crafted mail she had worn in

Riane, and Eirian regretted she had convinced herself she would never need more than leather.

"Always wear this. It will help with the weight." Picking up the belt from the table, Brenna carefully tightened it around Eirian's waist, asking, "How did you get such a good fit, Aiden?"

He smiled secretively and replied, "It would be inappropriate to make the comment I want to."

Brenna shook her head while Eirian started laughing, giving him a disgusted look.

"It's only slightly less inappropriate if I say it, but he has had me under him enough to know me well!" Eirian continued to laugh.

"Honestly, the two of you!" Huffing, Brenna threw her hands in the air. "You really would have made a better man than woman, Eirian."

"Oh, absolutely! But I don't think Aiden would agree."

Winking at Aiden as his amusement turned into a slight scowl, Eirian made a few adjustments to how the mail and her belt sat. She glanced at the door to her chamber, tempted to fetch the armor she usually wore.

Those thoughts led her to say, "I'll need thicker tunics underneath, and this hood would be easier if my hair were short. My leathers will work over the top. They'll keep it in place, and the wards will add protection. I'll ask Harlow to go over the mail."

"You are not cutting your hair!" Brenna declared.

She put her hands on her hips and cast a look at the observing ladies. Elke approached cautiously, examining the hood sitting on Eirian's head. Her fingers tugged at the mail.

Elke said, "I can try some different styles that would minimize the bulk of your hair on the back of your head."

"Easier to cut your hair again," Aiden muttered.

He gave Elke a wary look and ran a hand through his short hair. Walking away from the table, Eirian stretched and moved to get a feel for the armor.

"While I agree, Aiden, I must give victory over the matter to Brenna," she admitted.

Aiden saluted and met her contemplative stare. Something in Eirian's gaze made him keep his hand in place. Brenna sighed, her eyes darting between them in frustration.

"You look like you want to say something, Your Majesty," he said.

Cocking her head to the side, Eirian shrugged, noticing the extra weight as her shoulders moved. Her mind went back to the day before, her stomach clenching at the enormity of her secret. To avoid the spiral of thoughts, she brought up Gabe.

"I learned something yesterday about a man you entrust with my safety."

"I heard."

"Why did you choose him? What made you pick him to guard me over other options?"

Hushed, her ladies looked between them as Aiden gripped his hands behind his back and shifted his stance. He caught the look directed at him by Brenna and suspected that she would have plenty to say when Eirian was not around to hear.

"Are you concerned I've made a mistake? I know his version of your conversation, and I trust him enough that I doubt he lied."

"I can't imagine Gabe lied. It was eye-opening to hear his story, but it makes me wonder why you picked him. You selected the men for my guard before I returned from Riane. What drew you to him? Why place him in my household instead of keeping him in the shadows."

While she waited for his answer, Eirian worked through several simple maneuvers. She attempted to push her fears from her mind, using the exercises as a focus.

"Do you think your father didn't have such a man serving him? Or your cousins? Ask the Duchess. She knows her husband has such a man. It simply my duty to have him at your disposal."

Pursing her lips, Brenna nodded. "It is true."

Chuckling, Eirian gave them an amused look. "I'm aware of his role. That wasn't my question."

"I didn't know what you were capable of when I made my decisions. Forgive me, ma'am, but I assumed you'd be the embodiment of a princess and need someone capable of anything close at hand. A man to do what others wouldn't be willing to do. Gabe sees things coming that most miss."

"Thank you, Aiden, I understand. He made me an offer that I'm sure you've contemplated. I was so tempted. Imagine how close he could get with a little help from me."

Aiden swallowed, nervous at the prospect of what she was suggesting. It required little thought to work out what sort of help Eirian could give Gabe.

"He didn't mention that. I assume you decided not to, but would you've told me if you had?"

Unwilling to answer, Eirian carefully removed the hood from her head, flinching when it caught on some hairs and pulled them from her scalp. She placed it on the table before she ran a hand through her hair.

"Perhaps. Do you think Gabe would've told you if I did?"

"Yes, I do. I don't think any of my men are more loyal to you than they are to me. So where are you going with this?"

"Ah, finally, you ask."

Eirian placed a hand on the back of a chair and leaned on it, giving Aiden a sly smile. He suspected he would not like what she would say.

"What I want is for you to include me in any future decisions like that. I'll know what you order on my behalf. I don't care for any arguments that it's better if I don't know."

Staring at her blankly, Aiden wished her order was a surprise. "As you command, Your Majesty. I hope it isn't something you come to regret."

"We shall see."

"Do you want to take that off?" Brenna cut into the staring contest between them, drawing Eirian's gaze.

Cocking her head to the side, Eirian considered her options before answering. "No. I'll keep it on."

"But you're meeting Lord Faolan soon. Is this the way you wish to greet him?"

"Yes, it is. I don't pretend to know what the Telmians expect of me, but I can show them what I am." Putting a hand to her stomach, she scowled and said, "Send for some refreshments, please, and wine."

Bowing stiffly, Brenna turned and pointed at Isabella and Bea. "Off you go, you heard your queen."

Watching the two ladies dip a quick curtsy as they hurried out of the chamber, Eirian stroked her fingertips over the mail covering her abdomen. She pursed her lips and glanced at the remaining two ladies and Brenna when the door shut. Eirian was not sure she wanted them around while she waited. Her mind constantly circled Nolan's revelation. It made Eirian nervous, the prospect of seeing Faolan when she was struggling with what she knew.

"Brenna, I need you to see Llewellyn and find out how it went when the Dowager and my father left. Please take Romana and Elke with you," she said, and gave Romana a knowing look. "Then check in with the chancellor regarding the upcoming council meeting and let him know I'm aware of certain matters they plan to bring before me. Make sure you tell him I'm not pleased because I'd made my choice clear."

Pressing fingertips to her lips, Brenna looked ashamed, murmuring, "I wanted to say something, but Marcellus told me Everett and Llewellyn planned to tell you."

"Next time you think you should tell me something, I suggest going with your instincts. Once finished with the chancellor, find Tynan and ask him if he sent the letter we discussed at the tournament."

Shifting from the chair, Eirian rubbed her wrist and turned her gaze to Aiden. Knowing Eirian would tolerate no arguments, Brenna nodded to the remaining ladies and crossed to the door, casting a look over her shoulder.

"Good luck with your meeting, Your Majesty."

Looking at the two guards hovering in the corner, Aiden noted the look they gave him, their eyes darting to Eirian. "Mac, Lyle. Outside. Knock when Lord Faolan approaches."

"Don't bother pressing your point, Aiden. You won't be remaining in the chamber when he arrives. I'll meet with him alone as we agreed."

"I wouldn't dare argue with my queen."

Snorting, Eirian turned and strode to the window to stare at the city beyond the walls. An argument with Aiden would provide her with a distraction. "It amuses me you can say that with a straight face."

Shuffling, Aiden pulled out a chair and sat, propping his feet up on the corner of the table. He stared at her back, aware of what Eirian was trying to do. Something was bothering her, and Aiden wondered what it would take to convince her to tell him.

"I'm offended you'd suggest I'd lie about it."

"Aiden."

"Your Majesty."

Arching an eyebrow at the look Eirian gave him over her shoulder. It amused Aiden when she pointed at him, and he wondered what she would say. Then, flicking her finger, Eirian used her magic to shift his feet from their position. The suddenness of her action startled Aiden, but he hid it with a smirk.

"And here I thought we were being all improper," Aiden mocked her earlier words.

"While I might make the occasional inappropriate joke, I'm your queen, and it would pay for you to remember that!"

Eirian took several deep breaths and pushed her fears away, turning back to the view. She heard the drumming of fingers, and out of the corner of her eye, Eirian watched as Aiden lifted his feet back up.

Aiden told her, "Oh, believe me, I never forget. I'm not allowed to."

"How are your preparations for our journey progressing?"

"I'm prepared. Still don't agree it's a good idea, and you can be damn sure I won't hesitate to knock you out and drag you away from a battlefield if it comes to it. But, magic or not, my job is to keep you alive."

Crossing her arms, Eirian rubbed her hands against the mail on her shoulders, muttering, "I doubt you'd be the only one trying, and I wish you luck."

"Why do you think I let you train with me? I know you very well, how you move, what you favor in a fight, your blind spots. Watching you with your prince has confirmed what I know. Your magic doesn't change those things," Aiden said, knowing his words would anger her.

"You've not seen what I can truly do, Aiden, not even close. That day in the woods? What I did to those men? That was nothing. If I didn't want you to get close, you wouldn't."

Eirian gave him a look over her shoulder, resting her chin on her hand. It dug into the gap between her thumb and finger, causing a discomfort she welcomed. Shrugging at her words, Aiden continued drumming his fingers, knowing her ladies would return with food soon.

"Majesty, you're good with a sword, even better with two, and I don't deny you're more than decent with a bow. However, you're not the greatest warrior alive."

"Did I say I was?"

He scoffed. "Your magic gives you an advantage. Just not against someone who, as you said earlier, has had you under him enough times to know you well."

"You're infuriating."

"I'd say the same thing about you, but that wouldn't be appropriate, and after all, I mustn't forget you're my queen. Especially when I've got you beneath me."

Turning around, Eirian's magic simmered as she growled. "I've half a mind to have you replaced."

"No, you don't. You like the way I push boundaries with you and the way I don't have any qualms about putting you down in a fight. It motivates you. You don't want people surrounding you who bow and scrape all the time, simpering as they try to make you happy."

"Do you know how to simper?" Eirian muttered.

Ignoring her magic, he said tauntingly, "Right now, you want nothing more than to strangle me, Eirian, but we know how that will end."

"Are you sure about that?"

"Oh, absolutely. It would end with you on your back and me on top. As it always does," Aiden replied with a smirk.

"You're enjoying this." Expression faltering, Eirian slumped against the windowsill, grumbling, "I've made a mistake by letting you win. You think you're better than me."

"You're right about me enjoying it. I always do, and by the powers, I mean every damn word. After what you learned about Gabe, I hope you stop pretending we're pleasant people. Because we aren't, and you aren't either."

"Captain—"

"Your nobles can pretend all they like, but they'd only take a life out of necessity. Me? I could slit a throat in broad daylight in the middle of a street with a crowd watching and walk away whistling. As could all the men guarding you, and importantly, so could you."

Wide-eyed, Eirian stared at Aiden with her mouth open as she tried to decide what to say. He was right. She knew it, and he knew it, but Eirian did not want to give him the satisfaction of agreeing. Jolting when a knock came at the door, she watched Aiden sit upright in the chair in a quick motion before they opened the door. Accompanied by maids, Bea and Isabella entered with food and drink.

"Thank you. The Duchess is busy with tasks, and I need the two of you to visit the seamstress. Let them know I require several thicker shirts to wear under this mail."

Leaving the window, Eirian approached the table without looking at Aiden and selected an item to eat. The two women exchanged looks, suspecting they had interrupted something.

"I'll arrange for a gambeson," Aiden said, watching her closely.

Shaking her head, Eirian returned with her food to the safety she imagined she had at the window. "No, that's unnecessary. A gambeson would affect the fit of my leathers. A few shirts I can work some wards into will be sufficient."

Quietly leaving the room to attend to their task, the ladies shared a look as Bea shut the door. Hearing the soft thud of its closing, Eirian sighed. She finished eating the slice of cheese and bread she had selected and glanced warily at Aiden. Stretching his arms and legs, Aiden smiled at her in amusement. It made Eirian shift, and her gaze dropped to the ground.

"You look at me like I might devour you."

"Because it feels as though you might!" Throwing her hands in the air, Eirian huffed in frustration at the growing smile on his face.

"Are you feeling a little frustrated, Eirian?"

"It's Your Majesty!"

Standing, Aiden crossed to the window and blocked her path before Eirian could move away. Leaning in to bring them face to face, he smiled darkly. She froze, knowing she should put space between them, but she did not want to. He smelled of eucalyptus oil and leather, the scent strangely soothing.

"You're about to embark on a journey accompanied by thousands of men who don't know you. They'll see you prancing around in your armor and wearing your weapons, making strategies with men they view as superior to you. They'll hear you're a fierce fighter, and your weapons aren't for show, but they won't believe it."

"They don't have to believe it. They just have to follow orders."

Aiden chuckled. "They'll want to test you and challenge your sensitivities. You're walking into a den of ravenous wolves thinking you can tame them."

She lifted her hands to push him, but he batted them away without flinching, and she said, "Captain, get out of my way!"

"No, you will hear me! Once we leave this city, you'll go nowhere without me. You don't know what you're walking into."

"I'm not stupid. I know."

Laughing, Aiden lifted a hand and gripped her chin, ignoring the rising swirl of magic. Eirian's eyes narrowed, and she contemplated showing him what she could do when pushed. He could see it and wondered if kissing her would shift that fire. Resisting the urge to find out, Aiden moved closer, pushing her against the windowsill. The edge of the stone dug into the backs of her legs, and Eirian's breath hitched.

"Oh, so you know what would happen if you got captured by a group of Athnaralan soldiers?"

Yanking her face free, Eirian said, "I'd defend myself."

"And we wouldn't want you to do anything stupid. It's safer if you behave and follow my orders so I can do my job and protect you."

"Follow your orders? I don't follow orders, Captain."

His hand stroked her neck, feeling the softness of her skin. Eirian could not decide if she wanted him to keep going, or if she wanted to strangle him. While she dithered over her choices, her hands rested on his chest. Her nails dug into the leather of his baldrics, but Eirian did not notice in her frustration, though Aiden did. Through the layers of cloth and armor, he felt the press of her fingers.

Aiden murmured, "You're the embodiment of what men talk about in garrisons. Every soldier makes jokes about wanting to experience a noble-woman, a princess, or a mage. They figure they're different to the women they're used to."

Eirian glared at him and replied, "I can handle soldiers."

"Can you? If you want a rough tumble with a soldier, say the word, darling. I'll happily oblige you. After all, I'm here to serve my queen for life."

The widening of Eirian's eyes made him chuckle. She did not move, and Aiden wondered if she was going to say anything. When she remained silent, he returned to the table, putting distance between them before he made a mistake by giving in to his desire. Eirian looked at the door, sensing Faolan. His arrival filled her with relief and dread.

"If you think you can frighten me, Captain, you're sorely mistaken."

Hearing a knock, Aiden shrugged and picked up an apple, biting into it as he walked to the door. "I'm not trying to frighten you, but I'm not about to let other wolves devour you."

"Don't fool yourself, Captain. You're not a wolf, and I'm certainly not a sheep."

He shrugged again and yanked the door open before Eirian could say any more on the matter. Faolan stood there, hands clasped behind his back and an amused expression.

Giving Faolan a bow, Aiden said, "My lord, Her Majesty is ready to see you."

Arching a brow, Faolan looked between them knowingly. "I'm inter-rupting. I can return when you're less busy."

"You're not interrupting anything, Lord Faolan. Please come in. The captain is leaving." Eirian waved at the table, her rings catching the light as she moved, saying, "Help yourself."

"I'll be right outside, Your Majesty, just a call away."

His smirk was challenging, and Eirian wanted to wipe it from his face. The look she gave Aiden had Faolan chuckling.

"I don't think that's a good idea."

Treading softly to the table, Faolan glanced over at the food while pouring two glasses of wine. Once the door closed, he held one out to Eirian.

"I think you need this."

"Thank you." Eirian left the window to accept the offering, murmuring, "I apologize. That was inappropriate for you to walk in on."

"I don't know what you're talking about!"

Smiling faintly, he sipped at the wine. Snorting, Eirian took a sip before setting it down.

"So, here we are. You have me alone as you wanted."

"Indeed, I do. You have questions for me, and I'll do my best to answer them."

Eirian sat on the chair Aiden had vacated and picked up her wine. Holding the glass to her mouth with both hands wrapped around it, she examined Faolan curiously. Her power was hiding, making Eirian wonder if she was holding it back without thinking because of her secret. Waiting, Faolan studied her in return, and Eirian pointed at the chairs next to her.

"I'm not sure how things normally work for you, but finding out what you want to know is easier if you ask questions. Unless you can read minds?" Sitting, Faolan rested his arm on the table with the glass firmly gripped in his hand and asked, "Can you read my mind, little Queen?"

"No, I can't. So why are you here?"

He smiled widely and answered, "Straight to the point. Now, why me specifically or?"

"Both."

"My king chose me because I'm one of his most trusted confidants. We came to make an alliance and protect you."

"What makes Endara so important that they must war over us?" Still frustrated, Eirian shook her head and huffed. "It will never end, will it?"

Tilting his head to the side, Faolan stared, and she felt as though she could drown in the deep green of his eyes. They were familiar, reminding her of the emeralds set into her mother's diadem, and Eirian wondered if they had known each other.

Faolan said, "War serves many purposes. But don't mistake our intention. Endara is not the reason we have come. You are why we're here."

"We're the same now that I'm the queen."

"No, you're not. For now, you're the Queen of Endara, but when fate and duty demand it, you'll simply be Eirian Altira, the mage."

Eirian frowned at him and murmured, "You suggest I'll give up the throne one day."

"Indeed. If the darkness is returning, you will." Lifting the glass to his lips, Faolan drained it and added, "But of course, if it's returning, then we may all do things we never planned on."

"What is the darkness?"

"Exactly what it sounds like."

Giving him a mocking look, Eirian reached for a piece of meat. "The absence of light?"

"I walked into that one." Faolan chuckled, then glanced at the window. "It's everything we fear, the part of ourselves we barricade behind walls because we know if it got out, people would run screaming in terror. It's a nameless memory you can never put your finger on."

"Are you saying the darkness is ourselves?"

"The darkness is more than that and has a tangible form. What makes it our enemy is it brings out the darkness in those it touches. It can turn a good man who loved his family and worked hard all his life into a ravening beast who slaughters everyone he cared for."

Eirian finished eating the slice of meat before leaning towards him. "The darkness is a magical being? A duine, perhaps? I don't know everything, not even close, but surely it can't be a human or elf."

"I don't know what it is, but you have my promise that the darkness is not a duine. I suspect the only one who can answer that question is my king, and Neriwyn won't tell me. Perhaps he'll tell you when you meet."

"I have no desire to meet your king."

Chuckling, Faolan reached for a slice of cheese. "You're probably the first to say that. King Neriwyn always gets what he wants."

"If you're half as beautiful as he is, I imagine that's the truth," Eirian replied with a smile.

"You're a warrior. You'd appreciate how Neriwyn handles his sword and, perhaps, the mercy he shows to his quarry when he defeats it."

"Why insist on meeting me alone?"

Faolan rolled his shoulders, rubbing the back of his neck, while Eirian watched him warily. His nose twitched. The floral scent he had noticed previously was distracting him, but it did not hide her nervousness.

"Perhaps I wanted to get a feel for you?"

"You don't need a private audience to do that," Eirian said, her magic responding to her frustration.

"Ah, but I couldn't play with you so easily with others watching," Faolan replied, and his magic surrounded her.

Wide-eyed, Eirian clung to her power as an anchor, tempted to push back at him. He was powerful, but she suspected he would not stand a chance if she dropped her shields completely. It was not something Eirian could risk. What she could not deny was the way his magic made her feel. A familiarity stirred the memories, and for once, Eirian embraced them as a distraction. She let the whispers fill her mind.

"You've made your point."

"Have I? Oh dear, was it a bit too much for you?"

"Not at all."

Faolan watched her shift uncomfortably on the chair with a smirk and chuckled. "I can take care of that discomfort for you. Just ask, and I'll call your captain in."

"No, thank you."

"You enjoy making yourself suffer."

Glancing at her hands, Eirian picked at the hem of her tunic and asked, "Tell me, do daoine ever disappear?"

Surprised, he blinked and said, "That is a strange question to ask."

"Do they?"

"Occasionally, and His Majesty always brings them back. But, most of the time, it's because they fancy a taste of mortal flesh."

There was a tiny thread loose, and Eirian picked at it repeatedly without looking at him. She knew her mother had come for reasons more serious than a simple dalliance with a human.

"A taste of mortal flesh? You make us sound like a meal."

Laughing, Faolan replied, "You're a feast to us, hiding behind your walls of propriety. I know you understand how it feels to feed off the emotions of others."

Eirian glanced at him and murmured, "I try to avoid it."

"I can tell. It's even more pleasurable during intimacy, which you also know very well. So, imagine how it feels to us when someone who has suppressed their innermost feelings for most of their lives surrenders to them. A feast indeed."

"Your approach is disturbing."

"Only because you're told not to use your magic like that. In doing so, you tie your hands behind your backs. Magic should be a part of breathing and feeling, and you need to learn to stop restraining yourself because it makes you weak."

Flattening her hands against her thighs, Eirian lifted her head to peer at him without meeting his gaze. Faolan spoke the truth, and she knew it better than others. She had spent so many years restraining her power, avoiding how it made her feel.

"You're right," Eirian told him. "We restrain ourselves from behaving like you because we have far less time to deal with the consequences. What happens to any offspring that results from your hunts?"

"They're duine and belong with their people. Daoine blood always breeds true. Why are you so curious?" Faolan contemplated her.

"Because my nobles want me to marry the Prince of Ensaycal."

Her quick answer seemed to mollify his curiosity, and Faolan said, "And you wonder about children? I see. Humans are always so fussy. You love each other and that is the only thing that should matter."

"But it matters," she replied, annoyed by his dismissive tone.

"What do you want?"

Pursing her lips, Eirian considered his question. "They expect me to marry, and when I suggest I don't want to? They dismiss it like I'm a foolish child who doesn't know what she wants. I've been a pawn all my life, and thanks to you, I now know I'll always be a pawn."

He shrugged. "If you don't want to marry, then don't. Take all the lovers to your bed that you wish. You're a mage, and you can prevent any undesired repercussions. All we care about is the Altira linage continuing, and you have cousins enough to ensure that. Though I suggest adding more magic back in."

"Do your people marry?"

"No, we prefer to be free and happy with whoever we wish. Though some remain together for a long time. We have the choice, and some make that decision."

Sighing, Eirian picked up the jug of wine and refilled their glasses, murmuring, "I wish it were that easy for us. We've gone well off-topic, though."

Picking up his drink, Faolan saluted her with it. "I wasn't aware we had a topic. Though if I can suggest something?"

"Dare I ask what?"

"Your captain has so much simmering below the surface. I'm surprised my sister hasn't set her eyes on him. I certainly would if he was interested in me. Thankfully, we've had no shortage of willing fodder."

Tightening her grip on the mug, Eirian stared at him blankly. "Are you working your way through my court?"

Smiling at her over the lip of his glass, Faolan flickered his gaze to the door to her chamber. "Definitely. I wish I could show you. It might help you forget about your prince in Telmia."

"You've made it obvious that you know about Prince Galameyvin and me." Swallowing, Eirian shook her head and added, "My court believes me to be an innocent woman because that's what they expect of Endaran noble-women."

"He's very disciplined, but not disciplined enough. As for your court not knowing, I suspect it suits you."

Frowning at the wine, Eirian hoped he mistook her fear for concern over what they might have learned from Galameyvin and not her fear of what they could learn from her.

She admitted, "I can't let anyone know because it would ruin my reputation."

"Why do you care about your reputation? It's such a silly notion. Besides, you said it yourself. You don't want to marry."

"I don't enjoy disappointing the people I care about. So yes, I worry about silly notions like reputation."

Leaning back, Faolan picked at the food, giving it a look. "No wonder you want to shove your captain against a wall. You've deprived yourself for months."

"I do not!" Protesting his observation, she scowled. "Do you know when I might face this darkness?"

Faolan gave her a look that told Eirian he saw through her lie and replied, "I can't answer that. It could be soon, or it might be years from now. That's a question you'll have to ask Neriwyn. If you end up at war with Athnaral, I imagine he'll make an appearance, and you'll have ample time to talk to him."

She sighed. "How do I defeat the darkness? Did you see it happen last time?"

He grew serious, and Eirian could feel the anguish in his magic. It concerned her.

"No, I was with the queen."

"You have a queen?" Eirian asked in surprise. "I've never heard mention of a queen."

"She was the first and our king the second. That is the way the gods created us. Her power was truly something to behold."

Draining his glass, Faolan reached for the jug to refill it, pain clear on his face. Reaching out, Eirian stopped him, her hand covering his on the handle. He looked at her.

"Was? What happened?"

"No one knows except Neriwyn. He says he knows where she is, and she's doing her duty. I fear she is dead. She had the gift of foresight, rare even for us, and something she passed to her son." Faolan turned his hand around, gripping hers tightly, saying, "You understand you can never speak of this."

"You think she foresaw the darkness returning. That's how King Neriwyn became aware and how he knows I have a part to play. You believe she killed herself because of her visions?"

"I don't know. She had so many who loved her, so many things to keep her going. I don't know why I feel like she may have."

Tugging at her hand when his thumb started stroking the inside of her wrist, Eirian murmured, "We can't always control how we feel. Sometimes, the things we feel become too much to cope with."

"Speaking from experience?"

Not letting go of her hand, Faolan stared into space thoughtfully, despite her tugging. Eirian paused, worried he suspected the thoughts that had crossed her mind many times.

"Please let go of my hand," she requested softly.

Glancing at her hand, Faolan released it with a faint smile. "My apologies, Your Majesty."

Flexing her fingers, Eirian returned the smile. "You spoke of bloodlines when we first met. What makes my family line so important?"

"Well, for a start, you descend from the first human mage. It was your ancestor who banished the darkness last time. Mages from your line have always been powerful. There is a great deal of magic in you, more than you realize."

"I want no more power than I already have. I'd gladly give away half of it as it is."

The look that crossed Faolan's face was unreadable, and a knock at the door startled them. "I gather our time is up."

"I feel like we barely covered anything. Do you intend to drag this out as long as possible?" Eirian shook her head, glancing at the door, grumbling, "You make me feel like I'm dizzy from spinning in circles."

Leaning forward, Faolan lifted her hand to kiss the back softly. "You misunderstand. We won't be leaving. King Neriwyn has ordered us to remain and watch over you. We can communicate with him if you find yourself at war. Or if we feel the darkness is coming."

Mortified, Eirian wondered how long she could keep her secret. "You aren't leaving?"

"No need to look so upset. You'll hurt my feelings. Count it as a blessing that your people are the lucky ones who get to know the daoine for the first time in generations. I'm completely at your service. Anything you want to learn about us, and I mean anything, just ask."

"I'm sure I won't need your services."

Faolan kissed her hand again before standing and drawing Eirian to her feet with him. "By the way, mail suits you. It makes you look like a harder quarry."

Withdrawing her hand, Eirian stepped away and told him, "I'm not your quarry, Lord Faolan."

Chuckling, Faolan closed the gap and placed a hand on her arm, leaning in to murmur, "You're the quarry of many."

A second round of knocking made him step away, smiling at her nervous expression. Shaking her head, Eirian reached for the hilt of one of her swords for reassurance.

"I know many would like to have me, but let me make it clear, you never will."

"We'll see. I know you're keeping secrets, and you fear us learning them. I don't have the same skills as my sister, but I have a nose for these things." Winking, Faolan headed for the door, saying, "Thank you for your time."

Taking a deep breath, Eirian did not turn to see who had entered as Faolan left. Listening to the footsteps, a hand landed on her shoulder and startled her. Turning, Eirian saw Everett looking at her in concern.

"Thank the powers."

"Went that well, did it?" Everett reached around and shifted the chair so she could sit. "You look fierce! Who had that crafted?"

"Aiden did. I swear everyone has gone mad today."

"He has always been good at being a step ahead, but I suppose he needs to be to cope with you. Why has the world gone mad?"

Plopping down on the chair Faolan had vacated, Everett grabbed a bread roll and pulled it apart. Shaking her head, Eirian picked up her wine and took a mouthful.

She asked him, "Tell me, is sex the only thing men think about sometimes?"

Everett almost dropped his bread roll as he stared at her. "What?"

"You heard me. Is it?"

"Did Lord Faolan try to seduce you?"

Eirian cocked her head to the side and looked up at the ceiling, muttering, "Thankfully, no, but he made certain things clear to me. As did Aiden. I've half a mind to have him punished, I suppose anyone else would. Am I too liberal with my captain?"

"Are you serious about refusing to marry?"

"I am. You'll marry, give me heirs, and all will be fine. But I want an honest answer. Am I too friendly with certain people?"

Everett nodded and said, "Having seen you with the elves, it's obvious you're used to being with friends. As for Aiden, I'm sure whatever he had to say came from a place of dutiful concern for your welfare."

"He implied that if I wasn't careful, I might end up raped by the enemy." Eirian finished her drink and reached for the jug to refill it. "I don't think there's enough wine in the castle to help me forget today."

"He has a point. Armies have a lot of men and not as many women. Men have urges, and war seems to make things worse. Women from the other side always suffer the most."

Blinking slowly, she glared at him and said, "Thank you for agreeing. It makes me feel better about insisting my ladies remain here."

Frowning, Everett finished the roll. "If we encounter Athnaral, you need to get away from the conflict. Aiden knows this. He'll get you away and protect you."

"No."

"You can't be serious."

"I'm sorry, but I won't be running away. I might only be one mage, but I have things I can do to tip the balance in our favor. Would you throw that away? I can hold my own in a fight better than you!" Eirian was adamant, pointing at him with her glass. "By the way, the Telmians aren't leaving. They're here to stay for a while."

Everett watched her drain the glass a second time, asking, "And getting drunk is going to help you deal with that fact? It's only the middle of the afternoon."

"Oh yes, I'm going to have a few drinks and maybe seduce my best friend or the captain of my guards. Perhaps both. Preferably at the same time. Men get away with taking lovers. So why shouldn't I?" Leaning on the table, Eirian peered into the jug and sighed. "I'm not in Riane. I know I can't bed anyone I fancy anymore."

"I understand you are anxious about everything, but do you think that is wise?"

He was not sure which comment bothered him more. The suggestion Eirian might try to seduce Aiden or that bedding anyone she wanted was not an option. Deciding to push it from his mind, Everett ground his teeth, agitated by the conversation.

"Why does it matter? Why are you lot so hung up on women not having lovers other than their husbands? I must send for some more wine. This is not enough to get drunk on."

Standing, Everett shook his head and grumbled in frustration, "Fine, have your drinking session! There isn't anything important to attend to. Just don't go gallivanting around the castle."

Holding up her glass, Eirian told him, "I don't make any promises! Besides, wouldn't you be happy if I ended up in Celiaen's bed? Then you could force our marriage."

"I told you before. If I thought it was what you wanted—"

"Yes, we know what I want matters a great deal to no one. I was born to fill a role, and by the powers, I'll do it, but I'll do it my way."

"Eirian—"

"Get out and let me drink in peace!"

TWENTY-SIX

Eirian leaned back in the chair with her arms on the table, and her magic gave off an air of calm. Nobles and small council members had steadily filtered in, surprise showing on half of their faces when greeted with the sight of her waiting for them. Her eyes followed the movements of those Eirian knew were openly against her decision, hoping that her act of singling them out would make them nervous. But, if her gaze was not enough, the smug curl to her mouth left them questioning their choices.

On either side, her cousins were hiding their defeat well, giving her nervous glances when they thought she would not notice. Eirian signaled for Gabe to shut the door when the last person entered. He wore a grim smile, knowing she had selected him because he made people nervous. Celiaen and Tynan were outside the chamber, unwelcome during the meeting. The impatience and hopefulness coming from Celiaen left Eirian feeling guilty for not warning him it would not go his way. The guilt only reminded her of her anger.

"Your Majesty." Sabine greeted her with a terse smile. "We weren't expecting your presence this early in the meeting."

"I'm quite aware. I suppose you were hoping to complete your plans to override my decision regarding the proposal from Ensaycal." Pointing at the stack of parchment in front of Sabine, Eirian arched a brow and said, "I'm surprised you support it, Sabine."

Sabine shrugged, holding her hands out in a gesture that mirrored her tone, saying, "Well, what do you know, we're both full of surprises! My concern is the financial stability of Endara."

Ulric smiled in amusement. "Our dear treasurer doesn't have faith the elves will honor the treaty if you refuse to marry their prince. I disagree. Paienven wouldn't disregard the treaty because you scorned his son. He's a practical man. The treaty benefits both kingdoms and has done so for a long time."

"Yes, but none of us can be sure of that!" Earl Baeddan shouted before shrinking back from the look directed his way by Eirian.

"I can be sure of that."

Seated beside Gallagher, his mother Kaie said, "How can you be confident of holding a much shrewder man to an alliance after refusing his son. As for some other concerns raised, so what if he is an elf? There is ample enough elf blood in Endara and in this very room."

Letting Kaie's words linger, Eirian leaned forward and rested her elbows on the table, linking her fingers together under her chin. Her magic oozed through the chamber, a reminder that she was powerful, and capable of doing things they could not. Eirian had worked out that just the touch of her power was enough to encourage them to listen to her. People stared, waiting to hear what she would say.

Smiling at Kaie, Eirian replied, "The only reason Paienven added marriage as an option is because Celiaen loves me. It's the result of a lovesick boy making demands and a vindictive father using them to teach him a lesson. Believe me, if I thought our alliance was at risk, I'd take the proposal seriously."

"That lovesick boy is older than any of us here. And more powerful!"

"It is still the demand of a selfish, lovesick boy who can't stand the thought of another having what he desires. A child who'd throw a tantrum because another child might play with the toy he wants. Celiaen has never been good at sharing, and I know that better than anyone."

Llewellyn looked uncomfortable, muttering, "You're harsh on the man you claim is your closest friend."

"And it pains me to speak so of him, but if it makes these fools understand the reasons for the offer, then so be it. I can make my peace with Celiaen. I will not marry the Prince of Ensaycal." Her eyes narrowed as Eirian moved her gaze around the room, saying, "Let me make it clear. None of you can force me to."

Wendel placed his hands on a book and told her, "Actually, Your Majesty, we can."

Sighing, Eirian startled them by using her magic to drag the book across the table to her waiting grasp. It was a heavy tome, but she lifted it with one hand, ignoring the protest of her fingers as they strained to keep a steady hold. If anyone could tell the action caused her discomfort, they did not mention it. Inclining her head at the book, Eirian arched a brow and let her gaze drift.

"No, you can't. You think you can because a law says the council can dictate the royal family's marriage arrangements. I'll call on your agreement shortly for another. However, you can't force me."

"But you just said—"

"Hush, Wendel." Marcellus scolded. "The Queen is correct, but we're talking specifically about her, not everyone else in the family now or in the future."

"Alright, tell us why we can't hold you to the law," Ollier said and cocked his head.

"Because I am, to quote our Telmian visitors, the Altira mage. Apparently, that means I get to lead us in a battle. I'm sure everyone has heard various things regarding our new alliance with Telmia. I know you've been meeting with them, some more than others."

There were coughs from multiple people. Everyone knew exactly what she was implying, but no one would speak of it in the council chambers. Very few court members had resisted the draw of the daoine, the lure of the strange appealing to most. They were a novelty, and no one knew when they would leave, so everyone willing to risk it was taking advantage while they could.

Eirian continued, "It comes to mind that me marrying and attempting to produce an heir directly puts that alliance at risk."

Ulric nodded and said, "Because the alliance depends on you doing your part in this darkness issue."

"Precisely. With that in mind, I think you'll agree marriage is not an option until such a time as I complete my part. Unless, of course, you want to make enemies of Telmia?"

Glancing at her cousins, Eirian saw their surprise. It had been a deliberate choice not to tell them beforehand what her argument was. She did not want them warning Celiaen, or anyone else, of what she had planned. Those forewarned would have prepared a counterargument and potentially overruled her.

Agreeing, General Cameron said, "We hope our alliance with the daoine will be enough to make Aeyren change his mind about war. So, we need to do anything we can to keep them happy. Though admittedly, the old fighter in me wants to see them in action."

"And what about this darkness they keep on about? Do you believe them?" Gallagher asked with concern, glancing at Kaie beside him.

"No offense, Your Majesty, but you aren't young. You don't have many years in which to produce an heir and a spare," Kaie said. "We can't risk waiting years for you to decide to wed, let alone waiting in case some mystery enemy surfaces. The powers know, perhaps it is the daoine themselves we have to fear!"

"My father wasn't an only child. He had two sisters who produced children with as much claim to the throne as I have. Everett is my heir, and Llewellyn is after him. So there are ample Altira's for the throne, and hopefully, by this time next year, there will be more."

Pursing her lips, she glanced at Llewellyn and shrugged apologetically. Her interference would annoy him, but Eirian was happy to use him as an excuse to keep two of her ladies in Amath and away from the risk of a battlefield. Since Llewellyn admitted his interest in Romana, Eirian had watched her closely, and she could not think of a better wife for him.

Llewellyn realized she was planning to mollify the council with his marriage and protested. "Wait, Eirian, please."

"Earl Baeddan, I believe you'll like this royal match far more than the one you were pushing on my behalf." Looking at Baeddan, Eirian ignored Llewellyn and added, "I admit the duke's choice surprised me, but on consideration, it is a splendid match."

Spluttering, Baeddan looked at Llewellyn. "We've only just started negotiating."

"Excellent. The Duke of Onaorbaen will wed Lady Romana, daughter of the Earl of Nareen. Anyone with objections can keep them to themselves."

Groaning, Llewellyn covered his face and asked, "What about Everett?"

"Don't drag me into this!" Everett said, holding his hands up pleadingly as he stared at Eirian.

"I'll start preparing the contracts." Ulric bowed his head, casting a look at the shocked nobleman and commented, "A most fortuitous match for your daughter, Baeddan."

"To bring us back to the original marriage subject, are you implying you have no intention of marrying?" another noblewoman asked.

Eirian smiled, silently reminding herself why she could not wed, and replied, "That is right, no intention at all. My line is secure, so it makes no sense to put my life at risk for the sake of children. I'm fortunate that I can make that call. My duty is to Endara, and I cannot serve my kingdom if I'm dead."

"Women give birth every day and don't die," Sabine said.

"And women give birth every day and do die. For example, Earl Adalardo's wife. Though fortunately, she gave him two children before that terrible day. Even greens can't guarantee a woman's safety. Right now, somewhere, a woman is dying in childbirth."

Giving an apologetic look to Adalardo at the mention of his dead wife, Eirian read the understanding in his eyes. She needed him to agree, because his support would add weight to her argument. Adalardo inclined his head to her, and she nodded.

"Our queen is right. Dead is dead. Let Llewellyn and Everett do the breeding and let her rule. With the threat of war, it's probably better if we focus Eirian on dealing with Athnaral," Adalardo spoke softly, looking at the two dukes.

Previously silent, Brenna surprised Eirian by saying, "Think of the example it gives Athnaral. They have expectations for women that we don't share, and our queen is making that statement loud and clear. Eirian is our queen, and she'll rule without the 'guiding hand' of a man. Who can argue with that?"

Several of the men made noises before staring at Everett. He knew what they wanted. They had voiced it to him and to Llewellyn. It was a suggestion that continued to make Everett uncomfortable. He had done a lot of negotiating to stop them from demanding Aiden's attendance at the meeting and talk them out of making the proposal. Cameron, in particular, had been vocal about the council deciding either way before they departed Amath. He had not fancied explaining everything to Eirian if his appeals had failed.

"It also reinforces to all of us and our daughters that we have a choice. This is Endara and women are equal here. They can join the army, inherit, rule, own businesses and land. Countess Kathleen, would you be happy if someone said that your husband was now master of your lands simply because he has a cock?" Brenna finished speaking and looked at Kathleen.

"When I asked, I didn't intend to give the impression I disapprove. I think it's wonderful, and yes, it does set a powerful example," Kathleen replied with a grin. "I have daughters, one of whom serves our queen. We are Endara, and yes, we are equal here."

"Excellent. I'm so pleased that you see sense. Let me deal with Celiaen. Our alliance with Ensaycal will continue as it has done for generations. The prince told me Paienven never expected us to agree to the match."

Eirian looked at each person, daring them to protest. Most of them looked away, unwilling to argue when her argument had support from influential council members. If Brenna and Kathleen agreed with Eirian, it would not be long before others did.

"If it is the matter of a candidate that isn't an elf, there is one that would suit you well. I think most of us would agree with his pedigree." Cameron glanced at Everett and said, "It's a matter of a little piece of paper and a signature."

Sitting up straight, Llewellyn was quick to say, "I don't think we need to consider other options for the moment."

"I disagree. I think that while the matter is on the table, we should nominate our other candidates for consideration," Kaie replied with a look at Gallagher.

Sneering, Cameron scoffed. "You can't be serious. At least my candidate stands a chance of being approved."

"There is no candidate you could bring before me, General, that would make me change my mind. So, don't bother," Eirian informed him before Kaie could argue.

The withering look she directed at Cameron made him incline his head respectfully. Then he glanced at Everett and wondered if Eirian knew who he was referring to. Everett had fought hard to keep Aiden out of the meeting, making him suspect Eirian remained clueless about the truth.

Huffing, Wendel finally said, "I concede that, for now, we've dealt with the topic, but we'll revisit it once we've finished with Athnaral. If it looks like Ensaycal might break the treaty, you'll beg the prince to reconsider and offer him whatever he wants to keep them on our side."

Eirian understood his point. "I agree. Just don't fool yourself into thinking I'll change my mind for anything less than desperation to save my kingdom. Now, we have more important matters to discuss."

Hearing the note of finality in her voice, Ulric pushed forward the next issue they needed to deal with. Working their way through, Eirian paid particular attention to Sabine's reports regarding signs of crop failure in some regions. It was a concern, and Eirian shared a look with Ulric, knowing he repeatedly met with the daoine. She had brought him into her confidence, sharing her concerns about signs of the darkness rising.

The subject was raised frequently, each time asking if they should believe the Telmians. Half the council expressed disbelief with the demands for tangible evidence and not the words of some strangers. Eirian wanted to tell them what Howell had informed her about the cases of madness. She understood their disbelief in it. Why should they believe rumors and stories with nothing solid to prove it?

While they worked, Eirian felt Celiaen's rising frustration on the other side of the doors. An image of him pacing along the hallway lingered in the back of her mind. He sensed her triumph and her fears in return, the exchange only making him more agitated. It was a downside of their bond when close. His agitation made her squirm in her seat, the sensation of it an itch down her spine. Tynan's calm seeped through the walls of the chamber, the only thing keeping Celiaen's rage in check.

Leaning so she could whisper in Llewellyn's ear, Eirian monitored the council as they completed the day's matters. "I need you to distract Celiaen and let me get away."

"Why?" he asked and arched an eyebrow, glancing at her sideways.

"Because it won't be pleasant when we talk. Celiaen was counting on you giving him what he wants and isn't prepared to find out he's lost."

Frowning, Llewellyn grumbled, "You don't want us to witness what happens when the two of you fight."

"I wouldn't call it fighting." She cringed at the prospect, admitting, "But you're right."

"I want to let you deal with him after what you did to me, but fine, for the sake of everyone's safety, I'll do my best to distract the prince. I hope you have a plan."

Chuckling, Eirian leaned closer, dropping her voice to whisper, "Do you think he would forget his anger if I let him find me in bed?"

Startled, Llewellyn choked on his sudden intake of breath, and Eirian sat back, giving him an amused grin. He was aware they were being watched, and did not respond, forcing himself to focus on Cameron's report regarding troop movements. Eirian knew she should pay attention to it, but figured she would have time to catch up on the information later. Turning to Everett, she met his stare, and he knew what she would ask.

"Help Llewellyn keep Celiaen distracted."

"You're playing with fire," he muttered, shaking his head.

Shrugging, Eirian glanced at the rest of the room, and he did the same. People were paying attention to their exchange, but Cameron kept talking loudly. His voice was enough to muffle what she was whispering to Everett, and Eirian took the risk to answer him.

"I know, but I don't want anyone else to get burned."

"Please don't do anything stupid."

"No promises."

Turning her attention back to the meeting, Eirian grew anxious as it ended. Rising to her feet to exchange pleasantries with people as they filtered out, she watched her cousins exit. Eirian did her best to hover in a group of nobles as she followed them. Then, catching sight of Celiaen arguing with the dukes, she hurried in the opposite direction to avoid crossing directly onto his path. Her guards trailed Eirian in confusion. Gabe was the first to catch up with her, easily matching her stride.

"Where are we going?" he asked.

"To the stables."

Kip said, "We're going for a ride?"

"No, I'm going for a ride. Gabe can come, but the rest of you remain. No arguments. I need to get away from the city as quickly as possible." She glanced at Gabe, noting the furrow of his brows. "Look, it's mage stuff. You under-stand?"

"The boss won't like this!" Kip declared.

Continuing to frown, Gabe nodded and said, "Kip is right. Aiden will have us flogged. With everything going on, he's worried about your safety."

"So, you follow me. Let the others run to Aiden and claim I used my powers to give you the slip. Tell him I'm running from Celiaen to get our disagreement out of the castle. If Aiden wants to chase after me, he can face the consequences. I'm your queen, and this is an order."

Arguing among themselves, her guards did not stop Eirian as she continued to the stables. The stable staff were quick to prepare Halcyon at her command. Accepting the cloak Layne offered, Eirian secured it around her shoulders and pulled the hood up, hiding her face.

"I don't like this, ma'am, but we'll do what you suggested. We'll give you a head start before we find the captain," he said.

Eirian watched Halcyon being led towards her and told them, "Don't worry, I'll be back before nightfall. Celiaen can find me with no help from you. It's not the first time I've made him hunt me, and I'm sure it won't be the last."

Quickly checking over the tack, Eirian hoisted herself into the saddle and patted the horse gently. Then, looking at Gabe as he mounted, she nodded to him. The look he gave her was unreadable as he pointed at the gates. Feeling Celiaen's approach, Eirian took the opening given to her and nudged Halcyon into a trot, knowing better than to draw attention. It pleased her that no one gave them a second glance, most seeing a pair of guards going on their way.

"So as fun as letting the much more experienced elf hunt you down sounds, do you have a plan?" Gabe asked, watching people as they trotted through the city.

"Yes, the same plan I always have with our disagreements. I roll with the blows and hit back. Just stay out of the way. I don't want you to get hurt."

Shouts reached their ears, and Eirian and Gabe observed an altercation between two men as they rode past. City guards swooped in to deal with it, but the crowd remained. Others ignored it, too busy with their day to care about what was going on elsewhere. It was warm, the creep of summer making itself known. Eirian regretted she was in a hurry to get away from Celiaen. She wanted to be free to wander the streets and watch life unfold around her.

Gabe commented, "You know Aiden is going to come charging out here looking for you. He's terrifying when he's angry."

"We're going to the woods, and you're going to linger on the outskirts. Don't get in Celiaen's way, but if Aiden shows up, stop him. Tell him what is going on. Tell him if he thought it was bad when he felt Baenlin's magic, it's worse when Celiaen and I are together. That might make him think twice."

Giving her an unreadable look, Gabe tightened the grip on his reins. He remembered the day at the training yards, the feel of her rage and the responding rage of Baenlin. Like all the guards, he had watched Eirian and Celiaen spar, but they always tempered their magic. But, from what Eirian was saying, the fight to come would not be one where they held back. As far as Gabe was concerned, it was unfortunate it would be too dangerous for him to observe them.

"Is this why you don't want to marry the elf? You get dangerous when you're mad at each other."

Eirian scoffed. "Now that you mention it, we could say it's a reason. We can be volatile together, and that doesn't make for good politics."

The gates loomed ahead, and Eirian sunk into the cloak, making sure the hood hid her face. They remained on the road briefly before breaking off towards the woods, pushing the horses into a gallop. Whipped back by the breeze, the hood freed her hair, and Eirian laughed, enjoying the freedom she felt racing across the land. Gabe pulled his mount up as they reached the trees and saluted as she slowed to a trot, slipping amongst the trunks.

"Good luck, Your Majesty."

Eirian drew to a halt, slipping from Halcyon's back, and removed the cloak, draping it over the saddle. Then she loosened the girth, using the time to make her plans. After her last visit to the woods, she released her magic to get a sense of the land and make sure no one lurked in wait. Frowning, Gabe approached and took the reins she offered to him when she finished unbuckling it from the bit.

She told him, "Don't worry, I'll be fine on foot. I imagine you'll hold Celiaen's horse as well."

Looking at the horse, he shrugged and said, "Well, at least I know you won't vanish. Not easily done on foot. Can you tell if he has followed?"

"Celiaen knows where I am. He always does."

Eirian made her way into the woods, treading carefully as she went. Watching her vanish into the trees, Gabe had to blink to make sure he was not going blind. Then, knowing she had used her magic to hide, he turned his gaze to the city, waiting for the sight of more riders. Holding both sets of reins, Gabe rested against a tree, kicking at a root impatiently. It did not take long before he spotted the solitary rider. Dismounting, Celiaen thrust his hand out, passing the leather straps with a snarl.

"Are there others?"

"Just me. We left the others behind."

He grunted. "Good. Stay out."

"Don't worry, I'm not stupid enough to follow you in there. Have a good hunt!" Saluting Celiaen as he took a similar path to his quarry, Gabe chuckled. "Yep, this is going to be fun to explain."

Leading each horse to separate spots, Gabe hitched their reins to low-hanging branches. Wandering away from them, he pulled a small thin knife from inside his bracer and selected a tree as a target. The blade shot through the air, hitting the small swirl in the trunk that he had been aiming for. A second weapon followed, landing beside it without knocking the first.

Yanking the two knives from the tree, Gabe said, "Apologies. This isn't personal. I'm just bored."

Chuckling, he twirled the weapons between his fingers and shook his head. Gabe did not know why he bothered to apologize to a tree, but returning to the spot he had been standing in, he studied it. The trunk was a twisting thing, rough-barked and reaching, but there was a shimmer to the leaves that did not seem normal. Casting a glance in the direction the two mages had vanished, Gabe suspected it had something to do with Eirian's magic.

She fascinated him. It was not just her talent with a blade or the willingness to kill that he admired. What Gabe had witnessed her do with plant life was the opposite of killing. He found it curious that Eirian was capable of both sides of the coin. Giving the leaves another look, Gabe let his knives fly, aiming for the same spot in the trunk.

It was an easy, repetitive action that helped him pass the time. If Gabe's predictions were correct, the men of his squad would have found Aiden and informed him of what was going on. They would do their best to delay him from heading to the woods, but he would find his way sooner rather than later. Gabe hoped his men would escape unscathed from the rage they would face for telling Aiden.

Pulling the knives from the trunk for the umpteenth time, Gabe detected the sound of hooves approaching. Sighing, he returned the blades to their spots inside his bracers and turned to face Aiden. He barely had the chance to take a breath before a fist came flying in his direction and connected with his face. Grunting, Gabe covered his eye, bending over and intending to distract Aiden long enough that he would back down.

"What the fuck, Captain?" he said.

Aiden rubbed his fist, growling as he replied, "Where is she?"

"In the woods with her prince. You can't go in there, Aiden."

"Like fuck I can't!"

Ducking the next fist swung in his direction, Gabe remembered what Eirian had asked. He needed to do what he could to give her time to deal with Celiaen before Aiden got involved.

"Stop acting like a jealous fool and think for a moment!" Gabe shouted at him. "You go in there at the wrong time, and they'll kill you."

"Eirian wouldn't hurt me," he said, turning to face the woods.

"Maybe, maybe not. Prince Celiaen certainly would. He's a red mage and views you as a threat. If they're pissed at each other, and you get in the way, you'll die."

Sneering, Aiden cast a look in Gabe's direction and informed him, "I can handle them. Both of them. However, when we return to the keep, you and your squad will face disciplinary action for failing to keep the Queen of Endara safe."

Angry, Gabe squared his shoulders and argued, "Now, look, Captain, the others didn't fail."

"Didn't they?"

"They followed orders. She could have used her magic on us, but she didn't! So we negotiated, and I accompanied her here. Punish me if you really want, but not them."

"Don't worry, I plan to."

Watching Aiden move into the trees, Gabe sighed. "Fuck."

TWENTY-SEVEN

Progressing through the trees, Eirian felt the tug of the bond to Celiaen. There was no way to hide from him without completely masking her magic, and that would leave her vulnerable, a risk she could not take. Confident she had drawn him far enough from the edge of the woods, Eirian slowed her pace to prepare an ambush. Drawing her swords, she nestled against the trunk of a large gum with the blades tucked against her sides as she sensed Celiaen closing in.

"Did you think you could ambush me?" Celiaen growled.

He slipped in beside Eirian, pressing his knife to her throat. Swallowing, Eirian did not move, feeling her magic rising to match his like an old and faithful friend. It was predictable. Even as the power pulled them to each other, it welcomed the conflict.

"It wouldn't be the first time."

Celiaen grabbed her arm and turned her, careful not to slice her throat. He had never done it before, but the depth of anger he felt was new. As much as he trusted his abilities, it was not a time to be overconfident. Then, flicking a look at the blades he had gifted her, he sneered, and her eyes narrowed.

"What did you think to gain out of this little game?"

"Privacy. We're alone, with no audience, no one to interrupt us. Just you, me, and our blades, like it used to be in Riane," Eirian replied.

Resting her head on the trunk of the tree, Eirian exposed her throat further, relishing in how the rough bark felt pressing at the mail she wore. Celiaen's grasp on her arm tightened, the edge of his blade lifting slightly. He recognized the shift in her eyes, the flicker of magic.

She murmured, "No one we can hurt except each other."

"You could've spoken to me outside the council chamber, told me we should go for a ride. I'd have been less furious with you."

"I've had days to linger on how angry I am while I worked on a reason against marrying you that would compel the council to agree. How dare you try to force me! How dare you use my council against me! The very laws I swore to uphold!"

Her voice was a screech, her anger ringing through the trees. Magic swirled around them, leaves rustling. It sent birds scattering, none willing to remain close. The birds were not the only ones fleeing, most creatures fearful on an instinctive level of what was happening. Celiaen had seen what she could do in a forest when angry. She had caught him in tree roots many times when trying to slow him down. Pressing in closer, he hissed in warning.

"None of your dirty tricks, dear heart. Just you, me, and our blades."

Eirian kicked at him, and Celiaen moved out of the way. Free from the knife at her throat, she held her blades at the ready. She carefully stepped away from the roots of the tree for fear of tripping. Eyes narrowing, he slipped his knife back into its sheath and drew his swords. The forest went still as the two mages waited for the other to make the first move. Magic lay like a thick blanket in the surrounding air, the bond magnifying their feelings.

"You know all about dirty tricks! I'm supposed to trust you, Celi, but you betrayed me."

"What did you expect me to do? I saw an opportunity, and I took it, just like during a fight! You find the opening, and you take it!" Celiaen snarled.

Swinging, he forced her to step back. Matching Celiaen's blows, she realized she was at a disadvantage. Reminded of the weight of the haubergeon, Eirian did her best to hide it from him. It was a wasted effort when he saw straight through her attempts. He always did. Nothing she did in a fight was a surprise. He knew her every move, every instinct driving her.

"If you love me, you would've respected my refusal."

"But I'm a selfish boy who can't share," he said mockingly.

She cursed Llewellyn, knowing he had gotten his revenge by telling Celiaen what she had said. His strikes continued, quick and testing, and Eirian parried them. He was holding back, taunting her with the fact he was aware she was off balance. No one could keep up with him when he did not check his abilities. It was one thing they had bonded over early on. They each understood how it felt to hold back their magic constantly.

"Why would I give up on what I want because you said no?"

"What I said—"

Flinching as she parried a heavy blow, Eirian felt her heel catch a root and glanced down, giving him an opening on purpose. Seeing what she did, Celiaen backed away and refused the opportunity. She did not need to look where she was walking. Most of the time, her magic saw for her, guiding each step before she placed her foot down. Shaking his head, he huffed impatiently while Eirian shifted, watching him warily. Then, changing her stance, she observed the ground between them.

"What, Eirian? You didn't think I'd find out? You didn't think it would hurt me? Well, you're wrong."

"I thought you'd understand why I said the things I did!"

Angry with him, Eirian felt the magic echoing her feelings, the thrum of it filling every bit of space in the small glade. Circling her, Celiaen watched and waited. His rage whispered, urging him to end it. It did not want him to kill her. It never wanted him to do that, and he would never hurt her. It urged him to end the fight and take the victory, so he could claim what was his.

"No, I don't understand. You're so infuriating!"

"You're not the only one to call me that recently."

Lunging, Eirian miscalculated his block and wound up on the ground, rolling onto her back as quickly as she could, intending to defend herself. It had been half-intentional because she wanted to get to talking without the weapons between them. Following her down, Celiaen pressed the tip of his sword to Eirian's chest while holding the other above his head, knees on either side as he straddled her.

"Enough, Ree, before you get hurt."

Letting go of her blades, Eirian lay in the grass and stared up the length of steel at his face, watching the flicker of magic in his eyes. Knowing she had released the weapons, the bloodlust faded from both of them. They had been in this position before, more times than she could remember, but never as angry with each other as they were.

"You're right. I'm going to get hurt. I'm not prepared for this fight."

"Why do you have to be so stubborn?"

Bringing his arm down, Celiaen tossed his swords to the side, remaining above her. His anger faded like the bloodlust had, taking Eirian's with it. In its place, the bond called to them, strengthened by the physical contact. It urged them to be closer, a constant whisper to surrender to the magic. Instead of giving in, they knew they had to resist it and finish their argument.

"You're one to complain about stubbornness. I probably learned it from you," Eirian replied.

Sliding his hands along her arms, Celiaen pressed her wrists into the ground and hung his head, staring at her. Eirian saw the hurt in his gaze and hated that she caused it. She never wanted to hurt him, but it always seemed to end up that way. Above him, the leaves drifted in the breeze and, watching them shift, she noticed the clusters of flowers. It created a soothing background, something she could focus on.

"Why Gal? What does he have that I don't? Why can't you admit you love me?"

Closing her eyes, Eirian sighed. The press of Celiaen's magic was familiar and welcoming, the mix with her own intoxicating. She felt their bond strongly, the pull of it demanding a surrender she was unwilling to offer. Eirian considered returning to the council and taking back her decision. If they ordered her to marry Celiaen, it would take away her choice, and maybe she could accept it. They would give her a logical reason to stop fighting.

"I'm sorry, Celi, I don't know. You want answers I can't give you."

Celiaen whispered, "I waited for you the other night. All night I waited, but you never came."

"What do you mean?"

"Your cousin came to tell me you were in a state and drinking. I know you don't drink because you fear a loss of control. Everett told me you'd suggested you might seduce me. By the powers, I was so hopeful. I waited, and after a while, I debated going to you. I guess I figured you might've been angry enough that seeing me would be all we needed."

Feeling the press of a tree root against the edge of her shoulder blade, Eirian shifted, and Celiaen tightened his grip on her wrists, settling his weight on her legs. The pain gave her a new focus to cling to and avoid the bond's drag. It was a better thing to use than the leaves.

Eirian told him, "I didn't get drunk. Let me up, Celi, please."

Smirking, Celiaen pulled her wrists together and held them down with one hand, bringing his free hand to Eirian's face to cup her cheek. She caught herself turning to kiss his palm, swallowing when he chuckled. He knew what she had intended to do. Tracing patterns against her skin, he let his fingers graze over her jaw and behind her ear, observing the flutter of her eyelashes at the sensation.

"I don't think so," he murmured. "I rather like you right where you are. You're mine, Ree, no one else can ever have you completely except me."

"You can't just claim me."

"But I did, and you claimed me. We're married, bound for the rest of our lives more tightly than a contract could hope to bind. We can feel each other's heartbeat."

Running his thumb over her lips, Celiaen leaned down until his face was a finger's width from hers. She stayed perfectly still, holding her breath in anticipation of his kiss. It did not come, and he moved, ghosting his lips over her cheek slowly while his fingers stroked the other. Anticipation made her squirm, earning a chuckle.

Nose flaring, Eirian whispered, "Celi, please don't."

"Don't what? You started this. You fueled our anger and ran from it, knowing I'd chase after you. Knowing I'd defeat you like I always do. Like you always want me to. This is how we end up this close time and time again."

Burying his nose in her hair, Celiaen inhaled sharply. Eirian smelled like flowers. She always smelled like flowers, and he wanted to know if she tasted like them as well. Every time he had lingered outside the room while she was with Galameyvin, the scent had intensified, becoming so thick in the air that he would choke on it. Despite the forest around them and the natural smells accompanying it, Eirian was a garden of flowers.

He told her, "I wasn't expecting you to give up so easily, but I suppose you weighed yourself down with mail when you haven't worn it in years. Either way, the victor gets the spoils, and I plan to take my time enjoying my win."

"Let me take it off, and we can go another round. I promise it will be a fairer fight, and I won't let you win again."

Attempting to twist her wrists free, Eirian winced when the root dug painfully into her back. Despite the wards on the layers of armor, it hurt more than hitting the ground had. A blow would have been preferable.

Celiaen's voice was low as he said, "Why would I let you do that when I have you where I want you? Hardly seems like a fair deal to me."

Narrowing her eyes, Eirian replied, "How about you let me up before I hurt myself on this blasted tree root digging into my back?"

"You ask so nicely, Ree."

Releasing her hands, Celiaen twisted himself and rolled onto the ground beside her, using his motions to pull Eirian over on top of him. With a smirk, he reached up and plucked a leaf from her hair. Balancing herself with her hands on his chest, she felt the result of their sparring and proximity. She suspected he had positioned her there on purpose to taunt her.

"Is that better?"

She huffed. "Well, now you can have a root in the back."

"If you're offering."

Eirian lightly punched his shoulder and shook her head. "That's not what I meant."

Celiaen stared at Eirian with his hands resting on her thighs. "You're changing before my eyes, losing your carefree streak. Something is weighing on you, and I can't figure it out. Why won't you confide in me like you used to? I've never betrayed you, and I never will."

"But you just did, didn't you? I turned you down, and you went behind my back, hoping to use my kingdom's laws against me. How did you think I'd feel?"

"We're inevitable, Ree. I feel it in the bond. Eventually, it will force us together. I know you too well. You'd hate to betray the man you married. You're so loyal it hurts, and your loyalty will tear you apart. So marry me, make me your consort, and you don't have to worry about it. Then, all of your loyalties would come together."

Glancing away, Eirian closed her eyes and opened her mind to their bond. She thought she would burst when their magic combined, leaving her breathless. Beneath her, she felt Celiaen like he was part of her, and she remembered what it was like when they fought together with the link open. Her mind conjured images of their blades swinging together with blood dripping from the tips and their movements a perfect mirror.

The dig of Celiaen's fingers against her scalp when he buried his hands in her hair was enough to redirect Eirian's thoughts. He pulled her down to kiss her forcefully, and she could not help responding. Grinding against him, she contemplated letting go before clawing back a touch of control over her magic. It would be easy to give in.

"Don't you dare bring up the bloodlust," he said, growling.

"I didn't mean to!" Hands trapped awkwardly, Eirian struggled and whimpered. "Celi."

Tightening his grip on her head, Celiaen kissed her again. She relaxed against him. The whisper of magic drowned out the voice at the back of her mind that tried to warn her not to do anything stupid. She wanted to whisper the truth against his lips, admit what they both knew.

He murmured against her lips, "Tell me what you're hiding from me. The secret weighing so heavily I can taste it. You fear it."

Stiffening, Eirian stopped moving and swallowed nervously. His words were like a bucket of water emptied over her head.

"Celi."

"I love you more than anything, Ree, and there is no one you can trust more than me."

"I know, but that doesn't mean I can tell you everything."

"Tell me, or I'll make you."

Chuckling, Celiaen let go of her head with one hand and slid it down Eirian's back until it was on her backside. Ignoring the painful drag on her hair, she pushed herself up and stared at him. She wanted to tell him everything. It had been the truth when he said there was no one she could trust more than him.

"You don't understand how serious it is."

"It can't be that bad." Moving his hands to her hips, Celiaen felt the mail and grumbled, "I should let you strip out of this mail before I have you on your back again."

"You're incorrigible! At least have the decency to focus on one thing."

Eirian grabbed at his hands, pulling them from her hip so she could roll to the side. Sitting on the ground beside Celiaen, she rubbed her face and sighed heavily. She had never kept secrets from him, and it was uncomfortable to do so.

He sat up and admitted, "I find you spill more when you are flustered. Take the mail off, we can go that second round, and when I have you pinned beneath me—"

"My mother was a duine."

Celiaen stared at her in shock and muttered, "I wasn't expecting that."

"By the powers, Celiaen, you can't tell anyone. Ever!"

"Eirian, do you realize the seriousness of this?"

She dragged a hand through her hair and nodded. "It's all I can think about. I try not to think about it, but that makes it worse, like when I came into my bloodlust. Nothing distracts me for long. I constantly fear the Telmians will realize what I am and reveal it to everyone. I feel sick from the constant worry."

"And angry. That explains why I've felt what I have from you. How did you find out?"

Crossing his legs, Celiaen reached out and grasped her hands, the touch calming her agitation. Eirian entwined their fingers together, focusing on the contact. She always felt safe when he touched her. However, the most peace she felt was when Galameyvin was on the other side of her, holding her other hand. Together, they provided her with a tether, and she wished he was with them.

"My last visit with my father. Nolan thought I was my mother and was going on about something. I played along to find out what it was. I wish I hadn't."

"Nolan knew what your mother was? He's kept this secret for years, but surely he realized it would come out? What will they say when you steadily get older without aging?"

Eirian said, "I don't know what either of them thought. Siani made him promise to remain silent. She came to Endara specifically to marry him and have me. Foresight, Celi, she knew the darkness was coming. She knew I had to exist."

"Which is why you believe them. It truly wasn't the first time you'd heard mention of it," Celiaen replied, feeling at a loss.

"Yes, and no. I'd heard things here and there that mentioned darkness, but the Telmians were the first to call it a threat. All I know is I wish I hadn't accepted the crown, and my father should never have let me. He should've talked me out of it, knowing what I am and what was in my future."

"A half-blood. The very thing you feared the people wouldn't accept out of a union with me, and it adds to the reasons you keep finding to avoid marrying me formally. How was your mother able to hide from her people for so long? I thought they're forbidden to leave Telmia."

Looking at her hands, Eirian stared at the seal and admitted, "I think Neriwyn helped. I didn't dare press for more details. She hid so I could be born here. I'm a pawn, Celi, tied to the strings of a fate set forth by gods that didn't stick around to watch."

"The Altira, that's what this is about, whatever it means. In a few days, you'll leave to tour Endara. I'll ride with you for as long as you let me, and we can claim I'm surveying the border for myself to report back to my father. Truth is that since we met, I've never wanted to leave your side, and Paienven already suggested I might spend a lot of time in Endara."

"I don't resemble them, do I? People have always made comments about how maybe I wasn't completely human. I thought it was because of my power, but maybe there is something else that we don't see."

He pursed his lips and replied, "Well, having finally met your cousins, you look like them. Certainly more than I look like mine. It's undeniable that you're related. Everett has the same eyes as you, and Llewellyn's sister has your smile. You don't seem to be anything other than human, but sometimes you look… different. The magic makes you different, and everyone has always put that down to the amount of power you possess."

Throwing her hands in the air, Eirian said, "But what if it's not? That's what makes it so frustrating. I don't know what might give me away. They're under orders not to leave. I suppose Neriwyn intends to make sure I remain where he wants me."

"I think we should keep going as we are. We keep it secret and focus on Athnaral. Whenever you feel like it's getting too much, come to me, and you can let it out. I can always distract you. After everything is over with Athnaral, there will be something else to focus on. Maybe I can ask the delegation questions that you can't."

"Like what? Who my mother might be? Have you had any correspondence from your father? Strange things are going on out there, and I fear what it means." There was a shadow in her eyes, and he frowned.

"Like what?" Celiaen echoed her question.

Eirian shook her head, saying, "It's a collection of whispers and shadows that plague me. Howell told me they've had increasing reports of madness. I feel like we need to send for help from Riane, but my deal with your uncle."

"So, you haven't suggested it to your council. I know what you asked of Tynan."

Sighing, Celiaen uncrossed his legs and bent his knees, resting his arms on them. She studied him, resisting the desire to pull him into a hug.

He muttered, "I still can't believe you made a deal with Baenlin."

"It seemed like a sure win. I guess it is now. Baenlin can't drag me to Riane if I run away to Telmia."

"He is persistent. If he found out about our bond, I fear what he would do."

Grinning at the thought that crossed her mind, Eirian held back a giggle and used it to tease him. "He loves power, and this bond makes us more powerful together."

"No way. No! Not an option. I do not share my toys, remember. We can run away to Telmia together, and Gal is there. I have siblings. My father won't miss me. The powers know I'm not his favorite, and he'd prefer it if I wasn't the firstborn." Throwing a stick at her, Celiaen gave Eirian a scandalized look.

"I think the archmage is a rather overwhelming presence. Baenlin's control is awe-inspiring, and I don't think he's a selfish little boy."

Growling, Celiaen launched himself and tackled Eirian to the ground. "No, Baenlin is an even more selfish man who'd destroy something he couldn't have to stop others from having it. Where do you think I get it from?"

Laughing, Eirian pushed at him half-heartedly, and Celiaen's laughter joined hers. He caught her hands, pinning her down with a smile.

"Get off me, you oaf. I think we've rolled around on the ground enough for today." She giggled.

"I disagree. We haven't rolled around nearly enough. Though you still have this blasted mail on. Who thought it was a good idea to give you mail?"

Celiaen lowered his face to kiss her, and Eirian eagerly met his lips.

"I did," Aiden said, his voice cutting through the clearing. "Looks like I found you in time, Your Majesty."

They froze, and Eirian blushed, saying, "Captain, we didn't hear you."

Aiden crossed his arms and glared at them coldly. "No, I suppose you wouldn't have. You were too busy playing games."

"I'm not playing games, and I made my intentions clear. Ree's teasing me," Celiaen said jokingly.

"Did you just call the Queen of Endara a tease?"

Eirian was not sure she had ever heard Aiden's voice so cold. Celiaen pulled a face and pushed himself off, staggering to his feet before offering her a hand.

He replied, "Apologies, I was still in the playful mood you interrupted."

Unwilling to look at Aiden, Eirian let her gaze drift over the roof of tree branches above them. She admired the way sunlight filtered through, casting an odd glow. The relaxed mood that had come over her after telling Celiaen about her mother vanished.

"I ordered Gabe to keep you out of the woods."

"He tried. I imagine he'll wear his black eye with pride."

Eyes narrowing, she crossed her arms and asked, "I take it this means we have to return to the castle now?"

"You'd be correct. If you weren't my queen, I know what I'd do to you. Both of you! I'm furious. How could the two of you be so fucking reckless?"

Aiden hissed, pointing at the discarded weapons. "You were so busy rolling around in the grass that anyone could've taken you out with a bow."

"You're disappointed in me." Eirian glanced at him as she walked to her swords.

"Damn right I am! If you're lucky, I won't tell Everett. I know how much you like it when you disappoint the people who care for you. Now, pick up your weapons and move your assess back to the horses."

Following the order, the two mages sheathed their swords and followed him, exchanging worried looks. Aiden's anger was palatable, and they felt their magic responding. Quashing it down, Eirian avoided touching Celiaen as they moved.

"I did this to keep our magic from potentially causing harm," she said.

"Fuck your magic. You're the Queen of Endara, and you shouldn't be out in the woods alone. I thought I made it clear to you exactly what I'd do to ensure your safety." Not looking at her, Aiden fingered the hilt of his sword.

"I'm your queen, Aiden."

Her words triggered his anger, and Aiden spun, slamming Eirian against a tree and knocking the wind from her. Despite his fury, he wanted to kiss her and chase the taste and feel of Celiaen from her lips.

"My queen? You should try fucking behaving like one, darling." Pointing at Celiaen when he moved to pull him off, Aiden growled. "Don't you fucking dare, Princeling, or you'll have a black eye to match Gabe. I've got no problem putting you in your place."

Releasing her from his grip, Aiden watched as Eirian coughed and glared at him.

"I should have you flogged."

"But you won't because you know I'm right. If you don't plan to marry the man, you don't go playing in the woods alone with him!"

Eirian caught the jealousy that flickered across his face as Aiden spoke and swallowed uncomfortably. It told her the whole reason behind his anger. She glanced at Celiaen, and he shrugged. He understood what Aiden was feeling, and as much as he disliked the fact it was over the same woman, he did not blame him.

Aiden ignored their silent exchange and continued, "Now, shut the fuck up and keep walking! The longer I take to return you to where you should be, the more lashes Gabe and his men will receive for not preventing you from leaving."

Saluting him coldly, Eirian shared another look with Celiaen before they set off. Winding through the trees, it did not take long to reach the edge of the woods, and they realized they had not gotten far before he had caught up with her. Gabe was waiting with the horses, his eye swollen and bruised. He gave the duo an unreadable look with his other eye before handing over their reins.

Draping the cloak over her shoulders, Eirian double-checked her tack before swinging into the saddle.

"By the way, Ree, you have a gum nut in your hair," Celiaen muttered.

His words earned him a dark look from Aiden. Running her hand through her hair, Eirian plucked the gum nut out and let it drop to the ground.

"Don't say a word."

TWENTY-EIGHT

The city's outer wall cast a shadow over the group as Eirian watched more nobles and guards join the chaos. Leaning forward, she rested her arms on the pommel with a bored expression. Brenna wore a similar look, her mount showing signs of impatience. Halcyon ignored the other horses, his ears flickering while his tail swished, ready for any signal.

In the distance, a train of wagons had already left. A cloud of dust hung in the air, marking where they progressed. Soldiers accompanied the wagons. Part of their duty was to ensure the road ahead was clear for the nobility. There was no breeze, a stifling heat making Eirian thankful for the shade, and she turned her gaze to the observant guard next to her.

"How much longer do you think, Merle?"

Merle shaded his eyes and looked at the sky before answering. "I don't know. I figure once Aiden joins us, it'll be time to move."

At the mention of Aiden, Eirian scowled. "Has he calmed down?"

"He's as calm as a swarm of angry bees."

Beside him, Fox scoffed. "I think I'd rather deal with the bees than the cap'n."

"There's no need to make Her Majesty feel any worse." Tobin leaned forward on his mount and looked down the line at Eirian, saying, "Our thanks for stopping him from having Kip and the rest flogged."

Brenna shook her head at Eirian. "You should have him replaced. I know he is who he is but the behavior he has displayed in recent days—"

"Has been almost entirely my fault. Aiden is increasingly paranoid, and I haven't made it easier for him. When we return, he'll settle down. Until then, we'll clash again." Eirian checked the positioning of her bow and quivers, making sure her sword was not interfering with her draw.

"He's not the only paranoid one," Merle muttered, glancing at his squad.

Arching a brow, she gave him a pointed look and said, "I'm barely armed compared to you."

Opening his mouth to argue, Merle stopped when her attention shifted to the approach of Llewellyn. He brought his horse to a halt and gave Eirian a cocky grin before pointing over his shoulder at the other riders milling around. Shrugging, she waited for him to speak.

"As much as I'd love to be touring with you, thank you for making me remain. I forgot what a headache this lot is. I'll enjoy running your kingdom for you."

"You know why I did it." Eirian smiled. "You have important things to do."

Glancing at Brenna and Isabella, Llewellyn grumbled, "When you decide on something, you don't lose time making it happen."

Isabella grinned, saying, "You don't know what you're in for, Your Grace."

"I don't doubt it for a second, Lady Isabella," he replied, and returned the grin.

"I know you're better suited to coming with me than Everett, but you were the one who had a bride in mind. If it had been him, he'd be the one staying." Eirian swiped a hand over her forehead to wipe the beads of sweat away. "Finalize that contract. I've signed my part. Then get on with making me an heir."

"You're making me feel like a prize stud, and I'm not entirely sure I like it." There was a puzzled frown on Llewellyn's face as he said, "But I suppose I can't complain. It's part of being who we are."

Eirian cocked her head to the side and replied, "Yes, it is, but I'm entirely selfish. I need you to give me heirs. If you and Everett don't provide, they'll put pressure back on me."

Scowling, Brenna shook her head, saying, "It's not the end of the world."

"I have my reasons."

"Yes, you've made that clear."

Her gaze flickered to the Telmian group further along the wall. Eirian felt nerves settle into the pit of her stomach again.

"Don't worry, Llewellyn, we'll have messengers going between. I won't abandon you."

He answered, "I'm a man of action, Eirian."

"I know, but you can't change it now. I see the reports, and I know you do a good job. Do your best not to send my kingdom into chaos."

"I suspect you're far more likely to send it into chaos than I am. Please, I beg you, don't make a mess and leave me to clean up. I'd make a bloody terrible king."

Llewellyn grinned at her. Frowning, Eirian watched the horizon without speaking before looking at the sky and scrunching her nose. There was a prickle of energy to the air, a sense that her magic recognized, and she knew what it meant.

"We need to get moving."

"Well, true, you don't want to be traveling late into the night."

"No, that's not it. There's a storm brewing."

Her gaze found Celiaen in the crowd of elves, his eyes turning to her when he sensed her watching him, and she wondered if he felt it too. Storms attracted Eirian, the raw power finding an outlet in her magic. Despite the trip to their first stop, the prospect of walking through lightning gave her a thrill.

"I won't pretend to understand how you know, but you're right. It's time everything got moving. Be careful, Eirian, don't get yourself or Everett killed. I'll look after things here, don't worry." Llewellyn sighed, turning his horse away, saying, "I'll find Everett and let him know."

"Thank you, Llewellyn."

Merle was watching her and said, "If we're not waiting any longer, I'll send Fox to let the captain know."

"Unless you fancy moving this lot through foul weather, then yes, we're going. Ask the daoine if they can influence the weather. I can sense it changing, and that's all."

Nudging Halcyon, Eirian felt his eagerness to move, his neck stretching out as he tugged at the reins. Signaling to Fox to find Aiden, Merle and the rest of the guards were careful to keep their mounts close to Eirian and her two ladies. Eirian wove her way through the groups to the road, where mounted soldiers waited.

Sparing them a sympathetic look, Eirian knew they would be hot and uncomfortable with their armor on in the sunlight. Though most only wore a hauberk and jerkin, she could testify to the discomfort on a hot day. It took nothing more than seeing Eirian guide her mount to the road to signal that it was time to move. Nobles and their retinues followed as Halcyon tread steadily to the front, where Cameron waited with other high-ranking officers.

Saluting, Cameron caught sight of Everett behind her and asked, "Ready to leave?"

"I've been ready for hours. We can't delay any longer. We need to move." Eirian leaned forward in the saddle and flicked a thumb at the horizon, explaining, "The weather is turning."

"Well then, after you, Your Majesty."

Cameron did not question her last statement. His years of experience had taught him that mages knew things he did not. Calls rippled down the line, and they started forward. Glancing at Everett, Eirian could see the question on his tongue and smiled at him before allowing Halcyon to match the other horses' pace. Not wanting to distract from the reality that she was leaving, she turned in her saddle and looked back at the walls of Amath. Her eyes sought the castle rising above it all with the bright blue sky behind.

Something tugged at Eirian's mind, a feeling of dread and the suggestion she would not be returning. She dismissed the feeling and reminded herself it was not the first time she had left the city. Despite her efforts, the shadow in the corner of her eye was present and tugged at her mind. Continuously glancing back as they moved further and further away, Eirian watched Amath grow smaller against the sky, shadows chasing at the edge of her vision.

"You're quieter than I expected," Everett said.

Her eyes scanned over the green land, broken only by crops and the odd stone wall built to keep livestock from wandering too far. "Am I? I have a lot on my mind."

"I understand. You said the weather is going to turn?"

"Yes, it is. I feel the change in the air. It's something I've always sensed. Hopefully, we'll reach the first town before it begins."

The shrill scream of a bird caused them to look at the sky, and Eirian's eyes narrowed at the form of a large eagle circling above them. Shaking his head, Everett's mouth twisted in a puzzled scowl.

"I wasn't aware we were bringing any hunting birds."

"That's not a hunting bird," she whispered.

Eirian turned to scan the lines of riders behind her. Something about the bird was familiar. It tugged at memories, and when she tried to recall them, they drifted out of reach. The sensation had always plagued her, but it was getting worse.

"What do you mean?"

"I knew it was possible, but I didn't expect to see it. That is a duine. One of our visitors is a shapeshifter." Unable to spot them, Eirian shifted back to facing forwards and shook the unease that had settled on her. "I imagine they have a way of communicating."

Awe filled his face, and Everett stared up at the bird, watching it circle, gliding on winds he could not see. He was not the only one who did so.

"Everyone knows those stories, but I didn't think they were real."

"I'd love to become a bird. Just imagine what the world looks like from up there! How did you know what it is?" Isabella was breathless, watching from her horse behind them.

"How do I know anything? Magic."

Laughing, Isabella continued staring and asked, "Do you wish you could do that?"

Contemplating the question, Eirian ignored the curious looks Everett and Brenna were directing her way. She imagined the freedom having wings could give her, wondering if she could learn to do it given the time.

"Without knowing how much power they need to maintain the transformation or the consequences, I can't say if I'd want to shapeshift," Eirian answered.

"You take the fun out of imagining," Brenna said. "I'd like to be a cat."

"A cat?" Everett scoffed.

Silent, Eirian let them talk around her. Her gaze flickered back and forth as frequently as her horse flicked his ears, her shoulders tense. She recounted reports of crop failure, watching farmers stop in their fields to observe them ride past. Farming was not something she knew much about, but she thought the crops surrounding Amath looked healthy. Her magic confirmed it and provided a little relief over the matter.

Thoughts of the darkness chased away the rest. She did not want to think about the mysterious threat, but the whispers dragged it forward. Her companions realized Eirian was not listening and fell silent, sharing looks behind her back. She swayed to Halcyon's movements, paying the horse no attention as her hands barely touched the reins.

Everett leaned back and gave Brenna another puzzled look, whispering, "Do you think she's meditating?"

"I'm not meditating," Eirian answered in amusement. "I'm observing and thinking."

"Dare I ask what about?"

Waving at a field of cattle, Eirian shrugged and offered the most logical of her thoughts. "I'm worried about those reports. What if the crop failure spreads? What is causing it? We had reports from Caerwel and Periyit. They're on the border, and I worry it is Aeyren's doing. But how could he be responsible?"

"Magic?" Brenna asked.

"I hope not, but if it is some sort of disease affecting the plants, I don't know how we can stop it. The magic we can stop. However, it would require a fair amount of power to destroy entire fields overnight. I could do it, but I don't know of any others who could."

Eirian did not mention her fear that it was the darkness. It was easy to guess how they would react to such a suggestion.

Everett cast a speculative glance at the bird overhead and asked, "You don't think?"

Shaking her head furiously, Eirian silenced him. "No. No, I don't. I don't think the Telmians would bother doing something like that. Athnaral would gain from pushing us towards a disaster. There hasn't been widespread famine in Endara for generations."

"It's not that serious."

"Yet. We can't know what will happen, but I want to inspect any affected farms we pass. I can discover if it is magic causing the problem."

"She's right. We have to think about worst-case scenarios. That's our job. We must prepare for the worst to protect the people and ensure we can provide for them. A hungry population is unhappy, and an unhappy population becomes rebellious." Concerned about her lands, Brenna added, "Raellwynt is the biggest wheat-producing region in the kingdom. I fear every day we'll receive reports our crops are failing."

"Oh, wife, you're stressing again." Marcellus sounded gruff as he brought his mount in beside Brenna and bowed to Eirian. "Majesty."

"Anything to report?" Eirian inquired.

Marcellus rubbed his chin tiredly and told her, "Nothing but complaints about the heat, and it feels like a storm is coming."

Laughing, Eirian shared a look with Everett. "I told you!"

"How do you know, Marcellus?" Everett asked, looking perplexed.

"I'm an old man. I can feel it in my bones."

Confused by Eirian's laughter, Marcellus looked at Brenna for an explanation. Brenna smiled in amusement and winked at him before she answered his unspoken question.

"Eirian made us move because she felt a storm brewing."

Arching his brows, Marcellus nodded and said, "I've heard mages can do that. Have you got an explanation for our circling friend up there?"

"It's one of the Telmians. Have we got eyes on them? I'd like to avoid questions about their motives by having the answers first." Stretching, Eirian patted Halcyon gently, the horse snorting as he walked.

"Yes, we do. I believe the elves are also monitoring them. I don't like them. They've been scandalizing the court. Why won't they leave?"

"King Neriwyn has ordered them to watch over me. Unfortunately, we can't risk their ire by refusing. I want them gone as much as anyone else." She paused before turning to him abruptly and saying, "What do you mean scandalizing the court?"

Isabella giggled. "He means they frequently visit different beds."

"That's hardly a concern so long as it was consensual."

Marcellus looked at Eirian in horror. "Excuse me?"

Waving, Eirian dismissed his shock and said, "They're new, beautiful, and mysterious. People want to experience it for themselves. The daoine enjoy the fascination to its fullest. My only concern is if they use magic to manipulate anyone."

"I don't know how you can be so relaxed about it!"

"I don't know why you'd expect me to be otherwise. I'm a mage, and I'm certainly not a child. I'm extremely aware of what goes on between consenting adults!"

Pursing her lips, Brenna looked between them. "Considering I have to live with both of you, I'd like out of this argument. However, while I know nothing about your activities when you lived in Riane, I know you haven't been indiscreet since you returned. There's no need to act worried, Marcellus."

Everett stared at Eirian with understanding, asking, "Riane didn't care what you did?"

"No, not really. The only time anyone gets involved is if it causes issues. Magic doesn't provide immunity from emotions. It heightens what we feel, and mages get jealous like anyone else. They start fights over lovers scorned," she replied.

Eirian picked up the sound of hooves pounding towards them. Heads turned as more armed men brought their horses in to surround them, and she met Aiden's displeased gaze. Scowling, she pursed her lips and tilted her chin up in the slightest of acknowledgments. Able to sense she was in no mood to speak, the nobles grew quiet. In the distance, Eirian picked the darkening line of clouds, and her worry grew.

Casting a look up at the shapeshifter, she waved at it, knowing the moment the bird sensed her. Eirian pushed through the guards and ignored Aiden's grumbling as she encouraged the horse into a canter to break free of the line. With guards following, she brought Halcyon to a halt a short distance from the column while she waited for the bird to circle down and land. Eyes locked on the form, Eirian sensed the approach of Celiaen, his companions, and other daoine.

"You can't break off from everyone like that!" Aiden scolded, and her lack of response infuriated him further.

Hitting the ground, the massive bird shimmered, and Eirian watched in amazement. The ripples of magic transformed the bird into the smiling and naked form of Saoirse, her red hair gleaming in the sunlight. Aiden was quick to shut his mouth, equally amazed as everyone else. Shaking his head, Faolan stared patiently at Eirian.

"The storm ahead. How long do we have?" Eirian asked, taking her time to give Saoirse an appreciative look.

"Do you like what you see?" Saoirse replied, batting her eyes at Eirian and tucking a curl behind her ear.

Smiling, Eirian nodded and told her, "Yes, I do. You're a beautiful woman, and I like beautiful women very much. Especially when they're beneath me. Now, the storm?"

Cocking her head to the side, Saoirse peered skywards, answering, "We'll cross its path before nightfall."

"I thought as much. Is there anything you can do?" Directing her second question to Faolan, Eirian met his amused gaze.

"While I appreciate the flattery in your assumption, no, there isn't." Faolan grinned and winked, leaning forward to ask, "Can you?"

Bristling at the hint of challenge in his tone, Eirian's eyes narrowed. She heard the snickers of two of Celiaen's companions, recognizing the voices as Link and Harlow. Like the rest of Celiaen's companions, they knew her abilities to manipulate a storm did not involve ending it.

"It was a simple question. I'm unaware of the full abilities you possess. This was a surprise," Eirian said, and waved at Saoirse.

"As we stand here talking, the storm continues to move. I'll take to the skies while I can." Eyes returned to Saoirse as she spread her arms, the strange ripple beginning as she transformed.

"She's right about the weather. We should pick up the pace, but, Ree, you've done similarly in the past." Celiaen pointed at the horses, saying, "Do you think?"

Curious, Faolan cocked his head to the side and asked, "You can control them?"

"No, not exactly." Eirian shook her head vehemently, explaining, "Twenty to thirty horses I can manage, but I couldn't keep this many calm. Best we push the pace and hope those who left earlier make it to the first town before the weather turns."

"And you don't have Gal," Alyse commented. "The rest of us blues aren't enough."

"I'll send men along the train to tell everyone. I don't suggest pushing too hard for the moment. We don't want tired horses if we get caught," Aiden said, glancing at the horizon. "If only we could predict the weather."

Tara muttered, "They try to in Riane, but it's never very successful more than a day out."

Nodding to the group, Eirian nudged Halcyon. "Well, let's not waste any more time."

Signaling to the men who had accompanied her, Aiden sent them racing along the line to pass the message along. Glaring at Celiaen when he started after Eirian, he followed and kept his gaze locked on the back of her head. He watched her grin at Celiaen before pushing her mount into a canter. The two friends raced with whooping laughter. Aiden followed, catching words on the breeze as they mocked each other, their horses a match in stride.

Eirian was speaking to Marcellus and Everett when Aiden caught up.

"We need to pick up the pace," she told them.

"I've sent men along the line to spread the order." Aiden nodded to the two noblemen and ignored the mocking look Celiaen directed at him when he spoke.

Everett sighed. "We should've left earlier. It is ridiculous how long it takes to get moving."

"Large numbers require time and coordination," Celiaen said. "It makes war a lengthy process. You can't maneuver thousands of troops with the snap of your fingers."

Brenna replied, "This is hardly thousands."

"No, it's worse. It's nobility!" Grinning, Celiaen cackled in amusement.

Holding up her hands, Eirian said, "Regardless, it's done! We need to move quickly but tiring no one out. Marcellus, do we have the equipment to strike a camp if we don't make it to the town in time?"

Marcellus shook his head. "It's all on the supply train. I hate to admit it, but no one thought about a storm hitting as we left Amath."

"Well, at least it's a late spring storm, and we don't have to worry about freezing."

Dropping a hand to Halcyon's neck, Eirian ran her fingers through his mane, feeling the coarse strands against her skin. She shared a look with Celiaen, remembering all the times they had found shelter from storms. He winked at her, and she smiled faintly.

"We should send a rider ahead to catch up with the train," Brenna said.

Agreeing, Marcellus turned to a guard. "I know the rider."

Remaining on the column's outer line, Eirian wanted to make the ride herself. It would be nothing to Halcyon to race the distance, and the desire for solitary freedom was strong. Glancing at Celiaen, she knew he could read the thought in her mind, and he shook his head, gaze flicking at Aiden on the other side of her. Rolling her eyes, she was glad Aiden could not see her face.

"What are you going to do when the old boy needs to retire?" Celiaen asked, watching the way she fiddled with Halcyon's mane as they trotted along.

Eirian frowned. "I haven't considered that."

"He's been your horse for a long time."

"A good ten years. I have awhile before I need to consider a replacement. Why?"

Celiaen shrugged, and his grip on the reins loosened as he said, "I suppose I brought it up as a light topic of conversation. He's getting gray hairs in his ears."

"Don't pay him any heed, Halcyon, my love. You're my good boy." Scratching his neck, Eirian smiled when the horse tossed his head. "I know, Celi. However, after I finish this, will I need such a mount? I won't be riding off on any adventures."

"You never know!" he said, a hint of sadness in his eyes.

"Do your parents go off on adventures?" Aiden asked.

Prepared to argue, Celiaen shut his mouth when Eirian gave him a desperate look and muttered, "No, I suppose you're right."

Frowning at them, Aiden could tell it was not what Celiaen had intended to say. Suspicious, he looked at the bird soaring above before looking back at Eirian. She gave him a wide-eyed, innocent look he knew was for show.

Aiden told her, "Should we see war with Athnaral, you'll be glad to never go on another adventure."

"You don't need to remind me that war is bad. I'm not a fool," Eirian replied.

Her flare of anger had the horses snorting and shying. Clenching a fist, Eirian pulled her magic back to herself. The last thing she wanted was to cause the horses to bolt.

She added, "You don't know what I've seen."

"Well, you're acting like this is a jaunt through the countryside. So, I'll keep reminding you."

Eirian saw the nervous looks on Everett's and Brenna's faces as they glanced continuously at her. The prickle of Alyse and Tynan's magic reminded her they were close, and she took a deep breath to calm her temper.

"I'm acting like it's a jaunt through the countryside because, if I recall correctly, that's what we've said it is. You attended many of the meetings where we discussed it. A nice tour of the kingdom for the newly crowned queen."

"I didn't think you were that good at pretending. You sure fooled me."

Aiden watched her nostrils flare as Eirian clenched her jaw. Muscles twitched in her cheeks, a warning sign of her frustration. There was a concerned expression on Celiaen's face that made him wonder if he had pushed a little too far.

"It hardly takes skill to fool you. Perhaps you don't deserve your position, Captain," Eirian said.

Smirking, Aiden encouraged his mount forward and replied, "Thank you for confirming my suspicions, Your Majesty."

Everett shook his head and nudged his horse. "I'll have a word with him."

Feeling the blood drain from her face, Eirian shared a look with Celiaen. She read the thoughts flickering through his eyes and took a deep breath, pushing her concerns from the forefront of her mind. Not trusting herself to speak, she watched the horizon. The further they rode, the darker it grew. Making its descent, the sun was creeping closer to the growing mass of dark, angry clouds.

Eirian felt the heaviness in the air. It made her sweat, even though the temperature was slowly dropping along with the sun. Dark stains appeared on the horses' coats, and a hand to Halcyon's neck came away damp. Wiping it off on her leg, she looked at the rolling green of the countryside and hoped farmers were securing their livestock.

Shouts from the front drew Eirian's attention to a rider approaching. Urging Halcyon, she hurried to meet them to the side of the road. She took in the woman with her hair pulled back in a tight braid. A flicker of recognition hit, and she realized it was the eldest daughter of the countess of Periyit.

"Your Majesty, the town isn't far. When I caught up with the train, they knew about the storm. They're making camp and will notify the town to prepare for you."

"Thank you. You know this land. Can you say if we'll make it before the storm does?" Eirian queried, bringing herself in next to the younger woman.

She replied, "Absolutely. We're close enough that you can pick up the pace without risking the horses."

Reaching out, Eirian touched the other horse and allowed her magic to flow through to the animal, refreshing its energy. Startled, horse and rider shied, the woman giving her a frightened look.

Eirian told her, "I shared a little energy."

"You can do that?" Her fear turned to amazement. "Thank you, ma'am. I'm honored!"

Giving the command to increase the pace, Eirian cocked her head curiously. "Why did the duke send you?"

"Because I'm one of the best riders in the kingdom, and I know the land and the town," she said with pride.

"She's right. That's why I picked her," Marcellus said as he joined them.

They watched people canter along the road in silence. Allowing a few more to pass, Eirian nodded at Marcellus.

"I trust your judgment, Marcellus, if I didn't, I'd tell you. Now, shall we enjoy this run and race the weather? Because the powers know I could use a run!"

"As you wish, Your Majesty."

Marcellus chuckled, watching Eirian's hands drop and let slack form in her reins to give Halcyon the freedom to stretch his legs. Remaining with him, the young noblewoman watched in admiration as she raced away.

"That's a fine horse. What I wouldn't give to get my hands on some of his breed."

Giving her an amused look, Marcellus remained to the side of the road to observe. He intended to join the tail, overseeing the slower riders.

"If you make yourself valuable to your queen, you never know what favors you might earn," he replied.

"I wish they'd chosen me as one of her ladies, but unfortunately, I'm the eldest. Your advice is smart. I'll make myself useful to her. Perhaps one day, I'll get some of the mage-bred horses and make my name as the breeder of the finest mounts outside of Riane."

"Your ambition is admirable."

She bowed her head at him and started towards where her father was with her siblings. Marcellus knew the countess had remained in Amath. Sighing, he turned his horse and made his way to the back of the line, casting concerned looks at the dark horizon.

TWENTY-NINE

A delegation of the townsfolk was waiting to greet them when they reached their destination. The local reeve stood to the forefront with the tall staff that symbolized her rank. Following through with formalities, Eirian was thankful when the reeve suggested they wait until after the storm to tour the town. Instead, they led her to an inn and showed Eirian where she could sleep for the night.

Eirian listened intently to the old woman while enjoying a bowl of stew in the large common room with a select few. As the storm closed in, it became hard to hear them talking, and the townsfolk excused themselves to return to their homes. Left in the inn with the handful closest to her, Eirian conversed with the innkeeper and her family. She enjoyed listening to what they had to say and learning about their town.

Isabella was the first to retreat to bed, Marcellus and Brenna following soon after. Everett remained sitting near the fire with a mug of warmed ale while talking to the innkeeper's husband. With conversation dwindling, her attention turned to the weather. Eirian excused herself and slipped through the inn's main door to stand on the porch. Rain cascaded from rooftops, water covering the ground, the puddles illuminated with every bolt of lightning that lit the sky.

"It's a beautiful night," Eirian told her guards.

Fionn spluttered. "You think this is a beautiful night, ma'am?"

"Might not be to you, but it's incredible to me. I love storms. Would you like to see?"

"Does it involve getting wet?"

Smiling, Eirian watched the lightning. The energy of the storm prickled over her skin, calling to her. It was different to the ones that battered the cliffs of Riane; the rain lacked the sting of salt that came with sea winds. Inhaling deeply, she loosened some of her hold over her magic and considered her choices. She wanted to run through the rain, feeling the mud between her toes while the power danced over her skin.

"Only if you want to, Fionn."

He watched her unbuckling her belt and said, "Wait, no, what are you doing, Your Majesty? You can't go out there!"

"Don't worry, Fionn, it's perfectly safe for me. Just watch and enjoy the storm."

"If you go out there, I'll have to send for the captain."

"I'm not stopping any of you from accompanying me."

Eirian shoved her weapons into Fionn's hands and removed her armor. Ignoring his continued protests, she stepped down and went out into the rain. No one else was outside except a few guards huddled under sheltered spots. Smiling in the storm's glow, she tilted her face to the sky and closed her eyes, relishing in the feel of the heavy rain pelting her flesh. Flexing her fingers, Eirian felt the energy of the storm as she turned in a circle.

Opening her eyes, she strode down the empty street, her boots squelching in the mud. She heard the guards' protests and almost felt sorry for them having drawn the short straw to follow her out into the rain. The deafening booms of thunder drowned out anything the men said, and Eirian peered into the darkness after each flash of lightning. Then, drawing a deep breath in, she smelled the scent accompanying the storm. It was always difficult to describe, but the first word that came to mind was fresh.

Her magic was wild, and she halted, following the urge to crouch and dig her hands into the mud. Gathering handfuls, Eirian enjoyed the experience of it oozing between her fingers to rejoin the earth. It flowed out to meet the storm, dancing between the connections in the energy. The link her magic had to the life that beat within the ground was stronger, and it made her more powerful. It always did during a storm, and it provided Eirian with a high she could not get from anything else.

"What are you doing?" Paxton shouted in her ear.

Eirian glanced at him, smiling at the way the water ran down his face and dripped from the end of his nose. There was no need for a mirror to tell her she looked the same. A sodden mess soaked through, with her clothes clinging to her as she moved. Later she would regret the wet garments, but she did not care for the moment.

"I'm enjoying the storm," she shouted back. "I haven't done this in months!"

His hand darted to his sword, and his stance shifted nervously when he caught sight of something moving in the darkness. Beside him, Tyler followed suit, preparing to draw if whatever it was they saw was a threat. But, whatever it was, it was not a person.

"What is that?"

Following his pointing hand, Eirian went wide-eyed as lightning illuminated a massive wolf. Its head was high with one paw lifted as though the flash of light had frozen it. At the sight of it, the two guards drew their swords and shouted. Meeting its stare, she recognized the eyes and reached out to put her arm across Paxton's path. He glanced at her, and she shook her head, signaling for him to back down.

Once he had sheathed his sword, Paxton offered a hand. Eirian let him pull her up, and, pushing a lock of wet hair out of her eyes, she stepped towards the wolf. Holding out a hand, she touched the wet fur and waited for the duine to shift back. Whining, the wolf moved away, and Eirian followed him into the open space beyond the town. Monitoring her guards, she crouched beside the creature when he halted.

"Why am I not surprised you're out in this?"

Cocking his head to the side, the wolf regarded her curiously.

"You want to know why I'm out in this, don't you?"

Eirian shook her head, sodden hair whipping across her face, and rested her hands against the ground. The touch of the earth allowed her to reach for the energy crackling through it from the lightning strikes. She could siphon it directly from the air, but did not want to give away everything. So instead, Eirian drew it from the ground, lifting her hands and letting the wolf watch as she pulled the sparks upwards out of the soil.

They danced between her fingers, glittering with power, and she waved her hand, releasing them. It was something that Eirian had always been capable of, and she did not remember the first time. Other things had memories attached to them, moments when the knowledge slotted into place, and she knew she could do it. But not storms. That had always happened, and Eirian assumed it meant it had been an early manifestation of her power. Something that had happened when she was so young that she could not recall it.

"Does that help explain my reason?" she asked him. "Or do I need to make a bigger show of it for you?"

The rain continued to empty heavily from the skies, lightning striking closer as the storm raged. Many flashes lit the sky so brightly that Eirian could have sworn it was daytime. Looking up, she studied the clouds. It was eerie, the glow of the colors unique to the situation. The ripple of magic beside her brought her power wholly to life, and Eirian did not push it down for a change. Instead, she tilted her head back further and closed her eyes against the rain.

"You're no ordinary human, Eirian Altira!"

Faolan's voice rose above the sound of the rain. Waiting to reply after a clap of thunder, she did not look at him. Eirian suspected he would see the anguish his comment caused her if she did.

"I've been told before."

Reaching out, Faolan drew Eirian to stand, and they faced each other. He saw the flicker of power in her eyes, like they were reflecting the lightning in the sky. It was not something he had witnessed before, not even among his own people. Something about it tugged at his memories, an occurrence that had frequently happened since his arrival in Endara. Tharen and Saoirse had mentioned the same feeling, but they had kept it between themselves. None of them wanted to worry the younger members of their group.

"Your power feels familiar, but it isn't."

Eyes wide, Eirian stared at him in fear, wondering if he had detected her duine blood. The thoughts she had pushed from her mind came crashing back. Faolan sensed the spike in her anxiety and debated leaving his questions for another time. He wanted to run with her through the storm while letting her power drive their every step. It was a powerful urge, a wild desperation that would have seen him howl if he had been in his wolf form. But, as much as he wanted it, Faolan wanted answers more.

"What do you mean?"

"I don't know. You can draw energy directly from the storm, can't you?"

The power made her skin tingle, and Eirian wished she had thought to strip before stepping into the rain. Magic like this always felt better when she was naked. Her fingers found the hem of her tunic, tempting her to undress. She wanted to stand naked and pull the lightning into her, just like she used to in the little walled garden on the cliffs on the outskirts of Riane.

"Not just from storms," Eirian informed him.

Leaning forward, Faolan cupped her face and pressed their foreheads together. Startled, Eirian lifted her hands to push him away.

"Let go."

The words made Eirian freeze. His magic washed over her, and she gasped, understanding what Faolan was telling her to do. The heartbeat pounding in her ears was louder than the thunder, and she released what little hold on her magic she still maintained. Joining the energy of the storm, their power made her skin tingle. It was different to what Eirian felt when sharing her power with others, including Celiaen.

Eirian felt their bond at the back of her mind and saw him standing with his head tilted back and fists clenched at his sides. Swallowing, she realized Celiaen felt it washing over him twice as the magic spread across the country-side. When she had taken the energy of a storm in Riane, Eirian had finished the night off with someone, the magic leaving her brimming with need.

Reaching across the bond, she caressed Celiaen, tempted to walk away from Faolan to join him.

Inhaling sharply, Eirian distanced herself from the bond. Then, taking control of the power, she pulled it out of the air and down into the ground, dispersing it into anything she could feed it to. It spread far, and when the light of day arrived, people would know the effects. She saw the sparks in the air in the corner of her vision. As she did, she barely felt Faolan let go of her face and stumble backward.

"What are you?"

A flash of lightning illuminated Faolan, and Eirian cocked her head to the side, noticing for the first time that his skin faintly glowed on its own. Then, riding the power, she raised her hands, daring the storm to strike her. She loved taking a lightning strike, the thrill more than anything else. He reached out, grabbing one of her hands, and his nails digging into her flesh provided enough distraction to bring her focus back to him. Sensing her guards closing in on them, Eirian snarled.

"Let me go."

Her magic surrounded them, ready if Eirian needed it. Faolan felt a flicker of fear but refused to let go. He had underestimated what she could do, and it made him question if Neriwyn had been aware. A voice at the back of his mind expressed anger at the thought he had kept them in the dark.

"Not until you tell me the truth."

"What truth? I'm a powerful mage."

Faolan blinked, drops of water glistening on his eyelashes. It had soaked Eirian through, but it almost seemed like the rain slowed around her. He added it to the list of things he was not sure he had ever encountered before. She was a puzzle he was determined to figure out. No matter what it took.

"You shouldn't be able to do this."

Sneering, Eirian twisted her hand from his grip. She spread her arms wide, inviting the lightning. If Faolan or anyone else needed to see something to prove she was not what they thought her to be, the storm would provide the perfect display. Better this than a field of withered corpses. One would inspire awe, and the other would have them clambering for her head.

"You don't get to decide what I can or can't do."

"Even with your bond to the elf and the extra power it provides."

"I could do this before the bond!"

The wind caught her words, and Eirian watched him struggle to hear over a clap of thunder. It accompanied lightning so close they felt it in the earth beneath their feet. She flexed her fingers, touching against the vibrations in the air she suspected no one else could see. For a moment, she wanted to ask Faolan if he could see them. Eirian figured he would be the most likely to understand what she was talking about.

"But you're human!" he shouted.

Nostrils flaring, Eirian glared at the naked man in the rain, his glow illuminating him. It was enough for her to see the wild growth she was causing. Facing her palms to the ground, she curled her fingers, pulling the energy up and drawing the plants with it. She loved making things grow. It was the most natural feeling in the world to her, and it came as easy as breathing.

"You said it yourself. I'm the Altira mage."

Turning, Eirian let her guards guide her back to the inn. They were silent, too amazed by what they had witnessed to ask questions. Aiden was on the porch with Fionn, and she met his angry stare with fierce defiance. Snatching her things out of Fionn's hands, she trudged past the silent warriors into the warmth and flickering light on the other side of the door. Everett was waiting, a steaming mug in his hands.

"I gather it's wet out there."

Opening her mouth to give him a flippant reply, Eirian shut it again and shook her head. The energy coursing through her made her unwilling to remain to talk. Everett could tell she wanted to leave, but the sight of Aiden lurking encouraged him to put aside the questions he had.

"I'm going to my room to change and dry off. I'll see you in the morning."

"Eirian."

Everett held out the mug, and she shifted her grasp on her things to accept it. The warmth felt good against the icy chill setting into her skin.

"Thank you, Everett."

Chuckling, he watched Eirian leave puddles in her wake. It would be a fun story to tell Brenna and Marcellus in the morning.

"Well, at least you gave the town something to talk about!" Everett called out.

"I'm good at that!"

Hearing stomps, he watched Aiden storm past and said, "I swear you're going to end up killing each other."

"Wouldn't that suit you?" Aiden muttered.

"No, not really. I'm rather fond of both of you. Remember what I said earlier. Please."

Giving Everett a dark look over his shoulder, Aiden snorted and followed Eirian up the stairs to her room, finding her juggling the things in her hands. His stride faltered, gaze taking in the shine of magic coating her skin. It was unmistakable. When she had been out in the storm, he had seen her illuminated in the darkness. They had watched her summon sparks from the ground and air.

"Is he still punishing you, Gabe?" Eirian asked.

Seated on the floor beneath a shuttered window at the end of the hallway, Gabe's eyes darted between Eirian and Aiden. He had not been outside, but he could tell from the puddle forming at Eirian's feet and the sheen of magic that something had happened. As much as he wanted to ask, he felt the weight of Aiden's anger.

"No, I volunteered to guard this exit," he answered, avoiding Aiden's glare.

Rolling her eyes, Eirian glanced at Gabe and told him, "I wouldn't sneak out that window. Did you see the pitch of the roof outside? Not the best spot to go."

Deciding he had heard enough, Aiden finished walking over to Eirian. He briefly considered helping her get in the door but did not, preferring to watch her struggle. If she wanted to put herself at risk and do stupid things, then she could suffer the consequences.

"What the fuck do you think you were doing? You don't go out into a storm like that!"

Balancing the mug in her hand with her belt and dangling weapons, Eirian answered, "I was enjoying the storm."

"Is that what you call it?"

Aiden blocked the doorway with an arm, stopping her from going in. With how close he was to Eirian, he felt the tingle of energy radiating from her. It was not the same as her magic, and he wanted to touch her to find out if it would give him a shock. Biting the inside of his cheek, he reminded himself not to get distracted and to continue to scold her.

"I call it being an irresponsible brat."

"Mind your tongue, Captain, and remember who you're talking to," Eirian said icily, and she tilted her head to glare at him.

"It's my job to keep you safe."

"So, you keep saying, and it's tedious listening to you. Now get out of my way!"

Aiden dropped his arm, letting Eirian pass. The rain had soaked her through, and he knew she needed to change her clothes. The last thing they needed was for her to become sick right at the start of the journey.

"And it's tedious having my safety measures ignored."

Turning on him with fury rippling through the magic surrounding her, Eirian snarled. "Do you still believe you can protect me? I can turn the power of a storm into magic for my use."

"Yes, I do!"

Her magic was beautiful, sparks becoming obvious as her anger increased. Aiden wanted nothing more than to push Eirian against the wall so he could kiss her. He felt the desire to bury his hands in her hair while he drew her rage from her and drowned in the power that she wielded. While the desire was not new, the intensity of it startled him. Clenching his fists tight enough that his nails dug into his palm, Aiden resisted.

Gabe watched them silently, toying with the silver charm he wore around his neck. The knot danced through his fingers, slipping quickly and without thinking. He was glad he was the one observing them. Most of his fellow guards would be quick to tell everyone else about the literal sparks arcing from Eirian to Aiden.

"What could you possibly protect me from, Aiden?"

"I'll do whatever I have to do to protect you from whatever I can," he answered. "Including yourself!"

"Fuck you!"

Kicking the door shut, she leaned against it and listened to the sound of Aiden dragging a chair. Eirian knew he intended to remain outside the entire night, and it put a damper on her thoughts of sneaking out. Carefully putting the warm mug down, she dropped her belt and weapons on the bed and crossed to the window. Running her hands over the wooden shutters, Eirian closed her eyes. Her skin still tingled with magic.

Reluctantly, she dragged herself away and started pulling her sodden clothing off. She exchanged them for the clean set Isabella had laid out on the back of a chair. Thankful for the fire, Eirian sat with the mug grasped in her hands and contemplated how she would avoid Faolan and his questions. Regret filled her and chased away the joy of the storm as she realized she should never have set foot outside in it with the daoine around.

Hearing a knock at the door, Eirian knew who it was. With the residual power lingering in her magic, she was unsure she wanted Aiden anywhere near her. If she had been in Riane, she would not have been in her own bed, and the thought still sat in her mind to seek Celiaen out. Storms recharged her differently from the sun, but they also left her hypersensitive in an intoxicating manner.

When a second knock came, she called, "What?"

Pushing the door open, Aiden leaned in the doorway, watching her in front of the fire. The flames did not detract from the glow of magic illuminating her skin. He reminded himself of what Everett had said on the ride. They needed to overcome their differences.

"I wanted to check on you and make sure there was nothing you needed."

"I'm fine. Thank you, Aiden."

"Eirian," Aiden said and sighed. "We need to stop fighting with each other over the slightest thing. Out here, it's not so easy to hide it.

Her brows arched, and she looked at him. She nodded for him to enter and shut the door. Eirian told herself that if she remained seated in front of the fire and Aiden kept his distance, they would be safe. Closing the door, Aiden took a few steps into the small room, clasping his hands behind his back as he stared at her.

"I thought you enjoyed fighting with me," she commented.

"And I think you like fighting with people for the joy of it. So for the sake of someone I love, I'm trying to apologize. I don't want to fight with you outside of the training square."

Frowning at his words, Eirian nodded. She wanted to ask what he meant, but it was none of her business. Aiden was the captain of her guard, nothing more.

"Apology accepted. I'll try to be more cooperative. I know you're doing your job, and I shouldn't make it harder for you."

Aiden smirked and said, "I accept your apology. Now, I suggest you go to bed."

Glancing at the bed, Eirian chuckled. "As soon as I'm warm enough. The bed looks far too cold to be inviting right now."

"Are you trying to bait me, Eirian?"

She was, but Eirian thought she would pretend to be innocent to his meaning. "Bait you? No, Captain, I was simply observing that I'm cold from the rain and the bed is also chilly. I'd rather sit by the fire than shiver beneath blankets with no source of warmth."

The fire crackled, a log giving way, and Aiden walked over to it. Giving her a sideways smirk, he crouched to throw more wood into the flames. Eirian watched him over the lip of the mug, flickers of lightning still present in her eyes. They did not help his desire to pick her up and take her to bed. He wanted to know if they would remain and if the energy that made her glow would throw sparks when he showed Eirian how much pleasure he could give her.

"Is that better?" he asked, wiping his hands off on his trousers.

Pursing her lips, Eirian hummed appreciatively. "A little."

Rising to his feet, Aiden told himself to leave. There was a dangerous gleam in Eirian's gaze that told him he was not the only one considering their desires. Everett would retire to the next room soon enough, and while Gabe was the only one in the hallway, the inn was not so large that people would not find out. He knew what the council had decided, and he would not risk ruining the alliance with Ensaycal. He could want her all he liked, but he could only offer her friendship.

"Good. I'll be right outside the door if you need me."

"Aiden," she murmured his name, and he did not move.

"Eirian."

Her eyes glittered, but the surrounding glow seemed subdued. Glancing at the window, Eirian cocked her head to the side and listened to the thunder.

"You saw me out there."

"I did," Aiden replied.

"That was only a small display of what I can do in a storm. When the sun rises tomorrow, everyone will feel cranky or amazed by the growth that appeared."

He knew what she was referring to and chuckled. "You turned the power of the storm into a garden?"

"You could say that. It's not something that Riane was aware I could do, and you're right that I was irresponsible by going out there."

"You forgot the brat part."

Eirian sighed. "Really?"

Crossing his arms, Aiden smirked, and Eirian rolled her eyes. Then, taking a sip of the ale, she returned her gaze to the fire, watching the shadows dancing.

"Can I assume that Prince Celiaen and his companions were all aware you can do what you did out there?" Aiden asked, although he knew she would say yes.

"Celi knows everything about me, Aiden."

It galled him to hear it, but Aiden reminded himself he had years to learn. He suspected that what Eirian needed from him was someone to talk to without expressing judgment. Not a simple task, but he wanted to try.

"Then why won't you marry him?"

She shook her head, murmuring, "Is it so hard to believe I don't want to marry anyone? The thought of being tied to one man who would expect me to only be with him is an uncomfortable notion for me."

The answer surprised him, but Aiden respected her honesty. "Do you love him?"

"I'm a queen, Aiden. Do you really think love comes into the matter, let alone desire? I know how this works, and I know what they expect of me."

Remembering the day of her coronation and his conversation with Celiaen, Aiden wondered if Eirian knew what he had hinted at. Glancing over his shoulder at the door, he debated if sharing was something he could bring himself to be comfortable with. He would never admit it, but when he put his jealousy aside, he admired Celiaen in many ways.

"You need to sleep, Eirian."

"Perhaps. Goodnight, Aiden."

Making his way across to the door, he lingered with his hand on the knob. Eirian did not move from the chair, her hands cradling the mug of ale while she stared into the flames. Magic still illuminated her skin, flickers of energy chasing over the parts of her that were not covered by clothes. There was an air of loneliness around Eirian, and his desires gave way to the urge to comfort her. While he could not hold her and tell her it was fine, Aiden could provide her with something else to focus on.

"By the way, Tara has Kenna watching your window."

Her lips curled, and Eirian glanced in his direction as he opened the door to leave. "Sneaky move, Aiden."

"You've made me up my game, Eirian," he replied before shutting the door behind him.

"Everything good?" Gabe asked from his spot on the floor.

Looking at him, Aiden sighed. After the incident with the woods, he had been angry with Gabe, but he was no longer sure he had a right to be. Not with the power they felt coming from Eirian on the other side of the wall.

"It will be. I think we came to an agreement."

Chuckling, Gabe stretched his legs out and waved at the window above his head. "She had a good point about the window."

Arching a brow, Aiden asked, "Are you asking to be let off?"

He shook his head, replying, "Nope. I saw the magic surrounding her, and I want to hear everything you can tell me."

"Go get us some warm ale if there is still any down there, and I'll tell you what I saw." Looking up and down the hallway, Aiden added, "Maybe get yourself a chair as well."

Scrambling to his feet, Gabe tucked his silver pendant inside his clothes, giving Aiden and the door a wry smile. "You know, Captain, by the time this is over, I suspect nothing will surprise you about what our darling queen can do."

Aiden frowned and watched him move down the hall. Sometimes Gabe was too strange, even for him, but it was not something he liked to linger on for long.

"I'm sure she'll always surprise us."

Gabe glanced back, and in the flickering light of the storm, Aiden thought he saw shadows shifting as he chuckled. "With war coming, I'm sure you're right."

THIRTY

Shadows crept closer, shifting over the walls of the tent. Laying on the bed with her hands tucked under her head, Eirian watched them dance. They disturbed her, their darker shade separating them from the natural shadows of the night. It was not just the difference in pitch that set Eirian on edge. Her magic niggled at her and tugged at her mind. The whispers warned her they were not what they seemed.

Eirian wanted to dismiss them and the whispers. It would be easy to blame the remnants of her nightmare on why the shadows disturbed her. Turning her face to the flaps of the tent, she wondered which of her guards had the unfortunate luck of standing on the other side. They were all close by, taking turns surrounding her temporary quarters while they headed northward across Endara.

With a sigh, she pulled her hands free and rubbed her face. The shadows seemed to shift again, creeping away from the bed. Rolling over, Eirian pulled the knife from beneath the pillow and clasped it tightly in her hand. It was a reassurance. Something solid to hold on to. She needed it after her nightmares because they always left her unsettled. There were no ripples of concern coming across the bond, telling her she had not disturbed Celiaen from his sleep.

"This is ridiculous," Eirian grumbled, and released the knife. "Just get up and do something. Anything is better than laying here staring at nothing."

Sitting up, she untangled herself from the blanket and swung her legs over the side. It was not as comfortable as her bed in Amath, but Eirian suspected it was better than what everyone else had. She was the Queen of Endara, and they had attempted to provide every comfort possible for the journey. Not that she needed any of it. Eirian had spent enough nights on the ground with nothing, and anything more than that was an improvement.

There was nothing else in the tent except a chest of her belongings. Laid out on top of it, her armor and clothing were waiting for the morning to come. Pulling off the chemise she had gone to sleep in, Eirian dressed in the trousers and tunic. The armor followed, her fingers working to tighten the laces of her jerkin over the mail. She felt tired and stiff, the poor sleep leaving a lingering effect on her body. When she finished dressing, she moved on to her weapons.

She heard the guards on the other side of the tent walls, the scuff of boots on the ground. They were aware she was awake, but Eirian did not expect them to say anything unless she set foot outside. Muttering curses at herself, she crossed to the door and untied the togs. When she opened it, she stared at Aiden standing there with his arms crossed.

"What do you think you're doing?" he asked softly.

"I want to go for a walk."

Stepping forward, Aiden pushed her back into the tent and out of sight. There was little privacy, but tents shared by his men and those answering to Marcellus and Everett surrounded them. He trusted his men not to talk about anything they overheard.

"You had a nightmare again."

Eirian nodded, admitting, "I did. Which is why I want to go for a walk. Please, Aiden. I'm not asking to be alone. In fact, I'd rather not be."

He wanted to say no, but the memory of her soft whimpers while she slept silenced his protest. Nodding his agreement, Aiden offered his arm to Eirian and waited for her. There was no scornful look directed at it, just a quiet sigh as her hand wrapped around his forearm. Then, propping open the flap to let her through, Aiden signaled to the other guards to follow.

"Do you want to spar?"

She shook her head, murmuring, "Not really. Could we just walk until we find a clear spot, and I can stare at the sky for a while?"

Giving her a sideways look, Aiden felt concerned by her response. He had expected her to say yes and use the opportunity to clear her mind. Whatever Eirian had dreamed about was clearly bothering her. Covering her hand with his, he guided her towards the edge of the camp. When they set up each day, he made sure he knew the quickest route out if Athnaral attacked in the night. Eirian did not speak as they walked. Instead, her eyes turned to the sky, watching the stars.

Soldiers patrolled the outskirts of the camp, and they expressed their surprise at seeing Eirian and her guards emerging from among the tents. Aiden greeted them as they passed, his presence reassuring the patrol that their queen was not being abducted. There was a space near to the edge where they could still see the flicker of fires dotted among the canvas and the figures of people moving.

Outstretching her free hand, Eirian allowed her magic to guide her to a spot with decent grass coverage. Releasing his hold, Aiden chuckled when she flopped to the ground with a grunt. There was enough moonlight to watch her stretch out on her back, arms folded beneath her head. Looking around at where his men had positioned themselves, Aiden took his time sitting down beside Eirian.

"Do you want to talk about it?"

Tilting her head in his direction, Eirian said, "What's there to talk about?"

"You could start with what your nightmare was about."

"I don't know."

"It's not the first time you've woken from a nightmare since we left Amath," he said.

Eirian sighed, and Aiden realized she had not intended to annoy him with her answer. It was not an attempt to draw him into an argument. She could have lied, but she trusted him with the truth instead. A faint smile graced his lips, the only thing betraying how pleased he felt over the realization.

"You don't remember what it was about."

"No, I don't. I rarely do." Sniffing, Eirian muttered, "Maybe it's better if I don't."

Wrapping his arms around his knees, Aiden looked at the sky and admired the glitter of the stars. The night was not chill, but the worst of summer was not yet upon them. He did not recall her having nightmares as a child, but he wondered if he would have noticed.

"When did they start?"

Her breath hissed through her teeth, and Aiden glanced at her. Eirian's brow furrowed in thought, eyes shut while she tried to remember when the nightmares began. She could not recall a time when they had not plagued her. Any more than she could recall not feeling the press of forgotten memories and the perpetual sensation of something lingering in the corner of her eye.

"I've always had them."

"It's not that uncommon. I've met many who suffer from nightmares. Particularly those who've seen combat."

"Aiden..." Her voice broke, and Eirian swallowed before saying, "Sometimes they disrupt my magic."

Flinching at the implication, Aiden was not sure he wanted to ask for more information. Ever suspicious of her secrets, he wondered if Eirian would have mentioned it if they had not left Amath. Turning back to the sky, he knew dawn was not so far away. Behind them, the camp had started to stir.

"What can I do to help you?"

Eirian removed her arms from beneath her head, stretching them out. The grass was cool, and she dragged her fingers through it. Sensing the ripple of her magic, Aiden chuckled. It was her favorite trick, but he doubted anyone was complaining. The horses were never short of grazing, and the ground was not as torn up as it could be. He had heard the daoine mutter about it, expressing displeasure with her flaunting the balance, and it made him smile every time.

"Other than waking me, I'm not sure you can. Whatever the nightmares are about, sometimes they get bad enough to trigger my rage. Fay would ward our room every night to ensure I didn't influence anyone. Then, when we left the city with Celi and the others, it didn't matter so much. They surrounded me and could contain it."

"Well, that makes sense," Aiden said. "I thought Tara was being helpful by always having one of her mages close by at night. She was, but not for the reason I thought."

Unwilling to admit that Celiaen was probably aware of her nightmares, Eirian replied, "Tara knows what I'm like. She's playing it safe and trying to protect everyone around me."

"You've talked to one of those blues about the dreams?"

"Repeatedly."

Aiden wanted to lie beside her and stare at the stars. As children, they had often collapsed on the ground after running around and watched the clouds drift by. Times when it was just the three of them. Briefly, he wondered where Everett was and what he would say about the situation. He wanted to mention it to Eirian. Anything that would prompt her to remember him. Shuffling about, Aiden relaxed back until he was stretched out next to her.

Watching him from the corner of her eye, his actions surprised Eirian. She had not expected him to relax his guard when they were outside the perimeters of the camp. It seemed like Aiden was always there, and she wondered when he took the time to sleep. People had claimed that she bordered on inexhaustible, but Eirian felt like Aiden had her beat.

"Do you ever sleep?" she asked quietly.

He chuckled, replying, "I was asleep until someone woke me up with her nightmares. My tent is next to yours. As it is every night."

"Oh. I'm sorry."

"Don't be. It's my job to protect you, and when I heard you cry out, I wanted to be available if you needed me."

Wriggling closer, Eirian pointed at the sky and traced a pattern in the air. Not looking at her, Aiden tracked her movement and worked out she was referencing a collection of stars.

"Are soldiers taught about constellations?"

"They're taught basics for navigation. I'm educated in a lot of things," Aiden answered. "Do you think every soldier knows how to dance like I do?"

Her hand slapped his chest, and Aiden laughed at the indignant noise Eirian made. She pointed at a different part of the sky where a string of bright stars sat.

"The Northern Arrow," Eirian murmured.

"It's one of the first we're taught."

"Do you think there were stories behind the names?"

It was an interesting question, and Aiden gazed at the blanket of stars. Some of the constellation names suggested they had a meaning, but he had heard so many stories that he did not know what might have a grain of truth. While he thought about them, Aiden felt Eirian creep even closer. Glancing sideways at her, he lifted his arms and folded his hands beneath his head.

"Yes, once. Whatever the stories were, they're lost to us now."

Aiden held his breath when Eirian pressed against his side, her head resting on his arm. It was uncomfortable, and he tentatively stretched out, twisting it around to place a hand on Eirian's shoulder. She shifted in, watching his face cautiously.

"Thank you," she whispered.

Eyes darting to locate the guards surrounding them, Aiden was thankful he could trust his men to keep their mouths shut about anything they saw. Catching strands of her loose hair with his fingers, Aiden rubbed the silken strands.

"While your attempt to be subtle about it was amusing, darling, you could have asked," he murmured. "Whatever you need, just ask."

"Before I left Riane, I never had to ask."

Lying there, Aiden let her roll onto her side and curl against him with a hand resting on his chest. It was not the most comfortable position, the weapons they wore proving a nuisance. Neither of them mentioned the discomfort. Eirian wanted to cling to something comforting to chase the lingering fear from her mind, and Aiden knew it. Beneath the stars and before the sun rose, they could be at peace.

She told him, "I know I make your life difficult, Aiden."

"I'm not sure difficult is the word I'd use."

"I can't promise it'll ever change."

"And I can promise my responses won't," Aiden replied.

"Captain!" Merle's voice cut through the darkness.

Sighing, Eirian pressed her face into his chest for a moment before rolling away. Quickly sitting up, Aiden watched Merle approach cautiously while she muttered under her breath. Eyes darting between them, he regretted interrupting whatever had been going on but knew the message he had was important.

"I thought you were asleep," Aiden said

"I was, but Nick woke me while looking for you."

"What happened?"

Hearing Aiden's tone, Eirian sat up and looked at Merle. She did not bother to echo the question, knowing that he would answer.

"Scouts reported seeing Athnaralans. The general wants everyone up and moving."

"We're half a day away from Forrestfield," Eirian stated. "What sort of numbers?"

"Don't know," Merle replied. "But considering once we hit Forrestfield, the land is in our favor…"

Holding out a hand to Aiden, Merle braced himself. Snorting at the sight, Eirian scrambled to her feet and gave the two men an amused look.

"Hold his hand often, Merle?" she quipped.

"Only when he wants to kill you."

Laughing, Eirian banished the remnants of her nightmares and focused on the news. Shooting an amused look at her back, Aiden dusted himself off. With a shake of his head, Merle waved at the camp.

"I ordered the men to pack. Crossed paths with Gunter. He said the duke was on his way to meet with Cameron."

Aiden did not need to hear it from her to know what Eirian wanted. Grabbing her arm, he turned her to face him, dismissing the sudden flare of her magic in response.

"You don't leave my side."

"I'd never dream of it, Captain," Eirian muttered. "Shall we go speak to Cameron?"

Looking between them, Merle wondered if there was something more to the exchange than simply Aiden's concern for Eirian's safety. He had seen them cuddled together on the ground, but it was something he would not talk of to anyone.

Keeping his hand on Eirian's arm, Aiden asked, "Did Nick say where the general would be?"

"His tent. Western edge."

Not arguing, Eirian allowed Aiden to guide her back into the camp. Guards surrounded them, a barrier of blank faces that discouraged soldiers from approaching. There were no nobles in the section they were hurrying through, and she suspected it was the reason Aiden maintained his hold on her. She did not mind it, the contact continuing to provide a tether against the press of anxiety.

News of Cameron's orders had spread. People hurried about organizing meals while others dealt with breaking down the camp. Watching them as they passed, Eirian could not help envying the soldiers. They chatted easily with each other as they worked, none of them appearing bothered by the early start.

It would not be the same way within the nobles camp. Eirian imagined the complaints as most would just bandy about.

Catching the amused smirk on her face, Aiden asked, "What's funny?"

"I was thinking about the histrionics the nobles would put on."

"Histrionics?"

She chuckled. "Seemed right to me."

"You really are more warrior than noble."

"I hope you're not just working that out," Eirian said jokingly. "Because I have news for you."

It was his turn to chuckle, and Aiden caught the look Merle cast over his shoulder at them. There was a hint of amusement in it, signs that it pleased him they were not arguing for a change. Merle had been his friend long enough to feel confident telling Aiden when he thought he was behaving ridiculously.

"Don't worry, I worked out you aren't much of a lady months ago."

"Except how it counts," Mac said to Lyle behind them.

Lyle flinched at the look given to them and muttered, "Shit, don't say that!"

Shaking his head, Aiden watched the grin on Eirian's face from the corner of his eye. He did not bother to scold the two guards in front of her. It would only end up in an argument, and Aiden wanted to hold on to the peace between them for a little longer.

"How many do you think the scout saw?" Eirian asked quietly.

"Enough."

"You don't think?"

Aiden squeezed her arm, saying, "Best to wait and hear what they have to say. General Cameron is probably taking precautions. You'll be safer in the keep at Forrestfield."

Her eyes sought the eastern horizon, checking for the glow of dawn. The part of her magic that allowed Eirian to draw on the sun's energy whispered that it was close. She felt the approach and the promise of warmth. Aiden squeezed her arm again to attract her attention.

"It's not my safety that concerns me," she admitted.

"Your safety is all that matters to me."

Ahead of them, it was obvious which tent Cameron was occupying. A lit fire was close by, people crowded around with their heads bowed in conversation. Others hurried in and out of the tent, often jostling into each other in their rush. Releasing Eirian's arm, Aiden nodded at where he expected Cameron to be.

"I'll come in with you."

Eirian shrugged, heading to the tent. People saw them approaching and were quick to shift out of the way. She was the queen, and no one wanted to risk inciting her ire, let alone Aiden's, by coming between them and the news within the tent. There were lanterns scattered around the inside, and someone had set up a table in the middle. Cameron stood over it, a hand resting on a map while arguing with Everett and Marcellus.

"What's going on?" Eirian demanded.

They turned, and Cameron looked relieved to see her there. He knew Eirian would side with him. Her decisive attitude was preferable to the arguments in favor of caution that the two dukes pushed. At her side, Aiden stared blankly, a hand lingering close to her elbow, as though to caution her.

"A scout arrived earlier with reports that they spotted Athnaralans along the border," Marcellus said. "The general wants us to leave now for Forrest-field."

Cameron opened his mouth to argue, but Eirian was faster.

"I agree."

"We need to ensure your... Wait... you do?" He feigned surprise and added, "Thank you, ma'am."

She arched a brow and smirked at Aiden. Exchanging looks, Marcellus and Everett prepared to plead their stance with Eirian.

"Of course I agree. Unfortunately, we're not in the position to adequately defend ourselves if the Athnaralans decide to attack. There are far too many civilians here, and we need them safely out of the way." Eirian stepped forward to look at the map on the table. "I've studied the maps. Forrestfield is on the edge of land that doesn't lend itself to combat."

"That's right." Cameron agreed.

Everett huffed in frustration. "I don't think we need to rush. People will panic."

"We're an enticing target sitting here. If we know they're there, they know we're here. Did the scout give numbers?" Aiden directed his question to Cameron, ignoring the flash of annoyance on Everett's face.

"No, no clear idea of numbers. Going off previous reports, it's likely to be at least a company. So far, the sightings have only been of companies and not full legions," Marcellus informed them.

Pursing her lips, Eirian considered their choices. Either way, the decision would receive opposition. Nodding to Cameron, she watched his eyes narrow and his stance shift. It was clear he expected her to urge caution.

"Let's get to Forrestfield. I'd rather we have the safety of the keep to retreat to and the local expertise. Then, if Athnaral makes any moves, we can slow them down while the others escape." Grinning, Eirian said, "Besides, a company or two is nothing we can't handle."

Chuckling in relief, Cameron replied, "I'm not sure there's enough of you mages to make that much of a difference."

"You'd be surprised."

Glancing away, Eirian considered telling them the truth. She knew what she was capable of without lifting a sword, and stirred by the prospect, her magic whispered the challenge. It wanted to find out how many she could destroy before it became too much. Her fist clenched at her side, and Eirian felt Aiden's hand on her elbow to remind her of his presence. Looking back at the others, she forced the power down and smiled faintly.

"General, issue whatever orders you feel best. I know the reports have only been of companies, but where companies gather, a legion will eventually form."

"That's right. I suspect they're waiting for an order to form, and until then, they'll continue to patrol the border."

Aiden grunted. "Let's be honest. They know the queen is here. So what's stopping them from ambushing us and attempting to capture her?"

"Nothing," Everett replied. "We're in the open here, and it would be nigh on impossible to ambush us. Unfortunately, Forrestfield doesn't have the same advantage."

"No, but it's got the advantage of walls, secure supplies, and an entire garrison of soldiers."

Pinching the bridge of her nose, Eirian silenced them. She was not interested in listening to them argue when she had already decided.

"That's enough! Everett, Marcellus, go placate anyone who's got an issue with these orders. Remind them what'll happen to their precious skins if we're attacked. That should shut them up."

Holding back his laughter, Cameron appreciated the scolded expressions the two dukes wore as they bowed stiffly. Aiden shifted out of the way to let them pass, his eyes darting from Eirian to Cameron.

"General Cameron, I've told you previously that you can count on my support," Eirian informed him. "As my captain remarked earlier, I really am more warrior than noble."

"I understand, ma'am, but I also understand you have to keep them happy."

Placing a hand on the hilt of a sword, Eirian shook her head. She knew most of the nobles remained in denial over the prospect of war with Athnaral. It was not a stance she could afford. War was coming, and they needed to be prepared to fight.

"Fuck their happiness because it doesn't matter if they're dead. They can complain all they like. It's the advantage of being alive."

"I look forward to seeing you tell them that to their faces."

Choking, Aiden did not appreciate the impact of Eirian thumping him on the back. He stared at Cameron in surprise while she laughed, her hand remaining where it had landed.

"They'd riot," he commented.

Cameron laughed. "I know, and it'd be hilarious. They're here for decoration, nothing more. The most use we could get out of them is throwing them in the path of anyone pursuing Her Majesty while you get her away."

Laughter fading, Eirian's face fell at the suggestion. Her hand slipped from Aiden's back, and she shook her head.

"It won't come to that. We can't sacrifice people."

"Sacrifices have to be made during war."

"We're not at war yet!"

Magic crackled around Eirian, and Cameron stepped back as a precaution. Aiden remained where he was, the prickle of power making his skin crawl. He wanted to move. The whispers that clawed at his mind put him on edge. They called to him, urging him to draw his sword and cut down anyone who dared defy his queen.

"Put your claws away, ma'am. I don't intend to throw them at Athnaral, but we must be prepared to make sacrifices to protect Endara." Cameron's gaze shifted to Aiden, and he said, "Captain, perhaps you can encourage some restraint."

Understanding the message, Aiden placed a hand on Eirian's arm and murmured, "We should make sure they've packed your things, and you need to eat."

"I need to speak to Celi."

The magic faded, but the clench of Eirian's jaw suggested she was not happy with Cameron. Aiden kept his hand on her arm and encouraged her to turn and walk out of the tent. Outside, the sky had lightened as the sun appeared above the horizon. A smattering of stars was still visible, their shine remaining for as long as possible. Sighing, he wished they could return to the spot on the grass and the peace of the moment.

"The dukes didn't look happy," Merle commented, taking his place on the other side of Eirian.

"Where's the prince?" Eirian asked, ignoring his words. "I expected him to make an appearance."

Scratching the back of his neck, Merle replied, "I saw one elf briefly while you were with the general. A lanky man with spikey hair."

"Sounds like Tully."

"He double-checked the orders and went again."

Mouth twisting, Eirian nodded. Her eyes swept over the transient gathering before settling on a location. The bond told her where to find Celiaen. At the other end of it, she sensed his awareness and knew he was waiting. Feet moving, she started in his direction, only to be stopped short when Aiden tugged on her arm.

"Where are you going? Our tents are this way," he informed her, waving in the opposite direction.

"I told you, I need to speak to Celi."

Scowling, Aiden continued to grip her arm. Merle and the other guards watched cautiously, keeping a tight circle around them.

"No, you need to come and get some breakfast before we leave. Whatever it is can wait until after you've eaten."

"Really?" Eirian grumbled.

"Yes, really. Food first."

Sighing, she let him pull her toward her tent. Eirian wanted to argue and insist on going to Celiaen first, but she understood why Aiden wanted her to eat. Her stomach grumbled at the thought, a reminder that if the worst happened and Athnaral attacked, she would last longer with food in her body. Magic made them burn through energy quicker. Something she had to remind her ladies of frequently.

There was a tug at the bond, an acknowledgment of her desire to see him. It told Eirian he would seek her out when he was free. The camp was a hive of activity, soldiers and servants busy breaking down tents while nobles fluttered around. Aiden was careful to pick their path through, keeping her away from the bulk of nobility to prevent any potential arguments that might arise.

When they reached their tents, Gabe oversaw those guards who had remained. They dismantled most of their tents; the men working efficiently and without argument. Isabella was busy inside Eirian's tent, taking care of her things. The sight of her caused Eirian to flinch. No matter what Cameron suggested, she could never throw her people in the path of the Athnaralans to protect herself.

"Good morning, Your Majesty," Isabella said cheerily. "I found bread, but not much else. No one has made anything for breakfast."

Accepting the cloth bundle, Eirian watched the guards swoop in to dismantle her tent. Unwrapping the parcel, she smiled at the collection of small red fruits that surrounded the chunk of bread. Popping one in her mouth, she caught Gabe watching with a faint smile and knew he was the one responsible for the fruit.

"Where did you get the lilly pilly fruits from?" Eirian asked.

Isabella shrugged and waved at Gabe, answering, "He gave them to me when he heard me complain bread was all I had for you."

Giving him a nod, Eirian kept eating the fruit first. The bread would be easier to shove into a pack and eat while riding. Returning her nod, Gabe went back to his task. Keeping out of the way, Eirian and Isabella watched the guards work. Sensing the approach of Celiaen and several of his companions, Eirian turned to observe them dodge around the men.

"Want some?"

Holding out the bread to Celiaen, Eirian smiled at the arch of his brows. Nearby, Tara snorted and elbowed Alyse.

"Is that all you've got?" Celiaen chuckled and ran a hand through his hair, saying, "We had porridge."

"Kels?"

"Of course."

Eirian huffed. "My guards could take lessons. Gabe found some fruit for me."

"I heard there's been a sighting of Athnaralans. Have they crossed the border?" Tara asked.

"Not yet, that we know of," Aiden said, returning to his place beside Eirian. "But they decided we'd head to Forrestfield sooner."

"Good idea. I hope you weren't an idiot and argued against it, Ree."

Rolling her eyes at Tara, Eirian muttered, "As if I'd do that. You'd box my ears."

Celiaen said jokingly, "Pity you're the queen, or we could send you out to keep watch."

"You think I'd share the fun with you after your recent antics?"

Covering her heart, Tara pretended to be hurt and asked, "What about the rest of us? We haven't behaved like fools."

"You know I'll always share with you, Tara."

Shaking his head at them, Aiden did not understand how they could treat it like a joke. He suspected there was something they were not saying. It had to be another one of Eirian's secrets, and he felt his stomach turn at the thought she was still lying about her abilities. After her display during the storm, he dreaded what else she could do.

Crossing her arms, Alyse looked at the three warrior mages in concern and said, "There'll be no need for that. Letting any of you near the Athnaralans is asking for a bloody mess to happen."

"Who said anything about blood?" Eirian muttered, sharing a look with Celiaen as he picked at the bread in her hands.

"You know exactly what I mean."

Sighing, Celiaen agreed, "Alyse is right. We need to keep you away from the Athnaralans and the risk of an attack."

"No need to rush the start of this war if we can avoid it," Tara added.

Lifting her gaze to the morning sky and the dapple of colors remaining from sunrise, Eirian's mouth twisted. She agreed with Tara. The longer they could delay a war with Athnaral, the better. But, as confident as she was that they would win in the end, Eirian did not want to contemplate the number of people who would die.

"Maybe we'll get lucky." They stared at her in confusion, and Eirian shrugged. "You never know, maybe King Aeyren will realize it's a bad idea and change his mind. We might be worried about nothing."

Aiden hoped she was right, saying, "We have Telmia as an ally now."

Meeting Celiaen's eyes, Eirian knew he was the only one who understood her fear. He knew almost everything she knew. All the fragments of information she had picked up. The comments, the rumors. The truth of her heritage. He knew everything except the whispers at the back of her mind that warned of what was to come.

Those whispers Eirian kept to herself, along with the increasing press of forgotten memories. She did not know what would happen in the weeks to come, but she knew she would do everything she could to protect her people.

Thank you for reading!

Go to 5310PUBLISHING.COM
for more great books you can read today!

If you enjoyed this book, please review it!

Connect with us on social media!
@5310publishing on Twitter and Instagram

Subscribe to our mailing list to get exclusive offers, news, updates, and discounts for our future book releases and our authors!

READ THE NEXT BOOK IN THIS SERIES: BLOOD OF HUSKS

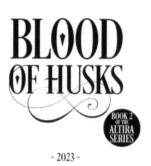

BLOOD OF HUSKS

BOOK 2 OF THE ALTIRA SERIES

- 2023 -

JOYCE GEE

The Kingdom of Endara is at war and Eirian refuses to be the soft-hearted queen the enemy expects. Among her growing collection of secrets is one that can help turn the tide of battle, even if it means that her people might turn on her. She knows she can buy the precious time needed for reinforcements to arrive, but she will have to break her promises to the ones closest to her.

Duty to her kingdom has always been her driving force. To save the lives of her people, Eirian knows it is no longer worth keeping her power hidden. To cling to her precarious position as queen, she holds some secrets close to her heart while allowing others to be revealed. But behind enemy lines awaits an enemy as old as the world they inhabit. One that seeks to destroy everything in its quest for revenge.

"I am the monster I feared."

Eirian's allies are too far to keep the enemy from crossing the border into the Kingdom of Endara. To keep her freedom and save her people, she will do whatever she can to buy time for reinforcements to reach them. Even if it means showing everyone why they should fear what she is capable of.

With Celiaen gone from her side, the only person Eirian can trust is her stalwart captain. Aiden knows she is keeping secrets, but so long as they do not threaten her safety, he tolerates it. All he can do is offer comfort when the price of her choices becomes a burden she struggles to carry alone.

The arrival of a mysterious king and his army spurs the real enemy into revealing themselves. Eirian knows it is her duty to stand against the oncoming darkness, even if it costs her everything.

SCAN ME

You might also like...
HONEY BEAUMONT

Once upon a time, an unlikely hero was born out of servitude. Honey Beaumont, our hero, strived to do right by everyone and see justice prevail no matter the consequence. He dreamt of the intrepid Adventurer's Guild and helping those who can't help themselves.

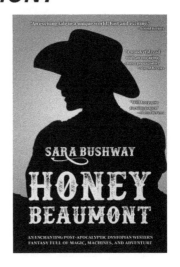

Every day our hero persevered the wrath of Byron, his owner. Helping those around him doesn't fill Byron's pockets, bringing out anger in his boss. One day, Byron brutally attacks Honey after a wealthy client offers to help Honey leave the life of servitude and be free. After the attack, Honey was scarred, disfigured, and with a grudge. He begrudgingly left his home and the love of his life behind to move into a new and luxurious home.

Honey mingles amongst those in the new house and learns about the world's inequalities, especially between the nobodies and humans. But with his new owner forbidding him from being independent, Honey has no other choice but to leave this new luxurious life behind.

Freedom for Honey meant joining the Adventure's Guild, becoming a hero, and helping his family leave the horrible place he used to call home. Will Honey be strong enough to take on Byron? Only time will tell.

"The combination of dystopian pre-war chaos with the familiarity of the Old West creates an adventurous and threatening backdrop for the plot."
    —Rachel Le Mesurier, author of *The Musician's Promise Series*

"A wonderful read with an engaging, sweet protagonist. Wonderful, evocative writing. It was a pleasure to get to know Honey, this fascinating world the author created, and ride along for all his adventures." —Starred Review 5/5

"Reading this was amazing! Following the main character throughout this book and watching him grow and change was so wonderful. I only wish I could read it for the first time again. I guess I'll have to reread it" —Starred Review 5/5

You might also like...
ARTIE'S COURAGE

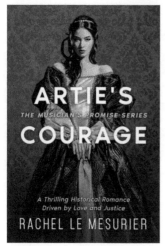

A courageous farm girl's life is changed forever when she falls in love with a charming street musician, opening her eyes to the cruel mistreatment of Mexico's mine workers and compelling her to stand with them against their oppressor - the man she is marrying.

Esperanza lives a charmed life. The daughter of a wealthy landowner, her family is thrilled when she attracts the attention of the handsome and mysterious Don Raúl, opening the door to a glittering life of opulence for them all.

However, a chance encounter with a charming street musician forces Esperanza to open her eyes to the cruel underworld of Mexico's mistreated working classes, and she begins to doubt everything she ever thought she wanted.

As the people begin to rise up in a bloodthirsty revolution against their oppressors, Esperanza is forced to make choices that she hoped never to face. Esperanza's decisions threaten to tear apart her family, her heart, and the country she loves.

In this brutal world where a few careless words can cost lives, will the price of freedom prove to be more than what she is willing to pay?

Led by strong female characters, ARTIE'S COURAGE turns the common damsel in distress trope on its head. Based on real historical events, this thrilling pageturner story of love and courage in the face of adversity follows characters on an emotional journey through laughter, tears, passion, and heartbreak.

"A rip-roaring, romantic adventure that is impossible to put down." —Starred Review

"A well-written and well-researched story against the background of early 20th century Mexico." —D. Wells, author

"Class intrigue, dynastic maneuvering, and dangerous politics against growing civil unrest in pre-revolutionary Mexico. Can an unlikely friendship blossom into more? I couldn't put it down, and nor will you!" —Jennifer Nugée, editor

Lightning Source UK Ltd.
Milton Keynes UK
UKHW010038090223
416653UK00002B/124